I0657692

UNLEASHED

A Stranger Root of Wrath

Sincere Echoes

This book is a work of fiction. Names, characters and incidents are the work of the author's imagination.

Any resemblance of events or person, living or deceased, is entirely coincidental. Although, many of the locations are real, they were only used to make the story believable.

Copyright by Free Taboo Publishing llc. All rights reserved.

No portion of this book may be reproduced, stored in a retrieval system, or transmitted in any form or by any means, including electronic, mechanical, photocopy, recording or otherwise without the prior express written permission of the publisher.

"Unleashed"
- Sincere Echoes.
"Free Taboo Publishing llc"
Copyright © 2024
ISBN: 979-8-9865779-6-8

Dedication

To my wife Jennifer, may the years continue unfolding our greatness to one another.

We in this for life, you and I, I love you and to my children; Angel, Kamryn, and Sincere, your dad's always been there, even though I couldn't be there due to no fault of your own.

I love you all equally...

Acknowledgment

To all of the readers, colleagues, close family and friends...

I want to send out a few special acknowledgements to all of the people who saw me through this and came out on the other side, still at my side.

I don't just owe you one Crybaby, I owe you forever, a good woman who vowed to be there, "for better or for worse."

To all of my Children; Angel, Kamryn and Sincere, we hardly know one another, but we soon will. Dad's coming home.

To my playa partner, friend and esteemed colleague, Taboo... We did it, Slim! We said we were going to go print and here we are, Free Taboo Publishing, LLC. Grindin' by all means. The only thing that stops the hustle is the hustler themselves... We on to great things, Slim, the past is behind us now. Let's give 'em back which was never ours to begin with. 91 years ain't stoppin' you, I gotcha Slim, we in this together!

To my D.C. homies, Fed-wide/Nation-wide. Stand up! Slim, a soldier salutes you all! I'm puttin' on for my city. This ain't just "Anything"- "It's everything, Slim! It's injected, high-octane hustle! And you know I went "Cujo" with the pen in this, much respect and big salutes to all of my comrades who did it with me in the trenches. You know who you are. We held it down, stood a hardline, and paved the way. They say blood only makes you related, loyalty makes you family. "We all we got" if we don't do it for ourselves, who will? Plan, Prepare, Pursue-That's the blueprint for success. When everything else fails, believe in yourself, if nothing else, and get it the hard-way..

Also, to Free Minds Book Club and Writing Workshop out of Washington, D.C. You've been there when most haven't! Thank you Free Minds Family, Sincere Echoes heading to the top, from rock bottom and I'm bringing a March of Mighty Men with me.

To all of Baltimore, MD and P.G. County, MD and those Virginia homies: "I said it, it shall be done."

To the Hill Family; Nate Hill and Jazmine Moore, at Jazmine.moore@moorehelp.org. Thanks for your support and encouragement in seeing that my poetry makes headlines.

Lastly, to the few others who I can't forget to mention, but there are so many more: Byrd, Scrappy, Bone, Tone, D-Boy, E\Easter, Rotknot, Money, Debo, Kic-Doe, Bleed, Mal from Virginia, and to James El, Los, Dro, Lin and Star from PA... We said it Slim! "If we gonna do it, let's do it big!"

Then I have to close this right, to the Creator, He gave me the talent and pointed me towards my purpose. "When all else fails me, you remain consistent." Thanks to my Lord and Savior, I'm nothing without you, for I am Blessed.

Well, that's it, get ready for Part II, UNLEASHED AGAIN, I promise you it's a sick trip. If I missed you, forgive me, I got you on the next go round...Real recognize real. I just separate the trees from the forest... Think on that...I'm out.

Sincere Echoes/Redz.

UNLEASHED

Stigmas-
crossbred with statistical enigma
makes way for a "new endangered species"

Oppression-
attached to the neck like choke chains Systematically restrained,
while the bias standard remains the standards, with prejudice and
injustice hidden within
the, "Stars and Stripes" of our lawful banners.

Innocence-
subjected to a pigment handpick Deathwish when raised, those officers
hands are bloodstained.

Justified-
the law wipes their guilt clean.
History, has not been erased.
Histories repeating itself today-
a systematic replay.
Accountability's now at stake
These acts of violence will not go silenced, nor swept under the rug, nor
decorated with a badge, as a Metal of Valor.
If another one bites the dust,
that Unleashes the blood lust.
Hell hath no wrath like,
when a conscious mind is uncaged.

Sincere Echoes

Prologue

Standing in the darkness of his living room, alone, in a one bedroom apartment on the North-West side of Washington, D.C., known as Le Droit Park, he peers through a slight crack in the vertical blinds, as the faint glow of the television illuminates the walls behind him. He listens to the newscast as the reporter recounts to the public about another senseless murder against an unarmed black man. This time, by the hands of another decorated officer, who claims it was just a tragedy, an instance of mistaken identity.

The news reporter continues: "...the off duty officer John St. Clair was investigating a breaking and entering in his neighborhood, when the officer approached the young man of 15 years of age, whose name is being withheld, he mistook the cell phone he held in his hand as an apparent gun. The officer wasn't available for comments, but the authorities investigating are ruling the shooting at the moment, as accidental..."

Just as the news reporter signed off and the newscast went on commercial break, the anger inside of him exploded into a fit of uncontrollable emotions, and he lashed out in a fierce outburst of rage, tearing away the blinds, throwing blurring blunt fists, punching against the wall, and flipping the only piece of furniture in the living room over, with so much force, that the recliner went sailing with a crushing impact against the wall on the other side of the room. He paced with blind rage coursing through his veins, seething.

When the newscast returned from commercial break, he had heard enough and the anger had taken a hold of his senses. He forced his foot through the television screen, shattering it on impact, as he continuously stomped it with a blind fury. Smoke and sparks were coming from the electrical circuits, causing an acrid burning smell that filled the room.

Then, with thoughtless action, he kicked the plastic milk crate that the television had been sitting upon and it bounced off of the wall and ricocheted towards the window and smashed the glass, causing it to shatter into a thousand fragmented cracks. His veins were still on fire and his anger wasn't anywhere under control. As he leaned against the wall facing the glass, he began cursing aloud, saying, "Fuck this shit-fuck these bitches....they just keep killing us....they're getting away with genocide, while we can't get away with nothin! How in the fuck are they doing that?" he said to himself, talking to nobody in particular.

"Killing us! Murdering children for being in the wrong place at the right time! Young men and women for being black, and then justifying their action on the basis that they are all convicted felons, like that's enough reason to die over."

"That's what you call protecting us?" he vents, voicing these questions in a thundering octave, as he screams at the walls, to himself. He then slams his back forcefully against the wall and slides down, positioning himself mournfully as he pulls his knees to his chest.

Breathing heavily, he began to sob and repeat in a whispering mantra, "This isn't right-this isn't right- this has to stop-this has to stop," over and over as he rocked his shaken body trying to console himself. "Look at what they've done to our lives, they misuse the system, the power, they use the justice system to imbed fear in us all, to destroy us, our families, and our communities, all under the guise of the law." Spewing these words, with spittle dripping down from his trembling, frightened lips, he continues. "They've charged me for crimes that I haven't committed, defeated me in court with lies, while I tell the truth-" Then balling his fist and pounding the sides of his face and violently pulling his hair, he screams, echoing on the empty apartment walls as he cried out, "My skin is a lie, my skin is...a crime. I'm living in a world of lose-lose."

For hours, he remained in that sitting, defeated position, rocking himself to sleep, as the flood gates of tears came, then dried but left white salt trails formed from the warm salty tears. A fitful sleep is what he is beginning to fade into; drained and completely discombobulated, from the passionate emotions he has released. He had truly been zapped of all energy and common sense. He slowly falls over to his side and balls up tightly into the fetal position, and quietly drifts away.

It wasn't until 4:30am, in the wee hours of the morning, that he had risen in a damp cold chill, from the carpeted living room floor. The darkness shrouded around him, as he tried to open his sleep-heavy eyelids, and focus his vision, while peering through the darkened space around him. He was accustomed to awakening such hours, for his body was on a natural time clock. This had become a necessary habit since his incarceration. He rose like any other morning, but now, he was no longer behind locked doors, awaiting his breakfast, as he had once done for many years during his illegal incarceration. Although he regained his freedom, he definitely didn't feel "free," under any defined sense of the word.

He had no job, even though he was intently and actively looking for employment, due to his criminal history, he was fatefully denied. He also had no family, due to the many years spent in the penitentiary, his family had long ago given up on him, before the judge had even hit his gavel with any sort of sentence having been set in stone. Such was very common for a lot of the black youth from the inner city hoods, and their families, who don't want to deal with them on any level, they use the justice system as their escape route to abandon their children or family members. This ruse is used almost as much as an excuse for why they couldn't be there to help or even stand in their corners in the times of their worse adversities. He realized over time and through personal experiences, that family wasn't family anymore, that it was only a word that was overrated, used without knowing its true meaning. Because to him, blood only meant that you are related. Loyalty is what makes family, and he had gotten more love and support from total strangers than anyone, and that had become a part of the norm for men like himself. Those people with his skin complexion that had been through his same struggles and tribulations, those are his people, his family. He managed to make it through the years by being resilient, and he's had to learn to take the bitter with the sweet, especially after being sentenced to 17 years for a case that he truly wasn't guilty of. But 12 jurors and a lot of speculation, as well as some falsified evidence with the fact that he was appointed a counsel that was lazy and incompetent while working for the prosecution was enough to place the last nail in his coffin, so to speak.

As he stood before the broken window, staring out into the dark complex of the apartments, listening to the quiet morning transform into the subtle hustle of activity, his mind was racing with past thoughts of his torment, these memories that wouldn't be allowed to be shaken loose. Rubbing the coarse hairs of his scruffy beard, he decided to take a shower and rinse away the confusion that was utterly cluttering his mind.

With the hot water spraying from the shower head set to his desired temperature, he stepped in, to allow the heat of the water pounce upon his skin. As he stood beneath the powerful hard spray and let his aching muscles absorb the steamy heat, the tension began to slip away from his exhausted body. He placed both of his palms flat against the tiles of the shower wall, and let his arms sustain his balance, as he rinsed away all of the troubles that were playing in his aggrieved mind. But when he began to soap himself, powerful images burst forth into his mind's eye. He saw the pictures so vividly, and the grotesque images seemed too real for his imagination to ponder. Watching the images reenact and take place all over again, like a demented scene from a horror flick, on replay, he could almost smell the vile acrid scent of copper, the stench of spilled blood, like a slaughter house flooding his nostrils.

He was taken aback, the shock from such vividness of imagery and the effects it had upon his senses had taken him by surprise. He knew then what must transpire, he was going to take the law into his own hands. Seeing a picture that was bigger than what anyone else could ever imagine. This was going to take the world by storm, and put the fear of God in the minds of all those who claimed to be our protectors. The ones who serve, those they deem are worthy and necessary to serve or punish, and those they believe are culprits, when in fact, many of them are culprits themselves as they judge and arrest. They are judges, jurors, and executioners in many cases, long before the case even goes to trial, and guilt is ever established. As of lately... these same protectors of the public, seem to be more executioners than they are cops, and since these protectors are so busy protecting, killing us, who is going to protect them?

Chapter One

May 18, 2020 Monday

1:50am Fredericksburg, Virginia

"Pull over, Stranger," Lisa snaps, from the back seat. Lost in thought, Stranger continues cruising down the interstate as if he never heard her words. Trapped in the headlights and the parallel lines, he remained oblivious to all that is going on around him.

"Stranger, did you hear me?" Lisa demands, with a hint of irritation in her voice. Again she grills, "Stranger! Pull Over!" displaying her aggressive attitude and annoyance in her voice, to no avail, trying to evoke a response from Stranger. As John erupts in his venomous tone from the passenger seat. "What, Lisa? What the fuck now? Every five minutes you want something, Stranger should've left your worrisome ass where he found you," John spews in his usual berating manner. "You know what? Fuck you, John!" Lisa replies, as yet another argument ensues between the two.

Stranger's train of thought is broken when the gas light pings continuously, alerting him that the fuel is low and the imminent need for a refill. "Would you both shut the hell up," Mike states, from the back seat, sitting along side Lisa, and her relentless barrage of insults and verbal threats.

"Damn, neither one of you can shut up for two seconds?"

asks Mike, venting his frustration at Lisa and John's nonstop onslaught of verbal altercations over the last few hours, and of being trapped in a car with the two. "Damn, do us all a favor, can both of you shut the fuck up!" Mike says, with exasperating annoyance.

Finally the silence ensues and Lisa, being Lisa, just has to have the last word, "Fine then, tell John to mind his own business and stay out of mine!" she says.

To that, John replies, "Lisa, get the fuck outta here, you don't even got no business, no life, no family, and no man for that matter," and snickers at his hurtful comments toward Lisa.

That is when Stranger speaks up in Lisa's defense, bringing the senseless argument to end, "Leave her alone, John," Stranger mildly stated, as if he himself is tired of the bickering between the two.

Just as he approaches an exit off of the interstate to refill, he notices a state trooper speeding towards him in the rearview. Maintaining the proper speed, he signals to exit from his lane, baring right onto the exit ramp. He keeps his eyes on the fast approaching Virginia State Trooper, as he takes extra precautions not to trigger any unneeded attention to initiate a traffic stop. Stranger, in a calm voice, says, "Everyone chill, the cops are behind us," and when Mike goes to turn around to see for himself, John scolds him, "Mike! What the fuck are you doing? Don't turn around, that's gonna make the cop suspicious, dumbass! Stranger got this, just chill the fuck out and act normal."

At the top of the ramp, Stranger signals another right and slowly merges into traffic while maintaining perfect speed, calm, and keeping his attention poised between the windshield and rearview mirror. Pulling into the Exxon gas station, and directing the car towards the pump, he notices the state trooper follows him at a safe distance and parks his cruiser at the curb at the far western side, where he can't be easily watched.

Lisa says, "Stranger, I think he's watching us. He's just sitting there staring at us." To which John replies, "He's a cop, Lisa, they watch everybody! What do you think cops do for a living? They watch and arrest people, dumbass!"

"Fuck you!" Lisa snaps just as Stranger gets out of the car and proceed towards the cashier window to pay for the gas. He notices out of his peripheral vision that the state trooper is peering at him fiercely behind his mirrored Aviators, such a cliche, Stranger thinks. It does make him nervous though, and the uneasiness only solidifies his notion that something bad is about to happen.

Turning to head back to the pumps, without even paying for gas, Stranger is in panic mode, speeds to the safety of the car. He starts staring at John and Lisa, who both stare back at him with a look of discomfort written on their collective expressions. Panic evident in his actions, he snatches the driver's side door handle and opens the door with a yank, pausing momentarily to gather his thoughts, and then Mike, coolheadedly says, "No, Stranger, this is not the time or the place, too many cameras, brother, patience is a virtue." But just then, John takes center stage again and forcefully says, "Fuck that Stranger! Take that mini baby bazooka and send Mr-I-got-eyes-on-you to a place he's never seen before where he can watch you from the clouds, that nosey motha-fucka!"

"Stranger no!" Lisa exclaims, "not here, Mike's right!"

"Fuck Mike," John snaps, "he's too damn cautious, and that's his problem right there. He don't understand 'get'er done', when it's time to get'er done!"

Mike stares at Stranger for a second, relaying an unspoken message, not even falling into the argument trap that John was so infamously known for, as a way to cause havoc, chaos, and confusion, in the midst of a moment when common sense and thinking were needed.

As the message was received, Stranger eased himself behind the steering wheel, put the car in pumps. The state trooper and Stranger locked eyes for a moment and remained that way until their cars passed from view.

Signaling a left turn and pulling off from the gas station, Mike suggested from the back seat, "Pull over at the next gas station, we still gotta get some gas, don't we?"

"Yeah, we do," Stranger replied a little down heartedly, causing John to say, "Oh, shit, here we go, damn I forgot to bring the party hats and streamers for this sissy ass pity party

Stranger brought me along for."

"Would you shut the fuck up, John! For real," Lisa booms from the back seat, "this is not the time for that!"

"Shit, it seems like it's never the time for anything, according to Mike, Mr. Patience-is-a-virtue back there."

Just as they are in the thick of the conversation, the state trooper bursts out of the lot heading in their direction. Lights flashing, sirens blaring, and in hot pursuit of them. "Fuck!" Stranger snaps with anguish, "he's on us, what the fuck now!"

Mike says, "Pull over, it's two in the morning, it's just us and him out here, now is the time! The rooster comes home to roost!"

"What the fuck is you talking about, Mike?" John exclaims, "Stranger's from the fuckin' city! He don't know shit about farms or roosters and shit, smartass! All this metaphorical shit you keep spewing. You want to tell him something? How about you tell him how we're gunna keep from going to jail tonight," John vehemently says, then added, "or tell Rambo here how to draw first blood, you fucking prick."

"Shut up, John!" Lisa said heatedly, "you always got something to say but you ain't sayin' nothin' you fuckin' dumbass!"

"Shut up everybody!" Stranger snaps, "let me think, let me think," he says to himself. John sarcastically replies, "Some good that will do," and rolls his eyes.

"Just pull over," Mike says, placidly.

Looking into the rearview mirror and staring into Mike's eyes, he bares to the right hand shoulder of the road and puts his car in park. Lights flashing like a carnival ride, the tension in the car rises. "What now?" John asks, but only silence fills the the car's interior, enough to hear a mouse piss on cotton, as his old celly used to say. But, the eerie silence is broken when the state trooper taps the driver's window with his flashlight. Stranger rolls down the window and continues to stare intently out of the front windshield, as if the trooper is nonexistent. The trooper states, "I need your license and registration, sir, and please keep your hands where I can see them."

Stranger goes to retrieve his credentials, but, instead, pulls his weapon from the console and levels the barrel on the cop with no resistance or hesitation. Stranger pulls the trigger of the .357 Smith & Wesson revolver three times, causing the trooper to back pedal with his hand covering the hemorrhaging wound in his neck, and falls down in the middle of the street. Unable to breathe, he lays there staring at the empty sky.

As Stranger unfolds himself from the confines of his car, he approaches the dying trooper and stares down at him, seeing the dwindling corpse and unloads three more shots into his face. With a sinister smirk on his face, he says, "You're the second of many more to come," leaning closer to see the officer's name and badge number. Officer Bloom #271.

He tears the badge from the officer's chest and removes his

gun from the deceased trooper's holster, then says, "you won't be needing these where you're going," then placing the items into the pouch of his hoodie, turning and getting back into the car and pulling away, he smiled to himself.

As soon as the car pulls onto the pavement, John says excitedly, "Now *that's* how you get'er done! Take no prisoners, only take badges and guns..."

Chapter Two

May 18, 2020 Monday

4:15am Fredericksburg, Virginia

Arriving at the scene of the fallen state trooper, Fredericksburg Homicide Detective Vince McNealson stands at a distance, as the crime scene unit does their job with pictures and collecting evidence. Det. McNealson paces the surrounding area, and looks for unnoticed clues or evidence of who might have been the culprit of such a heinous crime against a respected officer of the law. But as of lately, the net would be too large to cast due to the recent officer shootings involving unarmed minorities of black and brown ethnic backgrounds. Then there was the fact that this particular case seems more personal than any other homicide that he's ever investigated throughout his whole career.

Once Det. McNealson finished his cigarette and spoke with the medical examiner for the city of Fredericksburg, he took notes with the Crime Scene Unit's lead investigator, and got a few more details as to the evidence that may or may not be useful to the investigation.

Det. McNealson had asked that all the evidence be put on 'Priority' status and told them that he wanted everything on his desk in 72 hours stat. He was not walking lightly on this matter, and he was hoping that the dash cam from the state trooper's cruiser would shed some light and give the investigation a boost in the right direction. At least of the vehicle that was involved, even if the body cam footage revealed no true suspects at the moment.

While speaking with the other officers at the scene, a call came in across the radio of a possible arson of a vehicle a few miles south, off of interstate I-95. All available units were called to the scene of that crime now.

Just as McNealson's phone rang, he noticed something he didn't take note of before: The seclusion of the area, the darkness, and the absence of a street light and isolation from public view, which draws him to wonder, 'why would a veteran officer of 15 years put himself in such a compromising position?'

Upon answering his cellphone, he saw that the caller was one of the Detectives of his unit, Det. Matt York, who then told him that he needed to come down the road to the Exxon gas station, where apparently Det. York had found something that may be helpful to the investigation. Det. McNealson told Det. York to hold tight as he was wrapping things up at the crime scene but that he would be there shortly.

After tediously and meticulously combing the area for clues to the murder case, he released the scene for closure and headed out to the Exxon gas station as per request from Det. York.

Upon arrival, he was introduced to the new information as to the whereabouts of Officer Bloom, just before his ultimate demise, as he watched video footage of Officer Bloom, just sitting in the parking lot of the gas station before speeding off only moments later, after what appeared to be a car that he may have been suspicious of. But, upon further viewing of the tape, Det. McNealson took notice of something that not only looked off, but it felt off as well.

During the time span 1:51am to 1:57am, a car had entered the Exxon gas station and pulled to the pumps, momentarily followed by Officer Bloom. The driver of the car, a dark blue or black late 90's model Crown Victoria, proceeded to the window in which to purchase gas. At least Det. McNealson believed that was the intent.

Upon even further viewing and repeated reviews, he noticed that the driver was a little over anxious and looked to be totally focused on Officer Bloom as he sat stationed at the far end of the gas station's parking lot, against the curb, just past the pay phone and air pumps. Then Det. McNealson saw what seemed to be fear or paranoia take place as the driver hurriedly turned and proceeded back to the automobile and hesitated before getting into the driver's seat.

That momentary pause is what Det. McNealson perceived as aggravation or even confusion. Yet, even with the color video footage, he couldn't get a clear view of the alleged suspect due to the dark hoodie covering his head. Nor was he able to see if there were any other occupants in the car because of its dark window tints.

After interviewing the store clerk, another officer arrived at the gas station to see what help was needed, if any. When Det.

McNealson heard the officer relaying the story of a car arson down the highway, he was stuck with a possible clue when the officer said that the make of the vehicle had been a '98 Crown Vic, but also that the car had been part of a murder/carjacking out of Washington, DC, earlier that evening.

It was at that moment that Det. McNealson began to receive the notion that the two unrelated events were in fact one and the same, and party of the same crime spree that had taken place over the span of the night.

Immediately, Det. McNealson took off towards his unmarked cruiser and headed towards the scene of the arson with flashing lights as he was speeding close to 90 miles an hour. He sped down the interstate speaking frantically into his cellphone ordering them to cordon off the area and wait for crime scene techs to arrive there to collect any evidence or possible fingerprints.

But, it wasn't necessary when he arrived, because there was nothing left of the vehicle to print or take any evidence of. The only thing distinguishable was the District of Colombia license plate. Everything else was torched beyond recognition, and any evidence that may have helped was unattainable. Det. McNealson knew he wasn't dealing with an open and shut case, he was going to have to put in some real work, and real hours.

Chapter Three

May 18, 2020 Monday

4:30am Richmond, Virginia

Rest Stop - I-95

Sitting on the top of a picnic table at a rest stop just outside of Richmond, Virginia, along the I-95 south bound interstate, Stranger takes a much needed break to clear his head. With all of the constant nagging and bickering between his friends; Mike, Lisa, and John, he needs this moment to smoke a cigarette and grab a bite to eat in peace, leaving the others to do whatever they needed to do before they got back on the road.

Stranger feels sleepy yet relaxed at the moment and he is listening to sounds of the darkness and the slight awakening of the travelers on the interstate. He remains motionless as the clouds of cigarette smoke pass within his picture view and form silhouettes in the beams of the moonlight. His mind drifts onto memories of a distant past, as his hindsight takes shape in his present mind state. Daydreaming about the pain of those yesteryears, until Lisa's voice brings him back to reality.

"So, what now, Stranger?" Lisa asks nonchalantly, as if all that has happened in the last few hours is a part of the norm for them.

"I don't know," Stranger replies, "I guess we keep going, ain't no turning back now." Stranger states the last part as if he has no choice in the matter.

Then Lisa speaks up, "You know, we could go back home," as John steps in and exclaims, "And do what? Get stereotyped, harassed, and shot to death? All because we're black?"

"Who the fuck are you kidding, John? You're not even black, you stupid mutha fucka!" Lisa shouts at John as he just stands there looking bewildered, like this was a new revelation to him.

John blinks. Then he double blinks his eyes again, as if the words that Lisa just spoke finally came to dawn on him. John then seems to get the truth of her words and finally acceptance seeps in. He snaps back, "Ok! And your point is? I'm a reverse Oreo cookie dumb ass, I'm white on the outside, black on the inside, and for your information, Miss Black America, bullets don't got no racial picks, the fucking police DO!" John spits venomously, "and if they gunna shoot Stranger, well they better have two bullets in that gun, one for him and one for me! Ain't that right, Stranger?"

John looks to Stranger for confirmation of his comment. But Stranger just sits there as if he hasn't heard a word that was said. John blurts out, "Good! What's understood don't need to be said!" As Lisa bursts out laughing, she says, "John, you're so fucking stupid boy! The adage goes: 'What's understood, don't need to be explained' stupid!"

"So what! Same thing-they're close in relation! Just like human beings, we only have different shades of skin, everything else is the same, right? We're all brothers and sisters, if you ask me," John replied.

A little bit perturbed for being singled out by Lisa, John walked away feeling like an outcast. Stranger, seeing this, made Lisa clean it an up. "Lisa, John's an asshole, but he means well, and I am his only friend, so go make it right," he tells her, seriously.

As she walks off toward John to apologize for the sake of her friendship with Stranger, "You handled that pretty well," said Mike, appearing out of the clear blue. "Thanks," replies Stranger, "so, what's on your mind, bro?" Mike asked Stranger.

"Man, I can't call it slim," replies Stranger, "I just hope this isn't all for nothing."

"Well, it can't be all for nothing if it means something to you," Mike says, not questioning Stranger's intentions.

"Now you know the rules."

"Don't start something you can't finish, right?" Mike asks. "Yea, I know the rules," says Stranger, sounding a little bit dejected, "I'm all in Mike, ten toes down and two feet deep."

"Good!" says Mike, "let's get going! We got places to be and a few cops to meet," he says in a way that can only mean that he is serious.

Jumping off the picnic table, Stranger says, "Let's roll then!"

Climbing into the front seat of the new stolen car, John calls, "Shotgun!" and jumps in the passenger seat, closing the door behind him.

Just as they all pile in, a police cruiser pulls into the rest stop, not even paying them any attention, Stranger backs out of the parking spot and slowly pulls away.

As the officer heads toward the rest room, oblivious to his surroundings, he doesn't notice that brake lights have been applied to the car passing, and the car came to a stop. Stranger looks into the rearview mirror at Mike and Mike smiles and nods his head in answer to the unspoken question. Approval.

The door to the rest room opens and Stranger walks up to the urinals where the officer is relieving himself. Stranger begins fiddling with his zipper, as if, to pull his member out to urinate. But instead, he turns to face the officer and asks, "Officer, is this too big for me?"

When the officer looks down, he was caught off guard staring at a big Glock 17, cocked and ready for action. Without warning, the shots rang out, filling the officer with holes. But Stranger wasn't done humiliating the dead officer yet. He repositions the officer, leaning him face first into the urinal, as he removes the officer's badge and then his gun from his holster. Officer Ramirez Badge #1873.

Standing there admiring his work, Stranger then wipes down Officer Bloom's gun and drops it, then stuffing Officer Bloom's badge into Officer Ramirez's mouth, whispering to himself, "Now that is taking a bite out of crime. For every one of mine that you kill, I am killing two of yours."

As he was walking out of the restroom, hoodie clad, placing Officer Ramirez's badge and gun in his hoodie pouch, he acts as if this was just another day at the office.

Chapter Four

May 18, 2020 Monday

5:00am Spotsylvania County, Virginia

Upon arriving at the crime scene in Spotsylvania County, Virginia, Detective McNealson was greeted by the Spotsylvania County's lead investigators for arsons, Detective Joseph Dabney, as well as Spotsylvania County's Fire Department's Chief Investigator, Inspector Franklin Morrison.

With the formalities out of the way, Detective McNealson gave the two a brief summary of the crime that was committed in his jurisdiction and why he believed the two crimes may have been committed by the same suspect-or suspects. The information that was given to Detective Joseph Dabney began to expound his intake on the potential coincidences between the two crimes, by not relenting that the two were indeed a part of the same scheme of crime spree.

Detective Dabney being a four year veteran as a detective and on the force for six years, was very suspicious of other fellow officer's motives when it came to their seniority rank, due to the fact that a lot of officers and detectives use the backs of others to climb onto, in order to rise in the ranks and succeed into positions of higher authority.

Being that Detective Joseph Dabney was one of these types whose questionable integrity held no moral bounds. He refused to see the likelihood of the two crimes being related, plus, the fact

29

still remained that he himself, was not relinquishing his case over to another Detective from another jurisdiction. Nor was he giving in to becoming a stepping stone for another black man to rise in the ranks above him. He believed not only that he is of a superior mind and superior work ethic, but also, he is superior in race. So, no matter how convincing Detective McNealson was in his theorization of the relating factors in the two crimes, Detective Dabney was going to be the juggernaut that remained unimpressionable and unmovable in his exception to the rules of standard procedure.

Realizing that he wasn't getting anywhere with Detective Dabney, Detective McNealson used the reverse tactic and played the role of subordinate and asked Detective Dabney for his opinion, relying on the superiority/inferiority complex of the other detective to play his hand, and in fact, it did.

Once detective Dabney saw that he could lead the two investigations and thus play a better position in the overall stakes of the closing of his case with the capture and conviction of the suspected cop-killer, he would be making a bold statement. A statement that he, in fact, was an elite detective, in a class of his own, while his career would be sky rocketed.

This was the exact narcissistic thinking that Det. McNealson was banking on, and indeed, Det. Dabney fell right into his trap, so McNealson downplayed his position, and asked Det. Dabney all the questions as if he was the unsuspecting, inexperienced rookie, speaking to a veteran whom he looked up to and deemed to be larger than life.

The results were as he planned. Not only did he get more privileged information, he actually went a step further and got Det. Dabney to agree to work with him and his department, with the agreement that McNealson would give Det. Dabney the lion's share of the credit once the killer was in custody, or even better, in the morgue.

In turn, Det. Dabney would relinquish what information that he saw fit and lead the investigation from his end. That alone would be a boost for Det. Dabney if he helped solve this homicide, with all the recommendations and pats on the backs that he would receive. There wasn't any way Det. Dabney wouldn't move up to become lead detective in the Spotsylvania Homicide Division once he had taken all of the credit for the closure of the case.

While canvassing the scene for any clues, the two detectives juggled theories and bounced presumptions off of one another as to what the motives for the first crime leading up to this apparent crime spree were. Detective McNealson made a show in the face of inferiority saying, "Detective Dabney, do you mind if I reach out to the Metropolitan Police in D.C. and find out what evidence they may have in the armed robbery/carjacking in which the car that is surely a part of this arson, is a part of their ongoing investigation as well?" Detective Dabney paused while shining his flashlight upon the ground in search of any plausible evidence and states, "Well, since it is the automobile in question that I'm-I mean we're-investigating, I think it would be best if I spoke to them and got a handle on how the investigation is going on their end. I also got some clout with them guys out that way. I'll report any findings that may rise out of it to you and we'll see what we come up with. How's that for a start in search of a finish?"

McNealson responded with a smile. "That sounds fine to me. I believe with your experience, you will be able to get blood from a turnip!"

Both men laughed at the jibe and then shook hands, promising to stay up to date with one another's findings.

As McNealson walked away, he never took notice of Detective Dabney's arrogant smirk and the slight pompous way in which he slowly nodded his head in a self perceived victory over Detective McNealson's homicide case.

McNealson stopped short of the car and shifted his eyes to the back driver's side window, allowing him to see in the reflection, the knowing look. The look from a man who had no good intentions. Detective Dabney's reflection showed him to be a snake in the grass. A snake of the worst kind; a cruel, venomous and dangerous snake.

In turn, McNealson quickly turned to ask yet another question, only to peer into the eyes of what he could only attribute as something sinister, and thought to leave well enough alone, but instead, "Detective, I'll be in touch, have a good morning sir," he said, climbing into his car and then driving away.

Upon reaching the top of the hill at the peak of the incline, his phone rang. Seeing that it was Detective York, he answered with a passive tone, "Yeah, what's up, Matt?"

Hearing the details that Detective York just broke down to him through the receiver, he instantly replied, "I'm on my way," and, flipping his sirens and lights on, he sped away.

Mentally reviewing the recitation of facts and details that were just given to him, Detective McNealson was seeing the truth for the first time, that this was big. Much bigger than anyone was taking notice of at the moment. But he wasn't going to be distracted by any smoke and mirrors. He knew there was someone on the loose that wasn't only deadly, but extremely atrocious and stopping him wasn't going to be an easy task.

Chapter Five

May 18, 2020 Monday 6:10am

Richmond, Virginia

Rest Stop - I-95

An hour later, Detective McNealson reached the off ramp for the rest stop in the area of Richmond, Virginia.

Skidding to a stop by the area cordoned off by police tape, McNealson sat in the car for a second and surveyed the area first as he lit a cigarette and took notice of who was there in attendance. The Richmond 'First Response News Team' was already broadcasting to the public about its findings. Then came a light tap on his driver's side window.

Rolling down the window, Detective York said, "Man, you're not going to believe this!" To which Detective McNealson replied, "Try me, I once believed in fairies, unicorns, and dragons. Oh, and don't forget the Easter Bunny and a fat guy who breaks into people's houses and leaves gifts, only after stealing cookies and milk!" With a slight snicker, Detective York said, "You got me there, Vince."

"Yeah, I know," replied McNealson, "So, what you got for me?" he asked. "This is our man!" replied Det. York. "How so?" asked McNealson again.

Getting out of the car, Det. McNealson is taken aback by the sheer audacity of this suspect. The nature of the crime was an enigma within itself, but the complexities and boldness in which the crimes had been committed showed only one thing to McNealson at the moment: There is a pattern presenting itself and this isn't a crime of the run-of-the-mill spree killing. This is premeditated, and yet spontaneous, which meant there is no telling who the next intended victim could be. But, the pattern shows that the main common element of particulars is the 'victim', which seems to be cops.

After speaking with the investigating tech team and lead detective for Richmond Homicide Division, Detective McNealson and Detective Jacobs went and evaluated the scene.

Upon entering the bathroom, they both took notice that the officer had been using the urinal at the time of his demise. The fact supporting this conclusion was that Officer Ramirez's flaccid penis was still protruding from the zipper of his trousers and the floor around him was covered in what was a puddle of his own urine, apparently. Plus, the fact that the initial shots were point blank, close proximity and the victim was indeed facing the suspect upon impact, indicated that both men were using the urinals at approximately the same time.

"This wasn't a cowards killing, where the killer sneaks up from behind and shoots, as in execution style. No, this was a bold, fearless killing. The suspect was intentional with the murder of his victim," observed Det. Jacobs. "Yeah, he was, but there's more to this murder," replied McNealson. "I'm all ears," replied Jacobs.

Det. McNealson began to readjust his assumptions in a way that he now held a strong belief that the suspect went painstakingly out of his way to make personal contact with officer Ramirez, being that the suspect was on the far side of the bathroom, at the urinals, behind the officer. Det. Jacobs interjected by asking, "how do you know that the suspect wasn't already at the urinal when the officer came into the bathroom?"

"Well, let's take a moment and think about it," said McNealson. "You're an officer of the law, on duty, and it's the wee hours of the morning, at the rest stop that apparently nobody else is at. Would you nonchalantly walk into a bathroom, and put yourself at risk of being caught off guard? Or would you wait until nobody was in the bathroom before using it yourself?" asked McNealson, which caused Det. Jacobs to see the logic in his question.

He then stated to McNealson, "You know, Officer Ramirez has only been in the force for 2 years, which technically still makes him a rookie." But Det. McNealson countered with, "well, rookie or not, common sense would tell any officer of the law that, being in the bathroom at 4:30 in the morning, with nobody around, while being preoccupied with using the restroom, and thus, the use of his hands are preoccupied, fiddling with his zipper and pissing, are all things that a cop might want to take into account, well, I would, if I was in that position, don't you think?" asked McNealson.

"Well, you do have a good point there, now that you put it that way," stated Det. Jacobs. Then he added almost as an afterthought, "I wouldn't have come in here unless the bathroom was deserted in the first place. I would have waited until all occupants had left first."

"Precisely," said McNealson, "This was a very rare and unexpected situation Officer Ramirez was in, and I don't think the situation was premeditated to begin with," said Det. McNealson.

"Okay, so what's with the using of other cops' guns and significance of the other cops badges being left behind at each of the murders, what's the statement that he's making?" asked Det. Jacobs. "I can't really call it right now," answered McNealson.

Just then, Det. York sauntered into the bathroom and said, "Vince, can I speak with you?"

McNealson looked intently at Det. York and said, "sure, Matt," and excused himself to step outside.

Once out of earshot of anyone that might hear their conversation, Det. York started. "Vince, you know this is becoming a Federal matter now? This case is going outside of our jurisdiction and look at the direction and distance this crime spree has taken. I mean, from Washington, D.C. to Richmond, Virginia, and now two separate counties in between them. I think this may be out of our league here, Vince," said Det. York.

McNealson contemplates his options and calculates his choice of words before speaking. He finally says, "I think you're right, Matt, but let's first see what we can shake from the bushes before the FEDs yank this case from beneath our feet."

Pausing a second, McNealson then adds, "by the way, that first homicide fell inside our jurisdiction and that was a fellow officer, so I kinda got a vested interest in catching this murdering psychopath myself." Detective York stood there nodding his head, and saw Vince's logic in the matter, but, Det. York understands that the longer they take calling in the Federal dragnet, the chances are that more cops could end up dead. But, McNealson is not only his partner, but his friend and comrade in arms as well.

Noticing the look on Matt's face, McNealson said, "Don't trip Matt, if something turns up in a couple of days, we got him, and if not, I'll hand it over to the FEDs and let them do what they can. But let's see what we can come up with on our own first, it hasn't even been a total of 6 hours yet." Detective York dejected said, "I know, I know, but look at all that's happened in that time! A carjacking, two cop killings, which are obviously related and now a car arson, all in four different jurisdictions. This is going to make us fall flat on our faces if this goes wrong, ya know? But hey, I'm with you all the way, I just hope this ain't one of your hero syndrome moments where you feel you can save the day. Remember the last time..." McNealson felt the sting of the words, along with the memory that he had long ago buried in the cold grave of his soul.

A time back, he had allowed his daughter to be abducted and murdered when he could have prevented it, but instead, he forced his way into the investigation and got so wrapped up into a preconceived assumption of his suspect that he violated department regulations by having personal ties to the victim and being the lead investigator responsible for the apprehension of the suspect.

When it came out during the trial that a conflict of interest was this obvious and in fact his role was a key factor in the case, it had caused an adverse effect. But also the fact that the evidence was supposedly planted to frame the suspect caused the worst effect. A retrial was given to the defendant and key evidence was inadmissible, due to the accusations, but it wasn't the evidence that had ultimately found the defendant guilty. It was the jail cellmate of the defendant that had testified that he had admitted to killing a cops daughter and gave specifics.

Chapter Six

May 18, 2020 Monday 7:30am
Durham, North Carolina

Lisa yawns, then stares right into the eyes of Stranger, as they're sitting at a stop light waiting for it to turn green. Stranger watching the going ons from the rearview mirror and catches Lisa's eye while doing so.

"Good morning, Stranger," Lisa says, but Stranger only nods his head in reply. "So, you're not talkative today, huh?" she asks, being flirtatious.

"Oh my God, Lisa! Would you shut the fuck up! Nobody wants to talk to everybody they see this early in the morning but you!" John says grumpily.

Sitting up and stretching his cramped body, hearing Lisa up mutter incomprehensible comments under her breath, as John turns around in the front seat and eyes Lisa, shooting daggers from his ice blue retinas and fumes, adding, "I was sleeping soundly until the sound of your voice brought me back to the unpleasant look of your face. Do you know you sound like a female version of Urkel?"

Lisa stares intently at John and begins to spray him with a barrage of malevolent remarks. Finally, Stranger interposes, asking, "Lisa, are you hungry?" Knowing that Lisa loves food more than she loves belittling John. Then John blurts out insidiously, "Damn! I guess Lisa's the only one hungry, huh? Ole

Farmer Joe here goes to graze his cow, while he awaits his roosters to come home and roost! Man, we don't got that kind of money, you know she eats more than all of the starving kids in Zimbabwe do, with a year's worth of ration!"

"That's enough John!" Stranger replies to John's demeaning onslaught against Lisa.

As he pulls into the parking lot of McDonalds and searches for a vacant parking space, Mike asks from the back seat, "Where are we, Stranger?"

"Durham, North Carolina," Stranger replies. "Looks pretty laid back out here."

"Looks can be deceiving, sometimes cause the most conspicuous goes unnoticed, just like that police car sitting across the street that was tailing us a few miles back."

"I know, but I'm not worried about him," replies Stranger. "I know you're not," says Mike, "I'm not asking you to be worried, I'm asking you to be observant, if not damn overtly-observant."

"Hold up, wait a second, Mike," interrupts John, "is 'overtly-observant' even a word defined in the Websters dictionary?" asked John.

"Does it matter?" asks Mike. "As long as Stranger understands the magnitude of the message I'm conveying to him."

"Mike, what the fuck are you jibber-jabbering about back there? You're talking like you got your fucking D.E.G. or some shit like that!" John vents sarcastically, intentionally trying to belittle Mike's intelligence. But Mike doesn't bite into the bait and hook that John set out before him.

Instead, Mike redirects the attention to the more pressing matter at hand. "Well, Stranger, I got a feeling we're being watched again," states Mike seriously. "Me too," says Lisa, then adds , "I think we should leave, and find somewhere else to eat."

Stranger sits quietly for a minute allowing the opinion of everyone to sink in, until he decides to go with the consensus and started the car again, backing out of the parking spot. He slowly headed to the back of the lot where another exit was accessible and turned into the natural flow on the morning commuters traffic.

A few miles later, Stranger pulled into a cheap motel and parked, getting ready to open the door, Stranger said, "I'm gunna get us a room so we can relax a little and get some much needed rest."

Then as he proceeded to get out of the car, he hears John's last comment, "make sure they got a big ass pasture out back so you can graze your cow, you know she's hungry."

"Fuck you, John!" Lisa vehemently yells, "I can't stand your retarded ass!" Stranger, rolling his eyes, slams the car door and walks away.

Opening the door to the motel's front lobby, the door bells announce his arrival as the cashier appears from the back office and grumpily greets Stranger with a "Good morning, how can I help you?" This attitude implicitly relayed the message that this person didn't really want to be bothered or to do any work at the present moment, but Stranger replied with a somber "Good morning" of his own, and asked for a room, in which he paid for in cash on the spot.

While filling out the information card, Stranger's attention was diverted to the news broadcast on the TV which was providing the public coverage of the homicide of a Richmond, Virginia state trooper, Officer Ramirez, "...who was discovered by a civilian at a rest stop off of I-95 near Richmond, Virginia. Details were not yet released but some sources say that the officer was shot several times and there was no suspect or persons of interest at the time." The Crime Stoppers hotline was given for any information, "...that anyone who may have the ability to help in the investigation to capture the person or persons that committed this heinous crime against a decorated officer of the law..."

Upon hearing that newscast, Stranger returned the information slip, retrieved his key and left without giving off any impression of his guilt, or his discomfort in hearing this news.

Once in the room, the four of them got comfortable and turned on the TV set so they all could find out if there was indeed no suspects or any details being given about the case. Mike exploded. "You see, Stranger, they don't even comprehend the seriousness of our actions. This deserves a more aggressive approach, if you ask me," Mike says, heatedly, as he paces the small confines of the room while Stranger lays on the bed and stares at the ceiling, trying to sort out his own thoughts and loopy emotions.

A couple of hours later, Stranger rises from the bed and asks Mike, "'Where's Lisa and John?"

"They left," Mike answers.

"Well, I'm going to get something to eat, you going?" asked Stranger, but Mike shakes his head 'no' and continues to watch TV as Stranger left the room and headed down the motel's walkway. He saunters in a state of contemplation oblivious to his surroundings and comes to the sidewalk where the street has a steady flow of traffic, and waits for a break in traffic to cross the street. But, just as he begins crossing, he notices that the same cop from earlier at the McDonald's was posted across the street from the motel, at which he was now staying.

Stranger immediately played it safe and acted as if nothing was amiss, but knew in his mind that this couldn't be a coincidence. Not twice in one day. Instead, he proceeded to the neighboring fast food restaurant, a Wendy's. Entering the establishment, he decided to eat there and keep his eyes on the officer from a safe distance of the restaurant's dining room window.

After 45 minutes of picking at his food, and dragging out the procrastination stage of his subterfuge, Stranger realized that his physical presence was drawing unwanted attention, believing that some of the patrons of the restaurant were beginning to take notice of his poised state of quietness, Stranger gave off an air of unease and restive anxiety, due to his constant peering at his surrounding, watchful for anyone that may pose or be deemed a threat.

So, instead of sitting there and further experiencing this discomfort, Stranger composed himself and gathered the trash from the table, then headed to the trash receptacle, discarded the wrappers and placed the tray on top of a stack of trays on on the hutch. Upon heading towards the exit, Stranger caught sight of an approaching vehicle that pulled into the parking lot. Freezing in his position, he scrutinized the automobile and came to the conclusion that the car was that of an unmarked unit. With the hairs on the back of his neck prickling, he backed away from the door and looked around nervously, head on a swivel, his eyes alert for any sign of a threat. He finally spied a sign for the restrooms and headed in that direction, seeking to isolate himself from this sense of danger.

Once he entered the restroom, he surveyed the bottom of each stall and quickly approached the last in the row, with nobody else in the restroom with him. Stranger burst through the doors of the stall and swiftly slammed it shut, locking himself within the small space of confinement. After hastily wiping down the toilet seat and taking a seat, Stranger began to get a hold of his worrisome emotions and formulated a strategy on how he was going to outwit the opposition.

Thinking back to the many chess games that he played in prison, he started to mentally move the pieces in his head. He called this mental engagement. A war within the mind, where one can see the moves and counter attack preconceived moves that one hasn't yet made. This was Stranger's strange way of staying ahead of the curve and out-thinking the thinkers.

About ten minutes later, the restroom door opened and footsteps could be heard echoing off the tiled walls. Trying to peer through the slight gap between the stalls partition, Stranger caught a glimpse of an officer staring intently at the stalls. So, Stranger flushed the toilet for the effect that he was taking a dump, and he even poured on a cough or two for the added dramatization. When the officer's radio announced a call for all available units to respond to a domestic disturbance, the officer turned on his heels and burst out of the restroom at a breakneck speed.

Given this opportunity, Stranger took this impasse and wasted no time nor energy in relieving himself of this impossible situation he had found himself in. Standing up, Stranger replaced Officer Ramirez's gun back into the pouch of his hoodie, and made his way out of the restroom as casual like a man without any worry in the world, but also trying not to attract any undesired attention to himself.

Once outside and crossing the parking lot, Stranger took note that the officer that had been staked out earlier, was no longer present, so he made his way to his room without any incident.

Entering his room, he found there was total chaos in store for him. John was ranting on and on about him leaving without him and leaving him to graze his cow, while Mike was adamant that he needed to talk to Stranger, and needed to sit tight until nightfall because there was apparently an APB out for the grey Ford Taurus with Virginia plates, that had possibly been used in connection with the murder of a Virginia state trooper.

Hearing this news, Stranger became wary and he began to get agitated with John and his antics because this was not the time to be a fathead, and Lisa seemed to be at a stage of breaking down from all the acrimonious and hateful remarks that John had been dishing toward her. Stranger was at his wits end and the stress was mounting up on him. He wouldn't take much more.

Mike saw what was occurring and proceeded to defuse the situation, speaking abruptly, "John, chill out Slim, can't you see you're making matters worse?"

John stares around the room, catching everyone's eyes, and realized that he was being made out to be the bad guy. He actually didn't see anything wrong with what he was doing, he believed everything he does was normal, and everyone outside of him, had to either get with the program, or get hurt in the process. But, being that his antics were affecting Stranger, he decided to nip his crazy behavior in the bud, out of concern and respect for Stranger. So, John conceded and sat down on the bed crossing his arms in the typical way in which John does when he's trying to be passive or doesn't get his way.

Then John does the unbelievable which causes the others to stare at him mutely, mystified, when John said, "I know I've been a pain in the ass, and I'm sorry." Almost as if he actually meant it, until he rolled his eyes towards the ceiling and released an exasperated breath, like it took every fiber in his being to let his pride go and say those words.

Mike approached Stranger, who now sat on the edge of the bed with a look of disheartened doldrums and defeat. Squatting down to eye level, Mike places his head upon Stranger's and said, "let me speak to you a second, bruh! Come on, step into the bathroom for a minute."

With the door closed behind them, Mike took a moment to sort out his thoughts before speaking. When he did finally speak, he said, "I know you're wondering if you're doing all this for a cause, or just because. I know that crushing feeling that's taking center stage inside you, I can feel it too-shit, I've felt it more times than I can count. But here's the thing Stranger, these cops are killing our kind, they're decimating our futures and eradicating our seeds, our youth at the rate of one-per-minute. They're killing us in the sunlight for all to see. The authorities that are meant to protect us, are physically exterminating us and doing it in the name of justice."

"We're not being racially profiled anymore-this is a massacre of the masses, and our so-called forefather gave them this authority over 400 years ago. The laws aren't to protect us, they are put in place to wipe out our race, and they're doing this legally, the generations yet to come are being erased from existence long before they even get to actually exist. Yeah, I know some of our own kind don't care about anyone but themselves, but there are those who do, and there are some of us who will stand in the face of adversity, and Stranger, you're one of those 'us' that I'm speaking about right now.

"Yeah, this may not be right in some people's eyes, but who made the rules, and who made the rules of right and wrong? It's only right when they killing us, but is it wrong when we follow the law of the Bible: 'Eye for an eye'? Or, do we just turn the other cheek and keep marching in the street with an uncertain outcome in our horizon? Let's finish this and make the statement that enough is finally enough! That 'Justice' will no longer see 'Just Us'!

Taking a moment to see if this has sunk in, Mike turned towards the door and said over his shoulder, for added emphasis, "You know Stranger, I really look up to you for doing this, you're doing something a lot of us don't have the courage for, and that's big in my eyes. Bigger than the world seems, Stranger-bigger than the world!" Then he left the bathroom, shutting the door behind him, leaving Stranger to sort out his muddled thoughts on his own.

Half an hour later, Stranger exited the bathroom with renewed vigor, he came out and stood at the window, peeling back the curtains to peek out the happenings in the parking lot. Saying to nobody in particular he says, "we gotta get rid of that car, they on it, they got a precise description of it and I know where to get another, but what do we do with the car we got now?" John blurts out, "We burn it! Let me set it on fire, like the last one-Mike got to help with that one, let me do it this time," John excitedly rants on.

"Nah," replied Stranger, "That's too much attention!"

"I think they may be suspicious of the car in the parking lot now, that's why I believe the cops have been staking the place out," John cuts in.

"Wait a minute! You mean they already on us?" Lisa asked desperately.

"I think so," replied Stranger calmly.

"Then why haven't they come in here with a task force and dragged us all out of here?" asked Lisa.

"Because, Lisa," says John.

"Because what?" asked Lisa.

"Because they know Stranger got a room full of farm animals and they don't want to kill an innocent cow!" replied John.

"Fuck you, John! You're such an asshole!" Lisa says vehemently. Both Stranger and Mike just stands there smirking, trying not to laugh, at the way John and Lisa both banters one another, constantly, even in the midst of overwhelming darkness.

Then Stranger answers Lisa's question, saying, "the reason why they haven't come to get us is because I never gave the car's description on the motel's information slip, I wrote 'walk-in' where vehicle information was. The cashier went to the back office when I was checking in, so they can't possibly say for a fact, that we came in an automobile, that's why the cop sat across the street, to see who would go to the car. That's what I believe, and I think when it gets dark, I'll slip out and get us another car."

John said, "I'm going with you this time."

Chapter Seven

May 18, 2020 Monday 10:00pm

Durham, North Carolina

Slipping out of the motel, using the back window that faced a thicket of backwoods that was good camouflage and perfect concealment for Stranger and John to move around without being on display.

When they reached the edge of the trees facing the main avenue, where traffic moved at a slow and steady pace. Stranger relayed to John his plan of action, pointing to an Auto Mechanic Shop, 'Mike's Auto Machine Shop' that was across the street, he said, "There are cars all around that lot, and chances are, from the run down look of the red brick building, it may be easily accessible."

Then he pointed to where the back of the shop faced another patch of wooded area, Stranger said, "that's where we'll hide and wait, until the timing is right to make our move."

After crossing the street and vanishing into the darkness and dense thickets of the woods, Stranger led the way through the Labyrinth of trees and branches, until they were directly behind the auto shop. John, eager to get to the mission at hand, was halted by Stranger, who was taking his time, to light a cigarette and scope out the surveillance in the area, looking for any potential threats, when Stranger finishes his cigarette and says, "come on, I think I see a way in, cover me."

John remains silent, cautious not to make any mistakes because this is the first time Stranger has allowed him to accompany him on any 'adventure', as John calls them. Ducking down to be less noticeable, they proceeded to move between the rows of cars. Stranger came to a stealthy halt, listening to surrounding sounds that can alert him if they weren't alone. Once satisfied, Stranger traversed the darkness with clandestine rigor as he eased up to the rear of the building with John beside him, just awaiting instructions on what to do next, if there was to be any given. John was a criminal in his own mind, even though he hasn't committed the actual 'act' of a crime. He definitely knew how to impersonate a career criminal, so he followed Stranger, step for step, mimicking every action as he pantomimes Stranger's every move.

While peeking around the edge of the building, John asked, "What is it, Stranger? What do you see?" Stranger doesn't reply. Then the curiosity of not knowing what's going on begins to get the best of John and he sticks his head out around the corner, causing Stranger to react, pulling him back into the shadows. He began cursing John out through clenched teeth, saying, "stay the fuck behind me, don't move unless I tell you to!"

When Stranger turns to make sure John understood him. John saw the intensity that made him realize that Stranger was as serious as AIDs, strokes, and heart attacks. So, John scooted back a bit, and played his position.

When Stranger beckoned him to follow, John followed

closely, keeping an eye out in front, as well as back of them, to ensure they remain safely undetected and that nobody gets the drop on them from behind.

As Stranger found what he believed to be a point of entry, he tried prying at the vent cover with his hands, but gained no access. He then went towards the front of the building and sought out another point of entry, but this time he used the sole of his Timberland boot, and donkey-kicked in the glass window at the bottom of the garage's service bay door and then squatted down to case his surroundings to make sure nobody saw him enter into the building. Once Stranger was sure that he hasn't drawn unneeded attention, he climbs into the broken window and begins his search of the whole service area.

With nocturnal eyes of a night owl, Stranger swiftly moves about in the darkness and settles in on the peg board where the keys to the cars were hung. Noticing that there were keys that were labeled with tags on the board that was also labeled with 'done/completed', Stranger began snatching keys from the peg board. He then entered the waiting area and quickly moved behind the counter and took to searching through the drawers and hit the jackpot when he found a small box-like safe that had been left open that contained pouches of money that were probably meant to be deposited into the bank. Rising to a standing position, stuffing the keys and pouches into his pockets, Stranger was alerted to the presence of an approaching vehicle.

A police cruiser pulled into the front lot and parked. Its strobe lights were flashing, but without the sound of sirens. The officer stepped out of his vehicle and closed the driver's side door, peered suspiciously around the surrounding area, and pulled his flashlight from his utility belt to begin his search. Stranger reached into his hoodie pouch and removed the badge and gun, while standing in the shadows of the waiting area. As he stood watching out of the window, he then made his way to the service area, approaching the bay windows and stood there like a mannequin in a window dressing.

The officer neared the bay window to peer in, lifting his flashlight to get a better look into the darkness of the service area, and was met by the haunting sight of Stranger's gun. John screams, "Now, Stranger! Shoot him NOW!" from behind the fear frozen officer. Just as several booms shatters the glass bay window, echoing in the distance. The officer met his demise and his maker simultaneously, as he falls in a crumpled mess.

Standing over the officer's fallen body, John looks down with the most sinister of smiles Stranger has ever seen on his face.

After climbing out of the hole of the shattered bay window, Stranger said, "Let's go!" To which John answered, "Hey, wait, what are we gunna do about him?"

"Leave him," Stranger replies.

"That's not very smart, Stranger," replied John.

"How so?" Stranger asked him.

"He'll be too easy to find, we need to make it a little harder for them to find him, don't you think?" John asked. "I mean, we also need a head start to flee this area, and if we leave him here, our chances of escaping undetected diminishes a great deal, and we need to find a new car too," John reiterated.

Stranger takes in everything John spoke on and decided to go along with whatever John was conspiring to do with the officer's body. "Alright, what we gunna do with him?" Stranger asked. John smiled and said, "Let's play 'Hide and Seek'."

With a puzzled look, Stranger stared at John like he had spoken another language, so John took notice and clarified himself. "What I'm saying is-we hide him-they seek, or find him," John says for a clearer understanding about his proposal.

"Oh, alright," Stranger states nonchalantly. "But first, we need to hide his police cruiser so it won't be easy to find," John points out to Stranger, and then without a second thought, Stranger hurriedly rushes over to the police cruiser, opens the door, and climbs into the driver's seat. He starts the car, then switching off the strobe lights, he pulls the car to the back of the lot and parks it between an old school bus and a long-body movers truck that both look as if they haven't moved in years. With the car well hidden, Stranger jumps out of the car and pulls out a set of keys and presses the key fob to locate the vehicle he is searching for.

When the car's lights lit up and he peeped its location, Stranger rushed over and popped the trunk. He then went to where the officer laid and squatted down above him, snatched him up by his shirt collar and began dragging him across the blacktop like he weighed nothing at all. John stood there watching all of this, and said, "you know, I would have helped you Stranger, but I don't do the dirty work stuff, I'll leave all of that to you..."

"Yeah, whatever," Stranger replied at a distance. When he got the officer lifted into the trunk of the car, Stranger removed his badge and gun: Officer Folk, Badge #454 and placed them into his hoodie pouch. He then reached into the trunk with Officer Ramirez's Badge #1873 and shoved it into his mouth, then placed the barrel of Ramirez's gun to his nose, shooting him twice. "That's for being so damn nosey, ma-fucka!" Stranger said, dropping Ramirez's gun in the trunk. He shut it and casually walked away like nothing ever happened.

Chapter Eight

May 20, 2020 Tuesday 9:20am

Fredericksburg, Virginia

Just as Det. McNealson enters his office at the Fredericksburg Homicide Division, his phone rings. "Homicide, Detective McNealson," he says. Listening to the caller, he says, "Yeah, yeah, I remember, so how can I help you?" he asked the caller. The news that was relayed to him jolted him to a befuddled standstill, causing him to brace himself for support when the caller exposed intricate details that weren't privy to the public.

Det. McNealson tried to convince the caller to come to the department headquarters so his statement can be taken and placed on the record. But the caller denied any involvement and refused to get entangled with political drama that was unfolding in relation to these murders. Even with all of his charisma, his promising and coaxing, Det. McNealson couldn't get the caller to agree to his pleas to come forth, to further help with the investigation in the murder of Officer Bloom.

So instead, McNealson asked the caller to recap his laconic statement, while he briskly took shorthand notes of the sparse but irrefutable detail, in which, the caller gave description to, and therefore admitting being a witness of the actual crime that took place. With further coercion from McNealson, asking him to come in and be a good law abiding citizen, helping with the investigation to relieve the streets of this violent killer, but the caller abruptly hung up, leaving McNealson reeling from the information he was just given. When his partner, Det. York, knocked on his door and lumbered into the office, York took notice to the melancholy feel that was pungent in the air, seemingly almost stuffy and suffocating.

York is a youthful and energetic guy who hasn't let the theatrics of the job burrow into his skin and spirit like chiggers, allowing irritations, stress and blatant uncontrollable attitudes to manifest.

Det. York realized earlier on in his career as an officer that these attributes were consistent with the job and that not every officer of the law was a good officer, but York knew that McNealson was indeed a good detective, he also knew that McNealson was one of the officers who took his authority to the borderline and crossed the threshold into a criminal haziness of upholding the law, and breaking the law by applying the law as he saw fit. Although Det. York and McNealson weren't just partners, but friends as well, he had to admit that when Det. McNealson was in a typical mood, he could be ruthless and uncompromising.

York sat down in front of the desk and interlocked his fingers and sat his hands just below his sternum, leaned back, and crossed his legs. Judging the situation before his eyes and knowing his partner the way he does, he allowed McNealson to open up on his own, which he'd eventually do, but browbeating him into revealing what was on his mind, was like beating a dead horse, there was no good in it, nor was there going to be any accomplishment, because Vince McNealson was one of those type of men, that if you try to back him into a corner against his will, he'll turn into a rabid possum and attack you. So, Det. York put on his patient face and braced for the coming tidal wave of whatever was eating away at McNealson to come to a swell and then surge forth in a rant of investigative technicalities. Staring at Det. McNealson with passive intensity, York waited.

Feeling those benign blue eyes penetrating from Det. York, McNealson drifted from his reverie and said, "Matt, I just recieved a call from an unidentified caller who gave me some interesting facts about our case that wasn't revealed to the public." Det. York sat placidly and continued to bore holes into McNealson's conscience to make him cough up all of the beans, not just some of them. Taking a moment to evaluate Matt's face and noticing that Matt was waiting patiently for the dialogue to take shape and become apparent. McNealson lifted his handwritten notes which laid upon the desk blotter and began reciting almost verbatim, all the accounts which were given to him by the undisclosed caller.

Looking into Det. York's eyes, McNealson said, giving a run down of the information he learned: "At approximately 2:05am, on the morning of May 18th, the caller in question, was leaving from a club down the road from the scene in which Officer Bloom was murdered. He was about to turn onto the road when he heard 3 shots, then, 2 or 3 more, a few seconds later, he noticed that red and blue lights of a police car were illuminating the area, and, thinking in that moment that another cop was shooting 'yet another undeserving victim' due to the rash of police shootings taking place across the nation, the caller said he did, his words, not mine, 'not want to be another victim or another notch on the police's belt'. The caller then stated that after a few seconds, he turned onto Route 3 and headed in the direction of the shots because he had to get on the interstate to get home. Approaching the scene, a blackish '98 Crown Vic was fish tailing away from the scene of the crime, heading in the opposite direction and turned onto the ramp heading south bound on the I-95 interstate.

"The caller then stated that he passed the scene and noticed a cop laying in the street, which looked like most of his face had been torn away. He then got on the interstate and headed in the same south bound direction as the alleged black Crown Vic had gone. Well, upon driving on the interstate, the caller, noticed a car very similar to the car which pulled away from the scene of our murder investigation. The caller stated that he was coasting when the car came into sight, driving normal, at a speed of approximately 70 MPH. He stated that he himself, was doing about 75 to 80 MPH. When the car came into view, being that he was in the middle lane and the Crown Vic was in the far right lane, he was approaching the car, on its driver's side-and guess what?" asks McNealson finally. "Our caller got a real good look at our shooter. The caller said that when they were side by side, the driver of the Crown Vic turned his face towards him and he got a perfect view of him. He even said the guy was a male of about 25-30 years old, and wearing a black hoodie. He also said that the look on our guy's face was impassive. I asked the caller if he could describe the killer's face, and he said he could. When I asked if he'd come in to help with the investigation, he asked, 'why should I? you cops are killing us by the day and getting away with it'. He said that we are quick to launch a full scale investigation when one of our own gets murdered, but, what about them? He was saying, 'who's to say if I come in you won't be trying to link me into this crime? Making me part of it, cause I have knowledge of it? I'm black and in you people's eyes, 'black is bad' and then I'm a felon, So that's another strike against me there. Young, black, and felonies equal prison, life and death. Now you do the math!' Then the caller went on and I quote 'besides, I only called to let you know that I know, I saw, I heard, and NO, I ain't helping.' He then said, 'I also knew that car that went up in flames in Spotsylvania County, that was his car, how do I know? Because the Crown Vic had taken that exit, I was driving right beside him when he got off the interstate on that county's ramp'. Then the caller boasted, 'Yea, I can even pick the dude out in a photo lineup. I know every detail of his face-I got the memory of an elephant'.

Then McNealson told Det. York how he tried to get the young man to come in and speak with him so he could learn more. He even told him how he had pleaded and told him that he wouldn't be in any trouble and he promised he would keep him safe. Det. McNealson looked steadily at Det. York and said, "guess what he said, before he hung up? 'You protect me! Yea right'!"

Detective York sat stoically still before he spoke. The silence that followed McNealson's recount of the phone call he received could be felt like the stifling heat of an enclosed attic in the middle of a heat wave summer.

After a few minutes of hashing over the details in his head, Detective York unfolded his legs, unlocked his fingers and sat forward, hunched over with his forearm supported by his thighs. He leaned forward slightly and peered into Det. McNealson's eyes, and said, "Vince, this crime was brazen, petulantly cross, and screams insatiable, if you ask me."

Giving McNealson a minute to comprehend what he was saying, Det. York continued, stating, "I know we won't find this killer in Fredericksburg nor in Virginia, period. But I believe this spree isn't over!"

Chapter Nine

May 20, 2020 Wednesday 9:40am

Fredericksburg, Virginia

There is a knock at the door, and the conversation between Det. McNealson, and Det. York, is interrupted. McNealson waves the female officer into the office and asked her, "how can I help you?" Officer Shelly Spoon, the Homicide Unit's secretary, prances into the office with an air of conceitedness, interlaced with flirtation, making her the trademark for a sexual harassment case, if one was to engage in her antics. She approached the desk and presents the lab results and crime scene findings and said, "I'm waiting on the reports from Spotsylvania County. They told me that as soon as they're in, they will forward the reports from their investigation of the arson to us." Waiting to be dismissed, Officer Spoon stood boastfully, smiling like she wanted to be congratulated for winning the Miss America competition and a job well done.

Det. McNealson opens the file and sits down. Noticing that Officer Spoon is still standing there, he says, "Is there anything else, Spoon?" Shocked by his inattentiveness towards her presence and sheer lack of desire, in regards to her smoldering wantonness, she gracefully spun about on her heels and sashayed out of the office, but not before announcing that she would be available if they needed her assistance. Turning with an exaggerated flamboyance, while tossing an auburn colored ringlet of hair over her shoulder, she glanced back at McNealson tacitly implying that she was personally available for him. She then sauntered away towards her desk.

Det. York let an exasperated breath out, then said, "she's an accident waiting to happen." McNealson countered, "she won't be *my* accident, I sure ain't falling for the 'banana in the tailpipe'!" causing them both to burst out with laughter, the two detectives sharing a light banter together, but, just as quickly they got back to the task at hand. Det. York then shot McNealson a stern look, and said, "so...now that we know this murderer has moved out of our jurisdiction and can most likely be a serial, don't you think we should follow protocol and bring in the FEDs to maybe dragnet the area for the culprit and put a lid on this, before he strikes again?" Det. McNealson seemingly ignores his partner's query, as he peruses through the file of reports and evidence collected by the crime scene lab, looking for any connection or thread of evidence that could possibly give him a suspect to pursue.

While delaying the unavoidable question of Det. York, the phone rings and Det. McNealson answers impulsively, "Homicide, Detective McNealson."

"Yeah? How are you today, Special Agent Smart? How can I help you?" He stayed there listening to the agent's lengthy response for a minute. Then, McNealson answered, "Yeah, I have that case involving the homicide of Officer Bloom in my jurisdiction." Looking up from the file, into the eyes of Det. York, McNealson's face took on the dreaded look of a man who was just hit with some egregious news. Det. McNealson lowered his head in a shameful manner and answered, "Yes, I was there and-" He was cut off from explaining himself, McNealson said finally, "Yes, I realized there was a definitive connection with the two crimes, but I-" Cut off again, he listens to the agent's response.

Finally fed up with the Big-Me-Little-You song and dance, McNealson interrupts and says vehemently, "Look here Agent Smart, I'm investigating the murder of a fellow officer who was killed in my jurisdiction, adherent to protocol, I was under the assumption that Detective Seth Jacobs, from the Richmond Homicide Division was going to call you in, being that it didn't become a serial murder spree until the badge of my murder victim, Officer Bloom, was located at the scene of another murdered officer, 51 miles away, in Richmond, Virginia!" Fuming into the phone mouthpiece, Det. McNealson voiced his frustration in his defense and said, "Well, you do that!" then disrespectfully broke the connection with the agent by slamming down the phone.

Peering across the desk at Det. York, McNealson peevishly barks, "there you go, the FEDs are officially involved now. So get out of my office and do what a detective is supposed to do, investigate something, Mr. By-The-Book Barney!"

Unfazed by the inflamed hostility of Det. McNealson, Det. York didn't heed the irate comment but instead, he deliberately began poking holes in McNealson's angry facade, with an inquisition into what was said to him on the phone.

As McNealson began to reiterate the conversation between himself and Federal Agent Bradley Smart, he divulged that Detective Jacobs, the lead homicide detective in the Richmond murder, called the FEDs in, first thing that morning, and since then, there has been 3 more officers killed, connecting each by the removal and displacement of the murder victims badge and gun. While adding insult to injury, each victim was shot by the previous victim's gun, which was randomly left at each scene, but the most extreme aspect of these cases , are the manner in which the previous officers badges are being haphazardly positioned at each scene. McNealson went on to fill in Det. York on how the FEDs are placing blame on their department for failure to follow protocol, which led to the death of three other officers in three different states.

After relaying the last bits of their heated exchange,. McNealson sat stoically at his desk, waiting for Matt to say something. When nothing was spoken, McNealson admitted shamefully, barely above a whisper that he had "dropped the ball on this one." York, being the kind of friend and partner that he is, also agreed, saying, "Yeah, we did," taking on half of the blame so McNealson wouldn't have to shoulder all of the irresponsibilities and repercussions on his own. He felt they were partners, and they would face the wrath together, what else were friends for? As the silence carried on for a moment too long, Det. York unfolded himself from his seat and headed to the door. McNealson stopped him short and asked, "Where are you going?" York replied, "I'm 'bout to go do what detectives do, go investigate something."

Seeing that his comment eased the tension in his partner, when McNealson smiled approvingly. Det. York turned and proceeded out of the office, leaving McNealson to sort out his own thoughts in peace.

When passing Officer Spoon's desk, Det. York glimpsed Shelly watching him intently while sensually biting her bottom lip, feigning nonchalance with her flirtatious intentions. As Det. York passed by her, he shook his head in disapproval and said, "Officer Spoon, get it together, this isn't the time or place for those sort of antics." Seeing that his direct approach caused her to be crushed and instantly embarrassed, York continued on towards the elevators, never taking a second glance back at Officer Spoon.

Chapter Ten

May 20, 2020 9:47 Wednesday

Washington, D.C.

J. Edger Hoover Building

FBI Headquarters

Special Agent Bradley Smart, a 13 year veteran of the FBI's eastern division, and the lead investigator in the last serial murder crime spree, stares at the phone in disbelief, as the detective that was previously on the other end, hung up on him in a self important manner. This caused Agent Smart to feel a streak of vindictiveness brewing in the bowels of his guts. Picking up the phone, he made the appropriate calls to somebody who knew somebody, who was somebody and that somebody was going to make Detective McNealson's life a living hell, and Smart knew that he was going to be the cause of this effect.

Upon hanging up the phone, and leaning back in his plushly upholstered desk chair, he steepled the tips of his fingers at the base of his chin and smirked at the potency of his strength and effectiveness in a game of chess he would be 10 moves ahead right now, closing in on a check mate.

Just then, Agent Dennis Drapper, Special Agent Smart's junior investigator, stuck his head in the doorway and said, "Brad, let's get suited and booted, duty calls! We got another one in Durham. This one's been cooking in a trunk since Monday."

Special Agent Smart leaped from his seat and burst like a storm cloud towards the door. Exiting the office, he insisted that Agent Drapper walk and talk, filling him in on the facts of the case as they darted down the isles between the cubicles that filled the Bureau's main office. Agent Drapper informed Smart that the scene has been cordoned off and secured, awaiting their arrival. Drapper advised that he had dispatched the FBI's special Investigation Crime Scene Unit to the scene with orders not to process the scene until their arrival or their consent.

Emerging from the bank of elevators and crossing the Headquarters main atrium, Special Agent Smart asked Agent Drapper, "Could this case somehow be connected to the three other cases?"

Agent Drapper confirmed his suspicions when he said, "Yeah, it's an Officer Folks of Durham, North Carolina's Police Department. He's been MIA for the last two days. They found him in the trunk of a car at an auto shop, his police cruiser was parked in the same lot. I was informed that whoever did this really did a number on him," Agent Drapper relayed to Special Agent Smart, while climbing into the passenger seat of their unmarked 2018 Ford Explorer, just as Special Agent Smart jumped in on the driver's side and hit the push button start, and when the engine grumbled to life, he started peeling out of the parking lot at a breakneck speed. The auto shop was buzzing with a swarm of officers from the Durham Police Department. When Special Agent Smart and Agent Drapper came to a sudden halt in front of the auto shop, just mere feet away from the crime scene tape that cordoned off the area from anyone compromising the integrity of the scene. Quickly locating the lead investigator for Durham PD, Smart was given the intricate details of what was known through their immediate investigation about the heinous murder of one of their own. Once the information was plausibly considered, Special Agent Smart and Agent Draper allowed the scene to be processed by the FBI's Special Investigation Unit techs. While the crime scene was being evaluated, Smart sent Agent Drapper to collect any information or evidence that may have gone unintentionally overlooked by questioning the other officers that were hanging about, as he took a casual stroll around the rear of the parking lot, looking for any evidence that could've gone unnoticed. He looked at the placement of the Officer Folks car and then looked back across to where the body of Folks was disdainfully disposed off and left to rot in the trunk of a Nissan Altima.

The disfigurement of the victim was atrocious and left nothing of the officer's face for the medical examiner, or anyone else for that matter to identify. The crime scene lab techs came for fingerprinting, placing evidence tags all about, and taking pictures. Smart began surveying the scene, and noticed that there was a surrounding wooded area. He stood erect and glanced around, staring at everything but seeing nothing in particular.

When Agent Drapper approached him from the front of the auto shop, Smart said, "Dennis, there is a surveillance system here, right?"

"Yeah, we have the footage from only the last 24 hours though," replied Drapper.

"Well, that won't help us, huh?" questioned Smart rhetorically.

"No, I don't think it will," responded Drapper.

"I wonder if this suspect planned this, or he is just going off of a whim, and Officer Folks just happened to meet his demise by the hands of someone whose whole intentions are to kill every cop he encounters, or is he trying to tell us something and we're just not getting his message?" queried Smart to himself almost.

Just then, one of the crime scene techs approached and says, "Special Agent Smart, you're needed over by the body with the M.E." Special Agent Smart wasted no time with lucid thoughts and took off towards where the medical examiner was waiting for his arrival.

Medical Examiner Pamela Strouse introduced herself to him and then revealed the chilling find that she had come across while she was making an initial examination of the victim. She told Smart that the victim has an object imbedded in the back of his mouth, she then had the techs take pictures. Using the forceps from her medical bag to dislodge the object from the throat, just at the back of the tongue. They discovered an object that was a silver Virginia State Trooper's shield, badge #1873. Spl. Agent Smart knew from that very second that this was indeed the third victim in this evil, twisted plot of some sort of complex revenge against cops and there were two other victims that came before this one in two other states.

Agent Drapper called Spl. Agent Smart from the front of the auto shop and told Smart that the owner believes that one of the vehicles that was worked on earlier that day, the same day that Officer Folks was murdered, the vehicle was stolen, and so there was now an APB out for the black Charger with North Carolina vanity plates that read, SHOTIME. Smart takes a second to admire the irony of the plates versus the present situation, Smart made a logical guess and told Drapper to broaden the APB to all of the surrounding states.

When Agent Drapper walked away to put the orders in motion, Spl. Agent Smart was accosted by another officer from the Durham City DPD and the officer made a stunning revelation to him about a car that was found at a nearby motel, that was just less than a quarter mile away. But what was so revealing was that the car was a stolen 2001 grey Ford Taurus with Virginia tags, and the car was stolen from Spotsylvania, Virginia. Smart says, "hold up, where is this car now?" The officer answered him, "It's been towed, but there was something about that car that made me think that it was somehow involved in this case." Smart asked the officer, "how so?"

The officer peered into Smart's eyes for a few seconds before answering, then said, "Officer Folks was working a double that day, he was following that car, even sat on that car at that same motel from across the street, before it was initially reported stolen. I was on duty while he was staking the car out, and pulled up on him and he told me that he had a feeling about that car and how the driver of that car was acting real funny earlier that morning, at the

McDonalds down the road, but then the car disappeared out of the back entrance of the McDonalds and Folks lost sight of him due to rush hour traffic. Then he later on found it at the run down motel, and when investigating into its owner, he went to the motel front desk to find out which room the owner or driver of the car was registered to, but there was no resident on record who registered the vehicle with the office. So, Officer Folks was just sitting and waiting on the driver, when he got the report from the data base that the car was stolen." The officer waited a second to let Spl. Agent Smart take in all that he had said, before stating why he thought the stolen car and the homicide were related.

Once the officer was sure everything was fully communicated, he went on to say, "I think the two are related because the car that was stolen from Virginia was retrieved, and left abandoned at a motel. Then, at the scene of the murdered cop, at an auto shop, a car and money was stolen. Sounds like someone needed money and a getaway car if you ask me. Maybe the suspect of this murder was aware that officer Folks was on his trail and came here to get another car. Cause when the silent alarm was triggered, Folks was sitting up the street there," the officer pointed due east towards the lot, across the street from the seedy rundown motel. "He was the one who answered the dispatch call and said he was in close proximity of the alarm and would investigate."

Smart took all this information in and came to the conclusion that this officer had a very good theory, but not enough evidence or facts to lend it credence. It was still just a theory. But, a pretty good.

Chapter Eleven

May 26, 2020 11:00pm Tuesday

Memphis, Tennessee

"There's one right there! Stranger, do you see him?" John exclaimed excitedly. Stranger's focus is unaffected as he drove from Georgia, towards the city of Memphis, Tennessee. His thoughts were drifting back to the back roads of Augusta, Georgia, where Stranger was only a few hours ago, accosted by an Augusta Police Officer, while he was checking under his hood, having problems with the radiator...As smoke rose like dense fog around him, the officer asked him, "What's a South Carolina boy, doing out in the bush of Augusta?"

Standing on the passenger side, by the quarter panel of the 2012 Nissan Maxima, Mike said to Stranger, "seems some people don't know when to leave well enough alone." Stranger nods his head, as if he is listening to some melody, playing in the refuge of his mind. Then he looks at the officer, noticing his badge name, and says, "Officer Folks, there seems to be a problem with my radiator hose, or something."

The officer pauses momentarily, allowing Stranger's comment to register. He began by saying, "Well, ah, first thing is...my name's Officer Mahoney, and I think you have me confused with some other gentleman, but ah-you never answered my question-as to why you're out here in my sticks?" Stranger proceeds to work on the car, leaning down and fiddling with things under the hood that had no real meaning to the problem at hand, ignoring the question that was posed by the officer.

Officer Mohoney takes a step closer and starts to register suspicion, as intuition piques. He took notice that the radiator cap was removed and the steam was spewing from the radiator. Then, he realized that Stranger was inadequately tinkering with parts haphazardly, but Officer Mohoney began to badger Stranger as to his comings and goings. To which, he wasn't trying to answer. Officer Mahoney stepped closer to the front of the car, just in front of the driver's side head light, blocking the luminescence of the headlight beam with his body.

Beginning his questioning, he is only being confronted with an answering empty dark stare of Stranger's eyes, as he peered through Officer Mohoney's being. The officer froze, startled by the grim look. He began to step away, but the reaction of Stranger was brazen and stalk-like, as suddenly, Mike spoke with a seething abhorrence, telling Stranger, "Crush him! Crush Hiiim!" rolling his c's with his tongue and enunciating the i's. in 'him', like long exaggerated i's.

With swift, responsive speed, Stranger pulled the stolen gun from the hidden confines of his black hoodie pouch, and leveled the barrel on Officer Mohoney, telling the officer that it wouldn't be wise of him to play hero at this stage. He continued to call Officer Mohoney by the name of Officer Folks, and told him to raise his hands above his head. He then told him if he lowered his hands below his ears that he'd make sure he takes him to the family reunion of his relatives that have come to past.

Lowering himself to his knees, Officer Mahoney began to conjure up a plan to try to talk Stranger out of his demise. As he started to play the role of a caring cop. He said, "Son, what can I do to help you? There's something wrong here, and I just want to help." Stranger stared for a second. Gleaned in the direction of Mike and said, "Slim, do you hear this fool? He must think I'm just some dumbass, anything-ass-nigga, like him talking is gunna save him." Then, Stranger asked the officer, "you wanna save yourself?" The officer nods his head, without saying a word. Stranger persisted by saying, "Damn, Officer Folks, you was just talking a mile a minute just a few seconds ago, now what seems to be the problem? All those questions you were asking me, about why I was in this neck of the woods? Now, you's quiet as a church mouse pissin' on cotton."

Laughing at his own wise crack, Stranger takes note of everyone standing around him, and the officer. Lisa and Mike stand stoically, while John's hyped up over the exchange between Stranger and Officer Mahoney. John says, "ask him how many blacks he's offended, or how many times he's abused his authority and set a black man up to have him wrongly convicted of a crime that he didn't do?"

When Stranger posed these questions to Officer Mahoney, he instantly saw the officer tense up and began to quiver away in his own shell, but Stranger wasn't allowing that, he was going to get to the truth, or someone was going to die trying. After a few seconds, Officer Mahoney said, "Son, today is my anniversary-me and my wife has been together for 42 years and I just wanna make it home to her." Stranger thought for a second, then said, "Ok, answer my questions truthfully and you'll get to see her again." The officer took a moment to collect his thoughts, shaking off the terror he is experiencing. He began his recollection of a 'once upon a time'.

Officer Mahoney kneeled before Stranger, Lisa, Mike, and John, and stripped his soul down to bare bones as he revealed that he was the worst kind of law enforcement officer. The type that is vengeful against a race that has done him no harm. One who takes the shield and uses it against people he is sworn to protect-to further penalize and brutalize people for their ethnicity and not for their true crimes.

He began by stating a declaration that he's a true patriot of America, and that mankind shouldn't be held accountable for another man's short comings and poor people have it hard cause they don't work hard enough for it. He ranted on, and with a barrage of idiotic comments that were so Jim Crow-like, that he sounded like he was still living on a plantation, and still had slaves hidden away in the underground cellar. Who knew, maybe he really *did*.

He told them about how he thought black men were dangerous and lazy, and that society was doing away with them by using the justice system to mass incarcerate black men and other minorities. But the war against drugs and guns, is really a war against black men in general. Then, he said that he was only doing his civic duty, just as the rest of law enforcement, as well as what the justice system was doing.

He proclaimed that the laws that have been implemented were there to eliminate all black-kind and prosecute them to the full extent of the law for moderate crimes and to keep black men off of the streets and away from their families. That is how you tear down the family structure and the dynamics will then minimize the evolution of the black man.

Officer Mahoney, then made a statement that was blatant and overtly discriminatory, he said, "Ever since slavery days, the black man was powerful and strong. That's why we used them in the fields, to fill our crops and to pick acres on acres of cotton. They were strong as an ox, and they couldn't be broken back then, no matter how much he was beaten. But, when you terrorize his family, he falls into place-he becomes passive-so that's what's going on now, we're destroying his homes and taking his children and limiting his job security by making him a felon and taking all those rights away that makes him feel like a free man.

"In all actuality, he was just a dog on a leash and the law can yank him back and put him in the cage anytime they feel like it. The black man fits the bill, he looks the part. He's a criminal on sight, and he doesn't need to have been engaged in a crime, cause his skin complexion is the crime. He's guilty by association. His environment doesn't make him a product, it's his existence that makes him a product." As the officer knelt there huffing and puffing, with spittle foaming from his lips, he said, "And son it's been my civic duty to frame and convict as many blacks as my county jail can hold, I've put so many of you niggers away and shot so many of you back in the day, it's become part of the norm in our society. Take a look around you. Every cop nationwide is killing niggers and getting away with it. If you hadn't got the jump on me, you'd be a dead nigger right now!"

Mike screamed, "Crush! Him!" as Stranger brought silence to the night...

Pow! Pow! Pow!

Chapter Twelve

May 26, 2020 11:25pm Tuesday

Memphis, Tennessee Downtown

Riding down the street after entering into the city of Memphis, Tennessee, Stranger snaps out of his reverie, as John began excitedly pointing towards an empty parking lot at a neighborhood Quickie Mart. Driving down the avenue of Waltkin and Brown, John vehemently says, "Damn, Stranger, that cop was just sleeping in his cruiser all by himself and nobody was around, that was our chance right there!"

Stranger thought about it for a second, and remembering all the venomous comments that the Augusta police officer, Officer Mahoney, was lavishly boasting about, he signaled to the far left lane and made a U-turn, heading back in the direction of the officer that was sleeping on the job.

Mike said, "Stranger, park in the adjoining lot, there's cameras everywhere." Seeing that this was a true evaluation of the area, he drove into the next lot and parked behind the stores, in a darkened alleyway.

After sitting for a moment, he got out of the car and Lisa got out with him. Stranger asked, "where do you think you're going?"

"With you," Lisa answered without any hesitation. "Come on, Lisa, this ain't for girls," said Stranger.

"You right, this ain't for girls. But, I ain't no little girl, I'm a grown ass woman, and I want to see this one." Stranger hesitated a second while he contemplated what she proposed. Then he said, "Look, Lisa, stay out of the way and keep a sharp lookout for me," as they walked away from the car.

Rounding the corner of the building, he walked silently as Lisa rattled on about how this was all too much and that it was time for them to head back home. She tried to convince Stranger that they did enough and wasn't proving whatever it was that he was setting out to prove.

Stopping in his tracks, Stranger angrily took offense to Lisa's comment and said, "Lisa, you don't know what the fuck you talking about. There are cops out there killing blacks and getting away with it, they're using the law to justify their actions and they're only getting paid vacations for murder, but they call it 'paid leave' for the investigations of officer involved in shootings. Paid! Leave! Lisa!" Stranger reiterates. "And another thing, Miss Know-It-All, you wasn't wrongfully convicted of a crime you never committed. You wasn't assaulted and demoralized by officers who were sworn to protect you-you don't know shit! You're talking about something you have no clue about, this shit is bigger than me-it's bigger than us-I'm just making a statement that, if they can touch us, then we can touch them!"

Turning heatedly, Stranger proceeded to walk away with Lisa dragging herself at his heels. When they stepped over the curb, into the adjacent lot, Lisa stood at a short distance as Stranger prepared himself, pulling the hoodie's hood over his head and drawing the string tight, where his face was totally obscured from view of anyone lurking around or by the cameras that were used to surveil the property. Lisa was standing next to the car unseen by the occupant and said, "Oh my God, Stranger, she's a woman cop! We can't do this!"

Glancing in Lisa's direction, Stranger fumed with even more hatred and stated, "Then the lady officer that lied on me in court, and the lady officer that was in the pen that disrespected me and misused her authority to have her fellow officers jump on me and beat me up for no reason should get a pass too?" Stranger asked Lisa. 'Well?" Stranger posed to Lisa to answer his question.

Lisa dropped her head and fiddled with her fingers as she looked into the police cruiser, as a female officer sat there, fast asleep with her head leaned back on the headrest, unknowing that the reaper was just moments away from taking his claim. Lisa stuttered, "But..but... she's a woman Stranger..."

Stranger, ignoring her comment walked up to the drivers side window, stared in, reached inside his hoodie pouch, removed the police issued Beretta that he acquired from Officer Mahoney and with three sharp taps with the barrel of the gun against the window, the officer was stunned awake. Staring at the hoodie clad avenger and seeing the gun, she started to scream. But the scream was interrupted with two blaring blasts from Stranger's stolen gun. Shattering the glass and puncturing two simultaneous holes into the forehead of the officer, Stranger reached inside the car and removed the gun from her holster. Reading her name tag, he snatched the police shield from her uniform shirt and said, "Officer Hernandez, you won't be needing these, you have been permanently demoted for sleeping on the job, now you can go home and sleep for an eternity."

After stuffing her gun and badge, #119, into his hoodie pouch, he removed Officer Mahoney's badge. Badge #366. He then reached into the car, and yanking Officer Hernandez's jaw open, forcefully pushed Officer Mahoney's badge into her diminutive mouth and used his index and middle fingers to callously and forcibly thrust the badge deeper into the back of Officer Hernandez's throat. He then said, "There you go, Sleeping Beauty, now you really taking a bite out of crime." Lisa Jolts Stranger from his malevolent behavior by saying, "Stranger! Someone's coming!" Looking up, just barely above the police cruiser's rooftop, Stranger sees someone approaching in their direction.

Dropping Officer Mahoney's gun into her lap, he eases away from the police cruiser, staying low and stealthy, making a quiet getaway.

When they made it back to the car, Lisa stated, "Stranger, you didn't have to do that lady like that." Stranger grins with a sinister sneer and says, "The grass ain't always greener on the other side. I don't discriminate, women and queers have rights now too, and right now, she gets to die like any officer of the mutha-fuckin law! She wanted equality, well, she got it. Now, get the fuck in the car, or stay here with that bitch, it's up to you!" Stranger angrily states to Lisa.

With a tear streaming down her cheek, Lisa climbs in and closes the door, but not before stating, "This is wrong! This ain't you Stranger, what happened to you in the pen?"

Stranger takes what was said by Lisa and mumbled to nobody in particular, "Everything happened. Now…it's payback that's happening…"

Chapter Thirteen

May 25, 2020 10:00am Monday

Fredericksburg, Virginia

The main office in Fredericksburg Homicide Department was buzzing with activity, when Shelly Spoon rushes up to Detective McNealson and says, "There's an urgent call from a Detective Joseph Dabney. He says he needs to speak with you pronto and he's faxing some fingerprint analysis over. They'll be here shortly and I'll bring them as soon as I get them," trying to keep in step with Det. McNealson's speedy pace. "Thank you, Spoon," McNealson replies. "What extension is Det. Dabney on?" he asked. "Extension 1115, sir," Officer Spoon answers, just before she heads off to retrieve the faxed paperwork.

Pressing the speaker button and entering in the extension 1115, McNealson asks with no formal greeting to Det. Dabney, "what you got for me, Joe?" as if they were long term friends and on a first name basis. Det. Dabney said, "It's Detective Dabney, first off," saying this with a fume of indignation in his voice. "My bad, my bad, I thought we were colleagues on the same team and didn't have to be so formal." stated McNealson taken aback.

"Wrong again!" stated Det. Dabney.

"So, what's up, Detective?" asked McNealson.

"Have you received my fax yet?" asked Det. Dabney.

"No, it's on its way to me any minute now," answered McNealson. "So, what am I going to be looking at when I do get it?"

A moment passed, and Det. Dabney began relaying his findings over the past week, since the arson of the Crown Vic that was allegedly used in the murder of Officer Bloom in the jurisdiction of Fredericksburg, Virginia.

Detective Dabney began walking through his preliminary notes of the crimes that took place in Washington, D.C., before the subsequent murder of Officer Bloom and the arson in Spotsylvania County.

Relaying the facts to Detective McNealson, Dabney unloaded a detailed account of the murder and carjacking that happened in the North East area of Washington, D.C. on New York and Bladenbergs Ave, at an Econo Lodge Motel, saying, "The suspect approached the driver of a Crown Victoria and pointed a firearm at point blank range. The victim then handed over the keys when the suspect demanded them and his wallet. Adhering to the demands, the suspect was given the wallet which the suspect opened, and then he unloaded the weapon center mass on the victim." When facts were laid out, Det. Dabney then stated, "Now guess who the victim was?" Det. McNealson asked, "Who? Another cop?"

"Precisely!" answered Det. Dabney.

But the officer was an off duty, undercover cop, who was actually at the motel to meet with a confidential informant. The CI was standing at the door of room 218 when she noticed that the officer was being approached by a dark hooded individual, and watched the officer get shot several times.

Just as Det. McNealson was beginning to ask a question, there was a knock at his office door, and waving Officer Spoon in, she handed over the print out from the faxed evidence findings, and then Spoon left as fast as she had come in, but not before being hailed by McNealson. He asked "could you pull the files on the Bloom case and bring them to me asap?" Nodding her head, Officer Spoon spun on her heels to fetch the case records and evidence files of all the findings from the previous murders.

Det. McNealson continued to listen to Det. Dabney's recounts as he thumbed through the faxed notes, and was drawn to one piece in particular. Reading it over while barely keeping in tune with the conversation, he was having with Det. Dabney, McNealson halted the banter with Dabney by saying, "Hold up, Detective, it says here that the officer had a .357 revolver that he carried around on his person that was never retrieved at the scene. But also, the officer was shot with a .38 revolver, a Saturday Night Special. But that was the gun that was left at the scene, which was a stolen firearm in a robbery of a pawn shop in Silver Springs, MD. Is that correct?" asked McNealson.

"Yes," answered Dabney.

"When Officer Spoon returned with the files in hand and laid them on the desk, Det. McNealson asked her to locate the ballistics and firearm findings on the .357. She hurried back out of the office to accomplish the set task. Det. McNealson apologized to Det.

Dabney for the interruption, Dabney asked, "Are we really onto something here?"

"Yeah, and no," was the vague reply from McNealson, not trying to convey his thoughts and theories to Dabney. McNealson chose to keep it simple and just pass it off as a pointless hunch, "I think there's something off about the murder in D.C. and the one here in Fredericksburg," said McNealson.

"How so?" asked Det. Dabney. "Well, for starters, there was no badge left at the scene, was there?" asked McNealson.

"No, not from what I read," answered Dabney.

"Well, I'm wondering why? Unless..." Then the answers just jumped off of pages at McNealson.

"Unless what?" asked Dabney.

Pausing momentarily, reading the reports, he took notice that the original first killing had started with the undercover D.C. police officer, head of the Drug Task Force, Officer Richard Montgomery III, but that wasn't the revealing factor that drew McNealson's attention. It was the fact that Officer Montgomery was just reinstated after accusations of witness coercion, evidence tampering, falsifying CI's testimonies, planting narcotics on suspected dealers, assaults, falsifying records, and illegal search and seizures.

"It says here that Officer Montgomery has been on the radar as a dirty cop who did some real shady dealings, and it just so happens that Officer Montgomery was recently taken off of leave and reinstated to active duty after review committee justified his 'line of duty' use of force shooting of a juvenile, who was reportedly running away from apprehension. Montgomery cornered the juvenile in an alley on 1st Street, off of NW Florida Ave, where the shooting took place.

"Montgomery alleged that the juvenile pulled a gun on him and he shot the kid twice- the kid died on the scene. Being that Officer Montgomery was a white man and had a laundry list of accusations against him dating back to when he first became an officer, fresh out of the academy, ten years ago, this started a brush fire in the city of Washington, D.C.

"Once Montgomery was acquitted of any wrongdoings, there were relentless calls pouring in to dispatch with threats to do Officer Montgomery fatal harm. There was even a movement with thousands of demonstrators calling for action and for the removal of Officer Montgomery. They wanted charges of First Degree Murder to be filed against him," recited McNealson.

Det. Dabney then stated, "The officer wasn't found to be responsible for anything, so why make all that fuss?"

"Well..." Det. McNealson paused a second before reiterating the buzz, and answered by saying, "The juvenile that was shot by Montgomery was unarmed. There was never fingerprints found on the gun alleged to have been at the scene. The claim was that there was a gun found, but somehow the evidence was misplaced. All of the officers involved are collaborating this story as a show of unity and force that there was no foul play on Officer Montgomery's part.

"What do you think?" asked Dabney.

"I don't think nothing. I follow the evidence that are true, facts are truth. Theories are just that, theories," answered Det McNealson.

"So, you wouldn't stand with a fellow officer? Even in the worst of times, when they need you?" asked Det. Dabney.

McNealson waited a second before answering, just as Det. York entered the office. Staring at Detective Matt York, his friend and confidant, and stated without hesitation, "Yeah, there's some people you'd do anything for, or die trying." Then McNealson changed the course of the conversation by saying, "Look, Det. Dabney, I have some business to attend to, it would be nice if I could continue to receive your help in this matter." Playing up to Det. Dabney's narcissistic ego, he buttered him up a little bit more saying, "Cause you know I can't solve this case without your input and your superb investigative work and help."

With a prideful smile plastered upon his face, Det. Dabney said, "I'll be happy to keep digging to help solve this case, and if I happen to come across any leads, I'll contact you immediately." Before ending, he also added for the record, "Now, you know, if we crack this case, I want my just due, cause this could get me out of this arson division and into the big leagues with the real investigators, such as yourself," he shot back with his own portion of ego boosting.

Listening to Det. Dabney reveal his true intentions for helping out with this case, Det. McNealson said, "You're absolutely correct,

I wouldn't see it any other way. We're in this together, aren't we? We do play for the same team, don't we?"

"You're damn right we do!" answered Det. Dabney, with no sign of the earlier hostility, and with that, the two ambitious detective hung up.

Chapter Fourteen

May 25, 2020 1:10pm Monday

Augusta, Georgia

Arriving at the scene on a back road where the only residential home was just over the hill and down a dirt road, about three miles away, Smart thought these Augusta, Georgia backwater sticks were a convenient place to commit a murder and go unseen. With the scene tapped off and the FBI's Crime Scene Techs canvassing the area, taking photos, bagging and tagging any evidence that was in any way a remote possibility of being part of this crime spree.

Special Agent Bradley Smart lit a cigarette and proceeded to duck under the yellow crime scene tape that cordoned off the area from anyone compromising the integrity of the scene, or evidence that was being collected. Staring at the positioning of the police vehicle and the tire tracks left behind, Spl. Agent Smart took notice to the footprints and the drag impressions from the body being towed away into the menacing gloom of the dense woodlands that sat just beyond the old dirt road.

When finally, Spl. Agent Smart was approached by his partner, Spl. Agent Drapper, who was just speaking with the investigation's lead detective for the Augusta Homicide Division. Referring to his notes, Agent Drapper said, "Brad, this has got to be one crazy son of a bitch we're after." Tilting his head in the direction of the woods, but not commenting, Smart stayed silent.

Agent Drapper began to relay the findings, but he hesitated when it was time to describe the scene in which the body of the 67 year old veteran Officer Jamison Mahoney, whose badge, #366, wasn't present at the scene. But, left in its place, was the badge of a Durham, North Carolina Police Officer Danny Folks, badge #454. Pausing to break the news and the tension, Agent Drapper began to relay to Spl. Agent Smart that Officer Mahoney's murder was somewhat different than the 3 officers prior to this murder.

"How so?" asked Agent Smart.

"The way in which the badge was placed," replied Agent Drapper.

Staring into each other's eyes with unspoken words between them, Agent Drapper says, "It's pretty gruesome. Whoever did this is plain ass insane." With the ease of an old country western cowboy, Spl. Agent Smart asked, "Did what?" Agent Drapper knew this wasn't the time to pussy foot around. He began to disclose, "The body of Officer Mahoney was found in the woods, wasn't just murdered, it was desecrated," stated Agent Drapper. He went on to say, "In the three prior related cases where two of the badges of the officers were found in the officer's mouths." Pausing a second to let this sink in, Agent Drapper goes on to say, "In this case, Officer Mahoney didn't have a badge in his mouth, but the badge of officer Folks, was lodged into the recess of Officer Mahoney's chest cavity, which was brutally torn open and his heart was ripped out and replaced with Officer Folks' badge," then he went on to explain that, "a message was left on the hood of Officer

Mahoney's police cruiser, which was written in blood that is believed to be that of Officer Mahoney."

Spl. Agent Smart closes his eyes and lets out a exasperated breath, then asks, "What does this message say?" Agent Drapper stares off into the darkness of the woods and stated, "It said, 'This racist bitch died heartless' with a smiley face."

Spl. Agent Smart asked, "Was the heart relocated?"

"No sir," answered Agent Drapper. "There's no sign of it anywhere." But then added, "I think this was a murder of rage and hatred," which caused a visible reaction from Agent Smart.

"Why do you believe that?" asked Agent Smart.

"Well, the message was one-the ripped open chest and stolen heart was another- but three shots to the face, close range leaves no face left to identify him by. All these things together means that we're chasing a hideous, vile monster that has no respect for the law," replied Agent Drapper.

Moments pass between them before Agent Smart remarked, "Well, we better find this monster fast, we need reinforcements and we need to contain this lunatic, or we'll be finding dead police in every city. Cause once the word gets out, then we'll be chasing all of the copycats instead of the real serial killer."

"So, what do we tell the press?" asked Agent Drapper.

"Less is best, keep the details of this case close to the vest," replied Agent Smart.

Just then, the crime scene tech came storming in from out in the depths of the woods and calls for Agent Drapper, who then walked off with Agent Smart following his every step. They approach the tech, and Agent Drapper asked, "Yeah, what is it?" With a fragile expression on her face, she says, "Come with me, you need to see this."

Charging through the thick bush and dense foliage that lay in their way, they dodge lazy dead timbers and walk amongst the outer edge of what was considered the premises of the crime scene. Being careful to keep from compromising the integrity of the scene or any of the numbered tags that were laid out to show the discovery of each piece of evidence that was deemed to be a part of the crime scene. Coming to a halt in front of a tree, the crime scene tech pointed at the arrow drawn in blood on the bark of the oak tree pointing upward, as all heads and eyes ascended skyward and laid sight upon the missing heart of Officer Mahoney. Dangling from a crude made noose, attached to a branch of an oak tree, its meaning obvious.

Unbelieving, they all stared in hollow dread, at such a cruel act of intent on one of their own. With a silence that followed for a small moment in time, everyone tried to wrap their heads around the audacity of this killer's mind frame and what could've triggered this insatiable appetite of hatred and savagery.

Spl. Agent Smart yelled with such anger and venomousness, laced in the tone of his voice, "Get that down from there right now!" But the crime scene tech warily said, "I'm sorry sir, but I have to follow procedure, and that takes precedence." Then she turned and spoke softly, saying, "With all due respect sir, I will photograph and document the evidence as quickly and efficiently as possible, I do understand how disturbing this is for everyone to witness, but this is also a critical piece of evidence for this crime scene, and rushing through the preliminaries will only compromise the integrity of the case. I cannot and will not put this case or my reputation in jeopardy. I am to have emotional detachment in these matters, it's what I'm trained to do. Let me do my job, and I will give you all I have to catch the persons responsible."

The crime scene tech then stated that she needed to get back to work, if he expected her to process the scene and remove the human organ dangling from a noose. Just as she turned to walk away, Agent Smart's phone rang, breaking the death of silence that suffocated the moment. Upon answering and listening to the caller, confusion came across the face of Agent Smart, along with a tiresomeness of the stressful endless day, that didn't seem like it had an ending coming anytime soon.

With disgust and annoyance taking turns stomping on his patience, Spl. Agent Smart disconnects and turns on his heels, and allowed the weight of the moment to downtrodden him, with a heaviness that he couldn't dispel. Walking out of the woods and feeling depleted and defeated, Agent Drapper catches up with him and asks, "What's up, Partner? Everything alright?" Heading to his car, Agent Smart says, "No. No, I'm not alright. The killer just struck again!" He then left Agent Drapper with instructions to wrap up the scene and meet him back at the hotel. They were on a wild goose chase and they needed to get all of the rest they could get because the party was just getting started.

Chapter Fifteen

May 26, 2020 8:30pm Tuesday

Fredericksburg, Virginia

Detective Matt York sits at home watching TV. When the show goes to commercial, he heads to the fridge to get another beer and right when he sits the cold Bud Light down on the coffee table, he takes notice to the case file that Officer Spoon handed him before heading out of Homicide's main office. Picking up the file, he began to skim through the findings and brush up on the case notes.

As the commercials ended, the game trumped all else and setting the file down, he grabbed the beer off the coffee table, kicking his feet up, he reclined back into the comfort of the couch, sipping his beer and getting caught up in the excitement of the game. Bradley Beal, being one of his favorite players, was then fouled and Matt reacted like any other die hard fan would and called out the foul- from his living room- like he was actually talking to the referee in person. Setting his beer down, he did so clumsily, causing the bottle to fall over and spill its content all over the table. Jumping up to contain the spill from pouring onto the floor and ruining the case file that was laying haphazardly on the table. He tried to catch the mess before it became a bigger mess, but he didn't succeed, being that the case notes had beer dripping from the file pages.

After retrieving paper towels to soak up the spill on the table, and trying to unsuccessfully pat dry the pages of the wet case notes.

Matt took notice of something through the blurred wet blotted words on one of the pages. Taking the pages from the file folder, he set them out on the kitchen counter and dining room table to dry, but not before he examined the contents on the page that drew his attention. Then game night came to a cease and Detective Matt York settled into what he does best. Investigating.

Combing through each piece of the file as he jotted down notes of his own, the pieces began to come together in some form. Although they were only hunches, they were plausible hunches worth looking into. So, he called on a friend from Washington, D.C. Metropolitan Police Department and asked if she could look into the officer that was murdered at the Econo Lodge.

Pausing a bit to retrieve the name of the victim, he said, "It's a Richard Montgomery III."

The female officer said, "Oh, you mean 'Robocop'!"

Detective York asked if she knew him or was that what the streets named him? She said, "Know him? Boy please! That man was as shady as they come. He was more of a criminal than the criminals that he claimed to be ridding the streets of."

Curiously, she asked him, "Why you getting into all of that mess? That fool was a hot mess anyways." She said this last part as if she knew more than what she was letting on.

"I need the files on him if you can help, Tricia," said Det. York.

"Well, what kind of files?" Tricia asked.

"Nothing too personal, but I need a list of the people he got convictions on and maybe a list of the guys that may have been released from prison as of lately, who he might have testified against or was on his case load," said Det. York.

"How far back you need me to go?" she asked.

"Convictions as far back as when he was accused of any shady police work. As for the people released from prison, say two or three years back to present," said Det. York.

"Okay," said Tricia, nonchalantly. "Now, what do I get out of all this?"

"Whatever you want, save marriage and a child," joked York back to her, yet serious as three heart attacks. "I'm not ready for all that."

They both burst out in laughter at that comment, and Tricia stated, "Neither am I, but a nice dinner out on the town will do. Is that cool?" she asked shyly.

"Deal!" said York. "Call me when you get something for me, ok?" said York.

"Call you? I'll hand deliver that file to you, this is a night out on the town we talking about," laughing at her own comment, she added, "I got you, Matt. I'll start on it first thing in the morning."

Just before they hung up the phone, she made it her business to say, "I'll be seeing you soon." Then the phone went dead before he could even cultivate a response to her.

With all of the file notes scattered all over the place, Det. York began to pick apart the findings and build his own file because he knew there was something about this case that was going unseen. It was right there in his face, he just needed to peer a little deeper. He thinks that Detective Richard Montgomery III was going to be that one piece of thread that you pull on and the whole thing unravels right before your very eyes. He not only felt this, but he also knew that when shit stinks, you follow the scent to the source. Sometimes you'll find a dirty diaper, sometimes you'll find a dead body. Det. York was known on the force, as a blood hound, and blood hounds always follow the scent, until the trail runs cold.

Picking up his phone, Det. York punched in the digits and waited until the other party picked up the phone. After a few rings, the answering service chimed in, Det. York left a message and told the machine, "This is an urgent matter, I have some pressing news that I need to box your ears with and time is of the essence. Will you please return my call at your earliest convenience?" When Matt hung up the phone, he leaned against the kitchen island counter and let his eyes roam over the case file notes, sipping his Bud Light. He took mental notes and began to apply the 'what if' factors he routinely does when something is nagging at him, and he's trying to reach a conclusion and make something factual out of something theoretical...

Chapter Sixteen

May 27, 2020 2:00pm Wednesday
Minneapolis, Minnesota

Richmond County. Minneapolis, Minnesota. A place buzzing with activity and wonder. John's head is on a swivel as he is taking in all of the sights, but his eyes are looking for one thing in particular. Cops.

As they ride down a local street, Mike says, "Stranger, you think uh, we need to trade out vehicles?"

"Nah," answers Stranger, "I think we need to lay low till night fall."

John chimes in excitedly, "Yeah, so we can get us another cop under our belt!"

Then Lisa sucks her teeth peevishly and says, "There you go with that dumbass shit again, your bitch ass-"

"Bitch!" John screams violently, seeming ready to jump from the front passenger seat into the back seat. "Who the fuck you think you're calling a bitch, you nasty, trifling bitch! I'll beat your face in with my bare fists and drag your dead body out this car and leave you in the fucking gutter where your mamma shoulda left you!" said John, heatedly spewing his hatred for Lisa in a way he's never spoken to her before.

With spittle flying from his mouth and anger seething like a shark drawn to blood, John boils over and lunges over the seat in a blatant attempt to cause affliction against Lisa. But Mike chose that moment to intercede in the attempt and forcibly grabs John by the throat and squeezes down tight on his windpipe.

Mike's inhumane and merciless power exceeds his normally benign nature that only explodes into a violent rage when provoked and the cool amber of his slow burning coals are poked and coaxed into a inferno. With eyes bulging out of his skull, John is suffocated by the massive hands Mike has on his throat, until Stranger slams down on the car brakes in the middle of the street and tried to intervene between the two. Mike's mind isn't in its normal place though, but Stranger tried unsuccessfully to break the vise-like grip that is killing John, and begs Mike as a final option to let him live, Stranger says, "Come on Mike, settle down, bro! John didn't mean it like that! Come on back to us."

But it wasn't until Lisa spoke up that brought Mike back from such a far distance, saying, "Mike, chill the fuck out-you know John is a bitch and an asshole, but he's our friend and he don't deserve to die, not like this! Please let him go!"

With slow, unsure ease, the grip loosened and Mike came back from the land of the lost, when finally the calm settled in. Mike shoved John with a powerful thrust that sent him flying into the front passenger windshield and he found himself laying in the passenger floor board, trying to regain his composure and his breath. Then John being John, couldn't leave well enough alone, he had to say something, screaming at the top of his lungs, "What the fuck, Bro! Who the fuck shitted in your Wheaties? You strong ass, barbaric mother fucker! You tried to kill me over a broad!

Fuck this shit! Lisa, you gotta give me some of that pussy, cause you got these two mother fucking tender dicks ready to kill over that box between your legs!"

"Shut the fuck up, John! And get your ass up off the floor! Sit your dumb ass in that seat and don't say another fucking word," said Stranger with vehemence laced in his voice, finally having had enough of his antics.

As John slowly gathered himself and eased back into the front seat, Stranger slowly pulled off. Looking into the rearview mirror and noticed that Mike was once again staring out of the rear driver's side window as if nothing had just taken place, or he wasn't the least bit concerned about almost taking his own friend's life. Shaking his head, Stranger knew that Mike wasn't the one to mess with, he was a hair trigger on a fully automatic gatling gun. Messing around with Mike, a person's life expectancy will get cut short, for no other reason, than crossing an invisible line that you didn't even know you had crossed, until it was entirely too late to apologize to him for it.

Driving down the street, they passed an old abandoned house that looked like it had been unoccupied for quite some time. So, Stranger circled the block and pulled into the driveway. Waiting around to see if anyone was being attentive to their presence in the area, Stranger told everyone to wait in the car until he checked things out and found a way into the dwellings without raising any alarm. But before he shut the car door, he said, "All three of you better be alive when I get back here," and then he smirked at his little dig and closed the door, disappearing towards the back of the house.

With the sun setting and dusk settling in, this was a good time to get a little rest and figure out their next steps. Plus, they did need to find another vehicle as Mike had suggested earlier. Riding around in a white Toyota Camry with Florida tags that could possibly link them to the crime in Memphis, if anyone had gotten a good look at them and decided to be an upstanding citizen or try to phone in to Crime Stoppers for some sort of monetary reward. But with all of these eyes in the skies and human video cameras, it's a wonder how they even made it to Minnesota without every cop in the nation playing vigilante and hunting them down in cold blood.

With a smirk of appraisal for his own efforts, Stranger knew he had to out-think the thinkers. "They're on damage control," said Stranger to himself, "I'm the one causing the damage." Choosing an unboarded window and prying it open with a discarded metal bar, which was laying haphazardly in the back yard, he climbs in, taking a moment to allow his eyes to adjust to the darkness of the room as he lumbers around slowly in deaf quietness, being sure to not rouse anyone who might be already squatting in the abandoned dwelling. Once he cleared the rooms and makes sure the house is completely vacant, he goes to retrieve the others and make sure no one has taken notice of their arrival in the quiet solitude of the neighborhood.

Upon returning through the unlocked back door, everyone sat quietly in the living room on an old worn couch and chairs that were left behind like unwanted, derelict castaways. Everyone's train of thought was focused on the business at hand, of what to do next? Where to go? And how to get there?

Just as John begins pacing and Stranger's mind sets into problem solving mode, Lisa gets up and says, "I'm going for a walk to get some fresh air." John agrees to accompany her, like the earlier incident had never taken place. Stranger and Mike eyeballs them both as if they couldn't possibly be serious about being in one another's company. Then, as if John could read their minds, he said, "What the fuck? You think I'm gonna stay here with you two lunatics? I'd rather be with Lisa! At least she ain't try to kill me and I'm not scared shitless of her and what she can do."

Then, as he was about to leave out the back door, he says, "And if that makes me a bitch, well, then I'm a bitch! But one thing for sure, I'm not a dumb bitch!"

With that easing the tension with everyone, because it enlisted a reaction of laughter from everyone in the room, Lisa said, "Okay then, now bring your bitch ass on!" and John returned with a comment of his own. "I may act a bitch, but I can still fight like a man." Lisa replied, "Bitch please, you couldn't fight your way out of a wet paper bag, now bring your ass on and keep me company."

After the two left, Mike and Stranger sat quietly for some time. Then Stranger said, "What's up, Slim? You good?"

"Coolin'" replied Mike and then asked, "So what you got planned?"

"Well, this is the state where they been doing the most in, right? So, it's only fair to give back everything we've received," said Stranger, with a sinister glare in his eyes and a hint of brazen menace in his voice.

"Hmmm... sounds like you got a plan brewing in that big head of yours," said Mike.

"Naw, this ain't a plan, this is justice. For just us. And there's only one way to make a statement so poignant that it will never be forgotten," said Stranger. "I thought you was already making a statement," said Mike.

"Not of this magnitude, this will go down in America's history books, as America's worse police genocide," replied Stranger. "And guess what, Mike?"

"What?" asked Mike.

"The worst is yet to come," said Stranger.

"How so?" asked Mike.

"Since this is one of the epicenters for police brutality and police killing unarmed blacks, how about I make sure they have a funeral every single day for the next 30 days?" asked Stranger with a look so sinister, that Mike knew that Stranger wasn't joking in the least.

Then Mike asked, "So, you gunna kill one cop a day, for 30 days then?" Stranger just shook his head in the negative and remained silent for a few minutes to let what he was about to say take an impact like two speeding trains on a head on collision. When Stranger relayed his thoughts, Mike shockingly said, "Ain't no way!"

Stranger replied, "If there's a will, there's a way, and I will see this through. I want every cop in every city across the United States to fear going to work. I want a life for every life taken. Then I want a life for every cop that thought they was above the law. I'm implementing what I'm deeming as a *new* justice system. It's a system for just us."

"This is a purge, Stranger!" said Mike.

"Naw, Mike, this is rectification. A means to an end," said Stranger clarifying.

As all went silent in the house, the two friends sat in their own solitude, allowing their minds to wrap around the significance of what was to come.

Chapter Seventeen

May 28, 2020 10:45am Thursday

Fredericksburg, Virginia

Detective McNealson gets back to Detective Dabney on the findings from the file that was faxed over and the two agree to meet over lunch. Just then, Detective York barges into the office, slamming down a stack of papers and the Washington Post. Circled, was the headlines, "Serial Cop Killer Runs Rampant..."

Pausing for a second to take notice of the intense glare of scorn that sat upon Det. York's face, McNealson relayed his apologies to Det. Dabney and told him he'd have to get back to him later, ending the phone call at once, with urgency.

"What's all of this Matt?" asked McNealson.

"Clues!" said Det York. "'And I believe the system has a definite break in the chain," fumed Det. York.

"How so?" asked McNealson with an air of nonchalance that proved to Det. York that Vince McNealson wasn't catching the graveness of this situation in its entirety.

Opening the file and noticing that it was a stack of papers with endless names and various charges and dates. Det. McNealson looked up into the eyes of Det. York and questioned, "Fill me in, what am I missing here?"

"You're looking at undercover Detective Richard

Montgomery III's arrest and citation file over the last 20 years. There's also a list of ex-cons that have been released from prison in the last three years. Also, there's a list of complaints that were filed against Detective Montgomery.

"Okay, I already know about the complaints, but those same complaints have been cleared against Det. Montgomery," said Det. McNealson.

"Yeah, Vince, but you didn't look at the pattern that has taken place over the years, look deeper, partner, something was really amiss with that guy," said Det. York emphatically.

"Show me what I'm not seeing here, Matt," demanded McNealson. Turning around to close the office door to ensure their privacy, Det. York moved in closer to the desk and began reiterating his findings, as well as, his theories. He pointed out first, all of the discrepancies in all the cases and made a showing of how the complaints over the years were all signs pointing to negligence and obvious misuse of power, also dereliction of authoritative duties as an officer of the law.

Looking over the preponderance of the evidence that Det. York was blatantly forcing in his face, Det. McNealson had no other choice but to acknowledge the air of foul play, compromise, and cover-up that a blind man could see from a mile away, standing in the middle of a cornfield.

Then it hit him, as he looked down, the list of names and alleged incidents that took place over the years involving Detective Montgomery, as the disbelief turned into pure credence. When he set his sights on his own cousin's name. He knew that his cousin was a victim of foul play and the justice system failed him in a time of need. Staring at the name, Randle Palmer-Jones, accused of distribution of crack cocaine, possession of a firearm and maintaining a dwelling within 1,000 feet of a school, park, or church. It all came flooding back to Detective McNealson, of how his uncle's son was convicted and sentenced to 33 years. Then nine years later, he was exonerated of all charges due to ineffective assistance of counsel, witness tampering, falsified evidence, and what was the most detrimental to overturning his case, was the use of falsified testimonies from arresting officers. One being, Detective Richard Montgomery III, of Washington, D.C.'s metropolitan, undercover drug task force.

When his eyes roamed down the page, he also noticed a few others whose cases were compromised and were later overturned and exonerated as well. It took a moment before Det. York spoke out. Once his partner began to piece the puzzle together on his own, he asks, "Are you thinking what I'm thinking?"

Slowly nodding his head, Det. McNealson said, "Let's divide the list up between us. I'm going to bring Detective Dabney into the fold, we're going to need some help to tackle this many suspects.

"I already called Detective Dabney. He hasn't returned my call just yet," said Det. York.

With a look of befuddlement etched on his face, McNealson asked, "Why did you call him instead of me first?"

"It was him that put the initial file together, and it was him that started connecting the dots that got us to where we are now," said Det. York earnestly.

Taking sometime to allow his agitation to subside, McNealson weighed his words before letting them roll off of his tongue with reckless abandonment. "Okay, Matt, I see that there's some weakness in our partnership chain link," said McNealson.

"Naw, Vince, we good. I just needed to see where Det. Dabney was headed with this to make sure we weren't left out of the loop," stated Det. York seriously.

As they stared into one another's eyes to scrutinize the other's true intentions, Officer Spoon taps on the door and says, "Detectives, there's a Detective Dabney wanting to speak with one or the both of you."

Without breaking eye contact with one another, Det. McNealson said, "Send him in, Shelly." Officer Spoon took a second to observe if there was indeed some high tension filling the atmosphere of the office and began back pedaling out of the door, but not before saying, "If you say so," in her natural sassy, hoodish tone, closing the office door in her retreat.

"We good, Vince?" asked Det. York, throwing on a casual demeanor.

"Yeah, we good, Matt. We are partners, and brothers from another mother, aren't we?" asked McNealson.

"Yeah, we that," stated Det. York, just then, there was a light tap on the door and Detective York moved to open the door and allowed Det. Dabney to enter so that they could jointly get down to business without any need for formal introduction.

Chapter Eighteen

May 29, 2020 12:20pm Friday

Fredericksburg, Virginia

Taking a seat without invitation, Det. Dabney said, "Gentlemen, good afternoon." Then, turning to Det. York, Dabney adds, "Sorry I didn't return your call, I've been busy hunting down leads in this case, and it just so happens that I think I've narrowed down the list to about 10 potential suspects, whom could possibly have a real motive in all this entangled mess."

"Ten!?" boomed both McNealson and York in unison.

"Yeah, ten," replied Dabney.

"How so?" asked McNealson.

"Well," said Dabney, "it's called 'the process of elimination, and-"

"Hold up!" interrupted Det. York, "who are you eliminating? From the file you sent us, there's not much to go by," said Det. York.

"Well, sir, that's where you're wrong," said Dabney. "It seems every good investigator has what's known as a hunch. So, I followed mine, and it seems that Det. Montgomery wasn't a very well liked individual in the streets, or on the force."

Allowing this comment to settle in like a goodnight sleep, he goes on to say, "I dug a little deeper than what I initially sent to you in the file I had faxed over, and I compiled another one.

At that moment, Det. McNealson tossed the file that Det.

York compiled towards Det. Dabney, pointed at it, and said, "Is any of this in that file?"

Thumbing through the contents and offhandedly reviewing the file, Det. Dabney pushed his glasses upon the bridge of his nose and said, "This is a very thoroughly compiled file on Montgomery's arrest history and alleged infractions you have here. It seems I underestimated your investigative abilities, but there's still something you failed to do-" stated Dabney.

"And what's that?" asked Det. York.

"As I was saying before I was rudely interrupted, it's the process of elimination," stated Dabney. "You see, I went about this process by eliminating three key factors from your initial investigation into Officer Bloom's death. I took all of the surveillance footage from the gas station and noticed that the suspect in the footage was a young black male, between the ages of 25 to 30. Then I factored in that he was above average height of 6'1 to 6'3 and about 180 to 200 pounds, give or take. So, I went to my list of possible people of interest, which is about the same list that you compiled of actual people who could have a real motive behind Montgomery's murder. After a close evaluation of each individual, I began eliminating anyone who didn't fit the description of the suspect in the surveillance footage, narrowing the list down to about 30 individuals."

I then took into account which ones were still actively engaged in the streets, like, uh-the ones who've re-offended and are in custody at the present time, those who have met their untimely demise, and those who are still in the city limits at this present time. Whoever is doing these senseless murders can't be in the Washington, D.C. area and be traveling from state to state committing the murders at the same time. Nobody can be in two places at once."

Pausing for a second, Det. Dabney then goes on to explain further. "Now, here's where I had to play a little game called 'act as if'. So, I placed myself in the mind frame of a total lunatic, who has an absolute obsession-and hatred-towards cops, cause only an insane nutcase would go to these extremes in which this cold blooded killer has taken on, an insatiable appetite to commit, and I narrowed my list down to ten possible suspects that aren't dead, currently incarcerated, and whom are on the grid, as in presently being in the city limits at this moment."

After relaying his process of elimination to both of the detectives, Det. Dabney then pulls out a loose sheet of paper with the ten possible suspects, their last known address, and any associates or family members that could potentially help to reveal their whereabouts. With smiles upon their faces, the two detectives nodded their heads in approval and Det. York said, "Now that's one helluva hunch, if you ask me."

McNealson, in agreement, added, "Damn good detective work," then he asked, "So, what's next on the agenda? Where do we go from here?"

"Well, I have another hunch," said Dabney. "I'm all ears," retorted Det. york.

Slightly taking a breath before proceeding, Dabney said, "Okay, now all these suspects have two things in common. One: They were all locked up at one point in time by Detective Montgomery, and Two: they each were wrongly convicted and were eventually exonerated of their convictions, but only after doing a considerable amount of time, which wouldn't sit well with you, if you were in their shoes, would it?" asks Det. Dabney.

"Right," replied McNealson as Det. York sat awaiting the conclusion of Dabney's hunch.

"This is what I propose we do," stated Det. Dabney. "Since we know that the man that's committing these murders is not mentally stable, and seems to be missing a few screws, I think we should split up the list and go in search of the ones that are a couple of cans short of a six pack. But in order to do that, we need to get mental evals on these men from the penitentiary where they resided at. Like which ones were on meds, and what their afflictions were, and their diagnosis, if any. We can even interview the staff members that dealt with them on a daily basis during their stint, and maybe even their cellmates who might have known them personally.

At that moment, Det. York cut in by saying, "That all sounds good and we may even get some viable information from the staff members. But the cellmates, they are a different breed entirely."

"Naw, that's where you're wrong, partner," stated Det. McNealson knowingly. "You got convicts, and then you have inmates. The cons will be reluctant to talk to us, but the inmates are called inmates for a reason, they're the type of criminals that will let us 'in'," he said, emphasizing the 'in' part with air quotation marks, "…on everything they know. We may have to bribe them, but what's a little bribe to get the goods on these possible suspects? Think about all the dudes we've arrested over the years and how many were willing to send their own mammas up the river? Or sell their soul, or their firstborn child for a chance to walk out of that interrogation room?"

"You're right there, partner," replied Det. York, laughing at the many times those so called thugs and gangstas turned out to be bitches and snitches at the drop of a dime.

Then Det. McNealson took the lead and lifted the pen off of his desk blotter, starting to circle names on the list, pairing together the ones that were at the same penitentiary, so they wouldn't have to travel all over the United States to interview staff and associates of each of the men listed. With the names divided amongst them, they were going in search of answers for the missing pieces of this complex puzzle they found themselves caught up in.

As Det. Dabney and Det. York exited the office, heading towards the elevators, Det. McNealson leaned back in his desk chair, stapling his fingers together under his chin, closing his eyes to gather his thoughts, he said to nobody other than himself, "My, my, what a tangled web we're unweaving. But I'm hot on your trail. Yeah, Hot. On. Your. Trail." emphasizing each word with definite intention.

Chapter Nineteen

May 28, 2020 3:05pm Thursday
Memphis, Tennessee

Entering the morgue in downtown Memphis, Spl. Agent Smart and Agent Drapper were both still mentally reeling from the details that were laid upon them like a heavy burden by the investigating detective that was initially assigned to the murder case of Officer Rosie Hernandez. In his findings, he uncovered a semi -automatic Baretta 9mm, service pistol registered to an Augusta, Georgia Police Officer Jamieson Mahoney.

Also recovered was Officer Mahoney's badge, #366, which was removed from the mouth of Officer Hernandez's lifeless body by the medical examiner at the scene of the crime. After photographs and the initial examination into the unofficial cause of death were completed, it made the C.O.D as clear as day, due to the two large holes tightly grouped into the forehead of Officer Hernandez.

Spl. Agent Smart was also feeling contempt when he was given information from a witness that was present at the scene, who told the lead investigator that Officer Hernandez was asleep, and derelict in her duties, which was what ultimately led to her untimely demise as a 5 year veteran on the force. Officer Hernandez was careless in her actions as an officer of the law. But upon further inquiry into the preliminary investigation, Spl. Agent Smart was told that in the passenger seat of Officer Hernandez's police cruiser, she had open textbooks on criminal law.

Officer Hernandez was enrolled at the University of Tennessee, majoring in criminal law, with hopes of becoming a lawyer upon graduating and passing the Tennessee bar exam. Her goal wasn't to become a prosecutor. It was to become a defense lawyer, because she had believed that there were a lot of latino and black people being railroaded by the unjust criminal justice system, due to nothing more than the complexion of their skin and the communities in which they were subjected to live in and become a part of, whether voluntarily, or involuntarily.

With these thoughts playing on the emotions of the mind, Spl. Agent Smart became vexed in his determination to bring this case to a close and catch this insatiable killer, before another officer finds themselves at the wrong end of a gun, staring into the eyes of someone who has no regards for human life or the law which governs our society.

Officially, the body of the deceased Officer Rosie Hernandez, belonged in the custody of the FBI's Criminal Medical Examiner's office, but due to the lapse in time, and time was of the essence, Spl. Agent Smart allowed the head Medical Examiner, Dr. Francis Blake, for the city of Memphis, Tennessee, to conduct her examination and provide the cause of death and toxicology reports.

When Spl. Agent Smart and Agent Drapper were formally introduced to Dr. Francis Blake, they were whisked away into the morgue's examination room, where the body of Officer Hernandez laid on the stainless steel examination table, with the Y-incision peeled back, revealing the internal organs of the deceased officer exposed. The smell of decomposition and death was laying heavily in the cold air of the creepy morgue. Dr. Blake spoke candidly of her findings and rules the death a homicide by dual gunshot wounds to the frontal lobe by 9mm projectiles. When she finished her summation into her case findings, she lifted her glasses off of the bridge of her nose, allowing them to hang freely around her neck, looking intently into the agent's eyes, she softly stated with the surety of someone who's seen this type of act, time and time again.

"Gentlemen, the motive behind this is unclear to me. The heinous intent in which this woman was victimized, is grave and decisive. This doesn't have a feel of pointlessness, nor was this committed impulsively. As a doctor of biology, behavioral science and psychology, I can tell you through evaluation of this case that the person or persons that are responsible for this murder has a definite fixation, and his or her mania will only heighten into more erratic and violent behavior, leading to more murders, in a similar fashion."

Dr. Blake takes a second to let the severity of her final statement set in, before she adds, "This is a deliberate and patient killer. The mind of a thinker, that is not thinking about the consequences. He or she is only thinking about the intended message they are sending, and from what I'm seeing in this case, and have gathered from the news lately, their sights are set on Officers of the law. There's blood in the water and this shark is circling."

Spl. Agent Smart began to say something, but thought better of it, and decided not to let on too much of what he already knew. After changing the subject by redirecting the conversation back in the direction of Dr. Blake's conclusion and gathering any useful information that may have gone unnoticed by the initial examination of the scene, Spl. Agent Smart asked if there were anything else that she could find that may be useful to the case, and if she so happened to find anything in closing of this autopsy, would she notify him, as soon as possible. Dr. Blake took the card, and sat it next to her note book and went on to say that as soon as the autopsy report came back, she'd fax the findings and any other additional information that she stumbles on, if any.

Seeing them out, to the main entrance, they said their farewells. Dr.Blake made it her business to mention once again that the predator that they were after wasn't going to stop on his or her own. That this was an obsession of a grand design and that nobody was safe, at least nobody that owned a badge and gun. "This is a vile killer who has malicious intent and will stop at nothing until every last cop that crosses their path lies in a perpetual blood bath, there's going to be nothing but bodies left in his or her wake."

With that being said, Dr. Blake bid them goodnight and safe travels, as she turned to lock up behind herself, heading back down the brightly lit hallway to finish the autopsy of the deceased, Officer Rosie Hernandez.

As the two FBI agents got into the confines of their

government issued Crown Victoria, Agent Drapper turned to his partner and asked, "Brad, what do you think about her diagnosis of our suspect?"

Spl. Agent. Smart replied, "Sounds like she knows our boy personally, or something, at least she's been around his kind many times."

Then Drapper said, "I think she hit the nail on the head, if you ask me."

"Well, let's see what the real professionals in Quantico gotta say about all this...mess..." said Spl. Agent Smart.

Chapter Twenty

May 27, 2020

7:20pm Wednesday

With a plan in mind, Stranger set out to implement Phase One of his insidious game of cat and mouse.

Driving down a residential street, he took notice of a domestic disturbance between a black male and female, who were apparently drunk. The two were in an all out brawl in the front yard of their residence while neighbors stood by watching the scene. Stranger parked the car and sat quietly in deep reverie, watching the two tussle in their inebriated state.

John broke the silence with a comment of inquiry by asking, "What the fuck, Stranger? We just sitting here watching two fools beat each other up? We can go to a boxing match for that shit."

"Shut up, John!" Mike spat from the back seat.

"I wasn't talking to you, Mike," John shot back with vehemence in his voice. "I was talking to Stranger, the one that got us sitting here stalking a couple like he wants to put on his 'duh-duhn-duh duhns' and a cape and go save the day or something."

Bending the corner at an irate speed, with lights flashing, sirens blaring, two police cruisers pulled up to the ensuing chaos. When the officers jumped out of the car, they began to manhandle the combatants in the midst of the disorder. They never saw what was coming. Stranger slid out of the driver's seat and casually walked up to the maelstrom and removed the handgun from his hoodie pouch. In one fluid motion, he put the gun to one of the two cops head and fired two shots at point blank range. He then turned to the other officer who was on top of the male, cuffing him, and put two shots to the temporal area of this officer's head.

Standing over the dead officers, Stranger reached down and relieved both of the officers of their respective guns and silver badges, dropping the smoking Kel-Tec 9mm that had belonged to Officer Rosie Hernandez and her badge, badge #119, at the feet of both dead officers. Without any hesitation, he turned and walked down the street to the car, as if he had no care in the world, where he climbed in the car and drove off.

John was ecstatic when Stranger got in the car and pulled off with ease, saying, "Now that's how you fuck a cop over! That was cold hearted and calculated! We waited for them bitches to come and save the day and they couldn't even save themselves! Stranger"

"Shut the fuck up, John!" Mike screamed from the backseat, cutting John's comment off short. "Let's get rid of this car right now, everyone on the block just saw us leaving this bitch!"

In a calm and steady voice, Stranger said, "I already got that handled."

Two blocks later, Stranger pulled into a car lot and parked. Jumping out quickly, the four of them stood on the side of the building when Lisa said, "What now, Stranger? We walking?"

John chimed in, "No, Lisa, we're riding! We're all gunna climb on your back and ride your fat ass all the way into the sunset! Now shut the fuck up, and let Stranger think for a second-He's got a plan." Then, with curiosity, John turned to Stranger and said, "You *do* got a plan, don't you?"

Making sure the coast was clear, Stranger stepped off and told the others to wait there, that he would be right back in a second. He then vanished to the back of the building, only to return a few minutes later with a 2010 blue Ford Expedition. The police presence was as thick as fog on a muggy fall morning, but they weren't looking for a blue SUV, they were in search for a white Toyota Camry.

Making their getaway, Mike said, "Damn, Stranger, that was making a statement." Stranger stopped at a red light staring off into a busy intersection, and said, "Naw, that wasn't the statement I was trying to make. This one is..." and pulled into a parking lot.

With the SUV still running, he jumped out, jogging across the street, then opened the door to the Quickie Mart. Two officers stood paralyzed, staring down the barrel on Stranger's new Sig Sauer P225 9mm handgun. Stranger said, "Officers, you are being relieved of duty, goodnight and farewell!" blasting the officers and robbing the Quickie Mart because he did need more money to continue on his streak, but before leaving the store, he again shot both officers in the face and chest until the gun clicked empty. Dropping that gun, he removed the other officers P225 9mm service pistol from his hoodie pouch and shot into the already dead cops with the stolen officers' gun taken from the previous murder half an hour ago.

Just before leaving, he threw two badges on the ground next

to the two dead cops. The badges of Richmond County's MPD Officer Monroe, Badge #864 and Officer Burnheart, badge # 935. Retrieving the guns and badges off of the two officers, Stranger made a clean getaway.

When he got into the car, Mike, said, "Damn, four bodies in half an hour! Stranger, we need to chill now!"

Stranger looked into the rearview mirror and said in a menacing voice, "Chill- I'm just getting started, I'm dropping bodies all the way til sunrise! Four down, and many more to go..."

As Stranger pulled off in search of his next victim, he repeated his mantra out loud, to himself, "No love, No mercy!"

May 28, 2020
Early Morning

Mike, John, and Lisa, all sat in silence, as daybreak came and Stranger drove around the city of Minneapolis, Minnesota, in a state of complete turbulent tunnel vision, with death and destruction weighing heavily on his mind, when finally Lisa spoke up for the first time in hours, saying, "Stranger, it's time to get ghost! That's enough! How many more cops are you planning on killing? This shit is crazy! You can't be serious, Stranger! They gunna get hip to us, and this ain't gunna end well!"

"End well?" John burst in with an attitude of annoyance. "Lisa, you're not a fucking psychologist! What are you? A remedial math coach? We're way passed 'ending well' Miss-Catch-A-Conscience!

We won't see a jail cell nor a courtroom-what we're doing to them is the same thing that they've been doing to us! If they catch up, this is kill on sight, this is judgement day! So, how about you-"

"Shut up, John," Stranger said, cutting off John once again, annoyed with his belligerent antics and comments at all the wrong times.

Turning on the radio to catch the news, they could hear the reporter stating solemnly, "...ladies and gentlemen, there have been several tragic episodes that has taken place overnight, involving several decorated officers of Minneapolis Police Department. A reign of ruthless terror has been unleashed and has claimed the lives of 18 officers over the last 12 hours, the city of Richmond County is under siege and the mayor has implemented a curfew until the person or persons suspected of these heinous murders have been apprehended. At this time, there are no real leads or even a definite description, other than a black male, mid 20's to early 30's, medium height, slim build, and wearing a black hoodie, black jeans, and black gloves and shoes.

The suspect was last seen leaving a scene early last night in a white Toyota Camry, where he claimed the first two lives; of Officers Monroe and Burnheart of the Richmond County Police Department. It is also alleged that this suspect is part of an ongoing investigation into a series of murdered police officers in several states. The FBI is working in full cooperation in these investigations and are asking anyone from the public, who may have any information involving these recent murders to please call the Crime Stoppers hotline, you do not have to leave your name or any identifying information, tips can be left totally anonymous..."

As the news went to commercial, Mike spoke up, saying, "It's time to leave Minnesota, Stranger, your point has been made and damage done, you made a statement that won't be forgotten for the next 100 years, Slim. Let's hit the highway while we still can and leave this massacre in the rearview."

With everyone agreeing with Mike on his logic and common sense rationale of their situation, Stranger relented and said, "Well, I did make a statement that won't be forgotten nor misconstrued, Biggie said it best! 'What's beef? Beef is when I-see-you, guaranteed to be an ICU'," as he was bobbing his head to the silent beat that only he could hear.

Chapter Twenty - One

June 4, 2020 8:07am Thursday

USP Lee County,

Jonesville, Virginia

With Detective Dabney checking in with his findings, which all came back with a negative impression on him, Det. York tagged along with Det. McNealson, heading to Jonesville, Virginia, the home of Lee County, a United States Penitentiary. A maximum security federal penitentiary that houses federal max prisoners up in the mountains of western Virginia.

After going though several check points, administration reviewing the documents that the detectives had secured under false pretenses, they finally were allowed to enter the facility through the administrative office. They were greeted by a homely looking secretary that wore entirely too much make-up to be working in a prison. With her hair frizzed, facial foundation so thick that she must have applied it with a spatula, and her eye shadow with eye liner, made her look as silly as a 70's Go-Go dancer mixed with a circus clown. But her evil sneer showed when Det. McNealson tried greeting her with a handshake. She looked quite repulsed, as if touching his black hand, would somehow give her a disease.

McNealson took notice to her reaction and slowly lowered his hand, mentally acknowledging that she had a sever case of racism laced into her blood and upbringing. The secretary, with a look of distain said, "Captain Spires and A.W. Holmes will be with y'all in a few, have a seat." She said this with her nastiest hick-town accent, the two detectives looked at one another and knew instantly that the rumors in the wind about this penitentiary held some serious credence.

When Captain Spires entered the office and stood in front of the secretary, his look spoke volumes and one could tell that he wasn't in any mood to have some out of town detectives snooping around in his backyard, no matter what their reasons were. Their presence alone was a discomfort in itself.

Without knowledge as to why they were really there, Captain Spires spoke in a slow inquiring drawl, "And how can I help you fellas?" The smile on his face showed an evil intent, as he lifted an empty spring water bottle to his mouth and spit some brown nicotine from his Copenhagen stuffed lip into it, while standing wide legged, like he was ready for a show down at high noon. Giving the obvious impression that this country bumpkin was just as racist as his secretary.

As A.W. Holmes walked in wearing his protective vest, tan cargo pants and a red polo style shirt with the Federal Bureau of Prisons emblem on the sleeve, he presented his hand towards the two detectives for a firm handshake while sporting an inviting smile on his face. Detective McNealson knew that this guy wasn't a native of this town, probably not even from the state. Unlike his two colleagues, he didn't ooze with the rancid stench of racism. With the formal introductions out of the way, A.W. Holmes invited

Det. McNealson and Det. York to the back office where they could speak in private and shed light as to the reason they've come to Lee County.

When the four men took their respective seats around the long table, Det. McNealson opened a file folder flat and placed the first document on the table top. He then began to relay the story as to why he was there, what he needed and who could meet his demands. With most of his cards on the table, A.W. Holmes and Captain Spires were ready to play fair and lend their help in the investigation. They were saddened by the recent attacks against police officers. So, whatever information they could provide them for the investigation, they were more than happy to assist.

Det. McNealson placed a list on the table, and then print outs of four mug shots with a laundry list of charges for each man. He then said, "I also need to speak with these following staff members, and any other member that have come into contact with these four men during their stay here in this facility at one time or the other."

Demanding the files such as, psychology evaluations, medical records, housing assignments, and solitary confinement status reports, Captain Spires tried bringing their requests to a halt by stating that the files Det. McNealson were seeking were indeed private and would breech confidentiality as well as security protocols. But it was only short lived, when Det. York placed a warrant on the table for a release and also an order for all documents, inquiries, and files pertaining to this investigation, signed by a federal district court judge. Leaning back in the seat,

Det. McNealson said, "If you'd be so kind, I'd like to start with psychology records, and inmate central files, gang affiliations and housing assignments." He spoke in his best southern drawl. Smiling, he waited for the two administrators to figure out who was going to go fetch all of those files, when Captain Spires yelled out, "Carol! I need your assistance in here!"

Carol, the secretary, took her sweet time making it to the back office. But when she got there, she instantly got some real pep in her step when she realized the severity of the situation, as to not further infuriate Captain Spires any more than he already was about this situation.

The office became an interstate of traffic, along with the hustle and bustle of staff, and the entrance of prisoners shackled hand and feet, escorted by two correctional officers for security measures. Files began to arrive and stacks of them were placed on the conference table for their convenience in order to pursue their investigation.

As both of the detectives split up and set out to perform two separate tasks, one being the reviewing of files and taking notes on the possible suspects and also checking the mental background histories of each of the four individuals in question. The second being the interviews of staff and affiliates that were closest to any one of these men that they were compiling files of information on, trying to narrow down these their list of potential suspects.

Detective York took the file reading task because he was a stickler for catching the little things, and putting together tricky puzzles. Whereas, Detective McNealson was better suited to interview the staff and known associates, being known as 'The Truth Seeker' due to his efforts and style of questioning. Det. McNealson always seemed to walk away from the table with either the answers he needed or a confession recorded, which he never failed to do, as to date.

Chapter Twenty - Two

June 4, 2020 Noon, Thursday

USP Lee,

Jonesville, Virginia.

Four hours later, Det. McNealson enters the conference room, where he'd earlier left Det. York combing over a mountain of files for the four suspects in question. Staring at the file-covered conference table, Det. McNealson lowered his head slightly, and placed his lips upon the rim of his styrofoam cup of coffee and allowed his eyes to roam over the room. They finally landed upon his partner. Taking notice to the etched forehead, and the intense look of a noticeable strain upon Det. York's face, Det. McNealson beckoned Det. York's attention with a playful slow southern drawl to his voice, saying, "How's it goin' partner?" which caused Det. York to momentarily steer his focus away from the open file folder of one of the potential suspects in their investigation.

Det. York leaned back in the chair, clamped his forefinger and thumb to the bridge of his nose and quietly said, "Vince, you wouldn't believe some of the stuff I've read on our suspects." Then Det. York went on to fill in his partner on his findings and his suspicions of the rumored claims that are surrounding USP Lee County, up in these mountains.

Physically assaulting inmates by use of excessive force, is a common thing, as well as, the tactics that have been used against prisoners that have endured the afflictions of this inexcusable abuse caused by correctional officers, who have implemented the punishment which now seemed to consist of torment and malicious oppression.

Det. York held hard eye contact with Det. McNealson and stated, "Vince, I think this place violated every civil rights law in the book." Pointing towards his notes, he added, "Look here, Vince, these men were subjected to some seriously vile treatment by the officers here, and from the looks of these records, there hasn't been one person on this whole entire staff reprimanded or sanctioned for the use of excessive force or anything even remotely close to it. After searching through their records and evaluations of these individuals, it seems they've given the same excuse to every incident as to the reasons for these inmates being physically assaulted to the point that they needed serious medical attention. I mean from broken bones, to fractured skulls, even some self inflicted deaths, that weren't ruled as suicide, but as homicides, by the medical examiners in this town of Jonesville."

Once Det. York conveyed his disturbing findings to Det. McNealson waiting for his response, they both sat silently in the conference room, allowing the moment to pass, but also giving them the time to brood over facts and findings. Then Det. York began to reiterate what he found out about three of the four suspected men of their inquiry. He went off into a continual spiral of chilling details for each man. Some of the news he unveiled was consistent of only a person who was indeed mentally incapacitated or insane. The incident reports were somewhat creatively imaginative, and the evaluations were describing some of the most heinous atrocities of the utmost violent proportions.

Displeased, Det. York laid a file folder open on the table and said, "Vince, read this." In the small file was a mugshot photo of a youthful looking black male sporting a malevolent scowl that was seemingly etched into the callow flesh of his young face. Just below his photo was the general information of his physical description, date of birth, and known aliases in which the alleged suspect was known by in the streets. Det. McNealson scanned the left side of the file folder, then proceeded to the right side, only to be halted in his tracks, when his eyes fell upon the psychological evaluation case notes of a, Dr. Emily Anne Poole and her observations and diagnosis of Harold McDermott, a very mentally disturbed individual by the nickname 'Mayhem'. He was diagnosed to have severe mental disorder of psychosis and a very complex disorder of acute stress.

Reading further into the files and treatments of McDermotts' mental illnesses and his psychoanalytic evaluations, Det. McNealson began to get a mental impression into the extreme madness and erratic behaviors of Harold 'Mayhem' McDermott while he was housed at U.S. Penitentiary Lee County for the Federal Bureau of Prisons. But still, Det. McNealson wasn't totally sold on the specifics of Mayhem's incident reports, or the countless infractions he accumulated during his stay at USP Lee. These incident reports depicted an individual that wasn't just crazy, for lack of a better word, but maniacal and recklessly wicked in his pattern of erratic thinking and behavior.

Allowing his mind to sort out the facts from fiction, Det. McNealson closed the file folder, and stood up straight as a board, then turned on his heels and lazily said, "I got some serious questions that need some serious answers," throwing his words over his shoulder, Det. McNealson proceeded towards the conference room door.

Det. York said, "Where you going now?"

Replying, Det. McNealson said, "To the SHU," referring to the Special Housing Unit. "The only place I can get the answers to my questions."

Chapter Twenty - Three

June 7, 2020 9am Monday

Prince William County,

Quantico, Virginia

Pulling into the parking space at Quantico Marine Base, Spl. Agents Smart and Drapper, sat quietly for a few moments before words were passed between them. Staring off into a reverie of mangled thoughts, Spl. Agent Smart broke the silence in the car's quiet solitude when he blurted out from the clear blue, "Something tells me our perp, is one fucked up individual. I mean, seriously disturbed and demented person, whose express purpose is to single handedly deliver a clear and precise message to the police."

When Spl. Agent Drapper, chimed in, "You think?" adding the question sarcastically, saying, "I think he's someone who has a deeper reason for what he's doing, and there's something that we aren't seeing, because he has our own eyes in clouds when we should be looking at the ground." Head twisting in the direction of the passenger seat where Spl. Agent Drapper sat ranting on about some gibberish he'd never heard before, Spl. Agent Smart said, "Hold up here! What the hell does all of that stuff about clouds and the ground mean?"

With a slow smirk forming on his face, Spl. Agent Drapper replies, "This dude got our heads all in the countless clouds, we're wondering all the wonders about the countless 'whys' we're going to encounter, instead of being focused on the foundation of things, the direction he's taking us through, the nonexistent trail of clues he's leaving behind, that somehow connects to antagonistic reasons for him to unleash such brazen unrelating terror against the police force. Which if you ask me, is tactical and definitely obsessive."

After Spl. Agent Drapper concluded his thoughts, Spl. Agent Smart cracks the driver's side door and pushes it open. He then replies simply, "Well, let's see what the real professional nut crackers have to say about this, maybe they can make all this make sense to us."

As both agents climb out of the car, they head to the front door of a plain looking, windowless, beige, brick building, which unknowingly to the public, held the United States top bio-psychology and behavioral neuron-scientist and most scholarly expert in the studies of clinical psychology for the diagnosis and treatment of sever mental illnesses, behavioral and emotional disorders, psychoanalysis, and behavioral therapy.

The chief scientist, Herman Applegate entered his office and took position behind his immaculate desk. He intertwined his fingers on the desk blotter, stating, "So, Spl. Agent Smart, and Spl. Agent Drapper, it's a pleasure to make your acquaintance. So, how may I be of assistance to you?" saying his words with an air of official bureaucracy that spoke volumes of intelligence over the average human mind. Spl. Agent Smart began by unraveling the seemingly evil tales of psychodrama into these mysterious serial killings of decorated police officers at random and unprovoked times.

Chief behavioral scientist Herman Applegate sat rigidly still behind his desk, absorbing all the bizarre and intricate details of each case that was known up to date, like a Brawny paper towel. Once concluding the well spent tale of remorseless terror that had taken place over the last three weeks, Herman Applegate sat seemingly motionless for a moment. Then, slowly pushing his glasses up on the bridge of his nose, he rose to his feet and headed to a book case in the corner his of office and pulled a large heavily bound book from its confines on the top shelf. This book being the DSM-IV-. Diagnostic and statistical manual of mental disorders 4th edition. Still carrying on, in a stream of psychobabble, like a military cadence that never broke its stride or rhythm, Applegate thumbed through the thick bound manual, retaking his seat behind his desk. He placed the book on the desk blotter, opened it, and started summarizing examples of different mental disorders like he was having a normal conversation, and relaying facts that was not common knowledge to the ignorant and simple minded.

Halting Dr. Applegate in his barrage of endless clinical psychology jargon, Spl. Agent Smart asked the scientist to dumb down his summation into the different disorders, and without clinical terms that he was tossing around like a mental ball of common sense.

Pausing a moment, Dr. Applegate began to reiterate, and give a less complex description of the diverse behaviors and mental processes, making it more straight forward and simple to comprehend for the two FBI agents. He was going from one clinical term to another, also presenting examples of the many abnormal behaviors that are accustomed and consistent with each diagnosis.

Spl. Agent Smart's interests were piqued as he sat motionless, listening to the doctor stress his concerns and doubts as to what mental disorder their perp was suffering from. When Dr. Applegate began to compile, apply and characterize the various disorders to the perp in question, Agent Drapper expressed his belief that the perp seemed to be suffering from some sort of fixation with cops, through either acute stress or PTSD (Post Traumatic Stress Disorder).

Only now does he go on in his explanation into why, saying, "I think our guy is someone who's had some disturbing run ins with law enforcement due to the evidence that was left behind in the Augusta, Georgia homicide of Sheriff Deputy Jamieson Mahoney." Going on to state, "In the way in which Deputy Mahoney was murdered, and the acts that were committed against him, showed signs of repressed anger, and an abnormal fixation consistent to the behavior without any rational instigation." When Dr. Applegate divulged his thoughts by weighing in on the facts through the means of clinical studies, and said, "I have reason to believe that the perp you're chasing is suffering from a form of catharsis," only to go on in his explanation that something triggered this reaction, like it was most likely instigated.

All the while, Agent Smart sat quietly and mentally pieced together a mental and psychological profile of their perp when a scary thought hit him out of the blue, like a hit and run. Agent Smart then tossed his thoughts out there like a handful of intellectual confetti, and said, "So, if this is catharsis, you're speaking of, could it be triggered by something unrelated to the individual, but still have the effects that is relatable?"

Dr. Applegate pondered the question in his own mind for a moment, then replied, saying, "If I'm understanding you correctly, are you asking if our perp was triggered into committing this violent spree of vile acts due to some sort of ...outside influence?"

"Exactly!" replied Agent Smart, "Like say perhaps, all of these recent police involved shootings that doesn't seem justified from the outside looking in, when the victim is unarmed and a black male?"

Dr. Applegate brooded over the inquiry momentarily and without batting an eye, he succumbed to the plausibility of the statement and said, "I can't say actually for a fact that with all that's taken place, and the stress that the Covid-19 scare has placed upon society as a whole, that a person suffering from any form of a mental disorder or illness could or couldn't be triggered into a mania, or paranoia, especially if one is suffering from an acute form of psychosis as a guess, I'd say yes. I'd have to agree with the presumption of your inquisition, but I'd also add, the behavior is only going to lead to a more extreme case of violence, generally speaking. I get a sense that this persistent behavior is unalterable. Whatever event that triggered these psychotic episodes in this individual, I believe you are dealing with a very delusional person, whose sole intent is to right some unknown wrongs that have occurred against him or the experiences specific to a culture or group, such as a meme."

Taking some time to process the depth of the information they were being given, Agent Smart and Agent York both sat stone straight, allowing their minds to grasp the severity of the situation, only to accept the facts, in the face of their adversity: That they indeed were in a hare and turtle race to the finish line, and they were definitely the turtle, in this race running too slow to catch up. But they knew that without shedding some light of truth, they were going to need a traumatic change in events to catch this perp, and he wasn't making many, if any, mistakes.

They were dealing with one cold, calculated, and demented individual, who had a serious hard on for killing cops. But one thing is for sure and two things for certain, they had to catch him and catch him quick. All criminals make mistakes, there was no such thing as a perfect crime. But catching this particular person, from so far behind the ball, they were definitely going to need him to make some kind of mistakes. Hopefully a grave mistake.

Chapter Twenty - Four

June 4, 2020 7:30am Thursday
South West, Virginia

Driving along interstate 64, Stranger sat listening to John voice his opinion as to how he would proceed in rectifying all of the unjustified homicides against young men and women in the African-American communities by the so called 'Long Arm of the Law', which also seems to be lawless vigilantes working in tandem with other law enforcement agencies across the county under the guise heroes of The War on Drugs, guns and gangs.

It's a fact that this was the government's rendition of putting-the-hammer-to-the-nail and closing the coffin on the lives, families, and communities of all the minorities who are enduring the struggles and living under oppressed conditions.

Stranger slightly turning his head in the direction of John, who sat contemplative in the front passenger seat, ranting on about his views of how the system is systematically corralling the black youth and stripping them of their rights, freedoms, and fair treatment, with no intentions of enforcing justice or equality. Then, John blurts out, "It's a true fact! Stranger, did you know that in the constitution, that it was once written, that the black man is considered $3/5^{th}$ of a man, which gave them the right to enslave us?"

Stranger then breaks his silence of the reference of 'us' that John had taken the liberty to entitle himself as being a part of his race by saying, "John, you *do* know that you're not black, right? Not even light skinned or mulatto for that matter!"

The silence sits heavily like a fog for a moment in the stuffy SUV, when suddenly, John replied, feeling slightly insulted by Stranger's comment, which held to be true.

"Look, Stranger, oppressed is oppressed! The color of my skin doesn't eliminate me from feeling or being treated unjustly. I feel like I'm just as much twisted up in the system's finely weaved web of deceit and systemic racism as anyone else of color. You are my closest friend, and when you hurt-I hurt. When you're oppressed-I'm oppressed. Our connection is buried deeper than a mere color of our skin."

Waking up out of a sullen, fitful sleep, Mike, chimed into the conversation between John and Stranger, saying, "You can't be serious, John! You know damn well that you've never been oppressed! Not one single day of your life. You're only friends with Stranger because no one else will be your friend, and that's because you're such an annoying asshole, who is so facetious and sarcastic, that you can't help but offend and repulse any and everyone you come into contact with. So, shut your fuckin' mouth, and enjoy the fuckin' ride, why don't ya?"

John sat there with a perplexed look upon his face and quietly says, just barely above a whisper, "It seems someone woke up on the wrong side of the backseat."

Ignoring John's comment, Mike asked Stranger, "Where are we, Strange? We ain't in St. Louis yet?"

Stranger remained quiet for a few fleeting seconds, replying, "Naw, we ain't there yet, and there won't be a St. Louis when we do get there."

"What you mean, Slim?" asked Mike.

"I decided to back track a little, because I left some unfinished business in Jonesville, Virginia. That's where I'm really about to make a statement," Stranger replied, with an air of malice laced in the depths of his voice.

Agitated, Mike responded by saying, "Aww shit, Stranger, come on Slim, you made your point and your statement, now let's move forward, toward the West Coast, this region of the United States is hotter than Last Dab hot wing sauce."

"Naw, I think it's hotter than that," John blurts out, refusing to keep his unwanted opinion to himself.

"You see, Stranger, even John is making sense, and he's never made any sense to me before," said Mike, blatantly belittling John as if he wasn't even present. Stranger reinforces his standings by saying, "Well, me and John has been talking for a little while, while you and sleeping beauty back there caught up on your Z's, and I'm in agreement with all of what John spoke on."

"And what's that?" asked Mike. "Well, the Police Force is on high alert at the moment, so, it seems like a perfect time to switch things up and pursue another target, who deemed themselves to be above the law," stated Stranger.

"I don't get it, you're gunna have to elaborate on the specifics," replied Mike.

Frustrated, Stranger began unwinding a past tale that took a serious toll on him, causing him fear and anxiety at the hands of a few of Jonesville's correctional staff, which in turn, built a strong, loathsome resentment towards anyone who posed as a figure of authority. He began relaying in detail, the harsh treatment and abuse he endured while in the custody of the Federal Bureau of Prisons at USP Lee County. The traumatic events he was defenselessly left vulnerable to, were relentless and went on for extended amounts of time. Everyday, Stranger was in fear for his life, being beaten because he wouldn't allow the staff to disrespect him or berate him. Not even strip him of his pride or manhood.

Stranger went on to describe some of their acts as cruel intentional acts of attempted murder, when he had found finely crushed shards of glass in his food, and the many untold assaults he had endured when he was placed in four point restraints, and beaten unconscious, to the point where he lost his vision and his memory for days while he laid strapped to a mattress-less bed, only to have several different correctional officers show up every few hours and teach him a lesson in the art of falling in line. In their line.

When Stranger finished this story, Mike sat in the back seat, reeling with anger and dazed with a careless intent to seek revenge for all of the malfeasance that Stranger was subjected to while incarcerated for a crime he had never committed in the first place. Some unlawfully dirty narcotics detective out of D.C. had been pinning cases on innocent men for the purpose of 'Cleaning up the

Streets of D.C.', only to have the majority of the cases overturned on appeal when the head of the Metropolitan Drug Force was exposed for all of his wrong doings, and for being derelict in his duties. That person was none other than, Detective Richard Montgomery III. D.C.'s finest, yet worst detective to ever wear the badge and gun. When Mike broke the silence again, he said, "Stranger, whatever plan you've concocted with John, I sure hope it's something that legends are made of, I'm with you slim, all the way, whatever-whenever-however."

Stranger glared sternly into the rearview mirror, locking eyes with Mike, who was seated directly behind him, and nodded his head in acceptance and approval of Mike's self proclaimed admiration and loyalty toward him and their lifelong friendship.

When they pulled off interstate 64 and headed towards the town of Jonesville, Virginia, Stranger finally came alive and sat upright and alert with his head on a swivel as he drove. John took note of Stranger's sudden mood change and began to instigate some sort of reaction out of him by inducing the deeply seated hatred inside Stranger to rise to the surface, prodding and provoking him to come undone at the seams. John worked mechanically and relentlessly on Stranger's unsteady mind state by embedding a vicious need of wrath, along with a blatant need to unleash his pent up anger and fulfill the promise he had made to all those correctional officers at USP Lee, who set out purposely to cause him undue harm and distress. The chicken has finally come home to roost, and the statement that is about to be made, will in fact, go down in the history books as the most audacious and disturbing murders to date.

After some time of prepping and coercing on John's behalf, he sat back in the passenger seat and folded his arms across his chest like he was satisfied with his insidious plan, and patiently waiting for the fruits to ripen from all those savage seeds he planted in Stranger's mind as they drove along the interstate while Mike and Lisa slept peacefully in the backseat.

John held no smirk on his face, but he was definitely laughing on the inside. John wanted Stranger to, not only execute the threats that he had made against the correctional officers when he was incarcerated, but also, to stand firm on his mission to eradicate any officer who crosses his path, for the sole purpose and reason of righting those wrongs, with an eye for an eye. Or in this case, a life for a life.

As the quietness engulfed in the SUV, there was complete chaos boiling inside one person, which vibrated louder than a scream and Stranger was standing at the threshold of something legendary.

Chapter Twenty - Five

June 4, 2020 8:20am Thursday

Jonesville, Virginia

Waking up from a sound sleep, Lisa felt the air in the SUV was stuffy and heavy with a tension that was so thickly woven with solemn discomfort, she instantly knew she'd missed out on something. Raising the question, she asked, "What's going on?" Spoken in her suspicious, no nonsense voice, Lisa awaited an answer, but none was forthcoming.

She then said, "What the fuck ever, Stranger, I need you to pull over at the gas station, I gotta pee-please!"

"We almost there, Lisa, sit tight, I just gotta make this right at the light," Stranger replied.

Lisa persisted on though. When she saw a gas station to the left side of the street she said, "Damn! Stranger, the gas station right there! I have to pee NOW!"

Signaling to change lanes, into the far left lane, Stranger eases over and came to a stop, turning into the gas station parking lot. John, in turn, throws a fit when the course of action he'd put into place was being derailed by a woman who couldn't hold her bladder.

Suddenly, John began berating Lisa in his normal demoralizing way, saying, "Here we go again, catering to the one eyed hippo. You know Lisa, the more I'm around you, the more I feel like a fucking zoo keeper! Being around you is like taking care of a pet, and you're the reason why I never had one as a child!" John continued on in a fitful rant, when finally, Stranger intervened saying, "Enough, John, she's just waking up."

But Lisa blurted out from the backseat, "Naw, Stranger, I was about to punch his scary bitch ass in the head. Stranger, I don't know why you keep riding around with that coward ass bitch in the front seat anyhow! Oh, I know why-If the cops see his white ass in the front seat, they won't pull our asses over, but if he's in the back seat, they will think we kidnapped his punk ass, right off the street, and kill us all under the assumption that he's our hostage."

John came back with a verbal onslaught of his own when he stated, "No, Lisa, I'm in the front seat because it's illegal to ride around with your pet horse in the front seat. If Stranger keeps training you right, he just may be able to get you to learn to hold your bladder. Shit, I can't see why not, he's taught a horse how to talk! Yea Mrs. Ed! You fuckin' fat bag of piss."

John rattled on a barrage of insults that were meant to demean and belittle Lisa's self esteem, which makes her shut up and stare daggers into the back of John's head, when finally, Stranger said, "John, I said that's enough."

John cut his comments short in fear of making Stranger more enraged than he already was, and just sat quietly in the front seat, staring out of the windshield at nothing in particular, trying his hardest not to turn his head in Stranger's direction and locking eyes.

While Lisa was in the gas station, Stranger began gasing up the Ford Expedition, when surprisingly, a grey Chevy Silverado pick up truck, pulled up on the other side of the pumps, parallel to Strangers SUV. Climbing out was two of Lee County's correction staff, just as an Subaru Outback pulled up to the gas pumps in front of Stranger's SUV where two more staff members appeared, one heading towards the store, while the other, popped the gas tank and removed the cap to fill up the car with the gas nozzle in hand.

Stranger took notice that the correctional officer was indeed one of the individuals who had physically assaulted him while he was housed in the SHU at USP Lee. Stranger stood there holding the gas nozzle, when it all came back to him in a flash as he mentally began to relive the physical and mental torment he was exposed to not too long ago.

When the pump stopped, the tank being full, Stranger casually swung around the back of the SUV and reemerged on the driver's side only to open the driver door. As he reaches in, under the seat, Mike takes note to Stranger's peculiar movements and asked, suspiciously, "Stranger, what's up, Slim? You got that look in your eye." Then he zeroed in on what was demanding such intense concentration from Stranger, but before Mike could prevent the inevitable, things spiraled into a fiery ball of damnation, and Stranger was sure enough about to unleash hell's wrath on one of the men that he had promised to decapitate if he ever ran across him in the street.

Swiftly, Stranger closed the driver's door, reacting with stealth-like speed, he closed the distance between him and the officer. Before the C.O. could manage to turn around to face his

Judge, Jury, and Executioner, Stranger pointed the gun at him and said, "Walk. Don't look back, and don't make a sound."

The C.O. tried to reason with him, but his words fell on deaf ears as he was forcefully grabbed and pushed towards the side of the building and out of the public's view. When he had the C.O. out of sight, Stranger asked the officer menacingly if he remembers him. The officer replied silently by furrowing his brow as if he truly didn't know who he was. But Stranger quickly helped him recollect, saying, "Come on now, it's me, C.O. Greene. Oh, don't you remember ole Stranger?"

The cruelty of the words rolled off his tongue with such induced hatred, that Officer Greene stood motionless as his memory began to piece together the perplexed puzzle of where he had seen Stranger's face before. It all came back to him, flooding like a tsunami. "Oh, shit!" Correctional Officer Greene exclaimed, in awe, with trepidation tricking off of his words, like profuse sweat, rolling down one's brow.

But, before C.O. Greene could scream for help, Stranger silenced him with a serrated blade of a big hunting knife that he had retrieved from under his driver's seat, along with the police issued semi -automatic Sig Sauer P225, 9mm that he had seized from the last murdered Police Officer in Minnesota that had crossed paths with Stranger and paid the ultimate price with his life for the many bad seeds that the Police Force was willingly standing behind, like a gang of blue recruits that was being shielded by their shields.

With the precision of a brain surgeon, Stranger swiftly drew the blade across C.O. Greene's throat, which ended up in a full decapitation of C.O. Greene's head, as it fell off lopsided and smashed to the ground with a crunching thud. Stranger stood over his prized corpse and said, "I told you I was coming for your head and I never make promises I cannot keep." He then picked up the head by its hair and turned on his heals, heading back around the side of the building towards the gas pumps with a swaggering stroll, like nothing heinous had just taken place only moments ago.

Keeping his head down and covered by the hood of his black hoodie, Stranger approached the pumps and eased past the front end of the car that the deceased C.O. arrived in, and with blinding speed, snatched open the door to the passenger side where his next Lee County victim sat, unknowingly awaiting his demise. Stranger leaned in and violently went to work, impaling the C.O. with the hunting blade, until his body went deathly still.

John watched the action take place in front of him through the rearview window of the car. The look in his eye said he was being effectively entertained and impressed with the efficiency, and the quiet terror that Stranger was inflicting in broad day light, in the parking lot of a busy gas station without drawing any attention to himself. When Stranger rose up from the car's interior, he held in his hand two decapitated heads. C.O. John Downy and Peter Greene, two veteran C.O.s of the Bureau of Prisons, but just two men of several that Stranger had made the threatening promise to come back and behead. Opening the driver's side door of the SUV, he tosses both heads onto the floor board. He then shut the door and stepped off at a hurried pace, rounding the back of the SUV and disappearing from view. Lisa, John, and Mike all sat confused, with their heads spinning around on a swivel, trying to locate Stranger when a short second later, they caught a glimpse of him through the short passage way on the other side of the gas pumps where the Silverado pickup was parked.

Stranger was escorting another officer to the side of the building, where he had left the dead, headless corpse of C.O. Greene, but when they bent the corner of the building, the passenger of the Silverado, C.O. Pruitt, stepped out of the front door of the store, just barely catching sight of his friend and coworker, C.O. James Davenport, being forced around the side the building by some guy he couldn't quite see clearly because his head was covered completely by a dark hoodie. He was looking downwards, while aggressively pushing C.O. Davenport to continue walking out of sight.

C.O Pruitt witnessed the manner in which C.O. Davenport's uniform was being grabbed and shoved forcefully. His suspicions were piqued and he decided to follow to see what was really happening.

As he rounded the corner, he heard the voice of C.O. Davenport pleading with the hooded guy and decided to approach them from behind, only to be frozen in his tracks. When he saw his coworker step back laggardly and collapse to the ground, his confidence turned to pure terror. Just then, John rounded the corner and yelled out, "Someone's behind you! Stranger! Watch out!"

Spinning around in a low crouch, he lunged in the direction of the figure right behind him, plunging the knife, already dripping with blood, into the abdomen of C.O. Pruitt and slowly stood up, ripping open the stomach lining as he went. Stranger kept lifting the knife until he was actually sawing into the sternum with the serrated edge of the blade.

Listening to the unmistakable sound of death's guttural moans as the C.O. gurgled on the blood that was accumulating in his throat passages, Stranger stepped closer to his dying victim and began to whisper to him, saying, "So, we meet again, huh Pruitt? Well, it seems as if I *do* make good on my promises after all, and seeing the look in your eye as you take your last breath and your soul leaves your body behind, it's like a priceless work of art. It's, huh... Breathtaking! Don't you think?" Stranger questions with a low growl to his voice, as if he is refraining himself from leaping off into the deep end.

C.O. Pruitt falls lifelessly limp at Stranger's feet. Stranger again began to saw the knife vertically further up into the chest plate up of his victim, until he reached the base of the neck, only to reposition the knife horizontally, and saw away into the neck until he had severed the head from the base of the neck, just above the Adam's Apple.

The scene then turned even more gruesome as John stood watching and Stranger grabbed a fistful of the C.O.'s hair. Using his foot to brace the body, Stranger, for all it was worth, began pulling until the head tore away at the spinal cord with a sickening wet snap. John stood in quiet frozen awe, as he watched Stranger quickly revert back to the previous murder victim, C.O. Davenport, and began hacking at his body like he was gutting a deer in the wilderness.

John was feeling overly excited, especially to have witnessed Stranger's sadistic handiwork and true artistry in raw form. John approached Stranger from behind with an admiring grin plastered on his face, commenting. "Stranger, if this isn't making a statement, I don't know what the fuck is! I swear! I've never seen anything so richly fulfilling as what my eyes just beheld! Stranger, you're truly a master of the slaying craft, You're a-"

"Shut the fuck up John!" Stranger says, angrily, cutting John's comment off in mid sentence, and with fiery eyes, he shoots John a look over his shoulder that said all that was needed to be said. John started back-peddling, as he made his intent known, when he said, "I'll be in the truck." Then he hastily disappeared from sight in the blink of an eye.

Stranger looked around and located a discarded plastic grocery bag randomly laying about the ground. Immediately snatching it up, he quickly examined it for any holes. Satisfied that the bag would serve its purpose, Stranger grabbed up both decapitated heads at the scalps and tossed them both into the plastic bag like trash. Just like how those same C.O.s once treated him like nothing of worth by assaulting him, knocking him unconscious, unprovoked.

But just before heading back to the SUV, he stopped short and stood over the maliciously mutilated corpse of C.O. Pruitt, stooped down and reached into the open chest cavity and seized a hold of Mitchell Pruitt's still barely beating heart and dislodged it with a merciless yank. Rising to his feet, Stranger said crudely to the mutilated corpse, "I told you I was coming to get your heartless ass."

Constricting his fist tightly around the faintly pulsing heart, he squeezed with all of his might until the left and right ventricles were crushed, making a squishy sounding pop as the remaining blood began to drain. Stranger dropped the useless heart like discarded litter, and before rounding the corner, he pulled the stolen service issued Sig Sauer P225 9mm from his hoodie pouch and headed back towards the SUV. Reaching the gas pumps, he tossed the handgun on the hood of C.O. Greene's Subaru Outback. He then removed the badge of the last Minnesota police officer that was forced to resign on short notice for failure to uphold the law: Richmond County's MPD Officer Jeremiah Jacobs, badge #772, and carelessly chucked in on the top of the Subaru's hood as well.

Without breaking stride, Stranger continued to the SUV's driver side door, stopping only for a split second to survey the parking lot. Seeing that nobody had even noticed him. The only other person in the vicinity that was even remotely close enough to witness the brash of murders that had taken place, was the gas station attendant. But her attention was diverted upon the small television set that was airing the daytime show, Maury, to which she was all eyes and ears to. She was totally oblivious to all that took place around her as she sat surrounded by bitter carnage, a battlefield of unburied dead bodies that was laid to waste.

Climbing back into the SUV and callously dropping the plastic shopping bag on the floor board, amongst the other two decapitated heads that were carelessly thrown there beforehand, Stranger started the SUV, shifted into drive, pulling off from the pump area as if nothing was amiss.

It wasn't until several miles later that any words were spoken, when Lisa said, "Stranger, this is lunacy! I don't know what the fuck just took place back there or why, for that matter, but you need to pull over and get cleaned up. You're a fucking bloody mess." When Stranger didn't respond, Mike spoke up, nonchalantly saying, "Leave him alone for now, Lisa. Let him sort out his emotions. Those murders back at that gas station were personal, and right now, Stranger's dealing with some very heavy shit on his mind. Now is not the time. Plus, he needs to put some distance between us and that massacre that he just left behind."

Lisa took heed to Mike's rational thinking and fell quiet, but she definitely kept her eyes focused on the rearview mirror, in hopes of locking eyes with Stranger to relay the unspoken message that she was beyond upset with him, but at the same time, also concerned.

Lisa made a mental note to dig deeper into the meaning behind all of this, when things cooled down a little later. Until then, she would hold her tongue and mind her 'principles and qualities', or her P's and Q's, as the ole saying goes. But she definitely knew that Stranger was a train wreck waiting to happen. She just didn't know when it would happen, cause the wreck was sure to come, and soon, at the rate he was going.

Chapter Twenty - Six

June 4, 2020 12:30pm Thursday

USP Lee County,

Jonesville, Virginia

The sliding door rolls shut behind McNealson as he enters the SHU, or the Segregated Housing Unit, and is met by the head psychologist, Dr. Emily Poole. McNealson began to tick off a few of his minor suspicions to test the waters and see if Dr. Poole would take the bait, but she wouldn't surrender an inch. She remained composed at the hints that many, if not all, of the incident reports that were delved into, showed a lot of inconsistencies with unauthorized acts, and falsified statements filed by many of the staff members there.

McNealson then made a breakthrough, when he said, "Can you explain to me the procedures that are to be followed when an offender is placed into four point restraints?" Biting into the bait, he had laid, she went on to give a thorough breakdown of how the inmates are forced into total submission and compliance. She then had to further explain why excessive force was being used on them after they were placed into restraints, and why there wasn't any medical attention provided for those men, who had fractured arms, legs, skulls, or were beaten unconscious to the point that their injuries left them unconscious for days with head traumas, like contusions, lacerations and swelling, in a lot of cases.

Flustered, Dr. Poole tried to explain away the blatantly hostile and overly aggressive acts of use of force that were inflicted on the men. But, she couldn't come up with plausible reasonings as to why restrained inmates at their facility were practically beaten to within an inch of their lives on a constant basis. Realizing she was only digging herself deeper in the hole that was set for her, she expressed that she herself had done no wrong doings, and that in fact, she believed that there were a few times that some of the C.O. staff members were put in compromising situations and things may have gotten a little out of control.

Upon hearing this subtle admission that she had knowledge of criminal conduct and the use of excessive force, but had never once filed any complaint on the behalf of any of the prisoners in her care, made her just as culpable as those who were actually carelessly committing the acts of assaulting prisoners and intentionally covering up the dirty deeds with fabricated incident reports and withholding proper medical care, and mental health treatment.

When McNealson made the connection, he gave Dr. Poole a grave look and said, "Doc, if I were you, I'd be getting my affairs in order. I will be contacting Internal Affairs Division and letting them in on the little secrets that are being hidden in these backwood mountains of Jonesville, and just so you know, I will testify, at the Grand Jury hearings, if they decide to proceed forward with indictments against anyone who is found to be liable and are derelict in their duties. I'm having these records seized and sealed until IAD has completed a full investigation into these inner workings and the many violations of constitutional rights that are, and have been violated here, not only by the correctional staff, but by you and the administration as well. Now, let's see who'll start throwing who under the bus to save their own asses. This won't end well for many of you, and from what my partner has read in some of these files, you don't have enough explanations for the criminal conduct and corruption that's taking place behind these razor wires and gates."

With a look of defeat plastered on her face, Dr. Emily Anne Poole lowered her head in dejection and said, "Detective, is there anything I can do? You know-to help? I feel *so* guilty and ashamed right now..."

Smiling inside to himself, McNealson took a few moments before answering, "Well, you can help by helping me pinpoint our suspect. You can help me rattle some of those cages in there," he said, nodding his head in the direction of the SHU cell range where chaos and madness were echoing off the walls, by all of the offenders that were locked away from general population.

Nervously, she looked into his eyes and said, "Like-rattle them, how?" McNealson said, "I want to know everything about a guy names Mayhem, a Harold Mc-"

Cutting him off short, Dr. Poole said, "Harold McDermott, I know him all too well. What would you like to know about him that the files we've compiled on him didn't tell you?"

"I don't want what's in the file, I want what's been said," countered McNealson with a smirk.

Perplexed, Dr. Poole looked at the detective like he had lost his mind. Replying, she said, "Sorry, detective, I'm not following..." she said trailing off.

McNealson stared at her for a second longer than he should've and began to explain, saying, "The thing about criminals, and people in general are, no matter who they are, where they're from, or how crazy you think they are, they always find someone to talk to behind these walls. There's no such thing as secrets in the penitentiary, nor in the streets, not even in the church. If someone knows something about you, outside of yourself, it's no longer a secret. Most men like to trade war stories, and tell little white lies that are sprinkled with a fine line of truth. Find that truth and you'll connect to the real conviction inside that person. There's an art to it, just allow them to talk long enough and all their truths will turn to their lies, or either all their lies will turn to truths, your job is to distinguish the fact from fiction. Since you are a psychologist, this is right up your alley. I want to talk to anyone who may have been in close contact with Mayhem during his brief stay here."

Searching her memory bank, Dr. Poole said with an assurance, "There's only one person who Mayhem would let in the cell with him. Follow me," she said, and quickly stepped off, heading towards the cell ranges. Speaking over her shoulder, Dr. Poole said, "This should be very interesting to watch."

"How so?" asked McNealson.

"You will find out shortly detective, but I must warn you now, approach this guy very cautiously. This guy isn't your everyday psychopath, he's the worst kind," Dr. Poole cautioned him.

"And, what's the worst kind?" McNealson asked.

"The thinking kind!" she replied with contempt weaved in the meaning behind her words, as if she's went a few rounds with this guy and he had come out the victor on every occasion.

Det. McNealson took her implication as a challenge. He replied, "Well, this guy may need to go a few rounds with someone who's just as well versed in picking apart the brains and motives of the sick minded."

Pausing in her steps, Dr. Poole, turned around and said, "Detective, I'm quite aware that you seem to think highly of your mental capabilities, but please, let's not get this guy mistaken with the average nut case you've encountered in your profession. Mr. Dominic Mann, "Mannimal" , as he's referred to, is a very callous individual who is intelligent, with calculating patterns of thought. If I had to describe him in one word, "I'd say he's ingenious. So, if you think your just gonna waltz in there and 'rattle' his cage, as you call it, you're in for a rude awakening, sir, and furthermore, I'm practically willing to stake my 15 year professional career on the odds that you'll walk away from his 'cage' the rattled one," she said, making the air quotes with her fingers.

Ending her warning with her head slightly tilted to the left, a disdainful look etched onto her face, and not waiting for Det. McNealson to further voice his opinion to show his arrogance, Dr. Poole rebuffed any further comment that could possibly come from McNealson, by spinning on her heels and proceeding toward the cell ranges, uncaring he was following her or not.

Suddenly, stopping at the far end of the range at cell #235, Dr. Poole softly taps on the cell door and said, "Mr. Mann, could you please come to the door, I have someone here who'd like to speak to you."

The room was completely darkened and there was no reply. After waiting momentarily, she tapped again and said, "Mr. Mann, can you-"

At strikingly fast speed, a youthfully fierce face appeared out of the darkness. There was sweat pouring down his face and a look of stubborn defiance written in his expression. Golden hazel eyes glowed angrily, causing Dr. Poole to instinctively retreat backward from the cell door in a noticeable display of fear from this menacing individual.

Det. McNealson took mental note as he observed that the quiet terror that exuded from this individual was indeed a frightfully tense and intimidating feeling. Dr. Poole then slowly composed herself by gathering whatever courage that she could muster, to face this adversity. Stepping forward, she said, "Mr. Mann, good morning, how are you today?" Dominic Mannimal Mann stood staring with a real coldhearted callous stare, not replying to her query. He was waiting for her to proceed.

"COP!" Mannimal cut in with vehemence in his voice voice, "I spy a cop! I spy a bitch ass cop who thinks he's gunna get some answers from me about something he's investigating. I spy..." Pausing a second, he squints his golden eyes tight, as if baring down on the truth. "No, I spy a very pompous cop! One who's standing at my door seeking...yes, seeking the answers to the riddle he's chasing. But..." Mannimal steps away from the door and recesses into the darkness of his cell.

Both Dr. Poole and Det. McNealson stood there awaiting Mannimal's return, but to no avail. So, Det. McNealson steps forward to the cell door and begins to talk, like he was actually having a conversation with someone whom he was well associated with. He said, "Look, Mannimal, you're absolutely right, on all counts. Yes, I'm a cop, yes, I'm in a bind with this case I'm working on, and yes, this case is a real clusterfuck of a riddle that I'm either not getting, or not smart enough to get."

From somewhere in the deep and dark recesses of the cell, Mannimal yelled, "I'd say it's the latter, if you're asking me. But you aren't asking me, so let's do each other a solid and leave this dead body where it lays, cause I'm not into reviving dead situations. That's for doctors, nurses and paramedics, and I can honestly tell you that I'm neither of those."

Det. McNealson takes a moment to recourse and to counterattack the verbal onslaught that Mannimal had just unleashed. Then he said, "Hey Mannimal, I'm not asking you to rat on nobody, I'm simply asking if you'll help me to understand Mayhem. You do know Mayhem, don't you? I mean, you're the only person in the system that has ever lived longer than a day with him in the cell. In fact, you're the only one who could reason with him when he went off the deep end at times, am I right?"

McNealson asked a question he already knew the answer to,

but this was a tactic to get Mannimal to lower his guard and answer one question, which would loosen the nut from the bolt, so to speak. When no answer was given, McNealson went on to relay small details into the case, to give the appearance that he was truly stupefied and caught in a stump. To portray this with great precision, McNealson began recounting the gruesome details of the homicides and then brazenly asked Mannimal for his intake on what message he believed the suspect was trying to convey, and to who? But Mannimal kept the prized question, the one that would bring any trouble minded psychopath out of his hidden shell. That question was, "If you were trying to make a statement such as this, what would you do differently?" Like a child in a candy store, Mannimal seemingly took the bait. The young mastermind drew forward to the window of his cell door and stoically voiced a malicious rendition on how he would have committed these heinous acts against the precious law enforcement. Mannimal looked daringly into Det. McNealson eyes, and never broke eye contact when he said the most atrocious animalistic acts that could not possibly be imagined in the mind of anyone who wasn't a bonafide lunatic and standing on some very unbalanced beams of mentally diabolical thoughts.

One thing that stood out to McNealson, while he stood listening to the spawn of satan, it seemed as if Dominic Mann was truly the supreme personification of evil, and having this particular man incapacitated was for society's best interests as a whole. But it wasn't until Mannimal made the statement, saying, "If you're looking at Mayhem for these recent deaths of all these cops, I can tell you right now, you're barking up the wrong tree."

"What makes you say that?" McNealson asked, confused.

"Mayhem has a deep fear for guns that he never told anyone about but me," answered Mannimal knowingly.

Going on to divulge a detailed account as to how this fear of Mayhem's came about. He turned his attention towards Dr. Poole. He bore a hole into her eyes as he relayed the story that was told to him of how at a young age, Harold Mayhem McDermott, was playing alone in his older brother's room when he stumbled across a loaded handgun under the bed. While pretending to shoot at imaginary targets, his older brother burst into the room, unknowing that Mayhem was there and walked straight into the line of fire, when a startled child, Harold, was frightened into discharging his older brother's gun, killing him with one shot to the chest, causing a terrified child to hold his dying brother in his arms, as he expelled his last dying breath, staring vacantly into space as young Harold sat waiting and begged his brother not to leave him. Since that dreaded day, Mayhem fearfully vowed to never touch another gun again in his life out of respect for his brother.

"So, as I was saying, you're chasing the wrong guy, under a false presumption," stated Mannimal, with McNealson thinking that he did 'rattle the cage' enough to further question Mannimal. He was denied any further conversation because Mannimal stepped away from the door into the darkness of the cell, but not before saying, "this is just the beginning detective, wait till you see what happens next, you're not chasing down riddles and leads, detective, you are chasing the wind, so let me know when you catch it..." Mannimal spoke these last words as he faded to black.

McNealson was left staring at an empty, dark cell window and feeling like a fool for allowing a demented psychopath to take his puzzle apart and hand it back to him in scattered little pieces, like a teacher does to the student. Basically, he was just told to go back to the drawing board and start all over.

Turning to leave the cell range, McNealson felt like the tables had turned on him. He was sure he would 'rattle' this man's cage, and walk away with all of the answers he needed, but instead, here he was, leaving with more questions than answers, and he even felt like he truly was 'chasing the wind', as Mannimal had perceptively suggested he was. So, the $64,000 question was, whose cage was actually 'rattled' in all of this?

As McNealson and Dr. Poole began to head away from Mannimal's cell, he was accosted by an inmate a few cells away. This inmate was known as the jail house rat, and was named Gene James, who has been chased off of every penitentiary yard that he had ever been housed at, and here he was, again speaking when he shouldn't be and sticking his nose where it doesn't belong, in other people's business.

Shouting through the door, "Excuse me, officer! Sir, excuse me! Can have I a word with you? Please sir, I got some news that you can use!" Gene James was seemingly begging to get Det. McNealson's attention. Stopping abruptly at the inmate's cell door,

McNealson asked, "Yes, how can I help you?"

Mr. James looked around suspiciously, as if to see if anyone was watching him interact with this police officer, before he went on to spew his guts with tell tale indications into the investigation he had overheard Det. McNealson summarizing details into the homicides with Mannimal, only a few moments ago.

Mr. James said, "Officer, Mayhem isn't the guy you after! I know this to be fact!"

"'How so?" countered McNealson.

"Well, for starters, I know who you looking for, cuz this person was once my next door neighbor here on this same range, just few months ago," replied James.

Waiting to hear more of who this guy was referring to, McNealson remained quiet as he listened to this man speak a hundred miles a minute, going on to give detailed accounts of how this guy was a certified 'looney bin', when Mr. James said, "This guy used to talk to himself all hours of the day and night. He would say things like, 'when I get out, I promise you I'm gonna cut your heads off'. Then he would threaten the C.O.s when he thought they were putting broken glass shards into his food, and toss his trays out the food slot onto the floor, which would cause the staff to suit up and raid his cell, with their ERT or Emergency Response Team, and they would have their hands full with him, it would go on like this for days on end. Officer, if you ask me, I'd say this guy was serious when he told C.O. Pruitt that he'd tear his heart clean out his chest with his bare hands and squeeze it till its wrung dry. But, there's this one C.O. he really had a hard on for, because he cracked him so hard with the baton, that he was knocked unconscious for like 3 or 4 days. When he woke up, he screamed all day and night, until they went back in there and silenced him again." Mr. James admitted, "Yea, they went too far from time to time, but when they deal with crazy people, they had to meet crazy, with crazy, and they-"

Stopping him mid-sentence, McNealson asked Inmate James, if he had a name for this guy? Without hesitation, Mr. James blurted out, "Stranger! His name is Ben Strange, and I'm telling you now, if anyone's capable of these recent murders, he's your guy. "

Det . McNealson asked, "What makes you so positive about this?" Mr. James looks deeply into McNealson's eyes and said, "Cause he told me in the vent, to keep an eye on the news, that he was gonna touch at least one cop in every state across the United States.

"He's doing it all cuz these cops had to pay for what they're doing to us. He said 'He was gonna make a statement that wouldn't be forgotten for the next 100 years, and if you ask me, I think he's making one helluva statement!"

McNealson turned to look at Dr. Poole, who was standing there with a mesmerized look plastered on her face, and asked her, "Do you know about this guy and these threats?"

Slowly nodding her head, she said, "Yes, and Ben Strange, Stranger is what he's known by. He isn't your average psychopath by any standard. He's a special case, I suppose, and I'm afraid that

175

if this is him, who is committing these atrocious acts, you're gonna have to-"

"Clear this range now! Lock down!" yelled the two fast approaching C.O.s. "This facility has gone on complete lockdown! Detective, you need to come with us immediately!"

Confused, Det. McNealson looked from Dr. Poole, to the two huge, hulking white C.O.s, then to inmate James, and back to the C.O.s and asked, "What happened?"

One of the C.O.s said, "'That's above our pay grade, the only thing we're concerned with right now, is getting you back the to the administration building, we have to leave now!" the C.O. forcefully stated.

As Dr. Poole and Det. McNealson were hastily escorted off of the cell range, and out of the SHU, without so much as an explanation other than the facility was on lockdown, they both looked to each other, knowing it was bad.

They were not even close. It was very bad.

Chapter Twenty - Seven

June 5, 2020 11:00am Friday
Minnesota, Minneapolis

Landing at a secluded air field in the suburban outskirts of Minneapolis, Minnesota, Agents Smart and Drapper, were met by a small convoy of heavily armed FBI field agents from the FBI Midwestern Region office and whisked away into an awaiting black GMC Suburban.

Inside their SUV, the agents were greeted by two agents, one being a 14 year veteran, Lead Investigator, Spl. Agent Marcus Maddox, and his partner of 8 years, Cynthia Goldfield. After their initial formalities were made, the no nonsense nature of the FBI's reputation came into play. It was get down to business, as Cynthia Goldfield handed Agents Smart and Drapper their field files to look over and study.

While they were being briefed into the recent massacres that had taken place less than 24 hours ago, Spl. Agent Drapper sat, mouth agape, as he was trying desperately to mentally distinguish what the true motives were of the person behind these serial murders. Agent Smart broke his train of thought when he proposed that their assailant was now committing acts of rage, saying, "These recent murders were committed with the intent to unleash extreme anger, and terror, not on the public, but on the protectors of the public. Whoever this person just so happens to be, they've got some serious issues with law enforcement," stated Agent Smart.

When Agent Maddox chimed in, he began by stating his own impression, "I believe that the person responsible could be suffering from some sorta mental breakdown," and then looked to his partner, Agent Goldfield, who searched through some papers in her stacks of files and retrieved some behavioral science case notes and clinical study on social behavior and developmental psychology.

Locating some highlighted sections, Agent Goldfield began with hypothesis, that through a psychoanalysis study, a person's abnormal mental reactions are due partly to repressed desires that are consciously rejected but also remain subconsciously persistent, speaking in layman terms, she went on to state, "A person will push thoughts out of their minds, kinda like, talking yourself out of doing something that you know is wrong, only to have it resurface in the subconscious mindset, constantly lingering there, it remains persistent, like the thoughts that lay dormant, waiting to be provoked into action, so to speak." She then goes on to give some examples of different psychosis and mania that could possibly have been their perp's mental illness and those examples were: Schizophrenia, bipolar disorder, dementia, madness and paranoia.

As she went on to summarize the different illnesses, outside of their clinical interpretations, Agent Drapper cut in briefly to theorize that maybe their perp wasn't so mentally unstable after all, causing the interior of the SUV to fall into a deathly silence, as he waited for someone to reject his suggestion. Only then did he further prod his speculation when none of them challenged his opinion by saying, "It seems our perp is reasonably capable of being mentally stable, and just may have a fixation to commit murders against law enforcement because he just doesn't like cops, and he's making a game of this for his own personal benefit."

This caused Special Agent Maddox to question him, "What benefits could he possibly be gaining from all these senseless murders?"

"What makes sense to us, doesn't necessarily mean it makes sense to our perp," countered Agent Goldfield. "Reasons are reasons, no matter how plausible, or fleetingly misunderstood they may seem to others."

Listening to the agents voice their opinions as to what could be the mental capabilities of their perp while scanning the field files for information, crime scene pictures, forensic findings, anything to assist them in their mission. Agent Smart kept his mind objectively open to all of the possibilities that could possibly play a potential role in the madness that was unraveling, with more profound and bizarre behavior being displayed with each new merciless killing that had been committed.

It seemed to Agent Smart, as if their perp was actually displaying signs of being a cathartic and committing extreme acts of purging against the law enforcement community, as some kind of strange means of rectification. Whatever their perp's true logic was behind these erratic episodes, they were definitely based on exigent circumstances that looked to be building into something monumental, with an instinctively unprovoked initiative paving the way.

As the Suburban pulled into the underground garage in downtown Minneapolis, the team filed out and began beelining towards the elevators when Agent Drapper purposely hung back, trying to speak privately with Agent Smart.

While the two agents hung back from the crowd, they spoke in hushed tones. Agent Drapper felt the need to inquire into the noticeably irritated mood that Agent Smart was uncharacteristically displaying. Candidly he asked his partner, "So, what's up, Brad? You're carrying around a stolid mood like some heavy burden is sitting on your shoulders, what's up?"

Agent Smart tears his eyes away from the file he'd been reviewing the whole ride, and looks into his partner's eyes with an alarming vacant look. He then blandly said, "This case is eating away at my own sanity, Dennis. I mean, it seems we're chasing a ghost. We can't get a decent description of this guy, not even a slight understanding into this motherfucker's mental stability. All we're going on is a bunch of assumptions that aren't supported by actual facts, these clinical studies, and the undiagnosed interpretations of this guy are only further confusing this investigation rather than bringing us closer to apprehending him, we're basically wasting our time trying to understand his mental capabilities, and that's what's bothering me. I don't give a fuck as to what he's thinking or why he's thinking it," Agent Smart vocalizes his thoughts venomously, yet trying to keep his voice down, as well as, control the rage that is starting to boil over like a volcanic eruption.

"They are our fellow officers of the law that are being unceremoniously victimized in such deplorable manners." Agent Smart remarked heatedly, causing Agent Drapper to shush him in a lame attempt to quiet him down and bring his partner's voice down a notch. When the other agents spun around to see what all of the fuss was about, Agent Smart noted their disapproving stares they were casting his way, and immediately quieted down and regained his composure. Falling back into a professional tone, without giving any apologies or excuses for his sudden outburst, they all filed into the elevator and with the doors closing behind them, the silence ensued until they reached the 4th floor.

When the door slid open, the main office was deafeningly roaring with chaotic activity as other agents in the division office were energetically moving about as phones, hidden in tiny coves of cubicles, rang continuously off the hook. All the agents were aligned and hastily walking in unison like the legs of a centipede as they furrowed into a large conference room.

A long circular conference table was stationed in the middle of the room, as everyone present took an open seat. When the meeting commenced, they conferred and exchanged information into the findings of each investigated homicide that had taken place up to date and the power point projector was turned on. The pictures and compiled evidence from each scene were artfully projected on the screen. As all the agents sat there sickened and repulsed by the grotesque horrors that were being displayed before their very eyes, some couldn't hide their obvious contempt and hatred for the atrocious acts that has been committed against their own.

The Senior Official Agent for the Midwestern Region Violent Crimes Division began presiding over the meeting by hashing over the psychological clinical studies and the FBI's chief psychologist's hypothetical evaluation of their perp's suspected character, nature, and mental stability.

Spl. Agent Smart halted the discussion to chime in his own hypothesis, when he heatedly said, "Special Agent Forrester, pardon the interruption, but don't you think that all this statistical hoopla that we're spoon-feeding ourselves with is just a bunch of psycho-babble that's only slowing down our progress? I think it's safe to say that our perp is a bonafide psycho-serial killer who has extreme vendettas, so to speak, against the law enforcement community as a whole. It doesn't take a degree in behavioral science to fully understand the severity of these circumstances or the mental capacity of the individual we are chasing. But, what we aren't doing at this moment, is actively chasing him, we're basically evaluating him through a bunch of statistical gibberish that nobody, including yourself, has any clue about on a scientific level, and I-"

Interrupting Spl. Agent Smart mid-sentence, Spl. Agent Forrester said, "So, what would you deem the necessary steps to be taken, uh, Agent-"

"Smart! Special Agent Smart, of the Eastern Division, who

has been chasing this lunatic through 7 states over the last three weeks. I haven't caught a break yet, and if I may be frank, I've got a real hard on for this guy, and sitting here chomping on the bit is as irritating as standing in a pile of fire ants with no shoes on. Sorry if I seem a little bit volatile at the moment, but can we not lose sight of the fact that, while we're here hashing over our statistics and evaluations, we still have a certified lunatic who's boldly engaging in a widespread murder spree that doesn't look to be coming to an end anytime soon? As long as we keep chasing this guy with our hands tied behind our backs and our pants hanging around our ankles, we're never going to catch up or get anywhere close in this race."

Then he finishes by saying, "Our perp is very thorough and careful, to leave no trace evidence, we've not even been able to get a little bit of his true description, and he's not sloppy in how he's proceeding to kill officers, and he's not a narcissist who's seeking fame or attention. He don't even want notoriety, he wants to rectify something, and he's making a blatant statement that will not go unheard or forgotten."

When those final words were spoken to the group of agents, the senior agent stood peering in the direction of Spl. Agent Smart, and said, "Well, Agent Smart, you're dismissed to proceed with this investigation on your own, it seems you got all your I's dotted and T's crossed. You've got our perp pegged, so to speak. There's no need for you to attend this meeting, with the perfunctory attitude that you have about the way we're gathering data, to know and understand the perpetrator we're relentlessly pursuing, I guess it's safe to say you're free to go," Agent Forrester said, dismissing Smart offhandedly, as if what he was rattling on about was meaningless and wasn't worth the time or slightest debate in the least .

Rising from his seat with ease sans any noticeable vehemence or response, Spl. Agent Smart closed the evidence file which was laid open on the conference table, respectfully excusing himself from the meeting. He quietly closed the door behind him and casually walked down the hallway towards the bustling office area. Locating the break room, he sat down at a far table and thoughtfully sipped down a styrofoam cup of stale, lukewarm coffee, allowing his mind to brood over all of the evidence that he's been contending with over the last few weeks.

An hour later, as his partner approached the table, Spl. Agent Smart didn't even look up to acknowledge his presence or the deadpan expression that sat uncommon upon his face. Agent Drapper awaited for his partner to conclude the phone conversation he was having, before bringing him up to speed on the latest news that brought their meeting to an abrupt end.

Agent Smart hung up the phone, raised his eyes, taking notice of the look on Agent Drapper's face, saying, "What's up, Dennis? You feeling some kinda way about what I said back there in the meeting?"

"No," replied, Spl. Agent Drapper, "It seems we have more shit to worry about than what was said back in that conference room."

"How so?" asked Smart, with his brow furrowed.

"Well," said Agent Drapper, "It seems as if this case has just taken a turn for the worse, and the one thing we didn't need happening-happened."

"What happened?" asked Spl. Agent Smart, with a stone hard stare. "It seems there's been several cop killings taking place in different states, there are calls coming in from all over the country, now, that the news is out about cops being targeted and mercilessly killed, at will."

Looking into the eyes of Agent Drapper, with a frozen stare of shock fear weary looking face, Agent Smart asked, "Is it our guy? I mean, damn, what the fuck? Who gave the media the details into the case?"

"All those questions have no answers at the moment," answered Agent Drapper. "And quite frankly, the who, what, and whys, no longer matter at this moment. Our focus should be on catching this nutcase, if you ask me," stated Agent Drapper.

Sitting there in quiet reserve, Agent Smart's attention was diverted towards the break room door, when Agent Cynthia Goldfield strolled in and stood in the threshold of the doorway saying, "Fellas, we've got a serious problem on our hands, you're both needed in the conference room, asap."

Rising from his seat at the back of the break room, Agent Smart gathered his belongings from the table and marched towards Agent Goldfield where he stopped short of passing her and said, "I hope we're not gonna be mentally evaluating this go round, cuz as you can see, things are beginning to take a turn for the worse, and if you think what took place in this state just a few hours ago, is bad, you ain't seen nothing yet. It should be obvious by now that we're dealing with a psychopath, our job is to catch him, not evaluate him!" Brushing past her, Agent Smart proceeded towards the conference room at a swift pace with them on his heels, because this case was getting more bizarre by the day and not one second more needed to be wasted.

Chapter Twenty - Eight

June 4, 2020 11:40pm Thursday
Louisville, Kentucky

Ensconced in a secluded car wash bay in the suburban outskirts of Louisville, Kentucky, Stranger stood, semi-nude, with a car wash spray gun, blasting soapy water on his blood caked clothes while lost in thought with obvious conflicts weighing heavily on his mind. Finally, Lisa cautiously approached him and started to inquire into what was on his mind, saying, "So, what's up, Stranger? You good bae?" standing just behind him and keeping her tone cheery, in fear of enraging him all over again, as she'd seen earlier that morning at the gas station in Jonesville, Virginia.

Stranger kept silent and continued to rinse the blood from his black hoodie and jeans, but Lisa wouldn't relent in her inquisition, as she charged forward, not worrying about overstepping any unknown boundaries, when she loudly asked, "You know...I still want to know what all that madness was about the at gas station this morning. You really spooked me out with all that shit, ya know? Like, who does that? I mean, decapitation isn't something I'd thought you'd be capable of doing, seeing how quiet and reserved you are normally, and-"

Spinning around on his heels, Stranger had a look of contempt blazing like an inferno in his eyes when he replied, "Lisa, those men that I beheaded, got what they had coming to them, you don't have a clue as to the kind of maltreatment and torture they repeatedly inflicted upon me while I was at that facility doing time. Those cops deserved what I gave them, and I promised them on my dead mother's grave, that I was coming back for their heads, and I made good on that promise."

Lisa stood there transfixed for a moment, then said, "Stranger, I don't understand, help me understand what they did to you that was so bad for you to inflict such dire consequences against them in that sorta manner?"

Taking a few moments to recollect his memory, Stranger began his recount into the past. Beginning at the start of the apparent incidents, Stranger said, "It all started when I was in the Lee County USP, and I went to the box, or the SHU as it's called there, for recklessly eyeballing a female staff member. A nurse, who lied and said that I was gunning her."

"Gunning?" Lisa asked, clueless to the term he'd used. "What does that mean?"

"It means pulling on my dick, Lisa, you know? Masturbating in public, so to speak." Stranger answered with annoyance obvious in his voice. "They call it lascivious or obscene acts, done in a sexual manner." Then he goes on to detail the events that had taken place.

"I was brutally beaten in handcuffs as I was placed in a restraint chair and wheeled down a back hallway and continuously punched in the face by numerous C.O.s. Then, once I was taken into a holding cell in the SHU, the Segregated Housing Unit, the C.O.s took turns jumping on me, even when I tried to tell them I didn't do what the lady said I did. It only enraged them further, to the point where they started slamming me on my head, until I was unconscious for a period of time. When I woke up, I was handcuffed in four points to a steel bed, where they left me, and just kept coming in the cell and slapping me and punching me, every time they did a sight check. My head was split open and they left me leaking blood while the same nurse would come in and evaluate me from time to time, and say derogatory things to me, like, 'That will teach you niggers about looking at me like I'm a piece of meat'. She'd even whisper taunts to me like, 'Say something. I wish you would, I'll make sure they kill your black ass next time, you fucking sexual predator'."

Stranger relayed this story with tears welling up in the corners of his eyes. Then he went on to narrate how the C.O.s he'd beheaded had kept breeching his cell, beating him daily. Then he told her how they were urinating in his food and how they would crush light bulbs and put the shards in his food, to the point where he would refuse to eat anything and they would have to forcefully put him on an IV drip because he'd been on a 'food strike' for weeks at a time, in fear of being poisoned, or worse.

Lisa stood there listening to the horrendous stories with tears streaming down her face, repeating her sorrows of sympathy, by stating, "I'm so sorry you had to endure such terror and the way those people treated you worse than they would a rabid dog." Seeing the anger flare up in his eyes, Lisa said, "You're safe now, Stranger, they can't hurt you no more."

Then Stranger shouted, louder than he should've, "Fuck that! I made sure they'll never hurt another soul! I made sure of that! I told them bitches I was coming back for them, and that I would behead every fucking one of them! I promised them, Lisa! I promised them that I'd enter their homes and kill their children in their sleep! I put that on God and on my dead mother that I'd pay them back! That I was gonna rip out their hearts and squeeze it till it beat it last dying beat! And I did just that! I made them pay, Lisa. With their fucking lives, and now I got their fucking heads in a bag to prove it. I told them I was coming back-I told them!"

Stranger fumed with spittle flying from his foaming mouth and tears flowing freely down his cheeks, dripping off of his chin like steady droplets of water falling from a leaky faucet, while he shook like a man standing in the freezing cold winds of a winter blizzard. Stranger released his pent up anger and the fears he'd held hidden inside him like a memorable keepsake that weren't supposed to be harbored inside. Lisa stepped forward to pull Stranger into her loving embrace, when Mike steps into the clearing of the carwash bay and said, "Stranger, we got company, Slim," with John following closely behind him. Stranger went on high alert and quickly turned his head in their direction when he saw the darkened street become illuminated with a bright spotlight beam, the headlights of an approaching car, which caused Stranger to react with stealth like speed.

Lunging for the driver's door handle, he yanked open the door, dove into the front driver's side seat, and began to rummage around in the front floor board until he had found what he had been searching for. Slowly, he rose his head, just above the steering wheel and leveled his eyes towards to oncoming light, as the bottom of his windshield hid his face from being seen, making it look as if he was cleaning the inside of his SUV.

The car approached. Noticing that it was a police cruiser, Stranger remained calm and held his position in hopes that the officer wouldn't be coaxed into getting out of his vehicle and investigating as to why Stranger was washing his vehicle this late at night while almost nude. But the officer continued as if he hadn't even paid them the faintest attention. Instead, he parked at the opposite end of the car wash, cut on the interior light and just sat there sullenly studying the street and the cars that passed by. When Stranger took notice that the police officer wasn't concerned with him in the least, he quickly gathered up his clothing. He wrung them out of the excess water and then lifted the car wash spray gun to douse himself with the high powered spray, cleaning himself down of the dried blood from the earlier episode.

Expeditiously he had gotten dressed in the dampened clothing and went to peer discreetly around the edge of the car wash bay. Watchful, he took note that the officer wasn't paying attention to his surroundings in the least. John spoke in a hushed voice, "He's a sitting duck, Stranger and we need something he has."

"What's that?" asked Lisa in a whisper.

"His gun!" answered Mike. "We need that, if nothing else," Mike added matter of factly.

Stranger patiently observed the officer. As he took in the area, he began to formulate a plan for a clandestine attack, to catch the unaware officer off guard. Mike began to point out the hedges and the murky darkness of the unlit parking area at the back of the car wash.

Stranger said, "Y'all stay here, I'll be back." But Mike and John refuse his command saying, "Hell naw, I want in on this," Mike said, and John added, "I don't want in. I just want to watch. That shit I saw this morning is what horror flicks are made out of, I'm gonna have nightmares for the next 50 years after what I saw. That shit was enough to give me a massive hard on-"

"Shut the fuck up, John!" Mike fumed back in John's direction with a look of abhorrence written in his expression. John immediately took to silence without any of his usual sarcastic jabs being thrown back.

With Lisa always being the rational thinker, she said, "Come on, Stranger, Let's just go, that dude ain't paying us any attention, we can slip away without being seen and-"

"Go Lisa! Go sit your ass in the truck, NOW!" said Stranger, quickly cutting her comment in half, like a hot butter knife to warm butter. Back peddling, Lisa felt ambushed by the harshness of his tone and blatant disrespect in which he had cut her off, when she was just trying to be the voice of reason. It seemed that everyone else was just egging him on into doing another malicious act that was seemingly senseless to her at the moment.

Storming back to the driver's side door, Stranger opened it and reached in. Fumbling around for a second, he yanked one of the C.O.s decapitated heads from the bag by the hair. This one was C.O. James Lee Davenport. He closed the door softly, careful not to alert the officer of any unnecessary noise that would rouse his attention, and went on the move.

Crouching low, Stranger snuck to the opposite side of the car wash bay and used the darkness to conceal his fast approach at a perpendicular angle. Just out of sight of the officer's rearview and side mirrors, he was within a very close distance. Stranger crouched low again and waited a few moments, not being too eager for this kill, because the police cruiser was so close to the main street, and he didn't need any concerned citizens to catch him in the act.

He was listening for sounds of oncoming cars, as the silence of the night made itself prominent. Stranger quickly dashed forward from the darkness and closed in on the drivers side of the police cruiser with stealth and speed. Then, with a wide-armed powerful swing, he tossed the severed head of C.O. Davenport into the open driver's window with the velocity of a professional pitcher's throw. This caused a sudden distraction inside the police cruiser as the severed head streaked past the officer and slammed with a mighty thud, when it splattered against the passenger window, sending blood and brain matter flying everywhere in the front seat and shattering the window upon impact. But before the officer could gather his baring about himself, he was impaled center mass, by the serrated hunting blade that Stranger had in his clenched fist. Ensuring that it was a confirmed kill, Stranger then viciously dragged the serrated blade across his windpipe and stooped down low beside the driver's door, as if he was casually talking like a known acquaintance with the dying officer.

Mike and John stood by and watched in pure awe, as they listened to Stranger talk in a low voice to the officer. He was saying, "Good evening officer-" peeking into the car to get a good look at the officer's name tag, "Umm, Officer Patterson, is it not?" he asked the wheezing officer like he would surely answer, if in fact he could. Then Stranger said, "Today is not so much your lucky day, now is it, Officer Patterson? I guess you can say you have been relieved of duty, Officer Patterson, and you will be able to retire in the big Precinct in the sky, with all your other fellow comrades, who have fallen to the demise of what you so-called 'Boys in Blue', claim to be a...what do you call it? Ahh, that's it, a 'Brotherhood'. Well, now, you can be with the rest of your brothers, and arrest and falsely convict-as well as kill-committing unjust murders up there in-down there in-shit, anywhere else, but you won't be doing it here anymore."

After relaying his speech to the dying officer, Stranger reached into the police cruiser and unbuckled the strap from the gun holster, and slowly unholstered the late Officer Patterson's semi-automatic Glock 17 service pistol and snatched his police shield, Badge #296 from the breast pocket of his uniform and said, "Where you're going, you won't be needing these. But don't fret, Officer Patterson, there'll be more of your comrades showing up just as unexpectedly as you are.. many more! You can bet your corrupt ass on that, this won't stop just because your casket dropped."

Rising to his feet, Stranger reached inside towards the ceiling globe and switched off the interior light. As the three of them casually walked away back towards the dark rear access of the car wash bays, they climbed in the SUV and pulled off out of the rear entrance of the car wash, making their getaway, through the back streets of an adjacent residential neighborhood.

When they were in the clear and making their way out of the Louisville, Kentucky area, Mike spoke up and said, "Stranger, I think uhh, we need to get a new ride, Slim, this one is hotter than fish grease, and we almost out of gas. So, this may be a good time to switch out vehicles, you think?" Signaling into the right lane, Stranger didn't reply, he just pulled off Interstate 64 at the next exit and went in search of a place to stash their SUV and swipe a new one.

As they came into a small town called Florence, Kentucky, Stranger kept his head on a swivel, locating used car dealership and an auto body shop right next to one another. He realized that the town was fast asleep at this hour. He made a U-turn in the middle of the street and drove back to the auto body shop and pulled into the cluttered parking lot that was overflowing with numerous cars that looked to be in need of some body work. After parking, he waited while looking about conspicuously. Noticing something, he climbed out of the SUV and said to the others, "I'll be back in a second," quickly disappearing from sight.

Not returning for quite sometime later, Stranger snatched open the driver's door and reached inside with his gloved hands and grabbed hold of the plastic shopping bag handles in which the three remaining heads of the Lee County C.O.s laid decomposing. Lisa said, "Damn, Stranger! Hell Naw! I know you not taking those damn heads with us! This shit is getting fucking ridiculous by the minute and-Mike, you not gonna say nothing or try to talk some sense into him?" she asked Mike, looking for some sort of intelligent reply, but nothing intelligent surfaced when Mike replied, "Shit, Lisa, fuck you talking about? What makes sense to him don't have to make sense to us, he's making statements and proving points."

Lost in the meaning of what Mike said to her, Lisa looked about confusedly and asked, "What the fuck is that supposed to mean? Making statements and proving points? That shit sound like something you just made up on a whim." Lisa spitefully shot back at Mike, who sat beside her in the backseat of the SUV.

"It means he's using his actions to make statements, since pleading with those of authority with our voices doesn't seem to be working. Only because those in charge aren't listening when these same 'Society Protectors' aren't protecting us any longer, they're killing us at an alarming rate and getting away with it. And the points he's making? There were points along the way where none of this would've occurred. There was a-Pivotal Point, where things began to get critical; -Turning Point, where things could've been handled differently and the course of things as they stand now could've changed direction; and a -Point of No Return, where they did nothing about it and watched it all happen with no serious consequences as a recourse for all of their officers who got away with murdering innocent men and women of color, and this is where we are now. This is a means to an end, when they stop killing us, like big game prey, we'll stop killing them. Like the Bible says: 'An eye for an eye, a tooth for a tooth', and the newly revised version goes: 'Life for a Life'. What do you think is gonna happen if they catch up with us? There won't be no trial. No, we gonna die, if not in the street like dogs, then we'll most definitely die by lethal injection if we ever see a 13 and a half chance," said Mike, spewing philosophy like he had recited it from some philosophy majors textbook.

Taking a moment to soak in what was said, Lisa asked, "So, what's this 13 and a half chance shit you talking about?"

John burst into their conversation and said, "Damn Lisa, don't you know anything? It means: One Judge, 12 Jurors, and half a mother-fucking chance, long before we enter the damn courtroom! Now shut the fuck up, and get out the fucking truck, we gotta get moving..."

Sucking her teeth with obvious annoyance, Lisa rolled her eyes and said, "I ain't ask you, you stupid ass bitch!" saying the words with venomous abhorrence dripping off her tongue like a poisonous snake bite.

John snickered snidely, as if, getting under Lisa's skin was his intention to begin with, then he lashed back with a venomous bite of his own, when he replied, "Oh yea? Bitch, huh? Well, you're three types of bitches, you fucking gut wrenching whore! You're a nasty bitch-a dirty bitch-and one retarded stupid bitch who can't seem to get it through your head that you're so damn repulsive, that the three men you're constantly around don't even get any type of arousal out of your funky ass, and that's why, none of us has not even tried to make a pass at you, cause you're not worth the headache, the time...or the stank ass dick we're gonna have once we pull out of that abortion clinic of a pussy you have. You're nothing but a dog's face on a cow's body, smelling like a dead carcass, you simple minded bitch! Keep fucking with me and I'm gonna-"

"You ain't gonna do shit, you worthless, limp dick piece of shit! And if Stranger lets me get a hold of that gun, I'll blow your brains out!" Lisa spat back, only to be counterattacked.

John said quickly, "The only brains you're gonna blow out is with your mouth wrapped around the head of my dick when I bust off in the back of your throat!"

Simultaneously, Stranger and Mike both spun about on their heels and began to yell at the both of them to shut the fuck up and telling them how they were both getting on their nerves.

John, thirsting for the last word said, "Lisa started it." Then he burst out laughing at his hateful barrage of insults that he had unleashed on Lisa just moments ago.

When they filed around the back of the used car dealership,

they climbed into a grey 2016 Grand Cherokee that was already running and ready to go. Stranger was definitely gifted in the art of auto theft, as well as burglary. But he was on his own summit when it came to the art of capital murder, and murder in the first degree. He was a master of massacre, separating himself from any serial killer before him. Stranger was mercilessly bloodthirsty and had no intention of aborting his mission of touching at least one police officer in 48 out of 50 of the States, excluding Alaska and Hawaii of course.

The plot thickens as the Grand Cherokee pulls onto the Interstate ramp and heads west, looking for their next victim from that 'Band of Brotherhood' that believes that they are above the law...

Chapter Twenty - Nine

June 4, 2020 1:00pm Thursday

Jonesville, Virginia

After being escorted back to the administration office, from the SHU, or the Segregated Housing Unit, by the two Compound Correctional Officers, along with Dr. Emily Anne Poole, in pursuit, as his shadows, Det. McNealson took notice of the egregious dramatic change in the atmosphere within the office, as well as the downheartedness that was blatantly present by the staff by the way in which everyone had a dejected hangdog look of sorrow on their faces. The hushed silence and quiet sniffles that were tearfully displayed by the apparently racist secretary and other female staff members and nurses, only further enforced his premonition that something terribly wrong had just taken place. But he remained constrained from inquiring into the nature for such a sullen mood change which was exuding off of everyone that stood present by their lugubrious expressions and noticeably pained scowls. When Det. McNealson entered the conference room, where his partner, Matt York was reviewing the inmate files they'd requested, he immediately observed the frown upon Det. York's face and began to ask what was bothering him.

Pausing in his thoughts, Det. York slowly rose his head to meet him at eye level. Removing his reading glasses, he sheepishly rubbed the bridge of his nose with his forefinger and thumb, while gathering his wits about himself to relay the tragic news that he was woefully laboring over.

When the moment passed, Det. York leaned back in the swivel rolling conference chair, and began to recite the horrible news of the four correctional officers that were killed just up the street from the facility they were presently at, and the malicious manner in which they were murdered in plain sight for all to witness, but yet, the gruesome acts had gone unseen by the public.

Standing in a stoic trance, Det. McNealson was reeling from the likelihood that this incident had just taken place not even a mile away from where they presently stood, didn't sit well with him, being that not even 10 minutes ago, he was confronted by an inmate in the SHU that had stated in the same precise detail the method in which one of the suspected inmates they were there to investigate, had said he was going to commit the same exact acts in verbatim. What was so alarming to him was, the fact that, the inmate that spoke of these incidents just moments ago, was adamant in his belief that the inmate he had informed him about was not only more than capable of committing those heinous acts, but he had actually made those same verbal threats to some degree to the officers who worked in the SHU during his stint at USP Lee County.

Disquieted by the boldness of the recent accounts, Det. McNealson lowered his voice to a whisper and gave Det. York an unsettling stare. "Matt, pull the files on one of our suspects by the name of Ben Strange, his alias is-"

"Stranger," Det. York cut in with a look of dreaded nervousness, "I was just reviewing his file not too long ago, right before the news spread through this office like a four alarm backdraft of a restless fire."

Quickly lifting the file in question off the table, Det. York asked, "So, what gives you the inclination that this could be the guy we're after? Cause after reading his background, and his psych reports, there's nothing there that mentioned he could be remotely close to being responsible for committing these grisly acts. I mean, he's not even a violent offender in the least, maybe a couple cans short of a six pack, but nothing of violence anywhere in his record, so what gives-"

Det. McNealson, through clenched teeth, cut short Det. York inquiry and said, "I know because a jailhouse rat just told me not ten minutes ago that Ben Strange had made some very viable threats to come back and decapitate a few of these C.O.s and lo and behold, look what has taken place." Calling over his shoulder, towards the doorway of the conference room, Det. McNealson yelled louder than he should have, "Dr. Poole, I need to speak with you, it's very urgent, please! And thank you!" Saying this in a demanding voice that could not be mistaken, as if, he was asking, but more so, telling her that her presence was expected immediately.

Dr. Poole casually strolled into the conference room taking note that something was definitely amiss by the intensity of the stares she had walked in on. Closing the door behind her, Det. McNealson asked her to have a seat because there was some questions he needed answers to and only she was capable of answering them. The files they were in possession of at the moment, were not painting an accurate of picture of the man who was out there committing these unthinkable and merciless murders on the whim. There was a missing story behind these senseless murders and Dr. Poole was the only person at the moment who could provide the answers they were in search of. Det. McNealson's intuition told him that she knew more than these files actually detailed, this he was certain of and willing to bet $100 to a donut, that he was spot on, in his assessment of the deliberate incidents that took place at that facility.

Once Dr. Poole took the seat she was offered, Det. McNealson wasted no time beating around the bush with her, when he made the accusation that implied that the documents that he and Det. York had been reviewing seemed coerced and fictitious. Every incident report, in all the other inmate files that they were looking into, had been deliberately duplicated. As if every incident that took place at that facility had been re-created and signed off on by the correctional staff, and the inmates found guilty of by the DHO, or Disciplinary Hearing Officer. To further cement his point, Det. York began opening every file of each of their suspect inquiries and pointed to the statements made on each incident report.

Frozen in explanation, Dr. Poole realized that she couldn't hold up the charade any longer, for she knew the cat was out of the bag and to further commit to the deceptive cover up, was only placing her in the hot seat, as not only one of the culprits, but throwing herself under the bus as being the mastermind and a liability. She sat thoughtfully for a few minutes, then she surrendered and came clean to all of the accusations. But she also tried to rationally put the facilities staff members views into perspective, but failed miserably, because there wasn't any sane approach, nor real justification for the miscarriage of justice and civil rights violations that took place right in front of everyone's knowing eyes.

The more she talked, the more she dug herself and her professional career into a perpetual grave. The pain of releasing the pent up guilt and shame, was like lifting a mountainous weight off her shoulders that she had carried around for so long. She now felt as light as a feather, as the tears came streaming down her cheek bones and the most shocking details came steam rolling off of her tongue. Both Det. McNealson and Det. York sat mesmerized as the vivid descriptions were verbalized with such a memory into the past accounts, that her testimony of truth was hard to bear witness to. But still, they belted her with a myriad of questions and she answered to every one of those as if she was under oath, at the trial of someone who the prosecution team was trying desperately to put away, by the way she gave up the grave details and the names of the many officers and staff members who committed unspeakable acts against the inmates housed at Lee County USP.

After about an hour and half, the detectives were truly awestruck and bedazzled by the light that was shined into this psycho-closet-of-secrets that has laid dormant for countless years that they could hardly wrap their minds around the audacity of some of the staff members who was hired to work at a facility, only to use their authority as a measure to dominate and oppress with the brutal violence of the excessive use of force. All these under the guise of protecting and serving. Which seemed foolishly illogical if they were committing more crimes of violence than the men they were responsible for housing. With all of the file folders opened on the table and rehashing the many falsified incident reports, Det. McNealson concluded that IAD, or Internal Affairs Division, was definitely in demand to break up the corruption within the walls of this Federal Bureau of Prisons facility.

Having a few more questions for Dr. Poole to answer, McNealson said, "Dr. Poole, the guy in question, Ben Strange," turning the file folder towards her, and pointing to the mugshot photo of Stranger. "Is this the man that was evaluated under your care, and who you saw on a regular basis while he was housed in the SHU?"

Not even verbalizing her answer, Dr. Poole just nodded her head in agreement. Det. McNealson went on to say, "Could you please be so kind as to give us your own personal take on this guy, you know; his character, his temperament, his mental capacity and stability? Uhh..." He took a second to search his thoughts. "Things that these fake files failed to mention." Det. McNealson's right hand pointed finger, lightly tapping the open file of Ben Strange.

Pushing her glasses up onto the bridge of her nose, Dr. Poole softly her clears her throat and pauses momentarily before going into her own personal recollection of how she perceived Stranger upon their first encounter...

Dr. Emily Poole began by saying, "I believe that the first time I met Ben Strange was about 6 years ago. He was quiet and introverted to say the least . But that person had a side to him that was restless and powerfully hard to engage with. Ben Strange was brought into the SHU for reportedly committing some perverted sexual acts against a nursing staff member-"

"What kind of act?" asked Det. York.

"Gunning," Dr. Poole answered point blank, "an act of masturbating publicly," she went on to explain the term she used, due to the confused looks upon the detectives faces.

As she proceeded into her reminiscent tale, she told the detectives of her impression into the incident that brought Stranger and herself to first encounter one another. She said, "When I first met Ben Strange, Stranger is what they called him," she clarified to show that she had known him on a personal level. "He was strapped down to a bed and unconscious. The officers claimed that he resisted, but that was their claim for every aggravated assault they committed against the men at this facility. But, since there was no way for me to speak with Stranger at that time, due to him being knocked unconscious, I went to speak with the nurse who he supposedly made sexual advances towards, and I must say this for the record, the woman in question has a history of making false claims against young black men, not just at this facility, but at four other facilities that she has worked at before here. When I got to her, her statement had changed dramatically, from Stranger gunning her, to he was staring at her recklessly. So, I asked her which one it was, she took what I asked her, as me badgering her and she got defensive. She asked me, "What side was I on?" and I replied that I was on the right side. She responded saying that 'there is no right side, it's white or black, with spics and Indians not even counting. 'It was all of 'us' against all of them niggers' and she was starting to think I was against my own race! She voiced her racist thoughts openly and without fear of being overheard. So, I told her, no, I'm not against anyone. I'm just trying to 'get to the truth', where she cut me off, she fumed about 'truth' and claimed she told the truth and said 'that black ass nigger disrespected her', and she made sure that he got what he had coming to him, and if any more of them just so happen to even glance in her direction, she would have them strapped down and four pointed to a bed knocked the fuck out and bleeding internally as well." Dr. Poole began to tear up again and sniffled, as she wiped the back of her hand across her nose and went on with her story.

Dr. Poole began to tell the detectives about when Stranger woke up, three days later, saying, "It was obvious to me that something like brain swelling or a serious concussion had taken effect, because he didn't know where he was, or how he got there, or even what had happened to him. I honestly believed him at first, but as time went on, I came to realize that he knew a lot more than he was caring to admit. I believe Stranger was so embedded in the street life, that tattle taling was snitching, no matter what the circumstances were involved. He used to scream things like 'That's against street code! Violation! Violation!' and 'Snitches get stitches and die in the ditches'. It was as if I couldn't have rationalized a conversation with him, without him quoting some ominous street wisdom, that became the laws of which he lived by. But, as for his mental state, there wasn't much he would tell me about his growing up in the streets of Washington, D.C. I believed he lived a hard life, and the most surprising connection I made with him was when he comes to the door of his cell and the first thing he'd ask me was, if I had any books for him to read, or puzzles he could do. I realized then that in order for me to get into him mentally, I had to be the one who gave him the nourishment he thirsted for, knowledge, the challenge of puzzles. The completion of novels gave him a sense of accomplishment. I keyed into that, and used that key to open a few locked doors inside him, but that key I had wasn't a skeleton key, it didn't open up many. But I was willing to take what I could, when it came to Stranger. More so, because..." Dr. Poole contemplatively waits a few moments before answering. "He was special, I mean special on so many levels," she said this with a look of adoration lovingly written in her eyes.

"How so?" Det. McNealson asked, "I need a little more than that," pushing his question for a far deeper meaning.

Dr. Poole's piercing blue eyes peered into his, as she said, "Stranger wasn't just a product of his environment, he was a product of his own making. He-" she stuttered here. "He lived in a world, with in a world, with in a world.

Totally thrown off by her comment, Det. York halted the story by saying, "Whoa, whoa! Hold up! You mean, like the movie 'Inception'? You're gonna have to elaborate a little more into what all this worlds within worlds stuff is about."

Turning her head slightly, "There are three worlds he's living in: The real World, where society establishes the rules. The Penitentiary World, where the penal system establishes the rules, and His World, the world that he lives in mentally, where he makes his own rules. This is where he feels safe, where he governs himself. He self teaches. He self talks. He self learns. He sees that there is nothing irrational in His World. He takes everything literally, there is no figuratively speaking. In his World, he means what he says and he says what he means."

"Stranger doesn't have a sense of humor, there is nothing humorous he sees in this world or in the penal world, and most definitely not in his own gigantic galactic world that he's living in. This place he lives in is not safe for anyone around him because he's not alone in the world. He governs that world of his, but he decides from a counsel of friends, and he makes the final decisions based on all of their opinions together as a whole. Stranger is not a nut case, he's fundamentally sound, and very observant. He'll watch from a distance before he approaches, and approaching him without first engaging the gateway locking mechanism, is only gonna make him recede and become recluse. Which will make it next to impossible to get to know him, understand, or even have more than a one word conversation with him, the one word being yes, or no. There is no in between, such as maybe, kinda, or possibly. He's very direct and exquisitely impulsive. Meaning, he formulates a plan in his head at an alarming rate, it will actually seem impulsive on the surface, but in all actuality, he's thought it through from beginning to end. It's almost as if he's a mental mystic, when he talks, it's like he is prophesying and narrating a story when he does speak to you."

"So, you're saying we are dealing with a very intelligent psychopath?" asked Det, McNealson.

"I'm saying no such thing, Detective," answered Dr. Poole, "What I'm saying is...Stranger...has a very complex and complicated accumulation of mental cognitive disorders, but none are distinctive enough to stand out as its own diagnosed mental disorder. Let's put it like this, his disorder changes over a course of time, making it hard to pin point. It's kind of like, well, he goes through some sort of evolution process and his mental capabilities take on several characteristics of behavior and mental disorders at the same time. It's almost like a phenomenon, how he adjusts to the erratic differences that takes place within."

Then McNealson said, "So, correct me if I'm wrong, but this psychopath is really not a psychopath, or something like that? Is that what you're saying?"

"He's.. extraordinary, Detective, is what I'm saying. Complex and… anomalous, to say the least," answers Dr. Poole. "I'd say if I had to diagnose him, I'd compile the disorders of him being a cross between a DID, or Dissociative Identity Disorder, with MPD, which is, Multiple Personality Disorder, something derived from him experiencing anxiety through exposure to acute stress and Post Traumatic Stress. One being the by-product that developed after a traumatic experience from his past. Which brought about his Introverted Personality, with many shadows which are human alter-ego that personifies the negative side of his personality, and then processes in the characteristics of catharsis, paranoia, psychosis, and that leads to his erratic behaviors of extreme mania which evolved into a fixation, that may or may not have been triggered by any rational instigation or event," she explained with soft reverie.

She then went on to say, "Detectives, I've studied behavior neuron-science, and its behavior and mental processes. I've psychoanalyzed Ben Strange on many accounts and I can say without a shadow of doubt, that what took place not too long ago, with those four C.O.s that were decapitated down the road from here, wasn't a coincidence. That was an act of insatiable loath, it was...coldhearted and calculated, devised only in the mental of someone who could dream up such a debased defilement. Stranger has really detached and receded deep into himself, but one of the main things that sits heavy on my mind was how he would call out the names of the C.O.s he had confrontations with, and yell out on the range that it didn't matter when, where, or who was with them, he was coming for their heads. He would scream, 'I'm literally coming for your heads,' calling out the names, of C.O. Pruitt, Davenport, Greene, repeatedly all the time, like he was taunting them, purposely, and they would indeed react and set out to enter his room, forcefully. Because Stranger wouldn't take it lying down, he fought back against them every chance he got, but as always, he got what his hand called for, which was a lose- lose situation every time. But that didn't seem to bother Stranger too much, he would always smile that devious smirk he possessed, and reply with his own heedful comments like, 'you gotta get yours, I'm gonna get mine'. 'Laugh now, cry later, 'Protect your neck! Protect your neck!' 'You know what it is bitches!' He would say, 'Slaughter House is comin' for ya' and his most famous from Forrest Gump, 'Life is like a box of chocolate, you never know when you're going to get it'.

She got a look of terror in her eyes and went on. "Then there was this horrible lullaby that he used to sing, that still sits in my mind, like a nightmarish mantra," and she started to sing, low and shaky, ""Time is frozen, caskets a'closin', the flesh is empty, the soul's set free, no longer are you breathin', death has chose a season, for you to go to sleep, eternally in peace, eternally in peace, eternally in peace...' and repeatedly he would sing that horrid lullaby like the song that never ends." She told them this with vivid fear and misery written in the tone of her voice.

Detectives McNealson and York were both dumbfounded when she finished her tale of the events and her evaluation of Ben Strange, and they realized then, the pun his parents had made with his name when they had named him Ben Strange, as a baby. For they must have foreseen that their child was going to grow into something incredibly odd, because it seemed to the detectives, that he had been Strange, since childhood at the very least.

Wrapping up their questions with Dr. Poole, they asked her, "'Is there anything else that you can add that will assist us in this investigation?"

Taking a few moments to think, she lifted her head towards the ceiling and closed her eyes, in obvious deep thought. When she lowered her head and opened her eyes, the tears began streaming down her face when she said, "This is tragic, Detective. I've dealt with many cases in my tenure as a psychologist, and reviewed countless cares of psychopathic behaviors, but none is even remotely close to Stranger, he's...not gonna stop, if this is in fact him. Which I believe with every fiber in my being that it is him...and not just him. Many hims. Detectives, approaching him from a normal perspective isn't going to work," Dr. Poole stated with finality as she turned to look into the their eyes.

"The guy you spoke with in the SHU, Dominic Mannimal Mann is a demented, ingenious psychopath. He's very educated and callous in his thinking patterns, which makes him very dangerous. His only ally, and true confident is Ben Strange, and that is a concoction in which I deem no man should ever encounter in the streets."

"Why is that?" asked McNealson.

"Because rumor has it that those two made plans to do the bidding for each other. What one can't accomplish, the other will. Stranger has slipped your net because he didn't register on your quote, unquote, 'Crazy Scale'. He doesn't have any violence in his criminal history whatsoever, at least none that has been reported.

The only reason why you're onto him is because of what the jailhouse rat told you in the SHU . I can tell you right now, Mr. James made the worst decision of his life by speaking to you about Stranger," Dr. Poole finished her piece with such a calm nonchalance that she was dead serious in her delivery.

"What makes you say that?" asked McNealson.

"Because, I can almost guarantee you, that-"

With commotion running into the hallway, and the duces being alerted, which is a body alarm on the officers to call for immediate assistance-sounding off on the walkie talkies, one of which Dr. Poole had on her belt, she got up. When the call came that there was a fight in the SHU, just when Dr. Poole was about to finish her statement, another call was broadcasted through the speaker that a gurney and all available staff was needed, suddenly the radios squawked that an inmate was unresponsive having been stabbed several times.

As Dr. Poole sat her radio on the conference room table, she looked deeply into both detectives' eyes and said, "I'll bet my pension that it was the inmate we were just questioning down there, Gene James, and that Mannimal convinced his cellmate to butcher him for giving Stranger up to you. This, I am quite sure of, I've made a living out of knowing, learning, and basically adapting my own surroundings. I know who's who, and what's what, and the whys, without ever having to ask many questions, detectives." She then picked up her radio and called down to the SHU, asking the range officer, "Who was the inmate who is unresponsive?"

speaking in a natural tone.

When the call came back, the officer replied to her, "It's Inmate Gene James, cell #218, and his cellmate, Lovell, Moses Lovell, has been detained and placed in restraints."

"Officer, what is the status of inmate James?" she asked, awaiting an answer. When the call came back, it didn't seem to surprise her at all. "Deceased, inmate James has been pronounced dead at 13:32 clear," the SHU officer responded back.

At that exact moment Dr. Poole rose from her seat and said, "If you gentlemen don't have anymore questions or concerns that I can be of assistance with, I have to go and speak with both Inmate Lovell, and Mannimal and commend them on their job well done."

"Whoa! What the fuck do you mean by 'a job well done'?" asked Det. York.

"Detective, the wise can play a fool, but the fool can never play being wise. I know the name of the game, and I can play it with the best of them, and there were two that I couldn't play it with, and one is presently sitting in the SHU calling the shots, and the other is running the streets murdering cops. Now, I've got a job to do, I think you need to go do yours, or more cops are going to die. Now, have a good day Detectives, and if you need any answers to questions, I would be happy to answer and assist in any way I can," said Dr. Poole, turning on her heels to leave.

Det. McNealson held her up, saying, "Oh, Dr. Poole, one more thing. How long have you been in love with Stranger?" The look of undisguised shock struck her face, with embarrassment all over her rosy blushing cheek, Dr. Poole stuttered, "I..I. I have no idea what you're talking about, detective."

"Yeah, of course you wouldn't, Dr. Poole. It seems Ben Strange was a stranger to most, but not to all."

Det. McNealson shot his shot in the dark, and hit a bull's eye, by following his initiative hunch. "Let me find out this is some real life Joker and Harley Quinn-type shit that took place here in Jonesville," tossing the accusation around like a hot potato to see if she will catch it.

Dr. Poole replied, "Crazy is what crazy does, and as crazy as this may sound, Stranger never touched me, not once. But, when I got off in his mind, he got off in my panties. Every conversation I ever had with him, I walked away with a wet cunt and mixed emotions. I didn't love him, I had lust for him, but I was smart enough to not get attached. That was the hardest part, detective, all those many meetings with him, they were like being touched by frolicking fingers. I knew to keep my distance, but I couldn't stay away and there's a big difference between the two. There were times that I felt addicted to his mental, and relapsed by the need to converse with him, and to answer your question, Detective McNealson, it's been that way since our very first conversation. Minus the love part, of course."

When Dr. Poole left the conference room, both detectives look at one another, both in disbelief. Detective McNealson said, "She fell hard for ole' boy...she talked about him like he was some mystical comic book hero and she was his number one fan. I could see the love and admiration written all over her eyes. She couldn't hide it if she tried," McNealson stated, and blew out an exasperated breath.

Det. York asked, "So, what we gonna do now? Alert the FBI on all of our findings?"

"Hell naw!" Det. McNealson bodly answered. "I'm going to catch this crazy ass son of a bitch, believe that! Without the FEDs help, this is *my* case!" Det. York was depleted and couldn't believe his ears. His partner-in-crime was up to his old tricks again. York knew that this wasn't going to end well, but they were like Will Smith and Martin Lawrence in 'Bad Boys', they are 'Bad Boys for life'!

Chapter Thirty

June 5, 2020 1:14pm Friday

Minneapolis, Minnesota

The conference room was dense with a mass of FBI agents when Spl Agents Smart, Drapper, and Goldfield entered and took their respective seats at the round table. Senior Investigative Agent, Matthew Forrester, gloomily began to convey the extent of the tragic news that had just been gathered from the network within their organization, while the room fell into exasperation and obvious dissatisfaction.

Opening the meeting with detailed accounts of at least nine different states that were under the impression that what took place a couple of days ago in the state of Minnesota, had now, unleashed widespread terror throughout the United States. Those cities were: Little Rock, Arkansas; Kansas City, Kansas; Grand Forks, North Dakota; Columbus, Ohio; Birmingham, Alabama; Lake Worth, Florida; Saltlake City, Utah; Eugene, Oregon; and Mason City, Iowa.

It had come to their attention that the news media had released unsanctioned details into the most recent murders that had taken place, and this has in fact brought out the 'crazies'; the people who are seriously delusional, crackbrained, nutcases who are simply fanatics and fascinated with the unrestrained acts of serial killers. They take special interest in the demented schemes by reenacting those insatiable kills by way of copy cat killings, and will even try to take the credit for the overall primary scheme as a whole. This in fact, further complicates and compromises the integrity of the investigation. Now that the FBI were thrown off the scent of their prey, being that there was far too many new cases being intentionally brought into the thick of things that were in no way connected to the real killer they were hunting. Without any obvious tracks being left behind, other than the previous officer's badge and gun, being utilized as the only connecting pieces, it only further frustrated and then prolonged the killer's capture.

It was as if they were being led around like a mule, being driven by a carrot on a stick, which makes this case so heartbreakingly devious and profoundly intolerable to ponder, let alone, to engage in on a level that doesn't feel like they're being toyed with or trapped in a moment, where there is no assumed end. Unless, the killer gets cocky or sloppy in covering his tracks, or simply does something so bold and unpredictable, that he jumps too far into the deep end of his death pool, disregarding the fact that he doesn't know how to swim, and drowns inside of his own mistakes.

The list of possibilities are endless when it came to the game of human chess, where allies and opposition make moves according to strategy. But when one's own strategies become compromised, one must regroup and capitalize off of the disadvantages. Thus, becoming a strategy of its own, by playing to the faults and defaults of your opponent. This was human chess at its best, with a twisted derivative as its off spring. A precious life of a human lays in the balance of fate versus feat.

Spl. Agent Smart was quiet all along, as he withheld comments, when Agent Goldfield spoke up and voiced her opinion, as to how they should proceed, saying, "It seems we need to organize with all the Federal, State, and County law enforcement agencies across the United States. I think our perp is making his rounds with no obvious fixed course established, although his acts are maliciously premeditated and calculated, he's committing these murders without a certain order attached, like going from Tennessee, and bypassing four and five states in his wake, just to strike terror in Minnesota at a wildly unprecedented proportion. I believe something triggered him to beeline straight to that particular state and unleash his wrath, not being able to withhold any longer-"

Cutting in, Agent Smart spoke up, and gave his opinion of these most recent incidents, when he respectfully suggested, "If I may be allowed to elaborate and piggy back off of Agent Goldfield's assessment of this individual, I believe she is spot on in what she guesstimates. This individual has had a serious vendetta against law enforcement since the beginning of this case, which initially took place in the Washington, D.C. Metropolitan area. Our records show this was committed against a-'" He paused for a moment to scan his memory, then goes on to state, "...a Umm, undercover narcotics detective, serving on the Metropolitan's drug task force. Who believed to have been shifty in character, with having a considerable amount of his cases being overturned, due to shady police work, witness tampering, planted evidence, and falsified statements and testimonies. It seemed at first like the victim in question, was a victim of happenstance, until his personal weapon and detective shield were found hours later, in Fredericksburg, Virginia, on the body of a deceased Virginia State Trooper. When we recovered the dash cam video footage from the trooper's cruiser, it became apparent to me that our killer had every intention to not just kill, but to kill with blind fury attached to a personified cause. I believe this cause to be his idea of justice. Because there have been a rash of officer involved killings, he's not holding those certain individuals responsible, he's holding every law enforcement agency he comes in contact with responsible, as a whole, like the old adage says, 'birds of a feather flock together'. This is the same perception in which our fellow officers in arms have when they encounter the youth, a black man, or a minority in general, they generalize them all as threats to the community without much consideration into the incident at hand, they tend to overreact by their own presumptions. Thus, comes the use of deadly force without just cause. It is my belief that we're not dealing with an average serial killer, he's the exterminator, on a mission of eradicating our police forces, one officer at a time. My gut tells me that he doesn't have any intention of quitting anytime soon, and this won't end with us capturing him. Not alive, anyway."

With his synopsis complete, Spl Agent Smart leaned back in his seat, but not before sarcastically stating, "But by all means, let's continue wasting time speculating over this guy's fanatic, unevaluated mental state, while more decent cops get dealt a bad hand, as they cross paths with our boogie man."

Not even biting into the bait that Smart set for him, Agent Forrester stood stoically and resumed the conversation by saying, "Ok, it is understood we're dealing with a wacko here, but time is of the essence. We're gonna break up in groups of two and commit to the task of investigating these copy cat killings and determine which ones are viable prospects to being a part of this ongoing investigation, we need to collaborate, separate, eliminate, in the exact order! So, ladies and gentlemen, pair up and receive your assignment. Let's get the ball rolling because as of right now, we're too far behind the ball."

With the orders established, all the agents began to rise, busily moving about, like a collection of worker ants. Agent Forrester halted all of the movements, saying, "I need to speak to the following agents: Agents Smart, Drapper, Goldfield, and Maddox, please be so kind as to stay back, thank you."

Pulling his spectacles off of his face, folding them, and placing them into the inside pocket of his suit jacket, he waited for all of the agents to scatter and move about their tasks before speaking. Closing the conference room door, he eased back to the round table and sat on it's surface, leveling his eyes at the four remaining agents, like he was assessing them in contemplative thought. When he finally spoke, he said, "Agents, I've asked you all to stay behind because the task that I gave the other agents aren't remotely significant as the one I'm electing to entrust the four of you to."

He stopped long enough to let the importance of his message to be absorbed and sink into acceptance. He went on, saying, "Now agents, there's another aspect to this case that I didn't go into, nor was I going to because it was apparent to me that it is a wild goose chase and I wasn't going to allow this case to be propelled into the funhouse of smoking mirrors. I can be a pompous asshole at times, but I'm very perceptive to raw talent when I'm in the midst of agents when I can soundly say with unwavering assurance that they in fact, possess the instinctive nature and the investigation wisdom that is needed to rise in the ranks as prominent influential field agents with great promise to make senior investigative agents, or even reach the pinnacle within this governmental structure, to become the Director of the FBI. This is why I'm deliberately conjoining the four of you on this assignment. As of yesterday morning, in the small town of Jonesville, Virginia; one of many that houses federal prisoners of the high security convicts for the Federal Bureau of Prisons, USP Lee County, it is believed that at approximately 8:25am eastern time, four of Lee County's correctional officers fatally encountered our perp. This is reportedly at local a gas station, where in fact each met their demise publicly in the broad day light. There was not one witness that either saw our perp or even witnessed the audacious acts take place just feet from a routinely travelled main street and intersection.

"I'm told even the gas station attendant was oblivious to the four murders that had taken place in her presence. There is no connection other than the badge and gun of the last officer killed in our Minnesota case, Officer Jeremiah Jacobs, badge #772, which was found at the scene. But here's where things turn for the worse. Our perp's signature has transgressed into something disturbingly vile. Those four officers were decapitated and reportedly impaled with a serrated knife and none of the heads were recovered at the scene. There are more gory details that I care not to further elaborate on, which is why I'm dispatching the four of you down to that crime scene, to assess the complexity of matters, as well as, have you head over to the penitentiary and maybe get a line on what could've went afoul with these officers. I am a firm believer in 'no such thing as a coincidence'. But with the aggravated nature in which these particular murders were committed, it doesn't sit well on my conscious as a coincidental act. There's more to this story and our perp doubled back with an intended purpose. I need you four to uncover that purpose and find the links in this repulsive chain of dreaded acts..."

Allowing his statement to trail off and soak in, Agent Forrester rose from the table and lumbered over to the lectern, fetching his thickly compiled case files and headed towards the door. But he was stopped short as Spl. Agent Smart halted him when he said, "Senior Agent Forrester, with all due respect, why is it that you've kept this information from everyone else and chosen us? Wouldn't it be in our favor if all available agents worked collectively, in a tandem conjunction?"

Staring daggers into Spl. Agent Smart's eyes, Senior Investigator Forrester said, "We are working in tandem, they've got their task and you've got yours. We accomplish the ultimate goal. But, let me ask you this, would you rather be chasing the copycats that are just imposters, imitating our true killer? Or would you rather the real killer keep cork screwing us in the ass with his atrocious acts while we play like the 'get-along gang' and hold hands, making sure that everyone makes it across the street safely, and all shoes are tied, conjoined at the hip and stumbling all over each other's feet? They got a task, you got a task. Some are more important than others. I'm putting my best foot forward, as well as putting my best men forward, I'm making sure my next move is my best move. So, if you know anything about chess, I suggest you put away these kindergarten checker pieces and start analyzing this shit from a strategist's perspective, cause not everything is for everybody! Now fall in and move out!"

Stating his last command with such brazen bravado that there was no mistaking as to who was in charge, and what was expected of the four remaining agents, as he forged forward, exiting the conference room, leaving behind grave expressions and perplex wonderment on their faces in his wake. When the four agents rose from their seats, they left, determined in their tasks, ready to bring down the killer.

Chapter Thirty - One

June 6, 2020 7:01am Saturday

St. Louis, Missouri

Two days after the Louisville, Kentucky slaughter, Stranger and his clique of miscreants lumbered out of the dense thicket that sat at the end of a dead end street, discreetly hidden behind an old, derelict, industrial complex in St. Louis, Missouri, where they took cover and caught up on some much needed sleep, because their bodies were on the verge of shutdown due to exhaustion and lack of sustenance, to refuel their basic human needs. It wasn't until they were leaving Chicago, Illinois where they decimated the city's police force with three crippling blows of shockingly unexplained genocide that occurred just moments apart from one another, while each transient incident became a deplorably gruesome scene, where Stranger made certain that each of the three remaining heads he had taken from the Jonesville massacre, were left and displayed grotesquely as a testament that the reaper was unleashed and running rampant, in the midst of the chaos.

Taking a few seconds to allow his eyes to adjust to the rising sun by shielding his blurry eyes with his hands, Stranger began to stalk down the back street towards the main road where traffic was pushing by steadily, as Mike, Lisa and John followed at his heels like devoted lap dogs. When they approached the street corner, Stranger stood and began to survey both directions of traffic. Turning right to walk down the sidewalk with the flow of traffic, they came upon a corner store and sauntered across the parking lot towards the entrance.

Entering the store, where morning commuters were buzzing around. Stranger noticed that most of the customers were seemingly unaware of his presence, except for one person in particular, which was a middle-eastern, Arab cashier, who had observed him the very moment the doorbell chimed, alerting him of a customer's entrance or exit. With a courteous nod of the Arab's head, Stranger didn't even convey any sort of courtesies in return. Instead, he leveled the cold hard stare of a man who wasn't in any mood to exchange pleasantries at 7:30 in the morning, which the digital clock displayed on the wall at the far back end of the store, for all who entered, to see. After a couple of quick peeps with those all knowing, suspicious eyes, Stranger began to head down the main isle towards the coffee machine. With John and Lisa hot on his trail in pursuit, he began to fill up a 20 ounce cup of hot Java, while Lisa questioned as to why he didn't put any sugar or creamer in his coffee. John began to begin his verbal onslaught again, like placing a key into a lock and disengaging a locking mechanism.

John was out of his locked box and baring down on Lisa, when Mike approached them from behind and said, "John, don't start that shit right now. Shut the fuck up, before you even open your mouth, and go find something to eat, NOW!" Mike spoke his demands through clenched teeth, in hopes, that the customers nearby didn't catch on to their little short-lived dispute before it even began.

While John, on the other hand, took note of the way in which

Mike spoke to him, and backed away from him, slightly, bumping into Stranger, in his retreat, saying, "Come on, Lisa, let's go find something to eat, they gotta have a bale of alfalfa, or a medicated salt block around here somewhere."

Turning to make his hasty retreat in the opposite direction of Mike, with Lisa slowly following, but not without saying, her peace in return. "Sure, John, while you looking for a bale of hay for me, I'll see if they got Poise panty liners, because your bitch ass just pissed in your panties when Mike said what he said, and how he said it. Oh yea, they may even have a box of Ho-Nuts you can snack on or some Chump Chips, and you can wash it all down with a new drink out, what do they call it, Mike? Oh, yea, Scary Cola! That's it, then we'll-"

"Lisa, get your ass on girl and stop antagonizing him!" Mike spat at her, with an obvious grin of approval for her creative comebacks she unleashed without getting all caught up in her normal emotional tirades that seemed to be common of her, when it came to the verbal backlash between John and her. With a frisky smirk on her face, Lisa spun around on her heels and put a little extra twist in her hips as she provocatively walked away with Stranger and Mike, both looking on in good-natured spirits. Then, both Mike and Stranger burst out laughing when they heard Lisa's voice billow from the isle next to them, saying, "John, you know damn well I don't eat no damn chicken feed, and no, it's not the same thing as boneless fried chicken bites, you dumbass retard, let's find something to eat and stop playing, boy, come on."

With coffee, chips, and a gallon of water in hand, Stranger asked the others if they were good? They began to look around and act as if none of them heard him, only to have Stranger call them out on their antics. Once they exited the store, he said, "Y'all some cold-blooded kleptos," watching as Lisa pulled Little Debbie cakes, and Krispy Creme donuts from under her shirt, and sodas from her bra, and handed one to John and one to Mike, while John started pulling out candy bars and energy drinks for every one. But the most impressive of all was Mike, who unearthed the mother-load of snacks and alcoholic beverages, even some packs of generic cigarettes.

Stranger couldn't believe his eyes, for all this couldn't have happened in the short time they were in the store, which was less than 5 minutes, full of morning commuters. They all just laughed at each other as more items were being pulled out from unsuspected areas of their bodies.

Stranger knew of his friend's secret games of 'who can steal the most in 2 minutes' and there had been some very impressive heists that he had witnessed throughout the times he had been with them while they played their little game. But never really partaking in the action himself, Stranger was on some next level type of felony life sentence madness when he broke laws, never settling for petty crimes, and misdemeanors. He felt like why take a little when you can take it all? So, he never got into those little games with them because when he was unleashed, it was either, 'Balls to the Wall, or nothing at all'.

It wasn't until Stranger left the store that the owner, who had observed him upon entering his establishment, took notice to the hazy photo that the local police force had handed out to all the stores all over the city of St. Louis.

Jaber' Al Hari-Ri, the store owner and cashier, began surveying the description, and the photo enhancement of the suspected serial cop-killer that has been sweeping the nation like a wet-jet Swifter Sweeper. The hair on the back of his neck began to rise, for he was almost sure that the man that he had seen just moments ago, could in fact, be the suspect. When he had noticed the black and white Nike fitted baseball gloves hanging from his back pocket, and the way he kept his face shielded from anyone looking at him, that truly gave Mr. Al Hari-Ri, the impression that he was definitely in the presence of the suspect, as he stared at a computer generated description. As one of his longtime friends and honorable member of the St. Louis Metropolitan Police Department, came strolling into the front door.

Without hesitation, he told Officer O'Connel that he needed a minute of his time before he left. Nodding his approval and flashing his infectious smile, Officer O'Connel filled up a cup of coffee, then stood to the side of the counter and waited until Mr. Al Hari-Ri, finished up with the last of the customers, before turning his attention towards him.

Before speaking any words, Mr. Al Hari-Ri, placed the statewide APB for the suspect, on the counter and pointed to the murky subject in the drawing and vocally stressed his adamant belief that he had just encountered that suspect less that 10 minutes prior, saying that the subject had walked to and from the store by foot. Explaining further in details, of why and how he believed that his accusation of this man were, he said, "The guy was wearing the same outfit in this photo," stabbing his finger at the picture with vehement intent, to further stress his point that he had indeed seen that man just moments ago in the store.

Officer O'Connel took note of the description and realized that he himself may have just passed the same guy on his way to the store. Then asked, "Mr. Al Hari-Ri, did that guy have a hoodie on his head with a couple of plastic grocery bags in his hand?"

Nodding his head to concur that he was correct in his assessment, Mr. Al Hari-Ri pointed to the street and said, "Yeah, he began walking down this side of the road."

Officer O'Connel said, "I know, I saw him too, down by the old industry complex, walking down that back road."

Pausing a second, he stared at the photo a moment longer and Officer O'Connel said, "I didn't get a good look at him, but I'm sure we're talking about the same person." It took Officer O'Connel a few minutes before he placed the picture upon the counter and said, "It's worth looking into, I'm gonna go canvas the area, and check out the old warehouse complex to see if this individual is pigeon holed up in there somewhere," saying this with an assured smile on his face, he pushed off with his wide placed palms from the counter, and started to spin around on his heels before he was quickly halted by the store owner.

"Be careful, my friend, this guy had that look in his eyes!" squinting his eyes to coax his meaning deeper into his conscious thoughts, Mr. Al Hari-Ri further explained his meaning by saying, "Those eyes weren't... they weren't..." stuttering in his words, "They were tumultuous and troublesome. I saw Hades on the surface of his eyes. Nothing but death and destruction written on the windows of his soul! I was-" Halting Mr. Al Hari-Ri in his tracks, Officer O'Connel said, "Okay, okay, I get your meaning, save the theatrical rendition of Biblical Revelations of the Apocalypse of mankind, coming in the form of a maniacal human." Flashing his friendly smile again, O'Connel said, "Besides, you know I got my trusted partner, Duke, with me in the truck, and he can sniff out the one bad guy in a crowd full of bad guys. But, thanks for the tip, anyway! You're a very observant, true blue citizen, and we need more like you in this world!" With that being said, O'Connel saluted Mr. Al Hari-Ri and bid him goodbye. Turning to head out of the door and never looking back over his shoulder.

Mr. Al Hari-Ri stood behind the cashier counter, and spoke softly to himself, saying, "Yes, my friend, farewell indeed. Hell's gates are open, the seals are removed and the trumpets have been sounding for several weeks now. Yeah, you can fight fire with water, but you can't quench the thirst of an erupting volcano, the only thing you can do is run for cover, my friend, and let this volcano go back into remission." Speaking this wisdom to nobody in particular, as he watched Officer O'Connel's K-9 Police SUV pull off from the parking lot, heading in the direction of the old condemned warehouse complex.

Mr. Hari-Ri said a quiet prayer for Officer O'Connel's safe return, as well as, one for all of the officers that he had recently heard about in the news, or read about in papers, like the USA Today, which he combed through daily to keep himself abreast of what was happening in the world around him.

Chapter Thirty - Two

June 6, 2020 7:48am

Saturday St. Louis, Missouri

After several minutes of circling the property and doing some reconnaissance from a distance to see if in fact there was a detectable presence in the area, Officer O'Connel pulled his K-9 SUV up to the main entry way which was a padlocked gate that led into the complex. He took notice that there wasn't any visible padlock attached to the thick, rusted chain that wrapped around the steel poles of the two disjointed gateways.

Slowly unwrapping the chain, O'Connel kept his eyes peeled on the open property, looking for any movement in the distance. Once the chain was unwrapped and laid dangling against one of the gates, he lifted the latch that kept the gates securely attached together and pushed the two gateways open with a loud screeching squeak emitting from the rusted hinges that were barely durable enough to keep the gate fastened to the rest of the fence much longer.

Climbing back into the drivers seat and pulling forward, Officer O'Connel drove around the whole property, periodically stopping from time to time, to get a feel of the surrounding area and gauge if there was any sign of threat or danger, by using two of his senses: Sight and sound, while following the veteran police instincts that he had used to save so many lives, as well as his own, in his 10 years on the force for the St. Louis Police Department.

Parking slightly askew to the western side of the building structures, he climbed out of the vehicle and stood at the driver's side quarter panel, and peered around the derelict buildings from behind his dark tinted Oakley shades. While he kept his hand on the grip of his sidearm, a Glock model 19, 9mm, 17 round semi- automatic handgun.

When the caution of threat wore off, Officer O'Connel eased around the front end of his Ford Excursion and proceeded to investigate the structures up-close, even stepping into open doorways and shining his maglite, to canvass the darkness inside the buildings and peeking into broken windows to detect any unsettling movement that would cause him to call for immediate backup and have the area cordoned off from any possible means of exit. Although Officer O'Connel was being led down this course of action on a hunch from the Arabian store owner, who was mostly suspicious of everyone who entered his establishment that didn't reflect either his own Arabian ethnicity or a caucasian racial background. He didn't want to start a statewide uproar with a false and baseless claim that, the serial cop killer was loose in their city without some sort of proof other than some insinuating evidence or bizarre presumption that was gained from a composite sketch of a guy that no one can honestly say they've ever seen. But, Officer O'Connel didn't leave any room for error, so he took it upon himself to investigate the area, for the potential suspect, if this was indeed the location in which the alleged suspect was hiding in.

Climbing up on to a ramp that led up to a large bay warehouse door that didn't have an access window to peer inside, O'Connel just so happened to look upon the ground and was alerted to fresh tire tracks, which engaged his investigative senses to try and gain access at this point to search into the findings of why fresh tire tracks were present in an area that was long ago condemned and shouldn't have had any sign of traffic. When the barking from his K-9, Duke, began, O'Connel took a second to see what was triggering his four legged partner and noticed that there was some large ravens in the area, and a few scurrying squirrels moving about, which always got Duke excited, seeing them roam about. After checking that there was no initial threat, Officer O'Connel located a thick strap laying the on ground, crushed beneath the shipping docks bay door, and he began to lift the garage door by the attached strap. Slowly, the door rose upon its rusty rolling tracks until it finally made it to the last few feet with ease. There, parked in the warehouse's shipping bay area, was a 2016 grey Grand Cherokee with Louisville, Kentucky tags.

Approaching the vehicle with extreme caution, gun and flashlight held at eye level, O'Connel side-stepped along the back of the SUV and peered into the back windows. Seeing that the vehicle was empty of any passengers, he rounded to the front of the SUV, as Duke's barking became more incessant which sounded of roused anger, causing him to redirect his attention to the surrounding area of the warehouse which sat spookily still, in the dark recess of the abandoned facility that now housed nothing but vermin and ghosts. A bunch of abandoned, old machinery, dust, and an old vandalized industrial property. It wasn't until Duke's barking turned into fierce growls and high pitched howls, which meant that Duke was trying to alert O'Connel to something of a serious nature, causing O'Connel to cease his search and retreat back and to the K-9 holding pen in the SUV to check on Duke, and assess the situation from there.

Chapter Thirty - Three

June 6, 2020 8:05am Saturday

St. Louis, Missouri

"You heard that Stranger?" Lisa asked.

"Naw," answered Stranger, "I don't hear nothing but birds chirping." As he laid back in the grass area, sipped from the gallon of water, and started to bite into a chip. The noise could be heard again, an automobile moving in close proximity.

Alerted to the noise himself, Mike made his way to the edge of the tree line and stared out with watchful eyes. When he caught a glimpse of all he needed to see, he said, "Stranger, there's cops all around us!"

This caused Stranger and the others to hustle and bustle, moving about to gather things and take up hidden positions behind the foliage of woods to camouflage themselves with Mike pointing out his discovery. Stranger took notice that the police vehicle was a black K-9 Unit SUV and it was apparent to him that the cop in question wasn't doing much but following his routine canvass of his designated area. Not until Stranger repositioned himself, did he see that the gate was being opened and the cop was pulling into the industrial complex, then parking in front of the building that he had stored their getaway car.

"Damn! Damn! Damn!" John began cussing with anger in his voice.

"What?" asked Lisa.

"If he finds our truck, we're hit, is what. You don't hear that barking, Lisa?" inquired John. "If that cop lets that dog out of that truck, it's gonna get a line on our scent and come beelining straight to us if it smells us inside that truck." With a sound of reluctant acceptance, Lisa was forced to agree with John on his evaluation of the situation.

Mike asked, "What's up, Stranger? Wanna wait it out or what? We can always get away and steal another vehicle."

Staring intently in the direction of the gated complex, Stranger made no comment, but answered by moving forward out of the woods and making his way to the fence, quickly locating the cutout accessible way into the complex. He pushed aside the steel fencing and ducked into the hole, followed by John, Lisa, and Mike.

As they took up hidden refuge behind miscellaneous broken, weathered machinery which laid scattered about haphazardly throughout the whole complex grounds. They realized that their attention was brought back to the dog when it began barking again. Holding their positions, they didn't retreat out of fear when the officer began looking around, his eyes falling upon the squirrels that were climbing about some wooden pallets and a few rather large ravens that sat lazily about the structures surrounding the area. It wasn't until the officer began to walk up the shipping bay ramp and lifted the warehouse bay door, that the tension began to rise inside everyone.

Seeing the bay door roll up and the tail end of the truck was enough to rouse Stranger into action. He casually began to move forward and slowly made his way towards the drivers side of the K-9 SUV, pulling from his hoodie pouch, a Browning Hi Power 9mm, semi automatic handgun, one in which he'd taken from the last officer he'd slain in Chicago, Illinois, just a few days ago, leaving him in a very deplorable manner, as he peeled his dying fingers from its pistol grip. But the officer had never stood a fighting chance at survival against the strategic moves that Stranger and Mike had put into play.

Once Stranger came face to face with the fiercely growling and barking German Shepard, he stared at the dog through the tinted glass window and began making kissy noises to antagonize the K-9 even more. The back window was cracked, so the dog could breathe fresh air, but the K-9 was prying at the small opening with his paws and snout, trying to bite the glass with its fangs, whining and growling more at his failed attempts.

Stranger leaned forward and whispered, "That's it, boy, call your master, bring him to meet his maker."

Tapping the barrel of the gun to the tinted glass, inciting more anger from the dog, by tracing its barrel in circles and figure 8 motions, as the K-9 followed his movements with its huge head like the hand cannon in his grip was a chewy toy or tasty beef flavored treat. Stranger said, "Yea boy, its very tasty boy, ever ate steel biscuits that taste like gun powder?"

Then John approached the window beside Stranger with a wicked look in his eyes which reflected off of the tinted window, and said, "Don't trip, you fucking mutt, its gonna send you straight to doggie heaven, you worthless barking flea bag," snickering at his own antics. John continued peering at the K-9, which continued to bark insanely.

Hearing this, the officer exit the warehouse. Standing on the shipping dock, Officer O'Connel yelled out to his K-9 partner, "Duke! Whassa matter boy? You're going crazy for nothing! I don't see nothing out here, boy."

Slowly he monitored the surroundings and concentrated on every possible angle for any apparent ambush, but to no avail. He didn't see anything remotely close to being a threat. But Duke continued to bark incessantly and the sound of his crying whines and growls only made Officer O'Connel relent and jump down off of the docking platform and approach his vehicle.

Openly talking to Duke, he said, "You want out, boy? You wanna chase the squirrels and stretch a little? Huh, Duke?" as he closed in on the SUV. He began to approach around the front end of the vehicle on the passenger side when Duke howled like a wolf and slammed his large head against the window, as if trying to shatter the glass upon impact. But, Duke's desperate attempts weren't enough to halt Officer O'Connel from fast approaching the driver's side of the vehicle.

Stooping down by the rear wheel base with his right arm extended with the Browning 9mm trained at eye level, securely fastened in his grip without stress or strain, and his left hand firmly cupped beneath the barrel encircling the trigger guard, displaying a perfect marksman shooter's stance.

Stranger didn't waste any time. The very second that Officer O'Connel entered the crosshairs, he pulled the trigger in two concise bursts. Two smoking, empty shell casings were sent flying out of the ejection port, as one bullet landed squarely center mass into Officer O'Connel's chest and the other one penetrated his windpipe, sending him sprawling back on his heels, desperately grasping to retrieve his firearm from his holster, but Stranger quickly gained the advantage and quietly approached Officer O'Connel. Effortlessly relieving him of his weapon, while he stood wide-eyed and mouth gaped, struggling to staunch the flow of blood that was draining from his neck like a slaughtered pig. Officer O'Connel fell backwards against an old stack of broken pallets, and began to slide down until finally in a sitting position gurgling on the blood that was building up in his mouth. Choking off the foaming blood starting to drown him in his windpipe. His hand clasped tightly around his wounded neck.

Stranger dropped down to his haunches and looked into the body cam lens, saying, "another one bites the dust, boys and girls, that's all folks," snatching the body camera from the fastened strap on the officer's shirt, only to realize that the officer was wearing a kevlar vest. Taking notice to the fact that the first bullet he'd shot from his Browning, didn't penetrate the officer's chest plate, Stranger looked into Officer O'Connel's eyes and still saw life within those heartless pupils. He shoved the barrel of the Browning deep into the officer's mouth, shattering his front teeth in the process, angling the barrel upwards, he sent 3 consecutive death sentences to his higher consciousness. He thought it funny that the officer had a lot on his mind now. 'Better yet, he's a scatterbrain!' Stranger thought to himself, laughing.

Removing the smoking gun from his lifeless lips, Stranger took the barrel of the gun, tapping O'Connel's head lightly, he began explaining his reasons for doing the officer how he did.

When he finished tapping, he said, "Now, Officer," tearing away the officer's badge from his already ripped open shirt. "O'Connel, it is now? It seems you're a part of a band of brothers that have taken it upon themselves to take innocent lives of a certain race. Now, I know you, and many generations before you, has deemed yourself as...above the law, shall we say? And I believe it's time someone took a stand and recalibrated the odds-you know, take it back to the biblical times-'an eye for eye, tooth for a tooth', and a life for a life. So, I guess you can say I am my brother's keeper!"

Speaking the last bit with a hint of amusement in his voice, Stranger rose from his haunches, and began to turn on his heels.

John walked up and said, "What you say, officer? You love your partner so much you want to take him with you? Oh, he's a loyal servant and faithful companion, is he? Well, I believe they got room for his flea scratchin' ass where you're goin' too! Ain't that right, Stranger?" asked John excitedly. But before John could receive an answer from Stranger, there was a blast and the barking from the K-9 ceased instantly.

Staring into the back of the SUV holding pen, Stranger

forcefully reached into the shattered window and grabbed Duke's tail, yanked the slumped dog to a dangling moribund position and saw that there was still life left in the mortally defeated dog.

Then, the unthinkable took place at blinding speed when Stranger ripped the dying dog from out of the holding pen window and slams him to the dirt like a discarded rag doll, bringing Lisa from out of her hiding, when she quickly approached Stranger, shouting, "No! No! Damn you! Look at that poor thing, he didn't do nothing to you but bark-"

"Nothing to us?" Mike cut in, "Lisa, if that dog was to have been released from the back of that truck, 'it', defenseless looking or not, would've hunted us down like preys! It would've ripped our flesh and held us down until his headmaster over there," Mike thumbed in the cop's direction, "told him to let go. So, if you want to get all emotional over some dying dog, then you should've been a fuckin' vet and not running in this circle. That's an officer of the law too. That dog gets treated with more love and respect than anyone in the hood. They don't respect us, cops don't respect us, and a damn dog gets a metal of honor and buried like a fucking war hero with a 21 gun salute and shit. They don't even give capital to anyone who kills someone in the hood, cop or otherwise! But let a cop or his K-9 get killed in the line of duty, that mutha-fucka that did it is going down. Not for cruelty to a fucking animal, not even manslaughter, but the highest murder of them all, 'Capital Murder'! So, if you ask me, it's 'fuck that dog' and I hope he chokes on his metal of honor when he gets to doggy heaven!" Mike fumed as he finished his insensitive rant about why Stranger shouldn't leave the dog alive. But none of what was said by either of them was heard by Stranger, as Mike turned around to face him, only to witness a vile act being unleashed in front of his eyes. With the Browning 9mm shoved firmly up the dog's rectum, Stranger began pulling the trigger until the gun slide kicked back and the body of the German Shepard was torn into shreds with half of its upper violently cleaved, tattered and riddled with gaping bullet holes from the exit wounds.

Lisa covered her face with her hands and began to cry heavy tears when John said, "Lisa, get the fuck outta here with all this soft ass bitch shit, fuck that damn dog! And now you're crying over that mutt? What, you're a cop lover now? You love cop dogs cuz they uphold the laws? Or did you know that when Stranger got arrested for the case that he didn't commit, he was chased down by a cop dog and mangled by his relentless fangs, and Stranger didn't run cuz of anything he had done, he ran cuz he has a natural fear of dogs period. He's been that way since he was attacked as a child. So, how about you shut the fuck up with all of that soft ass crying over a dead cop-dog, bullshit!" John said, speaking in a voice that wasn't normally used when he went on banters of sarcastic arguments with Lisa. Lisa understood then, that John was loyal and empathetic towards only one person in the world and that person was Stranger.

Then, she watched as John tagged along, while Stranger savagely snatched the dog by the tail and ruthlessly dragged its bloodied remains along the dirty pavement, towards the warehouse docks and tossed the lifeless animal onto the foundation like a sack of potatoes. Then he returned to the corpse of Officer O'Connel, grabbed a hold of his left tactical Gor-Tec boot and began to haul the deceased officer along the same bloodied path as his K-9 partner, Duke. He continued pulling the body up the ramp and into the warehouse, where both partners were positioned in a very obscene way after Officer O'Connel was stripped of his uniform and bulletproof vest.

When Stranger returned to the K-9 SUV, he went through the truck interior and located another firearm other than the Kimber Pro Carry II, .45 acp pistol that he had already seized off of the officer's person. This was a Glock 27, .40 caliber semi-auto with 2 extra 17 round magazines loaded to the T with hollow points. He also found a gym bag with some personal clothes and $286 in cash in the console, next to a high powered maglite.

Placing all of the stolen items in the gym bag, Stranger climbed into the front seat of the Ford Excursion, started the SUV, put it in drive, then he drove it towards the warehouse, and then up the ramp and into the bay door opening, parking it beside the stolen Grand Cherokee. After switching out vehicles, Stranger began backing the stolen get away SUV out of the warehouse and down the ramp. When Stranger completed this task, he climbed out and said to the others, "Get in, it's time to move around." Grabbing the warehouse bay door strap, he pulled the garage door shut, while sauntering back to the SUV, he paused and took a look around. Surveying the surroundings behind his new dark tinted black framed Oakley sunglasses.

Chapter Thirty - Four

June 5, 2020 12:10pm Friday

Prince William County, Virginia

Detective McNealson was sitting in his car as Det. York pulled up beside him in the parking lot of the Potomac Mills Mall, in Prince William County, Virginia. They arranged this meeting with Spotsylvania County's Arson Investigator, Detective Dabney, whom they needed to give some subtle spin on the findings they had stumbled across at the United States Penitentiary Lee, in Jonesville, Virginia. When Matt tapped on Vince's passenger window, McNealson was so enthralled in thought, that he didn't even notice his partner pull into the area and park beside him. Popping the door locks for Det. York to climb in, they greeted like longtime friends, by fist bump and leaning back into the comfort of the cool-blowing air conditioning and form fitting bucket seats in Vince's new 2020 Yukon Denali as the poetic flow of Kendrick Lamar's "Good Kid Bad City" album played at a volume that could be enjoyed and listened to.

Staring woefully out of the windshield, McNealson sat in a quiet brood when York churned up a conversation by asking him, "So, what we gonna do with all this new found inadmissible evidence that we compiled under false pretenses with the falsified court order documents that were deceptively coerced from a Federal Judge, for an investigation we, not only have no jurisdiction over, but aren't even legally supposed to be investigating, let alone, entering a Federal Maximum Security Facility, and combing through confidential files of people who aren't even considered suspects in the true investigation of these serial murders! And last, but most definitely not the least, there are three, I repeat, three careers that are hanging in the balance on this little wild goose chase that is only going to get wilder the longer it takes to grab and bag whoever this crazy son of a bitch is that's unleashing...whatever it is that this crazy mutha-fucka is unleashing!" Det. York says with obvious built up concern for 'the coming' that is sure to come when their Jenga tower of trouble falls. Not if it falls, but when it falls.

Suddenly, there is a knock on the driver's side rear window, causing them both to jump. Detective Dabney came into view and said, "Good afternoon, detectives," as he opened the rear door and began to climb in without getting an invitation to do so from Detective McNealson.

Once seated and wiping the beads of sweat from his forehead with his shirt sleeve, Detective Dabney asked, "What's the news, Blues Clues?" with excited curiosity traced in his voice, like this was some treasure hunt that they were on, instead of being a possible decimation of all three of their careers simultaneously being shitted on and flushed down the toilet like some toilet paper.

"Hey, Joe, how's it going?" asked McNealson, putting on a facade like he was just as happy to see him and hand over all of their juicy findings, as Dabney was to see them. He reached down into the middle console seeking something, "It's all there buddy, everything we're gonna need to put the clamps down on this case. We found a little something, but not enough to make an arrest yet, I think we're close to figuring this out though," McNealson said, proudly pushing the case files towards Dabney, like his own prized possession, with a smile so widely attached, it couldn't be mistaken for anything other than good intentions, under the guise of misguided deceit.

Taking the file and skimming through its loose leaf papers and psychology analysis and evaluations, Dabney closed the file and asked, "Where's the information about the men we're investigating as possible suspects? I sent you my investigative reports for the guys at Terre Haute USP and Florence USP, but where's your reports on the Lee County USP and Big Sandy USP suspects?" inquired Dabney, who had scrunched up his forehead and gave off an air of suspicion weaved in his question to McNealson.

Smiling brightly, Det McNealson countered, saying, "Oh, that report," sounding nonchalant and shrugging it off as if, it only led to a dead-end for a bunch of loonies who got off from doing time that they obviously played a major role in committing. "Me and Matt, here, questioned them people and threw everything at their staff members, we even served the kitchen sink, to no avail. The only thing we walked out of there with is some serious war stories that are gruesome enough to give us nightmares for the next five years and a lot of policies and procedures mumbo jumbo," trying to ease away from the subject like a quiet cat burglar on the prowl.

Shaking his head in studious reverie, Det Dabney accepted

McNealson's explanation into what took place, but not without saying, "So, now that we're stuck in a rut, so to speak, how about we just hand over our findings to the FEDs in charge of this case and see if they can use the information we've compiled on the subjects to dig a little deeper than what we've already dug?"

"Absolutely not!" shouted McNealson, turning on him like a cornered possum, trapped by fear and his survival instincts.

Jumping back a little from the rash comment and the tone in which it was thrown at him, Dabney timidly said, "Okay, okay! Chill out my friend! No need to get all bent out of shape, I was just proposing an idea, that's all," throwing up his palms in surrender, up like he was under arrest.

Detective York stepped in to save the day, saying, "One reason why we can't do that is because, you know the FEDs don't like or play fair with local police, they feel they're above our pay grade, if you know what I mean? But another is..." Taking a second to let what he was about to send his way set on his conscience for a minute, "You know how we got those federal warrants from a federal judge under false pretenses, right? We didn't just break a state law, we broke a federal law when we violated the Federal Privacy Act, and not to mention, Civil Rights violations by digging into medical and psychological confidential records, not just us, but, you as well. This ain't gonna stop at a reprimand or a slap on the wrist, you know?" asking this to actually see if the severity of the situation has actually reached home and convinced him of the seriousness of their actions.

When the porch light of common sense finally turned on in his eyes, Dabney said softly, "Oh, now I see. This situation won't be overlooked and tucked under the rug or put in a file cabinet with a seal placed on it. We're in big trouble if this gets out, huh?" asked Dabney, actually shaking.

Shaking his head, Matt York said, "Now, it won't get out and I won't be sharing a cell with neither of you either. What's gonna happen is: we're gonna put this case in a casket and bury it away like it never happened-"

Cutting him off, McNealson vehemently said, "Fuck no! Matt, I'm not burying shit! This is my case and I'm taking this psycho down, even if I have to do it by myself, I'm a damn good detective and it happened in my county first!"

"Second," York corrected him, cutting him off.

Seething and fuming, Det McNealson said, "Fuck it! I wouldn't care when it happened, but it happened in my...my county, on my watch!"

"You know what?" questioned Det. York, "You sound real egotistical and thoughtless right now, and you're trying to justify breaking the law and the Constitutional rights of citizens to get the job done as a means to an end? It only puts you in the same light as the criminal, the same law you are sworn to uphold and protect, you're desecrating now by wiping your shit stomping boots on it!" York finished with a serious, yet defeated tone.

Seeing the two detectives demeanor become almost combative, Dabney began to panic and allowed his anxiety to soar skywards with the knowledge that he'd in fact, taken part in an illegal investigation, which could prove to be disastrous, if the truth surfaced that they indeed had jeopardized the integrity of a federal investigation, and broke countless laws and civilian constitutional rights, along the way. But that wasn't the worst of their problems. It was the fact that they compromised the investigation by withholding potential evidence and federal obstruction of justice, with their actions by hindering the quick capture of this murderously maniacal individual, sitting perilously heavy on his conscience. Dabney speedily grabbed the door handle and pushed it open, frantically jumping out of the SUV, he stumbled away in fear and apprehension, gagging and sweating profusely. He doubled over on bended knee, trying to catch his breath. Shaky hands began reaching inside his sport coat to retrieve his inhaler from the inside liner pocket, then he quickly clamored the mouth piece to his lips and sprayed three short bursts to open his restricted lungs from near collapse.

When Detectives McNealson and York gathered around him to make sure he wasn't in need of further medical attention, York asked, "Joe, are you good? You need help, buddy?"

Shaking his head from side to side, relaying a wordless 'no' as his answer, Dabney remained leaning against the bumper of an old Nissan Altima, and took several moments to breathe and contain himself, before he rose to his feet and swipe the sweat beads from his forehead. In an urgent tone, Dabney began to stutter, saying, "I...I...I gotta get back...to th...to the office. Call me later...if if you get any... new news, okay?"

Backing away from the two detectives like a cautious prey surrounded by two savage predators, Dabney made it to his unmarked cruiser, a late model Crown Victoria, fumbling with the key, as he nervously watched the two detectives stare at him from the other side of the parking lane, making sure his cohorts weren't going to try anything remotely close to what he has seen on TV and read in Mystery/Thriller novel in the past, he knew he was dealing with some real heavy shit on his plate and he was putting as much distance between him and the two shit starters as he could.

Deep in his heart, he felt that these two detectives were not from the same cloth as him and other decent, law abiding cops that protected the Liberty, Equality, and Justice of the system and all its citizens. This he was sure of, and he needed to rid himself of their presence immediately, because he knew, when you lay down with dogs, you wake up with fleas.

Chapter Thirty - Five

June 8, 2020 10:32am Monday
USP Lee, Jonesville, Virginia

Sitting out front of the guard tower at USP Lee County, awaiting approval from administration to be allowed to enter the facility, Agents Smart and Drapper, began to discuss their views on the new and terrible twist that has just been heaved onto their big platter of clusterfucks. They received the Medical Examiner's report and the crime scene findings for the four correctional officers slain in broad daylight at a busy intersection, that apparently nobody had any inkling into the savage atrocities that were taking place in the vicinity without raised alarm or eyebrow to this unexplainable a homicide.

This is why, the agents were now stationed just outside of the facility, a United States Penitentiary, to find the missing pieces to this puzzle. Although it was a fact to their knowledge that these four decapitated victims were indeed part of their serial murder case. It wasn't apparent to them as to actually why these correctional officers had to die in such a heinous manner. When Agent Drapper mentioned what he believed to be the motive-that the four C.O.s were just victims of circumstances, and casualties of war-Agent Smart quickly countered and argued.

"It's a possibility, but the probability of this just happening as a chance of happenstance was highly unlikely-being that the victims all had something in common, first being they all worked at the same place, secondly, their heads were removed-not just from their bodies-but from the scene altogether. Third, they all happen to meet their demise almost simultaneously. Because the video footage from the gas station video feed, showed that all four murders happened in less than 10 minutes span of time. The suspect knew exactly what he was planning to do, long before he actually did it."

"After watching that video several times, it wasn't a question as to what the suspect's intentions were, because the moment he had seen the two cars pull up to the pumps, he reacted like a man who wasn't doing the act impulsively. It was done deliberately, almost as if that was the same reason he had come to Jonesville in the first place. Premeditated."

Taking a minute to ponder the common sense rationale that was effortlessly tailored to fit the incident in question, like a form fitting tuxedo, Agent Drapper just nodded his head in agreement, saying, "You know.. wherever the secret lies, the trail of breadcrumbs definitely leads right to these gates."

This caused Agent Smart to base his own wisdom on that comment by saying, "The one thing about secrets is...if more than one person knows about it, it is no longer a secret, it's called common knowledge, and in the Big House," he said, motioning to the Maximum Security heavily razor-wired and double-gated facility to his right, then adding, "is the one place where there are no secrets. Some of the biggest federal rats in the nation are housed behind those walls. If we want to get the Big answer, all we gotta to do is go fishing in a big sea full of sharks. They know all, see all, and hear all, and above all else, there's someone in there that will give up all the goods for a little of nothing. Now we just need to locate what cubby hole the common knowledge we're seeking is hiding in, and we don't got a lot of time to do it, because we're on the clock like draft night, and it's ticking away, the longer we sit in this car, idling away, the more time is lost."

Not much later, a perimeter vehicle pulls up in front of their black GMC Yukon, and slowly approach the driver's side window, lazily saying, "If you gentlemen would follow me, we'll need you to surrender your firearms with the weapons officer for proper storage, before you can enter the facility per Captain Spires' orders."

Climbing out of their vehicles, Agents Smart, Drapper, and a few others that were there on hand, incase there were more shovels needed to dig deeper into this case, followed. This was going to save them time by using the unlimited manpower they had at their disposal. Falling in line, they all made their way behind the Lieutenant to the guard tower and surrendered their federal issued firearms over to the Weapons officer, to be locked away until they left the facility. Once the weapons were stored, they proceeded through the gates and headed towards the administration office area, where they were met by the warden of USP Lee County, Warden Bradford, and a Captain Spires.

When pleasantries were disposed of, it was Captain Spires' comment that caused an immediate red flag for Agent Smart's demeanor. He said, "Look here, gentlemen, the last time you were here, five men died that day and I hope this isn't gonna be another day where I lose four good men behind this crazy kangaroo you got hopping from state to state, killing the brave protectors of our nation. I-"

Freezing the captain in his southern good ole boy rant, Spl. Agent Smart interrupted, saying, "Hold on a minute, did you say, 'the last time we were here'? and that five men died?"

"Why, yes sir!" Captain Spires answered, hooking both thumbs into the arm holes of his black federally issued protective stab vest, and leaning back on the heels of his brown suave Desert Storm boots.

"I don't understand, help me to clarify something, has this been a recent event that you are speaking of?" asked Agent Smart.

"As recently as four days ago!" Captain Spires answered. "I know because I met them myself, and I can tell you right now that they didn't stroll up in here like you gentlemen have. They moved kind of like some local boys, if I recall correctly. I think they were some Virginia Homicide Detectives with federally signed warrants," Captain Spires said, as he sifted through his memory banks, trying to remember. Calling out to his secretary, he yelled, "Carol Ann? Hey Carol!"

"Yes, Nate!" replied the secretary. "I need you to pull up that visitation sign in log from four days ago when them good ole boys with those federal warrants came causing all that ruckus and unnecessary nonsense a few days ago," said Captain Spires, lifting an empty water bottle to his lips and spitting a glob of brown Copenhagen chew spit into the mouth of it, screwing the cap back on, and shoving the bottle into his tan colored tactical cargo pants side pocket, as he waited for the secretary to return. When she did, she was lugging with her a thick bound book and a pen tied to it by a string hanging from its binding like a book marker.

Expeditiously flipping to the dated page that the two detectives had arrived on, Carol pointed to the names with a chipped red nail of her index finger, saying, "There, that's their signature right there," proudly, like she'd just helped solve the world's hunger issue herself with her professionally proficient administrative duties in grand order.

Moving in closer to read the signatures, both Spl. Agents, Smart and Drapper, stood there dismayed when their eyes took in the signatures of both McNealson and York scrawled in black ink, just days prior, but also on the same day that the Jonesville massacre took place. As they studied the sign in log, they noticed that they had signed in at 8:45am, and didn't leave until 2:47pm that afternoon.

Turning to face the warden, Spl. Agent Smart asked, "Warden Bradford, what was the matter in which these men were investigating?"

"I've no idea at the moment. I wasn't at the institution until later that evening when I was urgently summoned to the chaos that had taken place that day with four of my staff members, and also an Inmate housed in the SHU," answered the warden. Then he went on to add, "The assistant warden, AW Holmes, was acting warden at that time, along with Captain Spires here, but they followed policy and procedure, because the warrants those men presented were in fact, authentic federal warrants. Captain Spires called to see if these men were who they say they were, and they-" pausing for a moment to think back. "I do believe they gave us a number to their supervisor, at the Homicide Division, a Shelly Spoon, if I recall correctly. Ain't that correct, Captain?" Warden Bradford asked the captain, to make sure he was accurate.

Then, Carol, the secretary, came rushing back into the room after overhearing some of the conversation, with a folder in her hand. Handing the folder to Captain Spires, she smiled her bright red-lipped smile and stood amongst the crowd of men like she was one of the boys. When Captain Spires thumbed through the file, he nodded his head in appreciation towards her and then handed the file towards Agent Smart, saying, "There you go, sir, that's the copies of the warrants and a list of every record they pulled from our file system. Also, there is a list of every staff member and inmate they questioned," Captain Spires added this to show just how zipped tight his security measures were, and how they weren't running no clown and circus show out here in the mountainous sticks of South Western Virginia.

Opening up the file folder, Agent Smart began to review the contents. He scanned the pages with a furrowed brow and then turned to one of the other Agents that came along to assist them, saying, "Take this folder, and contact headquarters! Track down the federal judge that signed this warrant and the Chief of Police in Fredericksburg, Virginia, I want Detectives Vince McNealson, Matt York, and Officer Shelly Spoon detained immediately! This is a sham, they're not investigating a homicide in their jurisdiction, they're investigating the unidentified suspect in these cases! Suspects we don't even have on our radar!" he said with an obvious irascible tone of voice.

Turning his attention back to Warden Bradford, Spl. Agent Smart asked, "Is there some place we can set up and get down to business?"

"Certainly. Follow me, if you will," replied Warden Bradford and they began walking down through the interior of the administration office towards the back hall, lined with several rooms for conference meetings. When they all piled into the conference room, Spl. Agent Smart commenced by issuing orders and assigning details to everyone that was present and wanted to lend a helpful hand. When all the staff members that were questioned were present, Spl. Agent Smart told Spl. Agent Drapper to assess the damage and find the missing pieces by finding what it is they were particularly interested in. He looked around the room at all the reticent faces, and honed in on one that seemed to have a lot to say without much to talk about. Stepping closer, Spl. Agent Smart asked, "And your name is?"

Looking up from downcast eyes, the woman answered, "Dr. Emily Poole, head of the Psychology Department, sir. What is it that I can help you with?" Dr. Poole quickly began asking a question before she was picked apart like road kill by this federal vulture-like individual. She had gotten the impression he was going to be a 'bull in a China shop' if she got entangled in a battle of wits with him, so she kept it casual and tried to give off the notion that she was every bit as concerned with their cause as they were.

When Spl. Agent Smart opened the file on the table, he pointed to a mug shot face. "Him-who is he? Where is he? What were those two detectives after? What did you tell them?- is how you can help me," Spl. Agent Smart pressed Dr. Poole, with a look of indignation written in his expression.

Leaning forward to get a better look at the individual in question, Dr. poole stated, "He's Harold McDermott, nicknamed 'Mayhem'. He was housed at this facility for a couple of years and spent more time in our special housing unit for every infraction you can think of and more that you can't, than he did on the yard. As of right now, I don't know his whereabouts, but I'm certainly glad he's not here where I'd have to contend with him. That's trouble with a capital T if you ask me. As for what those Detectives wanted: They wanted to talk to anyone who'd had contact with him and a couple of other guys that are all probably mentioned in that case file you're pointing at, and the one main person that Detective McNealson said, 'whose cage he wanted to rattle'. Well, he did that and it caused another inmate to lose his life that very day, not less than 30 minutes after he was done shaking and rattling things up a bit so to speak. Lastly, I didn't say anything that my case notes hasn't already said for me." Dr. Poole spoke in a way that was condescending and brash, but also answering every question with efficient ease without any extended discourse.

When the staff interrogation had come to an end, Spl. Agent Smart said, "The only thing left to do, is take a stab at this Mannimal character." Looking directly into the eyes of Dr. Poole, he turned from the conference table, towards the door and said, "Dr. Poole, shall we?" extending the invitation that he would like for her to accompany him, to further poke holes in her little facade of contempt and obvious concealment of information that sat heavily upon the cracking of this case.

Entering the SHU, Dr. Poole halted in her steps and spun around to face Spl. Agent Smart saying, "Agent Smart, I must warn you, just as I warned Detective McNealson a few days ago, this gentleman isn't your normal psychopath."

Tilting his head in perplexed misinterpretation, Smart asked, "So, what are you saying? I'm supposed to be pusillanimous and reserved when speaking with this guy?"

"No!" replied Dr. Poole, "I'm not saying that, I'm just forewarning you that, you are about to walk into a dark cave with a very deviant and vile creature who personifies the true meaning of real evil, or someone having an insidious nature. I'm not telling you to walk on eggshells, I'm earnestly persuading you to tread on thin ice, there is a difference between the two. The first, being: to be fearful, the latter being: to be cautious. But it seems you're all gung-ho and professionally prepared to go in there with your six shooter out and at the ready, cocked and locked, like this is going to be a show down at high noon. So, go ahead Yosemite Sam, do you, and walk right into his crosshairs!" relaying her metaphoric comments with a serious, unsmiling attitude. Dr. Poole, quickly spun around, taking off toward the ranges, and flippantly calling back over her shoulder to the awestruck agent. "Now, shall we?" reversing the table on how he had earlier displayed an unsettling way of nonchalance, when he summoned her upon leaving the administration's conference room.

With an arrogant smirk easing into the corners of his mouth, Agent Smart proceeded to follow at a slow, lumbering distance, trying to mentally prepare for what he was to unknowingly encounter, but was given such heedful caution approaching in a reckless manner.

As they entered the range and heard the catcalls, ear-piercing yells, as fists pounding steel doors began vibrating off of the walls, Agent Smart was caught in a whirlwind of spitfire comments that were shot at him from the many fierce faces that sat like savagely condemned souls behind locked doors. He couldn't hear himself think, let alone, gather his senses about himself. He was ushered to the last cell on the range, and told, "Here we are, agent. This here is Dominic Mann, 'The Mannimal', 'Mad Man', and I'm going to step back and let you have your way with him," she said, smiling at her facetious comment, like she couldn't wait to see who prevails in this mental tug of war, which is about to be a battle of arrogance vs. ingeniousness.

Stepping back from the cell door, Dr. Poole, joyously said,

"Dominic... Dominic, Mr. Mann, you have a company." Receiving no response to her summons, she again tried, this time smiling broadly and yelled, "Mannimal!"

In a blinding blur, the door was smashed into like an untamed beast was just unleashed, and was charging rampantly in the close confines of the cell. When the figure finally appeared, his youthful face held a look of stoic meekness that didn't resonate with the villainous portrayal in which Dr. Poole had described Mannimal. As if reading his mind, Dr. Poole stated, "Looks can be deceiving, huh, Agent Smart?" asking the unsettling question like she knew what Agent Smart was seeing wasn't in fact, what he'd envisioned him to be or look like.

Steadying himself, Agent Smart commenced his interrogation of Mannimal, by saying, "Good morning, Mr. Mannimal...it is, Mannimal, is it not?"

Without a response, Mannimal stood there rigidly stiff, boring holes in Agent Smart's face: with a placid stare. When he didn't receive an answer, Smart went on with his inquiry and said, "Look, Mannimal, I need your help, a few days ago, there was a detect-"

Slicing his words off in mid sentence, Mannimal said, "Look here, Slim, Agent whatever-the-fuck-your-name-is. Help isn't something you're gonna get from me. You stand a better chance raising those executed cops from the dead and getting statements from them. What I will give you though, is three things-"

Cutting off his statement, Spl. Agent Smart said, "It's Special Agent Smart, and why don't you tell me those three things, since you wanna be so helpful," smiling back at Mannimal like he had gotten something of substance from him, with the ruckus of the range in tumultuous confusion, as the convicts were spewing loud heated comments: at the Agent, as some even kicked and pounded deafening blows upon their doors, to cause incessant disruption.

With a sudden omnipotent voice, Mannimal yelled loudly, "SILENCE" causing the entire range to fall abruptly silent, where peace sat still, as not even a whispered word in defiance was spoken in rebuke.

Looking down the cell range in disbelief, Spl. Agent Smart was shocked at the dominance one man behind the locked door had over so many others in the same situation as him. When he turned to lock eyes again with the strange man before him, Mannimal unleashed a powerful bellow of a voice, and said, "First thing I'll give you is, a mind bending headache from trying to figure out the hidden meanings within my meanings. The second thing is, a lifetime of spine-tingling memories that will change your whole impression of how the human mind actually works. The third thing I'll give you, is, a time period of three seconds, to walk away from my door, before, I make you second guess your career choice as a Federal Bureau Investigator. Now, if you continue to stand I will, and I repeat, I WILL...make you wish you never made my acquaintance, cause you will walk away from here with more questions than answers. That's the three things I'm gonna give you. Anything else you're seeking is..." looking skyward, as if, searching while contemplating, "Is an unattainable endeavor, pointless on your behalf, Spl. Agent Smart. But I'm in the mood to entertain this little game of yours. So, how about you first tell me, what you need my help with, you smart ass, super investigative clown! Standing at my cell, like a man who has 9 life sentences for capital murder, for killing everything that ever crossed his path-is gonna tell you anything. So, let's amuse one another and see who's more thoroughly entertained in the end of this sitcom."

Taking a few moments to assess the situation, while staring intently into Mannimal's eyes, relaying an unspoken message that he wasn't in the least bit intimidated by his frivolous rant of insignificant threats, when he heaved an exasperated breath, to show he was annoyed with mannimal's scatterbrained immaturity. He lifted the file folder and opened it to the contents within and said, "Well then, let's entertain one another," only to barge right into the interrogation, by asking, "Mannimal, a few days ago a Detective McNealson, came by and questioned you about...it says here, your ex cellmate, Harold McDermott, a 'Mayhem', if my files are correct. If you will, could you reiterate what the detective was seeking from you?"

Mannimal, lowers his eyes in a piercing glare and replied, "Yeah, he wanted to know whatever that file there says he wanted to know," countered Mannimal in a way that said he was sticking to his guns and not helping the police in no type of manner to capture anyone involved in their investigation, but he then goes on to say, "Hey, look here Slim, this is what I will do for you," smiling a devious smile like he was playing a cat and mouse game with the agent. "How about you tell me a name in that file and I will tell you yes or no, to help you with your process of elimination-as to whether the person is in fact someone that you might need to investigate further, is that fair enough for you?" asked Mannimal with a straightforward look on his face.

Agent Smart answered, "Fair enough," only to eagerly look down into the file and toss a name out in thin air. "How about Harold McDermott, aka Mayhem?"

"No," answered Mannimal expeditiously.

"What about Desmond Placard, aka Crazy Horse?" asked Smart.

"No!" Mannimal speedily returned his answer.

"What about ummm.. .Jonathan Monroe, aka Jojo?"

"No!" came his reply.

"Well, what about Ben Strange, aka Stranger?"

"No," Mannimal answered, almost before he was done asking the question.

"I'm all out of names," Agent Smart said, "Well, that's all the names on the list, I'm glad you could be of some assistance," saying this somberly, he turned to leave, when Mannimal called out to him.

"Spl. Agent Smartass! Don't look so dejected, you learned something today..."

"Oh, yeah? What's that?" asked Smart.

Looking deep into the agent's eyes, Mannimal growled, "You learned that some men stick to a strict code of honor, and don't have no sympathy for a cop, whether they're dead or alive. And also, I could care less if every cop, correctional officer, school security, neighborhood watch-or little child who plays the game of 'Cops and Robbers' and doesn't play the robber-dies, by the whoever is behind these recent cop killing. I'm actually jealous, cause I didn't think of it first, but if I would've done it, I would've took it to the extreme and crushed the cop and his whole family, all the way down to the family's house dog. When I clip a family tree I dig it up at the roots, fuck them cops-and whoever don't like it-fuck them too. Now take that statement back to the FBI Director, and tell him I said, "Tighten up-this shit's about to get real interesting here in a lil' bit. Now, get your bitch ass off the run, because your soft ass is making my dick hard!"

Then Mannimal yelled at the top of his lungs, "ATTACK!" which sent the entire SHU into chaotic frenzy so intense that the fear of God, was ripped out of agent Smart's chest as he stumbled backward towards the wall with the look of pure panic written on his face, when all the yelling and beating on the doors, thundered like a hatred chant of riotous turmoil.

Taking off, running down the hall towards the gate, Agent Smart looks back, out of fretful fear and noticed Dr. Emily Poole casually strolling down the run, behind him at a very slow pace with a mischievous smirk on her face and her hands stuffed in the front pockets of her pants. The look in her eyes told it all, she wasn't a psychologist, she was a bonafide psycho, who felt at home with her own kind. She was the lioness in a den full of lions.

Chapter Thirty - Six

June 8, 2020 11:41am Monday

USP Lee Jonesville, Virginia

At a breakneck speed, Spl. Agent Smart hastily burst into the administration office, and made his way towards the hall where the conference rooms were, and barged into the room like there was a pack of wolves, hot on his trail. He cleared the room instantly of everyone who wasn't a federal agent. He then began to recite the story of what had taken place back in the SHU just moments ago as sweat formed, beading on his forehead while he spoke in several failed attempts to convey the story to be correctly understood by the other agents. He had to halt himself just to gather his wits about himself, then slowly reiterate the murky details so the others could comprehend the bizarre situation that had taken place, which actually sent the decorated FBI veteran spiraling out of control in sheer cowardly panic to the point he now stood before them, a mess, tongue-tied and speaking gibberish.

Spl. Agent Drapper said, "Relax, Brad! Calm down and breathe for a minute."

Staring with his wild eyes bucking out of his skull, Spl. Agent Smart excitedly yelled back, "Calm down? I'm way past calming down at this point, Dennis. Get the FBI Director on the phone, now!" he demanded. "At once!" he adds, stressing his point, then turned to the other two agents standing by and said, "One of you, get the BOP Director on the line, immediately. That mother fucker! That crazy mother fucker that's in that cell right now is one diabolical creature! He's not no fucking spawn of satan, that crazy son-of-a-bitch is Lucifer himself!" Agent Smart vented with heated vehemence, spittle flying from his lips, as he spoke in a wildly angry tone, looking like a wild mutt contaminated with rabies.

With a representative from FBI Headquarters at the J. Edgar Hoover Building in Washington, on the line, Spl. Agent Drapper covers the mouthpiece with his hand and says to his partner, "Calm down and prepare to speak with the Assistant Director, Brad! Compose yourself and explain what took place down there, then ask to expedite the process for an immediate transfer of Mr. Mann!" When Agent Smart got full composure of himself, he took the cellphone and began his recitation of the earlier event that took place with Mannimal, in the SHU. When he had finished summarizing the totality of the incident, Assistant Director of FBI, Adam Tulane, along with Senior Investigative Agent, Special Agent Matthew Forrester, made the conclusion that Mannimal was indeed a potential threat to the safety and security of the staff and inmates at Lee County USP. Thus they made an urgent request to the Federal Bureau of Prisons, BOP, and the US Marshals, to transport Dominic Mannimal Mann, to the Super Max ADX facility in Florence, Colorado, immediately, as soon as the ink dries on the transfer papers.

Hanging up with the Director, after thanking him for taking his request at face value, and putting in a special call to ensure that

Mannimal, was removed from that facility at once. Spl Agent Smart leaned back in the high backed conference chair and ran his fingers through his hair in an overly dramatic fatigued and exasperated manner. Only then did he look at his partner and say, "Dennis, he's a monster, I swear I've never encountered anything like that young man in all my years." Pausing to think back, he felt a shiver resonate through his body from just momentarily rehashing what took place with Mannimal, sealed behind a locked steel door, only further intimidated him, when he said, "and guess what else?"

"What?" asked Agent Drapper.

"He actually told me that he was going to give me three things, and..."Reflecting back to what was said to him, he said, "He was going to give me a mind-bending headache, a life time of spine-tingling memories that will make me change my impression of how the human mind works, and lastly, that sorry-mentally-screwed son of a bitch said he was giving me three seconds to get out from the front of his cell before he made me second-guess my career choice! And when he finished, he said, if I stayed there, I'd wish I never met him! And Dennis, all three of the things he told me he was giving me, were actually given!" Spl. Agent Smart openly admitting that he wasn't just scared shitless of Mannimal, but that he was in fact, petrified to the point that he actually thought about putting in his resignation because he never again wanted to come into any sort of close contact with anyone even remotely close to the type of person Mannimal displayed himself capable of being.

As Spl. Agent Drapper sat hearing his partner of the last 8 years speak so uncharacteristically fearful of someone, he knew then that the man in question wasn't just a threat. He realized that Mannimal was a detrimentally unsound super predator that had the super natural ability to almost hypnotically manipulate and control anyone who came into contact with him. Seeing his partner so mentally bent out of shape and distraught, he understood that something was amiss here, more than he's care to imagine.

When he looked towards the doorway, because his attention was drawn to a slight sound and sudden flash of movement, from the corner of his peripheral, Spl. Agent Drapper caught a quick glimpse of Dr. Poole, as she casually breezed by. It wasn't her presence that captured his attention, it was the bitter, discomforting glare in her eyes as she strolled by the open threshold, he felt the hairs stand up on his arms, and goosebumps prickle upon his skin with the weirdly suspicious way she passed by.

Reverting his attention back toward Spl. Agent Smart, he was asked about the status of Detectives McNealson, York, and their little secretarial accomplice, Officer Spoon. Smart wanted to know, if in fact, any of them were detained yet for their roles in impeding a Federal Investigation by withholding information as well as possible evidence.

Spl. Agent Drapper answered, "Yeah, we've detained York and Spoon, but Detective McNealson is off the grid and has fled our dragnet." Only to have Spl. Agent Smart shoot back at him, saying, "Find him, and find him now! Use all available resources to get him under wraps!"

Rising from the table, gathering his case files and suit jacket from the chair back, Spl. Agent Smart said, "Let's go talk to Detective York. He's got some serious explaining to do," closing with the comment, "Our job here is done."

He swiftly started moving towards the door way to exit the conference room, with Spl. Agent Drapper and the two other accompanying agents silently in tow. Then, meeting up with Warden Bradford and Captain Spires to brief them on what they'd put into play with Mannimal's expedited transfer, he explained how they should expect, Dominic Mann, to be removed from their facility, as early as the following day.

Shaking hands, they bid one another farewell, as Warden Bradford issued his apologies that he couldn't be of more help, but he wished them well in cracking this hard case and capturing the person responsible for all of these recent cop killings. Nodding his head in appreciation, Spl. Agent Smart and his team made their way out of the facility towards the outer perimeter guard tower to retrieve their weapons. They needed to get to Fredericksburg quickly, where they had two individuals to interrogate and get whatever information or knowledge they had been hindered from receiving and hadn't been made privy to. Time wasn't on their side, and neither was patience, at this stage in the investigation.

Chapter Thirty - Seven

June 8, 2020 9:18pm Monday

Downtown Oklahoma City, Oklahoma

Exiting the ramp off Interstate 40, and steering the Grand Cherokee into the normal flow of traffic in the downtown area of Oklahoma City, Stranger was thoroughly immersed in the belittling banter between John and Lisa, as the two continued to throw verbal insults at one another, over the long drive from St. Louis to Oklahoma, when John belted out, "Hey Lisa, gotta joke for you..."

Not playing into John's little game of disrespectful antics, she didn't reply. But John was only trying to amuse himself and pass the time at Lisa's expense. He said, "Ok, there was these three roosters sitting on a fence awaiting the sunrise, then came along a plump, fat little hen named Lisa. As Lisa walks into the group of roosters and looked about them, Lisa, the fat hen said, 'I'm looking for a rooster'. Being that there was three handsome roosters already there, the first rooster named Stranger said, 'I'm a rooster, are you looking for me?' Stupidly, Lisa the fat hen just stared. Then a second rooster named Mike said, 'I'm a big strong rooster, she's looking for me!' Again, Lisa, the big fat hen stood there looking dumbfounded. Then, the third rooster, named John struts his stuff in a circle, and said, 'No, no, no, she's looking for me!' But once again, Lisa, the big fat dumb hen just stares at the three roosters with a silly grin on her face. When rooster-Stranger asked Lisa, the fat hen, 'which rooster will do for her?' Lisa, the fat hen leaps up onto the fence as the sunrise peeked above the horizon, puffed out her fat hen feathered chest and cawed out for the whole farm to hear, "ANY-COCK-WILL-DOOOO!"

As the whole car burst into laughter at John's little jib at Lisa, she counters with her own joke. "Ok, so you got jokes, huh? Well, here's one for you, there was once three friends, one was Deaf, one was Dumb, and one was Blind. Deaf couldn't hear how stupid he really sounded, the dumb one was so dumb, he couldn't understand, just how dumb he truly was, and the blind one, was too damn blind to see that his other two friends weren't his real true friends. It was the blind, led the deaf. The deaf being led by the dumb, and nobody was leading the dumb one around at all, which is why the three friends, continued to walk around in circles."

Then John finished her joke by saying, "because the dumb was only following behind a dog, that was chasing her own tail, you smart mouth bitch!"

Again the car breaks out in hysterical laughter while Lisa sat back fuming at how she became the butt of her own joke. With Stranger's attention diverted from the surrounding area, he didn't catch the police cruiser merge into the turning lane on the opposite side of the street, where traffic flowed in the opposite direction in which he was driving. As the Oklahoma City police officer made a turn and accelerated in their direction, Stranger wasn't paying any attention to his rearview until the officer quickly approached his rear bumper and kept a steady pace. As Stranger slowed down a little by taking his foot off the gas, and switching on the left turn signal to merge into the left lane in a failed attempt to shake the tail, the police cruiser merged left along with him, maintaining a safe distance to counterattack any evasive attempts to flee. Holding his composure under the slow rising severity of the situation that he was presently engaged in, Stranger made a left turn at the first available break in the traffic.

With the officer having to wait before following, due to the regular flow of traffic, Stranger used the break to quickly pull into a parking lot of a gas station, leaping out of the truck to enter the store and get a better advantage. Now, he can reassess the options, when very creepily, the police cruiser eased just past the store front window, while customers were pouring in and out of the busy establishment. With his hoodie pulled over his nappy dreads, Stranger remained poised, hiding in plain sight amongst the other paying customers, that he doesn't even fret or show any signs of nervousness, when Mike comes and stands next to him in the cashier line, and says, "He's passed, but I think we need to recon the area first, Slim, before moving that truck."

Nodding his head in silent approval, he then steps to the counter and pulls out a $20 dollar bill and asked for Newport 100s and paid for two hot dogs and the Ruffles Sour Cream and Cheddar chips that he had quickly grabbed when he entered the store and turned down the chip isle, to take up the viewpoint where he could observe and not be seen by the police who had followed him into the parking lot.

Once he paid the cashier and received his change in return, Stranger asked if they had a bathroom. He was given a key and told the location. Snatching the key from the counter, he exited with Mike at his side, prompting him to glance around and seek out the officer's location, only to shift his eyes momentarily and spy the officer sitting across the street, parked in a secluded area, staring towards the front of the store, at what could only be watchfully seeking out who was driving the Grand Cherokee, Stranger presumed.

He opened the bathroom door, closing it behind him. Then, he took his gloves from his back pocket and placed the stolen Kimber Pro Carry II .45 ACP on top of the toilet tank lid and covered his face with his black biker mask. Snatching up the fire arm and switching off the safety, he chambered a hollow tip round into the firing chamber by professionally cocking back the slide and readying the firearm for a prompt discharge once the five pounds of delicate pressure was placed on the trigger for easy and efficient extermination of the lurking officer.

Upon ducking through the restroom door, Stranger slipped out of sight at the rear of the building and climbed over the wooden privacy fence that separated the station gas from the building behind, which was now empty of cars or witnesses. Landing in a hunched position, Stranger eased along the fence line to remain concealed from view and waited at a steep angle across the street from the parked police cruiser. When the coast was clear of any passing vehicles, Stranger readied himself, but paused when he sensed a single car approaching from just 50 yards away. At the precise moment the car was unknowingly lumbering past, Stranger took off in a crouched sprint toward the waiting police officer, using the passing car as a shield of cover as he crossed the street with the Kimber .45 in his hand. He approached the drivers side window at a blinding speed, where he unleashed four tightly grouped blasts through the open window into the officer's temple, cheek and jawbone, sending the cop's upper torso tumbling over into the passenger seat from the powerful impact of the .45 caliber slugs that just rearranged the configuration of his face.

Opening the driver's side door, Stranger removed the officer's Sig Sauer P220 .45 and snatched the shield from his uniform shirt, placing the two items inside the hoodie pouch where he also removed the St. Louis K-9 Officer Vernon O'Connel's badge, #5610. Repositioning the officer's face, he laid the badge on his forehead leveling the Kimber .45 barrel against the metal shield and pulling the trigger twice, ripping through the frontal lobe with two .45 caliber hollow tips, bursting out of the back of the head of Oklahoma City Police Officer Eugene Chase, badge #412.

Closing the driver's door when he was done and skittering away, back across the street, slipping into the darkness, only to come casually strolling back to the front of the gas station moments later. He still had the two hot dogs and a bag of chips he had purchased less than 5 minutes ago when he returned the restroom key, and climbed into the Grand Cherokee afterwards.

He started the truck and asked, "Anyone want any chips?" When no one answered, he shrugs his shoulders, peeling the aluminum foil open on one of the hot dogs and hungrily taking a bite, closing his eyes, and blowing a breath of anxiety relief from his nose as he ravishingly chews the hot dog with a joyous moan.

Backing out of the parking space, he turns on the radio to catch some tunes being that there was too much death in the air with the silence within the truck, added to the brutality that took place moments ago. Stranger was listening along to a hiphop song when the urgent breaking news tone beeped, sounding to alert civilians of news that was meant for prompt public knowledge.

The broadcaster announced the widespread national alert, a broad smile creeped into his face, as he slowly shook his head in contemplative approval. Knowing what he knew, if he was a betting man, he would bet the horse, the farm, and his last bottom dollar, that things were seriously about to turn for the worse. Because now, Hell's Gates were fully wide open, with all Hell breaking loose.

Chapter Thirty - Eight

June 8, 2020 8:15pm Monday

I-95, Virginia

Riding along the Interstate 95, with Spl. Agent Drapper browsing through file folders alongside him, Spl. Agent Smart's cell phone chimes and he activates the phone to speaker mode, when he saw that the call was from Spl. Agent Goldfield. Tiredly, he answered, "Hey, Cynthia, what's up?" sounding like he was a tiresome wreck and in need of some rest and some moment of peace of mind.

Spl. Agent Goldfield and Maddox had split up the investigation file and taken to investigating the homicide that happened in Louisville, Kentucky which is also connected to the Jonesville, Virginia massacre being that the decapitated head of one of the correctional officers, a James Lee Davenport was found at the scene of where another police officer was stripped of his life and dignity, at the hands of their suspects, whom they don't even have a definitive description of or any factual information that can shed light on who this person, or persons could actually be.

When Agent Goldfield revealed that they weren't in Louisville any longer, but actually investigating three more recent homicides of Chicago, Illinois police officers, which were also connected to the Jonesville massacre, because of the three remaining decapitated heads were being left in a deplorable manner, at each of the horrendous scenes. Spl. Agent Smart thought better of inquiring as to how the heads were left when Spl. Agent Goldfield said, "The sick bastard, viciously ripped open the abdomens of each victim, from the belly buttons to chest plate, with some sort of jagged serrated blade and pushed a decapitated head face up deep into the stomach, after he had removed all their internal organs, and tossed them about like some discarded trash."

She summarized the scenes without trying to churn her own stomach with the gory details, but she definitely knew that the man or men they were after, were playing for keeps by the way he was moving like an unseen bandit and committing insane acts of despicable proportions on the law officers of our nation.

As Spl. Agent Smart mentally rehashed all that had taken place since the very start of this investigation in Fredericksburg, only finding out it began with an undercover drug task force detective, Richard Montgomery, in Washington, D.C. Blowing out an exasperated breath as he started to inform Agent Goldfield and Maddox of his intentions to interrogate two officers who were keys in the door of this case being kicked wide open, and how he had them detained and in search of another that was possibly the connecting key to opening this door.

Spl. Agent Drapper's cell phone buzzed. Lifting it to answer while staring out of the windshield at the passing traffic, he sat there taking in what was being said by the caller.

A few seconds later, a look of startled revelations sprung to the face of Drapper, and slowly he turned to look in the direction of Spl. Agent Smart with a perplexing and astonished look upon his face, before stuttering out his words in a soft, timidly scared voice.

Agent Smart looks at his partner with confusion scrunching his brow, and said, "What's up, Dennis? Why you looking like you've seen a ghost?"

Only then, he heard a reply that he wasn't quite prepared for, when Agent Drapper stuttering, said, "We...we...Go back! Brad, go back-go-go back-"

Agent Smart cut in, asking, "Go back where, Dennis?" yelling at his partner with a tiresome anguish traced in his tone.

"He's gone, Brad! He's..." stated Agent Drapper.

Not understanding what was being said to him, Smart yelled, "WHO'S GONE?"

Handing the phone to his partner to hear for himself, Agent Drapper slammed dejectedly back into the passenger seat and closed his eyes, when suddenly, Agent Smart yelled, "What!" And jammed his foot down on the break pedal, veering uncontrollably as their SUV crossed through unoccupied lanes, stopping short of plunging down a hillside on the right side of the highway emergency shoulder.

With smoke wafting the air, and panic rushing in their muscles, Agent Smart bowed his head against the steering wheel in quiet prayer and with a single tear streaming down his cheek. He whispered, "Dear God, this can't be happening..."

Chapter Thirty - Nine

June 9, 2020 12:36am Tuesday

Spotsylvania, Virginia

Pushing through the cubicles with a purposeful walk, Detective McNealson comes to a stop at an office that read, 'Arson Detective Joseph Dabney' on the door name plate.

Pausing to collect himself, Vince lightly taps on the door, hearing Det. Dabney within, clamoring about, when he said, "Come in!" unbeknownst to him whom was actually knocking at his door. He was completely taken aback when the office door sprung open and Det. McNealson waltzed into the small cubbyhole of an office, saying, "Joe, good afternoon," staring intently at the Detective with an unsuspecting smirk on his face. He helped himself to one of the old stiff-backed office chairs stationed in front of his desk, meant for invited guests to sit in. But, McNealson wasn't invited, nor was he expected when he entered the office. This could be seen on the face of Dabney, as he sat behind his office desk with a frightful grimace plastered as his facial expression.

Only then did he inquire in a tone of contempt, "And what the fuck do you want, detective?" making sure it was apparent that there was definitely some disdainful hostility noticeably radiating off of him with a loathsome glow. Raising his eyebrows in shock, when hearing the detective boldly speaking to him like he wasn't as scared as a little coward mouse.

Taking a second to garner his mentals to dismiss the way he

was spoken to, Det. McNealson smirked deviously at the detective and said, "Now, Joe, is this any way to talk to colleagues who are in cahoots to further advance one another's careers?" posing this question to cement the fact that they started their union on the premises of stepping up the ladder of ranks and successfully solving a murder that has actually turned into a national threat of serial murders.

Detective Dabney sat glowering at McNealson, his mind reeling with cluttered thoughts of why was he sitting face to face with a man that he had no intention of ever contacting again since having their clandestine meeting in the secluded parking lot at the mall, several counties away from where they now sat.

Finally, Dabney relented and stated, "First off, we ain't partners, Secondly, we ain't friends either. Third, I was never in 'cahoots' with you or your partner when it came to breaking the law, and last, but surely not least, I don't want any parts of this investigation, nor have I had any dealings with the li... with the likes of someone like you," Dabney heatedly said, as he stammered his last words, trying to relay the message loud and clear that he wasn't going to be entangled in this web of deceit and lawless behavior.

Leaning forward, placing his forearms on his thighs, Det. McNealson tilts his head to the side and menacingly glares into the Detective's eyes, never breaking eye contact, in the extended time that lapsed before he spoke and said, in a low, threatening tone, "Look here, Dabney, I don't have to express the true seriousness of this situation being that it's apparent to both of us, that you are clamming up tight like frog pussy. But let's get one thing straight here, I'm not in the least bit afraid of being under reprimand for infringing on a few convicted criminals Civil Rights or bending few a rules for the greater good of capturing a serial cop killer. If anything, I'm gonna be considered a hero when I get this maniac strapped up to a lethal injection needle and I save countless blue lives in the course of my actions. I don't need your approval to continue this investigation. What I need is for your scary ass to remain hidden in this cubbyhole for a while and keep tightlipped about having any involvement in this investigation, seeing that you're a little tea pot and you may tip over and start pouring out shit that don't need to be spilled."

Smiling at the metaphoric jest, McNealson added, "Detective, this will get ugly, but I'm sure you get the gist of what I'm saying, and if you don't, you'll learn the hard way, I'm only gonna say this once, because I won't be here a second time, stand down, and act like nothing has taken place with us."

Rising from the seat, like the meeting was over, McNealson demanded, "Is this understood?" Spooked into compliance, Dabney briskly nodded his head as his droopy jowls shook like that of a lazy basset hound.

Without ever looking back, McNealson smoothly exited the office and headed toward the cluster of tightly bunched cubicles and made his way through. With the office door sitting wide open, Dabney sat nervously astounded by the inferred threats he'd just been jarred by, when he had finally contemplated his options, he came to only one conclusion.

Quickly picking up the receiver his office phone, he dialed a number that was scrawled out on his desk top blotter. Waiting for the phone call to be answered, he drummed his left fingers on the desk top, only to stop and swipe his profusely sweating forehead. When the receiving end was picked up, Dabney said shakily, "Hello? This is Arson Detective Joseph Dabney of Spotsylvania County Police Department. I'd like for you to patch me through to a..." looking at the desk blotter to find the name, "A Special Agent Bradley Smart, please." Hearing that Agent Smart was not available at the time, Dabney asked if they could pass on a message and gave his contact information also.

Upon hanging up with the FBI's Special Crimes Unit secretary, Dabney knew he was going to have to wiggle his way out of this vice grip, and he had time now to figure out what he was going to say to save his own ass and his career. Slumping back into the leather desk chair, he began to conjure up his exit strategy.

Staring off into the busy office area that was buzzing with activity and awaiting the return call so he could clear his name of any wrongful involvement in their Federal investigation, Dabney knew he was opening a gas can and flicking the flint of a lighter. While doing so, he was setting himself on fire in a attempt of trying to remain unscathed. The odds weigh heavily against him, but he was going to try anyways. He has to try. McNealson has left him with no other choice.

Chapter Forty

June 8, 2020 6:30pm Monday
USP Lee, Jonesville, Virginia

Standing on an uneven balance beam of disharmonious conflict while battling between being morally correct, and a personal infatuation that is being guided by a mental silk leash of beguiling allure, it hurts. Storming down the hall and coming to an abrupt stop in front of a steel door, then standing there, staring at the self contained face that held no tension or obvious fear, hurt more. Then, all of a sudden calling out towards the heat tempered glass, behind which was darkness, a result of the covered lights in the cell, Dr. Poole yelled out, "Dominic! Dominic! Come to this door right now, mister!"

Demanding, as if she was reprimanding a child. When there was no reply to her demand, she stepped closer, stared into the cell and said in a lowered tone, "Mannimal, please come to the door, it's imperative, this is no time for our little cat and mouse games, do you hear me?" Asking this time, and not demanding anything of a man who is under no obligation to move by a command or demand.

Slowly approaching the window from the darkened shadows of the cell, Mannimal stood, sweating with his shirt off, exposing his ebony carved body. Standing 6'2 at 205lbs, he has powerfully ripped muscle mass and a very youthful face at the age of 25. Mannimal wasn't just an avid workout enthusiast, he was in survival training.

It started when he had first come to the federal penitentiary for a capital murder of one guilty verdict but at least 12 other suspected bodies could be attributed to his work. The victims had either not adhered to his orders, or getting in the way when he is in the middle of committing whatever fiendish crime he was committing. It wasn't until the correctional officers at the different facilities throughout the penal system thought it was a good idea to partake in the politics of crime and punishment, by trying to assault him and use the act of force to bend him into forced submission by accepting their physical punishment at random times as a part of his 9 consecutive life sentences. He pleaded guilty to keep himself from getting the needle, so instead will live out the remainder of his life in prison.

But seven years later, Mannimal has been shipped to seven different yards and charged with over 20 counts of serious staff assaults, when he returned the many favors they had inflicted on him. Mannimal became known as the bone collector, due to his bewildering need to snap the bones of the staff members, just to hear their screams, yells and pleas for their lives.

It was amazing to him how all those hulking, large C.O.s were so brazen in numbers, but when you snatch their hand when trying to handcuff you, break their thumbs or clamp down on their knuckles and squeeze with a powerful death grip, on those enormous hands they so boldly wanted to beat other convicts with, they fall to pieces and drop down to their knees and become very compliant and docile. This is why Mannimal worked out three times a day for four hours a session, six days a week, because he knew those cowards were suiting up at any moment, and were gonna come marching down that hall, in full body armor and riot gear, to try and manhandle him.

But they learned their lesson about fucking with him months ago, when they tried that little six man breech tactic at 2:00am in the morning, only to realize that concussion bombs no longer fazed him. Mannimal has been sprayed with OC chemical agent so many times that he was immune to the spray's reaction to his skin and he knew how to counter the spray's extreme reaction upon the visual and respiratory systems. Mannimal was considered the DEFCON one, Navy Seals Commanding Officer Platoon Leader of Convicts.

So, instead of posing him any further threat, it was best to just leave him alone, unless one of those daring staff members wanted to take 45 days paid leave, for a job related injury, and be either, sitting at home on the couch rehashing over the event of how they got their arm in a cast for the next 6 to 8 weeks, or laid up in a hospital bed, with all of their extremities snapped at the joints, completely ensconced in a full body cast. It all depended on how much disrespect Mannimal felt they've displayed towards him, by not paying homage to the man, who is allowing them to go home to their loved ones at night.

Now, standing face to face, Mannimal snarled lowly and asked, "And what do you want! Emily?"

Staring into his piercing golden hazel eyes, Dr. Poole used her key to open the chuckhole and said, "Give me your arm."

Hesitantly, Mannimal backed away from the door and said, "My momma said there's three things you don't trust; a man who doesn't wear a mustache, a bitch who bleeds for 5 days and don't die, and a mutha fuckin' police! So, which one are you? The rat, the snake, or the pig?" Mannimal steps closer to hear her answer.

Taking in the severity of the question, Dr. Poole quickly said, "I'm the bitch that bleeds for 5 days and don't die, but at this very moment, this bitch is all you have and time's running out for you!" Following his intuition, Mannimal eased his arm out of the hole, and passively gazed upon into Dr. Poole's face, wincing when he unknowingly felt the burning pinch of the needle puncturing his skin, only to subsequently fall unconsciously to the floor, not hearing the chuckhole slam shut as he collapsed.

Looking into the cell, she began her Academy Award winning performance as she convincingly yelled, "Mr. Mann, get up! Mr. Mann, are you the okay?" she pushed the inquiry as if, to further play out the performance to be believable to whoever was within earshot of the cell, when she pressed the duress button on her walkie talkie, and yelled for the SHU's D-Range officer, saying, "Hurry, hurry! We have one unresponsive! Come quick! Cell 235 is unresponsive!" The approaching C.O.s came running down the hall with their heavy boots pounding the grey cement floor echoing off the hall's cinder block walls, as their keys jingled, smashing against their thighs. The four men came into view running and looked into the window, unable to see inside due to the lights being covered, to be able to make an assessment as to open the door or not, to check on the inmate's status. They deemed it necessary to contact the facility's Institutional Duty Officer (IDO), to get the decision as to what they were supposed to do, being that the inmate in question was none other than Mannimal, 'The Madman-Bone Collector'. He was supposedly, laying unconscious upon the cell's concrete floor, but they couldn't positively say, if in fact, he was or if this is some sort of ruse to inflict physical harm to another staff member.

Shinning a flashlight upon Mannimal's collapsed body, the SHU lieutenant, with the IDO's permission, made the call to pop the sliding door. The officers cautiously moved in, readying themselves for a possible ambush, but there was no movement as Mannimal laid sprawled out on the floor with a faint pulse beating from the carotid artery in his neck. Frantically, the C.O.s called for a gurney.

Dr. Poole detailed what she had witnessed when she approached, in a professional manner, offering her assistance, saying, "That man is not to be removed from that cell without restraints, I don't care if he flatlines in there, he's a violent offender and the policies and procedures for such should be adhered to the T," she continued her charade by adding, "That means leg shackles as well."

Briskly moving about to secure him in restraints and placing his body the upon a gurney for transport, the evening nursing staff, made the necessary calls to have an emergency transport of Dominic Mann to the emergency room, with the ambulance idling in the shipping and receiving bay, awaiting the arrival of the emergency response paramedics to return to the vehicle with Mannimal in tow.

The IDO stressed that there was definitely going to be an armed escort and a staff member in the ambulance with him, when Dr. Poole said, "I'm a licensed firearm specialist-and also the head psychologist who should be accompanying him, to ensure that he is treated correctly and to make sure that there is someone there to reassure him that everything is going to be fine. He's going to probably be very combative and confused through this traumatic experience, being that he is very distrustful of everyone."

As two transport C.O.s lumbered down the hallway behind the hurried stretcher that was now rolling out of medical to the bay where the ambulance was stationed for transport, Dr. Poole said, "Officer Rhodes, I'm going to be riding along with the inmate, in the back, just in case he wakes up on the way to the hospital, I need one of you," pointing to both Officer Rhodes and Meade, "to secure the black box on his restraints, under no circumstances is Mr. Mann's condition to be taken lightly due to the fact that he's unconscious!" Calling the shots, like a professional physician caters to the wellbeing of any patient in their care, especially one as dangerously unpredictable as Mannimal actually is.

With weapons checked, the two burly C.O.s sat tightly in the front seats of the Ford transport van, as the stretcher is hoisted into the back of the ambulance and Dr. Poole and the assistant paramedic, climbs in and slams the door shut behind them. A few moments later, the rear light turned off and the ambulance shift into gear and speedily pulls away with emergency blue and red strobe lights flashing, as they departed.

Checking the unconscious patient for any failed signs of life, the paramedic makes the conclusion that he should call into the emergency room to give them a heads up on their status and ETA. Climbing to the front cab, he grabs the microphone to the CB and scanner.

Dr. Poole seizes the opportunity and pulls a syringe filled with 20cc's of epinephrine, an adrenaline hormone that is used as a stimulant to counteract heart failure. Sneakily, she slips the tip of the needle into Mannimal's bulging veins and pushed the plunger down, releasing the stimulant into his bloodstream, waking him up within seconds. Lifting the handgun that was loaned to her by the facility Weapons Officer, Dr. Poole pointed the gun at the back of the unsuspecting paramedic's head, while he continued to speak into the CB radio, issuing the status and ETA. When the paramedic was finished, he turned around to check on Mannimal's status and sat staring into the barrel of the Glock .40. Raising his hand in surrender, Dr. Poole tossed a set of handcuffs on his lap and softly said, "Cuff your wrists and lock it to the wheel base of the stretcher. Now!" Quickly doing so, he kept his head ducked down as he was told to do.

Unlocking the master lock and undoing the waist chain from the black box, Dr. Poole moved with very efficient speed and uncuffed Mannimal's handcuffs and leg shackles. When the task was complete and Mannimal was completely free of any restraints. He sat and turned to look over his shoulder to see if the ambulance driver was aware of what had transpired. He wasn't. Turning to face Dr. Poole, Mannimal just stared a villainous glare and held his hand out palm open, silently requesting the gun from Emily's hand to be placed there without hesitation. Instantly, and without second guessing herself, she laid it in his palm lovingly and smiled to him saying, "As you command."

Leaping from the stretcher, Mannimal pushed forward to the front cab, but not before using the butt of the Glock to knock the fearful paramedic unconscious with a solid blow to the base of the neck. Climbing into the cab, Mannimal leveled the barrel to the temple of the driver and began slowly issuing orders, that he demanded to be followed. Slowing to a stop at a red light, the Ford transport van that C.O.s Rhodes and Meade were tailing the ambulance in, closed tightly on the bumper awaiting the light to change, when it suddenly hit Officer Meade, who was sitting in the passenger seat. "Why are we waiting at the red light?" Looking up from his iphone, momentarily, when Officer Rhodes replied, "All this is overtime anyway, so if Mannimal dies on the way, they'd be doing the world a big favor," laughing at his comment with a slight chuckle.

As the ambulance began to pull off at the light, it did so at an accelerated rate, with the van keeping pace at 75 MPH, tightly tailing the bumper. Abruptly, the brakes of the ambulance were suddenly applied, causing the speeding transport van to collide with the rear bumper of the ambulance at an unstoppable force, bringing the van to a crashing stop as the frontend was totally smashed when it hit head-on, releasing the airbags into the faces of both officers, who were jarred senseless and left discombobulated.

Two loud cracks sound off in the distance but neither officer could muster any muscle to move due to the sharp impact of the vehicles and the head-snapping blow in which the air bags rendered them helpless. The front driver side door was snatched open and four resonating rounds from the Glock .40 was released into the van, penetrating the heads of both C.O. Harlan Rhodes and Noel Meade, at close range.

Climbing inside the van to relieve both deceased officers of their firearms, Mannimal noticed their federal work badges with their faces and names on them and seized both badges and swiftly climbed out of the cab and ran back to the driver side of the ambulance, jumping in. He placed the truck in drive and pulled off with Dr. Poole riding shotgun, staring emotionless out of the windshield. Reaching over, flipping switches, Mannimal cut off the strobing emergency lights and eased away from the scene with only one witness to this whole madness.

Dr. Poole, who was not just an accomplice, but the brains behind it all. She couldn't imagine herself not being able to see Mannimal and deal with him on a regular basis, if he was transferred to the ADX in Florence, Colorado. So, she made that dangerous choice, and she was definitely ready to live or die with it. Turning to look in Mannimal's direction, searching for those tempting gold eyes, Dr. Poole asked, "Mannimal...do you trust me now?" Without a word spoken in return, Mannimal looked in her direction, as he maneuvered the ambulance through the streets at a normal speed, only to turn his attention back to driving the truck. Taking that as a yes, she smiled and quietly praised herself for finally being able to prove to Mannimal after all this time that she was definitely a trusted ally. She then said, "Go to my house, we have to get a few things, and dispose off this truck, I've been secretly planning this moment since the first day I met you, when you lovingly ripped my heart out of my chest and took my breath away."

Following her directions, Mannimal drove, remaining absolutely silent...speechless really, that he was in the streets again, about to unleash his terror. Thinking to himself, "Who said God doesn't answer prayers, or was it an act of Satan who had opened Hell's Gates?" It didn't matter which, as long as he was out... He would finish what he started years ago, but this time, he will do it at grand proportions.

Chapter Forty - One

June 9th, 2020 11:10am Tuesday

Vigilantly pushing the Yukon Denali down the highway with his train of restless thoughts drifting in and out of a vast bad land of evil possibilities, Spl. Agent Smart broke, the ensuing silence. "Say, Dennis, what do you think provoked those three officers to withhold their findings in this case?"

Shrugging listlessly, unable to answer the question he was asked, Spl. Agent Drapper continued to brood over the dire situation that was now developing to further complicate their investigation. They pulled into the parking lot of the Fredericksburg Police Department and filed into the front lobby, meeting up with the agents that had detained Detective York and Officer Spoon.

Once they were brought up to speed, Spl. Agent Drapper asked the detaining agents if there was anyone sitting on Det. McNealson's home and workplace to bring him in for questioning. The agent in charge detailed the strategy in which they set up a perimeter around the job and residence of McNealson. Spl. Agent Smart was pleased to hear that the agent systematically organized a corralling lasso to efficaciously detain the detective, where they would begin the process of prying open their strong box of secrets and placing the three indictments for conspiracy to impede a federal investigation by acquiring a federal warrant under false pretenses, conspiracy to commit perjury under federal oath, and conspiracy to withhold evidence in an ongoing federal investigation.

When Spl. Agents Smart and Drapper barged into the interrogation room of Officer Spoon, they could see that she had already been crying and hasn't yet understood the hole that she had dug herself into, playing a role in the two detectives' little game of catch me if you can. After questioning her for 45 minutes, they came to believe that she truly had no answers to their questions and told her she would be needing a lawyer, because although she knew nothing effectively helpful, she still played a part in this little charade of theirs. Leaving through the door and closing it behind them while she sat handcuffed to the steel table baffled by the realization that she was going to jail for doing something as minor as accepting a call and misleading the caller, by pretending to be their supervisor, and forging a few federal documents. Hanging her head in perilous defeat, Officer Spoon began to weep sorrowful apologies.

When the two federal agents burst into interrogation room #2, they knew this was going to be an uncooperative witness by the way he sat. With a grin sprawled across his face, Detective York cheerfully said, "To what do I owe this visit?" staring at Spl. Agents Drapper and Smart, as if he didn't have a care in the world.

When they revealed their findings and began making indictment threats, York said in a cool indifferent tone, "Well, it seems I'm knee-deep in a shit hole and there's only one thing to do here, agents," lowering his head, he closed his eyes and said, "The only thing I can tell you is...I'm gonna need to speak with my attorney. You're barking up the wrong tree, agents, and if my calculations are correct, isn't it about time for your suspect to be..." Staring off to the ceiling he finishes, saying, "Ahh- Hah! There he goes now, Bam! He just murdered another cop. So, while you're here pussyfooting around with us, you could be chasing the man who's got you running around chasing your own tail. My suggestion to you two federal agents whatever-your-names-are, is, stop picking around the problem and *solve* the fucking problem. The solution doesn't sit here with us, you need to capture that man who has you spinning your wheels in a ditch, stranded in your federal investigation with no possible leads, and no possible way of capturing him at this time, you're just grasping at straws and you're still getting the shit end of the stick! Now, if you would please, allow me to call my attorney, I am invoking my Constitutional right at this time to remain silent, which is protected under the Fifth Amendment. It's called, pleading the Fifth, bitches!"

Falling dead silent, Detective York, sat boldly staring at the two agents in their eyes with a vehement scowl on his face. Only then, to demand of the agents in a sarcastic tone, "And yet you still stand here, why?"

§§§§

Coming down the main street, about to turn into Fredericksburg Police Department employee parking lot, Det. McNealson noticed that there were a few too many federal vehicles stationed at all of the different entryways. Getting the premonition that something suspicious was going down, McNealson continued to drive down the street passing the entrance and parking diagonally from the headquarters, in a fast food restaurant parking lot on the other side of the street. Detective McNealson dialed York's phone, trying to get a line on what was making him nervous, but to no avail. Matt didn't answer the phone. When McNealson called into the office to speak with Officer Spoon, Homicide's department secretary, a volunteer replacement officer answered, saying that Officer Spoon was not available and asked how she could direct his call, only to state that Det. York wasn't available either, when he had asked for him instead. She began asking who she was speaking with. He answered her with a confident swagger, "I'm Detective McNealson," as if he was well known.

The phone line went silent, as if she'd covered the mouthpiece with her hand or put him on mute. When she came back, she asked, "Where are you right now?"

Sensing that the question was a weird inquiry for someone that he had never met, he answered with a question of his own. "Why? Who wants to know?"

Unsuspecting that there was going to be another question thrown back in her direction, the secretary said, "I'm umm, I'm ah..." trying to figure out how she was going to get the detective to reveal his location, she quickly lied, saying, "I mean, because Detective York wanted to know."

Realizing that there was definitely something wrong with this picture, McNealson said, "Tell him to give me a call and where is Spoon? Better yet, put whoever's in charge on the phone, agent and tell them to put you in acting classes before they put you in the field, you're lousy at it, you're not talking to no rookie here, the gig is up..."

The agent still tried to maintain the cover, saying, "I have no idea what you're talking about, detective."

But when McNealson asked to speak with another detective, he was derailed and put on hold again. This caused him to conclude that his suspicions were correct. Calling the one and only person he knew would give it to him raw and uncut, he called the Captain. Upon hearing what the Captain said, it solidified that he was in deep shit, and possible indictments were coming down from above. When the Captain said, "you better have a fish on the hook with this one, and I mean a mutha fuckin' hump back whale, not no damn guppie. They got Matt and Shelly, and now they trying to put a lid on this jar of bullshit by getting you! You're on your own, and I hope this phantom was worth it." Without waiting for a reply, he hung up.

McNealson sat in his truck, and began to ponder the what ifs, but came to the conclusion that since he started this, he was going to see it through, or all of this would be for nothing. He was definitely going all in on this one hand, but he also knew that he was gambling on his ass. His only hope was that he caught something on the river...

Chapter Forty - Two

June 8, 2020 7:20pm Monday

Jonesville, Virginia

After ditching the ambulance in a secluded woodland and briskly fleeing on foot, the two entered into the rear of a house where Dr. Poole led Mannimal through the kitchen and into the living room, telling him to feel at home. She merrily moved about, like they weren't now America's Most Wanted top two fugitives with an All Points bulletin out for the escape from a Federal Maximum Security Penitentiary and the murder of four people. Mannimal stood transfixed in the darkness and said, "Emily, this isn't some sort of game you're gonna walk away from unscathed."

Dr. Poole lightheartedly said, "We'll be fine, just let me get a few things and the money I've been saving, then we can leave and start our new life together." Reaching for his hand and taking him in her warm delicate grip, she told him to relax and formulate a plan for them as she leaned in and quickly pecked his lips. Looking into his eyes, she said, "Oh gosh, you're so fuckin' sexy! Those eyes of yours are simply breathtaking!" Giddy with radiant glee, Dr. Poole spun around and joyously bounded up the stairs, leaving Mannimal to himself.

When he began to poke about the downstairs, and open a door to the garage, he saw that there was a burgundy GMC Envoy stored there, and he continued to glance about, closing the door. He went into the kitchen and opened the refrigerator. Checking the contents, he reached in and grabbed a handful of seedless grapes and an Aquafina water bottle. Twisting the cap off and raising it to his mouth, he gulped down the whole bottle without taking a breather. When he finished, he tossed the empty bottle in the trashcan and reached for another, only taking a quick sip this time around. As he moved about the kitchen, eating grapes, he began checking cabinets and pulling out drawers, not in search of anything in particular.

After thoroughly examining the kitchen and all of its contents, he made his way through the lavish dining room and back into the kitchen, where he located a bar stool and sat at the preparation counter attentively looking about, sitting in the dark. As his attention fell on items he thought he may need, gathering them up, he made his way back into the living room and sat on the couch, while Dr. Poole dilly dallied about upstairs. She called out to him, asking, "Hey, Dominic, have you come up with our plan yet? Where do you think we should go?" Speaking as if they were just going on a vacation on the spur of the moment. She went on to ramble about how she had family in the mountains of Colorado, as well as Texas. Bragging about her family wealth while she stuffed several suitcases full of miscellaneous items that weren't necessary for the trip.

Then she yelled out, "Mannimal, what do you think about me taking my hairdryer and-"

"Emily, you won't be needing no hairdryer," Mannimal stated, cutting off her words. "In fact, you're packing too much shit!"

Slowly easing up behind her and putting his hand on her hip and nuzzling her neck and ear with his nose, and thick masculine full lips.

Peeking over her shoulder, Mannimal appraised the content of the suitcases and said, "Baby, baby, baby...what's all these for? You know we on the run, right? This isn't some weekend romantic getaway and then we're back home, living like the regular average All American family. Yeah, we'll be on All American alright! We'll actually be on *All American's* television sets, as they display our mugshots and descriptions on all TV Sets, as American's Most Wanted is what's really about to happen."

Taking a moment to fully accept the uncompromising truth of their situation, Dr. Poole said, "'You're so right, this isn't how I imagined all this to be. I mean...I've had so many transfixed dreams about us being together. I don't even know how to feel, Dominic. My emotions are all over the place, and... this... this don't even feel real right now, with you standing in my bedroom, with your powerful hand softly touching my hip, as the heat pulsates from your exquisite physique. It arouses me to the point I'm boiling over with pure lust and you're so...so dominating!" Dr. Poole gushed over the apparent effect that Mannimal was having on her.

Leaning her head of auburn hair against Mannimal's stone chiseled chest, Dr.Poole hugged herself lovingly with her own arms, while Mannimal nuzzled his nose into her hair and inhaled the clean, refreshing scent of ocean breeze scented shampoo, and her intoxicating White Diamond perfume that she learned that

Mannimal liked so much. When she had dreamed of this day, she dreamed that they made intense, passionate love. Wanting to fulfill her dream of this day, Emily said, "Mannimal, make love to me. I've waited so long for this day, please, please take me and make me whole. I'm incomplete without you, Dominic. My whole world revolves around you."

Using a strong grip on her hip, Mannimal slowly turned her to face him as they stood face to face, at the foot of her California Queen-sized bed. Tilting her chin up to look at him in his eyes, Dr. Poole gasped a sharp intake of breath when she got caught in the seduction of those enchanting golden eyes.

Shaking on timid legs, she said, "Oh my God, Mannimal, I'm cumming on myself!" as her sweet nectar oozed down the insides of her thighs slickly.

Mannimal replied, "You ain't seen nothin' yet," beckoning her to remove her clothes and surrender herself completely to him.

Wasting no time, she quickly peeled off her shirt, unhooked her bra, and unbuttoned her dress slacks, allowing her pants and soaking wet blue lace bikini panties to shimmy down her legs. They fell at her feet in a pile of discarded cloth.

Stepping closer to Mannimal and allowing the totality of her naked warmth to mingle with his heated inferno of flesh, she basked in the glow of his ebony skin, and absorbed the illumination of the moonlight that shown brightly through the master bedroom window. She stood on her tippy toes and brought her lips to his, beginning to trace her tongue along his thick bottom lip, as

Mannimal stood like a mighty titan before her with his eyes trained deeply into her grey irises. She hungrily pushed her tongue into his tight-lipped mouth, and clumsily fumbled to push his orange prison pants and boxers down his tree-trunk-legs, removing his massive penis, still in a flaccid state. Unable to contain herself, she kissed him with more intense vigor while fondling his manhood with slow, manual stimulation, until he stood rigidly stiff and dangling thickly between his legs, halfway to his knee caps.

When she realized the size of his penis, and encircled her fist around his enormous base, Emily exhaled an astonished breath of air from her lips and begged, "Mannimal, please be gentle. I've never had anything in my life close to this size of yours and-"

With whirling speed, Mannimal clamped his powerful hands around her diminutive throat, cutting off her words in her vocal cords, snatching her almost weightless body off of her feet, where she was suspended in midair, trying desperately to pry Mannimal's suffocating grip from her neck, while tragically at a disadvantage.

Squeezing tighter, with his veins bulging painstakingly from his hands, all the way to his sculpted biceps, Mannimal continued to apply pressure until he heard the spinal cord collapse and a crushing crunch of tiny vertebrae being pulverized by his unimaginable power.

Dr. Poole's eyes held vacant as she lifelessly gazed back into Mannimal's golden orbs, only to be tossed upon the bed carelessly and flipped over onto her stomach and brutally ravished from behind.

Mannimal pounded forcefully into her vagina, tearing her vaginal walls to shreds after he taped three kitchen knives to his huge member. While he crammed his massive tool like a piston in her, he gruesomely used a large chopping knife he had taken from the kitchen to saw her head off, at the base of her neck, severing her brain stem. When the horrendous act was complete, Mannimal stood motionless, observing his handiwork. Then he removed the taped knives from his bloody, deflated penis, as he pushed all three knives simultaneously into Emily's anus, venomously saying, "I told you I don't trust nothing that bleeds for 5 days and don't die. Plus, you ain't loyal to no one, you gullible, naive bitch! I wish the fuck I *would* trust a bitch who's really a snake in disguise."

Setting her decapitated head on top of her lower back, facing the door, Mannimal collected the guns and ammo she had packed, the large amount of money she had been saving for this special day, and the keys to the burgundy Envoy sitting in her garage. He is truly proud of his first work of art here today as the other four bodies did not allow him to express himself artistically. When the garage door opened, Mannimal eased out of the driveway and pushed the button to close the door behind him, as he sped away into the night, leaving Dr. Emily Poole and her house, a blanket of complete silence.

Driving along the streets, Mannimal came to the area where the accident happened. A police officer flagged him by, as he looked at the scene where he had left the two C.O.s and two paramedics in exchange for his freedom. Now, Mannimal was unleashed again and he had no intentions of being put back in a cage. It would be over his dead body, and this was to be taken in literal terms.

Driving past the officer, he tilted his head in a kind of salute and smiled as he headed down the street, towards the interstate, leaving behind the beginning of a long trail of dead bodies, and unleashing a part two of his killing spree...

Chapter Forty - Three

June 9, 2020 12:40pm Tuesday

Fredericksburg, Virginia

Fed up with the antics that Det. York had defiantly put him through, Agent Smart stormed out of the interrogation room with Agent Drapper close at his heels. When he approached the agents that had been sitting on Spoon and York, he gave them explicit instructions to only allow York's lawyer meet with him and to place a hold against both of the officers until they could acquire a Grand Jury indictment for the three of the officers for their involvement in the conspiracy to falsify Federal documents, and obstruction of justice.

He then pushed further and said, "Also, seek a pliable judge who will give us a cease and desist order for the investigation files of all three officers in question and get on this immediately! We are wasting time and we're behind the ball on this one, call me when the indictments are in hand."

Without waiting for the agents to respond on whether or not they understood the orders, Agent Smart and Draper proceeded down the hall towards the lobby at a brisk pace, when Smart's phone rang.

Answering, Agent Smart was disappointed when he told Lead Investigator Matthew Forrester, that he was planning to head back to Lee County Penitentiary to look into the recent escape of a murderous individual he had just met with a day earlier.

Forrester admonished him, saying, "That case is none of your concern, it has its own US Marshal investigation team, and you're already assigned to a case that you and about ten other agents can't even seem to get a lead on, much less actually come close to solving. So, if you didn't get whatever information you were seeking from him, then you're definitely not going to get it out of him now! You're putting more eggs in your basket than you got the strength to carry. So, I'm gonna unload that burden for you. What I need for you and Agent Drapper to do, is detour this little wild goose chase you're on and leave that to the US Marshal's office. You two need to head down to Quantico and prepare to be airlifted to St. Louis, Missouri, where two more victims have been found in connection with these serial murders that seem to have us all stumble fucked, and twiddling our thumbs over. Agents Maddox and Goldfield will be there to brief you on their findings, they're headed there now and should be arriving.." He paused to calculate their ETA, "around 3pm Central Time. I expect you to get a handle on this case, and Smart, this is not a request, this is my expectation."

With hearing enough of the Big-me-Little-you, authoritative hoopla, Agent Smart stood, thoroughly fed up with the rambling ons of Agent Forrester. He sarcastically replied in response, "Yes, sir, I'll get right on that, right after I jump through these flaming hoops, and go fetch your morning paper, sir!"

Touching the end icon on the iPhone touchscreen, he disconnected and began to walk out of the lobby in a heated, deep reverie, as Drapper trotted alongside him. When they reached the

SUV, Spl. Agent Drapper said, "So, Brad, what's up now?"

"Plans have changed, Dennis, Poppa Smurf is sending us worker Smurfs into the woods again, and nothing's changed, more deaths, and from my take on the situation, whatever's taken place in St. Louis, it's probably going to be a gruesome one. So, let's prepare ourselves and head to Quantico, they're awaiting our arrival for transport to Missouri." Climbing into the truck's front seat, Smart signaled the two accompanying agents to pull out and follow.

Clearing security protocols at the heavily guarded checkpoint booth of Quantico's Marine Base, they arrived at the landing strip and were greeted by Airforce Corporal Bernard Rowe.

Smart's phone rang again, and he answered in annoyance, "Yeah, what is it?"

Hearing the caller on the other end detail reasons for calling, Agent Smart snaps his fingers to get Drapper's attention and replied to the caller after some time, "Okay, so let me get this right, you're calling to alert me of an investigation that you partook in and didn't have any clue as to the illegalities or obstructing justice, while in furtherance of hindering a Federal investigation by withholding potential connections of possible suspects, when there are cops being murdered by this psychopath? And right now, you're only bringing this to my attention due to the fact-not to help us catch this suspect-but to clear yourself of any involvement with Detectives McNealson and York, and under the pretense that McNealson also made viable threats, while you are under the assumption that he might even kill you if you don't remain invisible and as quiet as a church mouse?"

Hearing the reply and stuttered excuses, Agent Smart said, "Ugh, Detective Dabney, is it? Are you willing to testify in front of a grand jury against McNealson and York, as well as, and Officer Spoon?"

Not having to wait long for his answer, Agent Smart said, "Great then, I'll be sending over two agents to place you in temporary WITSEC custody until McNealson is detained and the Grand Jury is convened. I will also need your complete cooperation, and your case notes on everything you dug up on the potential suspects, since you're claiming it was your fine detective work that got this ball rolling. I'll be sending the agents to you, so have all of the files and case notes prepared. You'll be federally escorted from Spotsylvania's Police Department under federal custody, and you will need to submit to a polygraph examination as well as give a full statement as to your involvement in their investigation. Under no circumstances is there to be any shady business from you or you'll be indicted alongside those other three, is that understood?" When the deal was verbally sealed, Agent Smart told Det. Dabney to sit tight, and not to leave the office or contact anyone else and that the agents were on their way shortly.

Hanging up, Smart turned to look in the direction of the passenger seat, where Drapper sat listening and said, "Send Starsky and Hutch behind us to Spotsylvania County Police Department and put a Detective Dabney into WITSEC custody, and add witness tampering and conspiracy to commit murder to the indictments of McNealson, York and Spoon."

Chapter Forty - Four

June 9, 2020 4:20pm Tuesday

In Flight, Quantico, Virginia

Sitting in the plush seats of a Federal Transport Jet, right after take off, Agent Smart received a call from US Marshal Clayton VanDoren and was immediately flabbergasted by the news he was hearing, the details of how the scene of the accident occurred and how the two ambulance paramedics and two transport officers lives had been taken. It is a baffling puzzle that was going to take some time to put together, especially without any witnesses to help piece it together for them.

VanDoren went on to disclose the intricate details of how they entered the house of the prison's Psychology Director Dr. Emily Poole, they were still reeling with queasy stomachs of the scene that Dominic Mann had left behind, saying that the man was a demented lunatic. They would have never imagined any human was capable of the madness that they were witnesses to.

Only then did VanDoren give Agent Smart some helpful clues when he revealed that in the bedside nightstand drawer there were several notebooks that were obviously used as diaries by Dr. Poole. In their close examination of these memoirs, were detailed accounts of Dr. Poole's infatuation with Dominic Mann. VanDoren said she wasn't just enthralled with that man, like she was an insatiable devout follower in an imaginary cult, she was summoning every fiber of her being to keep her from falling under his control while in his presence. The Doctor was in need of psychological evaluation herself. Well, it was too late for that now anyway. She had been transfixed and wantonly unbalanced with eccentric lust and love, intertwined, taking a chokehold of her senses. She was a walking mental nutcase, posing as a Penitentiary Psychology Doctor, in charge of some of the most violent felons to walk the face of the Earth.

It wasn't until Marshal VanDoren began to rehash findings that were located in several of the diaries that caught Agent Smart's attention. When it was mentioned that there were several individuals that were mental objects of her desire and that she had detailed explicit emotions and lustful intentions that were never acted upon, but definitely imagined in very elaborate illusions. The descriptions were so raunchy and graphic, "the diaries could be sold out if they ever made their way into mainstream books stores under intense erotica," stated VanDoren.

Upon hearing this revelation, Smart asked, "Did she mention any other names? Other than Mannimal?"

"Yeah!" answered VanDoren. "Several at least, but the two that stuck out the most was this escapee Mannimal, and another mental monster by the name of..." He paused to study his notes. "Here we go, a guy by the name of Ben Strange, she calls him Stranger, and she describes him as a very intoxicating, exquisitely complex...uhh, anomalous man, who makes her have butterflies in her stomach and cream in her panties, ah....that's ah...verbatim, directly from the pages of her own diary."

When Smart asked about the whereabouts of the guy in question, Ben Strange, he said, "We don't know. He was incarcerated for 7 years, but his case was overturned a few months ago, and he was released."

Jotting down the information he had just been given Smart said, "So, what do you think Mannimal's plans are now?"

"I can't really say right now, Agent Smart, I can't wrap my head around this one," replied VanDoren.

"Well, I can tell you what I *do* now about Mannimal, at least," Smart said.

"What's that?" asked VanDoren.

"Well, you're definitely in for one hell of a ride that's not gonna be an easy capture, he's literally a genius on the IQ scale and he is superbly ingenious, clever, callous, and devious. This isn't gonna be a task, it's gonna be a fucking adventure, with a body count that will stack to the ceiling of the Sistine Chapel, if he's not captured right away, and I can tell you now, he's not going to go down without a fight." Smart said this with as much drama as he could muster.

Smiling like the person who was just described to him wasn't even a threat, Marshal VanDoren said, "I'm very confident that we'll get him back in his cage, and if not, we'll put him in a box. But either way, I always get my man. There are two things about a criminal that never changes, whether they're smart or not..."

"And what's that?" asked Agent Smart, awaiting the sanctimonious cop wisdom from this arrogant man who obviously thought too highly of his capabilities.

Boldly smiling into the phone, he says, "The first is: They're predictable and will always revert back to what they know best, and the second is: They'll make the same mistakes by doing the same things that got 'em into trouble to begin with. They're creatures of habit, Agent Smart, and most of them, you'll find right back in their old hoods. The others, you'll find 'em when they start committing crimes again, while they're still on the run. It's called: The Criminal Justice Cycle! It's like revolving doors, it never stops. It may slow down or speed up, but it will never stop. It's just like time, it never ceases. It just keeps recycling them over and over, back into the penitentiary. As long as there are criminals, I'll never be out of job, just like most criminals are career offenders, this job is my career choice. I spend my time chasin' 'em to get em behind bars. They spend their time runnin' from me, to keep themselves from being put behind bars. This is the adult version of 'Cops and Robbers', that's all. But, you're a federal agent, you already know this," stated VanDoren with respectful appreciation for a fellow officer of the law.

Smart replied, "Yea, I know, but I've learned something in all these years in the Bureau about a criminal."

"And what's that?" asked Marshal VanDoren with a hint of humor, enjoying the little banter in the battle of criminology wits.

"Well, I learned that most people know better, which in turn, results with the formation of the criminal, but when you separate a criminal from its element, they learn to adapt, it becomes a survival instinct. The laws of adaption! The thing about a criminal is, most are smarter than the average citizen, because they had to learn to adapt to several ways of life, when most only had to adapt to one way. Thus making them sophisticated integral beings that are cultivated and highly advanced in the criminal world, therefore making them terrorists of the communities and civilians around them. They understand the art of survival, and they've magnified the crime aspect on a larger scale now, they learned to make their own synthetic drugs, so they don't have to go to distant countries or cross borders, they only go to their own local store to gather the ingredients. They also build powerful structures that personifies the motto of 'Money, Power, and Respect', which are the three aspects men in our own governmental structure strive for. It's the three keys working in unison. The money have to be substantial, the power has to be commanding, and the respect will be given. You can't be broke, you can't be weak, and you can't be forceful. You can attain an illusion of success, but never will you remain in the hierarchy and sustain that success for an unforeseeable time, which lends credence to what I've learned: Most criminals will only succeed in what they do for a short period of time. But if they change their course of criminal thinking, they would change the game by readapting to new fundamentals and comprising legal empires that can't be dismantled. When the criminals master this, we'll be working for them, cause the power will change hands. If they teach their children this rule of success, we'll see a new world order. This is what I've learned in all my years of being with the Bureau and in

Special Crimes, as an agent. Don't ever underestimate your opponent. The criminal is one type of individual that's resilient, and will keep setting up the pieces to play again, each time with a new strategy."

When at last the conversation between the two came to a close, both men had found a new appreciation for one another's point of view on the complicated intricacies of criminology, but both knew what they knew, cause cops and criminals were alike in one nature, and that was going with what they knew best.

Chapter Forty - Five

June 9, 2020 5:00pm Tuesday

NewsCast Dallas, Texas

"This is Brett 'Magic Man' Copeland, with WKRSE, 94.3, and you're listening to, Tuesday's Traffic Jam, rush hour news..."

"Today the local authorities have put out a nationwide BOLO for a convicted serial murderer, Dominic 'Mannimal' Mann, who has reportedly escaped from a Federal Maximum Security Penitentiary in Jonesville, Virginia. Authorities say the recent escape was hashed by one of the facilities psychology staff members, who also has been found murdered at her place of residence. There's a $10,000 reward for the capture of this convicted fugitive. His description is as follows: He is a black male, height 6'2 and 205 pounds, short hair, hazel-brown eyes and he's believed to be driving a burgundy GMC Envoy, Virginia tag # DR POOL. To see his photo, you can log on to our website at www.KRSEhotnews.com. You can also see photos at America's Most Wanted #1 fugitive apprehension file, and if you have any information as to the whereabouts of this convicted murderer, we ask that you do not approach or try to apprehend him, but that you call our fugitive hotline to get in touch with representatives that will assist you. You can also call Crime Stoppers to leave any tips if you would like to remain anonymous."

"Also, in today's news, there's been a rash of police murders. The FBI are urging the public to help them locate a suspect in the recent serial murders. There's been an alarming surge of what authorities say are copycat killings, with no motive for these unrelated motivations. There's been at least four separate murders in separate states that they have detained suspects in all four of the murders, yet and still five or as many as 8 other suspects still remain at large. The details of these unrelated incidents remain sketchy, but authorities made it clear that all these recent murders are being thoroughly investigated and ask that anyone who may have any information or know of anyone who may be involved, should please contact your local police and report this information. The following states are under siege; Kansas, Arkansas, Florida, Alabama, Minnesota, Ohio, North Dekota, New Mexico Utah, and Oregon. They are all under curfew due to the police related shootings that have left several black youth dead."

"These cases are under investigation, and possible charges are now pending against those officers involved, says Prosecutor Edwards, of Richmond County, Minnesota. The recent massacre that took place in Minnesota on May 27th that left the police force in fear, only lasted for a span of 12 hours, is believed to be the handiwork of the serial- cop-killer that is yet to be identified, and is still at large. Authorities say the three slain officers in Chicago, Illinois on June 5th are also part of this murderous spree to target and kill random officers. As of right now, the investigations into all of these recent murders are ongoing and we are urgently asking the public for any help in capturing those responsible. There is again, a nationwide BOLO for an escaped convict who is deemed to be armed and extremely dangerous, please contact crime stoppers or your local police department with any information on any of these crimes that have been reported during this Tuesday Traffic Jam rush hour news with Brett 'Magic Man' Copeland, stay turned for more Hip-Hop and R&B at WKRSE, 94.3..."

Going to commercial break, Stranger sat contemplating all that he had heard, when Mike spoke out from the back, saying in a smooth, somber voice, "You hear that, Slim? They talkin' bout us, Slim, we making Prime Time news headlines," speaking proudly of their news debut.

Stranger replies, "Yea, they are, aren't they? I guess we made a statement and got someone's attention."

"Yea, we did," replied Mike.

Bursting into their conversation of congratulatory pats on the backs, John said, "What the fuck are you two roosters crowin' about? I mean, that little statement is like a small granule of sand at a beach full of sand, you really didn't make no real impression if you ask me."

"No one was asking you," shot back Mike, with a trace of piqued bitterness in his voice. "Better yet, how about you stay out of the conversation when me and Stranger are talking," Mike added point blank.

"Oh, you're the only one who can talk to Stranger and no one else has a voice, huh? Well, you know what? I got news for you, Mike, you're just a big, black, baldheaded psychopath, who manipulatively plays with Stranger's mind for your own personal satisfaction and you don't care about making statements and retaliating against the system and the people who are killing your own people. Nooo! That's not it at all, now is it, Michael?" John fumes, purposely vexing Mike with his ranting opinions of him.

Mike shouts from the backseat, "My name's not Micheal, bitch! And if you speak to me in that manner again, I'm gonna take that gun of Stranger's and splatter your brains all over that windshield and dashboard, I will completely erase your white ass from the face of the Earth, and push your worthless carcass out on the pavement without so much as to stop the car in the process. You better watch your mouth and count your blessings- this is the second time we've had an issue, there won't be a third. I won't be sayin' this again, I'll tell a child twice and an adult once, so that should tell you-I see you as a fucking kid, so play with someone else, and since you wanna play games, Simon says "Shut the fuck up'!"

Mike forcefully stresses his meaning by leaning forward and taking his pointer finger and mushing the temple of John's head with such menacing force, that John's head smacked the passenger window with a hard thump. John grabbed the right side of his head into his palm and yelped out, "Ouch! What the fuck, Mike? Alright! I get it, quit with all the bullying bullshit! Okay! No one wants to fuck with the big, bad wolf, cause you'll huff and you'll puff, and you'll blow my head off. Geeezus, you're such an ass-"

"John, shut the fuck up!" screamed Lisa from the backseat, sitting along side Mike, who was preparing to dive over the seat if

John continued talking. "You just don't know when to quit, do you?" asked Lisa, "John, you do know that you're not our friend, right? You're friends with Stranger, and there's nothing remotely close to a friendship between us and you. You're only alive because of Stranger, and as of right now, because of me! But, I won't stop him if you keep inciting him. You've been warned! And from the look of things and how they're playing out, this is your first and final warning, there won't be another one, you stupid mother fucker." When Lisa finished reprimanding John, he sat quietly vexed, mumbling under his breath intangible nervous jabber, as he rubbed the side of his head caressingly, while dispiritedly staring hard and uninterested out of the front windshield.

Coming back to the land of the living, Stranger looked into the rearview mirror and locked eyes with both Lisa and Mike, and shook his head with a smirk easing into the corners of his mouth. Then, to John, he said, "Hey, keep a lookout for a cop, this next one's for you, buddy, never mind them," as he extends his right arm out to receive a brotherly dap, tapping fists lightly with John. Only then did this door open for John to release the pent up comment he had been trying so hard to desperately keep under wraps.

"About fucking time someone kills something other than the positive energy I'm exuding! Everybody wants to kill the white guy, and you know, I just so happen to believe we're all very good friends! I'm the annoying one, Lisa's the fat obnoxious one, Mike is the cranky manipulative sharp one, and Stranger, he's the quiet, reserved, murderous one. Put all of us together and you got a toxic concoction that's gonna detonate and blow up in your face, eating away at your flesh like Lye, battery acid, sulfuric acid and muriatic acid, all combined toge-" John started before being interrupted.

"Shut up, John!" said Stranger, smiling at how easy it was to bring John out of his stupor and get him going again. "Just locate an easy target so we can get out of this state. Texas ain't the place to be dilly dallying in."

Just as they exited Interstate 35 and rounded the ramp to enter the city of Dallas, Texas, Stranger said, "So John, how do you want this one done?" Hearing Stranger's question to John, Lisa was quickly displeased and heaved her arms into a folded huff and blew out an exasperated breath, as she listened to John detail how he would like to make his statement reach national headlines. Listening along, Mike sat pondering the demented mind of John and actually had a newfound appreciation for the inner workings of his imaginative mind. Thinking to himself, "Now, that's some shit, that would really hit home and make headlines for sure."

While contemplatively driving around Dallas, Texas, Stranger realized that all of the cops they were targeting, were all riding around two deep in their cars. Also, following closely behind was an assisting unit. So, Stranger began to hash out a plan of counterattack against his strategic maneuver.

Pulling into a strip mall and retrieving the gym bag from the backseat, Stranger came up with a seemingly fool proof plan, with just one flaw. He needed to appropriate a vehicle to enact the getaway portion of his plan, so that once the chaos turned into a hazy overcast of disruption and the police begin to amass a blockade, setting up a perimeter, that can exceed miles. Stranger decided it was best to choose an area, and let his victim fall into his lap by laying in the bushes and unleashing terror from an advantage.

Walking into a used car lot, Stranger saw that there wasn't any salesman available, who spoke to him. So he leisurely strolled around the lot and was approached by a man.

"Good evening, sir," looking at his uniform he smiled and added, "Officer O'Connel, so how can I help you today?"

Spying the car lot for anyone within earshot, he said in a cheerful tone, "I'm doing fine, sir," extending his hand for a friendly handshake. Peering around again, Stranger said, "I'm looking for a new truck, I just moved down from St. Louis, as you can see, I'm an Officer of the law and would like to purchase a vehicle."

Smiling at Stranger approvingly, he says, "nice to meet another decorated officer, I'm a retired sergeant of the Dallas Police Force myself, and I must say..."

Pausing a moment to collect his thoughts, he actually took notice to the dried blood on the collar of the uniform and began to take in the whole picture. He decided to go with his gut, which told him that the man before him, was not who he was portraying himself to be. He finished his statement then, "Umm, you are in luck sir, uhh Officer O'Connel, I have the perfect vehicle for you, if you would follow me," trying to steer the conversation back into an unsuspecting salesman's pitch.

But Stranger stood steadfast and held his stoic mood under reigns saying, "I found what I was looking for Mr...what did you say your name was?"

Lost in analyzing his suspicion of Stranger's nature and the look of the wrinkled uniform with an obvious dried blood stain, the retired officer was very perceptive, taking notice, he answered the question by saying, "Oh yea, I'm Mr. Hammond, but you can call me Big Al," he said smiling. Then without so much as asking what car he preferred, Mr. Hammond spun around and said, "I'll be right back, uhh, Officer O'Connel, I'm gonna get some keys and a temp tag so you can do some test drives."

Just then, John strolls up beside Stranger. They both peered in the direction of the salesman who was obviously acting a little odd and didn't have a look of someone who was happy with a potential sale that could bring a commission they would receive once a car is sold. But, it was the look in his eyes, as he ascended the steps to enter the small office trailer in the middle of the car lot, that struck a nerve in both Stranger and John. It was John's comment that resonated clearly to his conscious thoughts, when John asked, "So, what car is he getting the keys for, Stranger? You never told him exactly what you was interested in, and you do know you have the dead cop's dried blood all around the collar of your shirt, don't you? Oh, and lastly, all the salesmen I know, they actually try to sell you on a car and give you a rapid-fire run down into the car's make, model, and special features. So, tell me Stranger, if you were a betting man, what would be the odds that this retired cop by the way, is getting keys and tags right now, versus, calling them good ole boys for a little assistance?"

Stranger, not wasting any time, took off at a sprint towards the office, climbing the steps, two at a time. He stood there staring through the glass front door, then ripped the door open abruptly, barging into the office, seeing that the salesman was hunched over his desk, speaking into the receiver of the desk phone.

Caught off guard, when the bells from the office door rang loudly, resonating with an echo throughout the deserted office. Mr. Hammond pointedly brought his attention towards the front office door and began to lower the phone receiver from his ear, when he was staring, point blank, into the barrel of a Sig Sauer P220, a .45 caliber ACP. He knew, and his gut told him this guy was bad news, but before he could explain away his reasons for talking on the phone, the dispatch operator came back on the line and said, "Thanks for holding, what is your emergency?" Those words sang like early morning birds chirping in a silent meadow in the stifling quietness of the empty office.

Approaching at a stealthy pace, Stranger seized the phone from the nervous salesman's hand and spoke into the receiver with a pleasant voice. "There's no emergency, officer, sorry to take up your time and inconvenience you. An honest mistake on my behalf, sorry."

The operator replied, "Oh no, there's no inconvenience sir, you have a nice day," before hanging up to answer more pressing emergencies in the Dallas area.

Dropping the phone, Stranger held the barrel trained steady on Mr. Hammond's forehead, as he desperately tried to plead for his life, saying, "Come on son, God don't like ugly, your problem's not with me, I've done you no wrong!" Stranger wanted to see if this was, in fact, the case when he said, "True, you did me no wrong, but let's look at something." Thus began the questioning, "So, how long was you on the force before you retired?" asked Stranger.

"25 years sir," replied Mr. Hammond.

"And in those 25 years, how many officer involved shootings of innocent black youth have you encountered?" asked Stranger.

"Well, ahh-I say, that's hard to say, I mean what's innocent these days? Most of the youth gang bang and carry guns and-"

"Cut the bullshit!" screamed Stranger. "How many were gunned down by a cop and there was no weapons, or reasonable explanation, other than he or she was black, young, and had a record?"

Stuttering in fear, he answered, "I'd say a few sir. But the officers were within their rights to do so, if the perp fled, or officers felt fear for their lives or the youth possessed a weapon, I mean I've had a gun pulled on me before, but I didn't have to kill the young man, he was just a scared kid," answered Mr. Hammond.

"That's good for you!" said Stranger. "Now, how many officers you know personally who's shot a kid and it wasn't justified, but he still got away with it?" asked Stranger, setting the trap.

Taking a few seconds, Mr. Hammond said, in a Southern Texas drawl, "I reckon, maybe three or four that shouldn't have happened, but they were exonerated of any wrongdoing."

He walked right into Stranger's trap. "But you knew that they were wrongful to begin with, yet you chose to stay silent, while another officer commits a murder of your own people and you stood by and allowed it to happen and then let it continue to happen three or four times."

Shocked by the revelation of the cold hard truth in Stranger's comment, Mr. Hammond lowered his head and said, "Now that you say it like that, it was my duty to uphold the law, even if I had to go against fellow brothers on the force."

Cutting in with venom in his voice, Stranger said, "And the light bulb comes on finally, and you see the light now, but it's way too late for those young men who lost their lives due to your obvious negligence and lack of upholding the law, even if it's against your own kind, and I'm not talking about black people either, I'm speaking on the boys in blue. Now who gonna pay for those mistakes that can't never be undone? We both know those weren't mistakes, they're actually intentional murders of black youth and you partook in the evil deed by knowingly standing by and doing nothing about it. Yeah, you're responsible, but you being a cop and having knowledge before and after the fact of these subsequent murders makes you just as culpable, if not solely responsible, officer Hammond-"

Pow! Pow!

He sent smoldering hot slugs tightly grouped into Mr. Hammond's forehead, causing his whole body to slam back into the swiveling desk chair. His mouth gaped open and his eyes staring heavenward, as if calling on Jesus to come and save him, while his arms hung limply at his sides.

Sliding the dead man back towards the wall, Stranger began to pilfer through the desk drawers. He opened the file cabinets only to discover that there was a safe inside, which had been left open. He removed the money, and with a quick survey of the room, found there was another, much larger safe, hiding behind a larger desk at the back of the room. When he opened the already unlocked safe, he knew he had hit gold when there was a Glock 17 handgun along with keys on a peg board for all of the vehicles in the lot. Also, there was new temp tags stacked, as well as several bank deposit bags filled filled with money. He then found the video recording unit that was currently recording his every move from all of the cameras inside and out of the office, covering the whole lot.

Removing the two video CDs and ripping the computer's mainframe from out of the rear of the safe, Stranger proceeded towards the door where he stood, then backtracked to the corpse of Mr. Hammond. He retrieved the keys from his pocket with his gloved hands. Stranger then switched the interior lights off inside the trailer, just before closing and locking the office door. He flipped the open for business' sign to 'closed' and casually moved down the steps with all of the stolen articles in hand.

Stopping at the back of a black 2019 Lincoln Navigator with

"26 inch black Asanti rims, he put a magnetized dealer tag on the rear end. John approached and said, "Did you leave something behind to show that this was part of our spree?"

Looking over his shoulder, towards John, Stranger said, "Yeah, I left the gun from Officer Chase there, but I didn't leave the badge, cause it don't matter if a badge is there or not, I'm not finished with Dallas yet, I got a message to send, and this one is gonna be monumental."

Climbing into the immaculately clean Lincoln, they both drove out of the lot, set to put the next phase of their reign of terror into play.

Chapter Forty - Six

June 9, 2020 6:43pm Tuesday

Dallas, Texas

Counting the cash in the darkened interior of the Grand Cherokee, Stranger used the cellphone he had stolen from Mr. Hammond, and made a call to police dispatch saying that he was a citizen that had been assaulted by someone and was in need of assistance. When asked about the description, Stranger ranted off a vague description of three individuals that had accosted and robbed him, and he mentioned that he was an officer of the St. Louis Police Department and was there on vacation.

Sitting in the truck, minutes after dispatch said she was sending a unit right away, Stranger hurriedly put the money in the other SUV and told the others to wait in the Lincoln for his return. But it was John's relentless pursuit that caused him to be taken along for the event that was sure to make headlines.

As Stranger pulled into a crowded parking lot, John rambled on and on, until Stranger turned to him and said, with a vehement scowl on his face, "Shut up, John, now is most definitely not the time for your theatrics, stay out the way and keep clear of the action, and get your ass back to the truck asap! Be there before I get there, or your ass is getting left behind. I'm not gonna go over this again because them cops are on the way and I need to be ready, so find your hiding place, now!"

With that said, John disappeared to go hide in a secluded little

334

cove by the dumpsters. Just as emergency lights came strobing into the McDonalds parking lot, Stranger is hiding underneath the already idling Grand Cherokee with two guns in hand. One being the Glock 17, belonging to Adam Abrams, the used car lot owner and the other, a Glock 27, belonging to Officer O'Connel of the St. Louis Police Department.

Stranger waited until the police cruiser came to a halt. Listening to the doors slam shut, he was alerted that there were only two officers present at the time. The officers looked around the busy parking lot of McDonalds, trying to locate their victim to make contact, but when they saw no one, they proceeded to walk into the McDonalds dining room, to make sure their vic wasn't inside, keeping closely grouped with other customers to ensure his safety. That moment of relaxed tension was enough time to give Stranger an opportunity to slide from beneath the truck and creep up towards the passenger side of the police cruiser. The trailing unit finally arrived, pulling into the parking lot to back up the first responding vehicle.

They were ambushed without so much as a warning that what they were arriving into was going to end as an atrocious massacre, and were helpless to prevent it. Stranger took notice to their vehicle pulling into the lot and not seeming to look in his direction before bringing their car to a stop just mere feet from the rear end of the parked police vehicle.

Before the two officers could react, a fast approaching figure ran and leaped onto the hood, crouching down in a shooter's stance, he unleashed several shots into both officers sitting in the front seats of their cruiser, killing them both instantly with a tatter of pelting bullets.

Stranger jumped swiftly off the hood of the car and quickly moved towards the Grand Cherokee. Climbing into the front seat, he lowered himself from detection as the first two responding officers began to come out of the McDonalds door, only then to be met head on by the front end of the Grand Cherokee, which mowed their bodies over, in the middle of a crowded McDonalds restaurant dining area.

Dizzily opening the door of the wrecked Grand Cherokee, obviously shaken up from the crash, Stranger climbed out and walked over the two helpless officers. Standing to over both bodies that lay in a pummeled mass of broken bones, he unleashed a buffet of bullets into the already defeated cops.

Then, reaching down, he picked up both of their of guns that laid strewn about and snatched their badges from their tattered uniforms, while all of the customers crouched down, watching every move, hidden behind chairs and trashcan receptacles. Some were screaming, while others, stood frozen with their hands stretched skywards as if filled with the Holy Ghost, just hoping not to be shot in the midst of the detestable act of savagery that had just taken place in front of their very eyes with no remorse or care for human life. Rising to his feet, Stranger peered around the room with a mask covering his face, and said, "My name is 'The Judgement' and this is 'The Statement'. If anymore youth die at the hands of any more cops, and they aren't truly justified in their actions in doing so, I will commence my reign of terror. I'm holding all law enforcement accountable, and make no mistake about it, since you all want to ride together, you can all die together, I don't care what city, town or state it happens in, the taking of just ONE innocent life, will cause me to take many of those, whose jobs are to prevent it. I am Moses, The Prophet, and I'll be sitting high on the mountain top, speaking with a burning bush until then..."

Before turning to walk over the rubble, Stranger dropped the badge of Oklahoma City Officer Eugene Chase, badge #512, at the feet of Officers Sandy Wood-Pratt, badge #282, and Jeremy Thompson, badge #5993. As he was leaving, he tossed the two weapons that were empty of bullets and ran towards the idling police cruiser of the first responding unit. Jumping in the driver's seat, he pulled off, leaving out from the rear exit of the McDonalds parking lot.

Reaching the getaway vehicle, John was sitting in the front seat with the most appreciative smile upon his face. Stranger climbed in, started the Lincoln Navigator, then pulled off on the back street, searching the rearview mirror to see if he was being followed by anyone. When he was sure he had made a clear getaway, Stranger proceeded to Interstate 25 and pushed the luxury SUV down the highway, heading west towards Fort Worth, putting distance between him and the scene he had left behind. Realizing that there were a few people there who were video recording his show, he was certain that by wearing the ski-mask and gloves, his identity still remained an enigma to the investigators. As long as he keeps his identity a mystery, he can keep getting away with his course of action for an untold amount of years. Only one mistake on his end, and this tightly weaved rope of visionary murderous intent will come unraveled. He thought it best if he laid low for a few days to see what is said on the news and how much of an impact tonight's statement will make on the world.

If he hears of even one young black man, woman or child shot by *any* cop unjustly, he was going to bring about life changing repercussions for the police force of whatever city he just so happens to be laying low in. Stranger wasn't going to quit until the cops quit killing his people and getting away with the murders. He knew anyone else would be charged with a murder, or manslaughter, so cops needed to be held accountable too. If prosecutors of that state won't prosecute, then the law will be taken into his own hands. The cops are watching us, but then who's watching them? That is the reason they were in their present situation now. But he had every intention of correcting that. Correcting all of the injustice in the system. He wouldn't stop until they did.

Chapter Forty - Seven

June 10, 2020 10:00am Wednesday

St. Louis, Missouri

After stopping at a local coffee shop and grabbing up a couple hot cups of strong morning joe and a few warm danishes, Spl. Agents Smart and Drapper made their way to the crime scene that was supposed to be a 'heart-wrenching one for the books', or so they were being told.

When pulling up to a fenced-in industrial complex, they took immediate notice that the surrounding areas were perfectly secluded spots to leave a body and not have to worry about anyone stumbling upon it, because from the looks of the place, no one has been beyond the fence line in months, if not years. The crime scene techs were moving about in hazmat gear and booties on their feet to preserve any crime scene evidence that may lay haphazardly around. Agent Smart parked on the outer perimeter of the crime scene tape, which pretty much consisted of cordoning off the entire complex due to the unknown factors, and not being able to positively pinpoint exactly what parts of the complex were actually part of the crime scene. Every door to every building in the surrounding area had police and FBI presence spilling in and out of each doorway, canvassing the grounds for any evidence.

Spying Agents Goldfield and Maddox from a distance, the two strolled up with streaming cups of coffee in hand, and stood a few feet away until Agent Maddox finished speaking with a man that looked to carry himself with the presence of a highly sophisticated professional, most likely a doctor or medical examiner. But it was the leather carry case that was eye-catching enough to warrant a plausible assumption that the weary looking man was indeed the medical examiner for that region of Missouri.

After the quiet conversation between the two was concluded, the medical examiner proceeded back towards an isolated building that was teeming with the FBI's investigators and crime scene techs, who were performing their individual tasks, collecting evidence, and photographing the yellow numbered evidence markers that were randomly scattered around the ground of the complex. When Agent Maddox was done with all of the inquiries that were being thrown at him from all directions, he stood there transfixed in deep reverie, as Agent Smart closed in and said, "Looks like things have taken a toll on you, Mark."

Taking a deep breath and exhaling through his nose, Agent Maddox said, "This one is just as bizarre as the last three we visited in Chicago. I mean, Brad, this maniac is taking these killings to a level of documented extremity that the human mind can't possibly conceive without there being some obvious mental instability that went inadequately diagnosed, but the point still remains: these acts aren't just cruel and unusual, there... there-there aren't any words in the English dictionary that can encapsulate the anomalies of the heinous acts that are being committed by our suspect."

As Agent Drapper looked upon the dejected agent, he asked, "So, what we have here, is a monster on a rampage then, huh?"

Hearing the words, but not having an easy answer, Agent Maddox just stepped back, and extended his arm, as if to grant them admittance into the macabre world of Helter Skelter.

Before they all moved forward, Agent Goldfield said, "I'm cool, I'm not ready to climb back into that circus tent of horrific visuals. That place in there is...Satan's den of Damnation, and I'll be damned if I step foot back through that threshold."

As Agent Smart began to walk by Agent Goldfield, he lightly touched her nervously fidgety hand before passing, to convey his empathy and compassion towards her, saying, "I'll be right back, hold it together 'til I return, okay?"

With her head lowered in a bereaved state of sickness, she just slowly nodded her head in acknowledgement and turned her back as she crossed her arms and stepped away without so much as a word in return towards his affectionate sentiments.

Upon entering the warehouse portion of the derelict building through the rollback bay door, the pungent smell of decomposing flesh sat heavy in the stifling heated air of the large room, as the agents made their way deeper into the gloominess they passed the K-9 SUV. Agent Smart took notice that the rear window was shattered and there was dried blood stains that left a stream patterns like tears running down the exterior of the SUV, which caused him to wonder what took place here. But when investigating further, getting a closer look, he continued to follow Agent Maddox, until he stopped and said, "This is where we located them."

Surprised at the plural enunciation of the word 'them', Agent

Smart said, "So, there's more than one person left at this scene?"

Stopping short mid-step and spinning around, Agent Maddox said, "When your eyes behold this scene, you won't forget these images, as long as you both shall live!" With interest peeked eyebrows, arched in discomfort, Agent Smart skeptically said, "Lead the way, Mark, not much is gonna disgust me at this late stage of my career."

But unbelieving to Agent Maddox, he said, "Well, we will see now, won't we?" spinning on his heels he proceeded without anymore comment.

When they came into an open area of another large staging area, bile rose into his mouth as Agent Smart stepped back in aghast dismay. The momentary glimpse of the horrific scene was enough to send Agent Drapper fleeing in trepidation, as Agent Smart stood frozen in a pond of fear, while he took in the totality of the gut wrenching scene in all of its excruciating detail. There, he unsteadily tried to maintain balance on wobbly legs, when his eyes trailed upward and saw that the two figures were the dead mutilated corpses of a male victim and an animal, he assumed to be the officer and his K-9 companion.

Slowly easing forward, the scene turned from horrid to sinisterly hideous and sickening upon closer observation. With danish and coffee rising like bile in his mouth already, the accompanying smell only instigated the vomit to come spewing out of his mouth like a fountain of uncontrollable torrid fluid. After several attempts to seize control of the regurgitated liquid, he finally pulled himself together and rose to his feet. Reaching inside his coat pocket, he pulled out a napkin from the danish, and began to wipe his mouth. Shaking his head in disbelief, as he looked upon the scene once again, he hoped not to vomit any more left over content within his stomach.

Once he was sure that he could proceed without incident, he stepped closer to the corpses that hung from the rafters by rusted chains and meathooks. Their heads were severed from their bodies and replaced by the others. Agent Smart was staring in awe, as he was looking upon a body of a human with a dog's head sitting atop of his shoulders, and a carcass of a dog with a human male's head jammed firmly in its place, with both corpses ripped open from neck to pelvis, their intestines hung spilled out of their bodies, dangling all the way to the floor, piled in a heap of grey decomposing ropes of maggot infested alimentary tube canal and feces. The arms and legs of the male were ripped from their sockets, suspended by thin tendons of fiber-like tissue that was barely holding up the weight of his limbs. While the dog's four legs lay scattered on the floor with vicious bite marks from what looked to have been hundreds of rats and vermin that had hungrily feasted on their remains. Along with noticing that the skin of the male victim was flayed, they saw that his torn away skin flaps hung like old, curled up, dried wallpaper.

Staring at the limbless victims with their mismatched heads sloppily attached as a repulsive joke, it caused Agent Smart to turn away and speedily retreat from the scene before he erupted in another uncontrollable fit of vomiting, or more accurately, dry heaving.

Clearing the building and inhaling fresh air, Agent Smart began to compose himself and regain his calm. When Agent Maddox came to check on him, he said, "Some sight, huh?" Without any words to form in his mouth to articulate how gruesome the scene was, Agent Smart just bowed his head in disbelief, and prayed quietly to himself that no one else, human or animal, living on God's green earth will ever again meet their untimely demise in such a manner as what he'd just encountered.

When Agent Maddox felt he had allowed enough time to pass before he began to unveil his findings. Agent Drapper and Goldfield joined in the conversation and listened to the compiled information.

Agent Maddox began by saying, "It is fact that the deceased man and the K-9 inside that building are none other than officer Vernon O'Connel and his K-9 partner, Sergeant Duke. Officer O'Connel is a 10 year veteran of the St. Louis, Police Department and a retired Army Specialist for training K-9 bomb sniffing dogs." As if reading from a profile history report, he goes on to recap the findings, "On the day of Saturday, June 6th, Officer O'Connel showed up for roll call with his K-9 partner, Duke, in tow, but at 4:00pm he hadn't returned to the station house at the end of his shift. It wasn't until June 9th, that the K-9's GPS transponder was emitting a weak signal, that gave too weak of a signal to pinpoint their exact location. However, it gave them an area of circumference of 10 miles in radius, but the cell tower's signal strengths weren't accurately identifying a precise area. It wasn't until, the news put out an APB for Officer O'Connel's whereabouts and a store owner, just down the road, due South, about a half a mile from here, called into the tips hotline and gave a detailed description of what took place. He was fiercely adamant that the man he saw in a grainy BOLO print out, was in fact, our suspect. He was so sure in fact, he coerced Officer O'Connel into investigating the area. He relayed the details that Officer O'Connel had gone in search of the alleged suspect without any backup to assist him, other than his K-9 Partner, and he came to the most secluded place in all of St. Louis, a condemned warehouse complex that hasn't been inhabited in the last 7 years. This was a perfect hideout, with perfect concealment, and a perfect place to commit an atrocious act without fear of being caught up.

Taking a look around, he points out the obvious escape routes and the ambush advantages. Then Agent Maddox made a proper evaluation when he said, "Look around Brad, this is a killer's nest, a playground -labyrinth of horror-"

Then, with anger rising in his voice, he added, "This guy isn't playing with a full deck, this is no longer a game of cat and mouse, this is a blatantly one-sided, odds stacked game of slippers count! I've reviewed the case notes in Kentucky and Illinois, but Minnesota was a fuckin' kill zone, like shooting fish in a fuckin' barrel. No one saw him coming and no one saw him leaving, and the only thing he's leaving is an accumulated stock pile of dead cops he's seemingly steam rolling in major cities, playing Peek-A-Boo, and he's the last person to see them alive."

Venting off his built up steam, he takes a moment to collect himself and says, "Now, what? What do we got?"

Looking in the direction of Agent Drapper, Agent Smart relays a message imperceptibly, that now was a good time to give Maddox some possible information that could be of help, at least give them a leg to stand on, and an identity to attach to the vague description that they were currently pussyfooting around with. Agent Smart said, "Hey, Mark, I think we may have a hit on the identity of our suspect, it may be farfetched, but it brings us a lot closer than where we're presently at."

"Nothing for the grand spiel of information," Agent Maddox said, "Well, what the fuck's the hold up? You want me to unwrap this shit like it's a birthday gift? Or are you gonna pass on the information to me by way of mental telepathy? Spit the shit out already!" causing Agent Smart to spill the beans.

He began by saying, "Look, this may be a long shot, but that incident at Lee County USP with the escaped convicted murderer and his female accomplice, whom just so happens to be the head psychology doctor who is now deceased by the hands of her lover; a convicted murder psychopath boyfriend. Well, the former Dr. Poole left behind some incriminating evidence that can cause a cesspool of shit to become stirred up, if IAD gets a hold of her personal diaries that were left in the bedside dresser of the victim's home. When US Marshals raided the premises in search of the escapee and his accomplice, they stumbled upon a horrific scene close in similarities to the last few murders that had taken place since the Lee County massacre. It's the decapitation of heads that are becoming the new unique trait that's connecting these murders. There are two men she spoke on, as having a fascination for, one being the escapee that is presently at large and the other being a young man by the name of Ben Strange, a resident of Washington, D.C., who was also falsely accused and found guilty of cases that were hinged against him unjustly by the one person where all of this murder madness started with, a Richard Montgomery, a Washington, D.C. Metropolitan undercover drug task force detective, who was found to have been playing dirty in the sandbox with almost all of his cases under review and the convicted being exonerated of all charges and released from federal custody. Ben Strange was one of those many men who was, not only housed at Lee County, but had some serious run ins with several of the C.O.s whose heads were decapitated at that gas station, and later found left at the scenes of subsequent murdered cops, that are connected to the exact same murder spree which we are presently standing at. One of many that has already occurred, but definitely not the last, if we don't put a lid on this can of worms, and fast."

Staring off into the clouds, Agent Maddox said, "Well, let's get a file compiled on this guy ASAP-"

"We already have it sir," said Agent Drapper, who stood to the right of Agent Smart. Then he went on to add, "When we heard the news and got a name, I figured what the heck, it beats a blank, so I called into headquarters and had them fax over every fiber of information we could dig up on this Ben Strange, and I must say, this guy's nickname fits him and his nature to the T. They call him Stranger, and his actions are getting stranger and stranger, with each new murder. I believe he's trying to tell us something and we're not getting the message he's trying to convey to us. If this is indeed our guy, my records show that we aren't going to be taking him down easily, he's what you call a thinker, but he has bouts of depression, and behavior and a lot of emotional disorders. His mental illness isn't diagnosed in clinical terms because he has many combined illnesses, which makes him erratic and unstable. He's prone to violence, but his thought process and patterns of thinking suggest that he's above average, and borderlines the IQ of a genius. The same goes for our escaped convict that's presently on the lam and already has five new bodies added to the already long list he'd amassed years back, in which he was doing 9 consecutive life sentences for. With these two men at large, the nation is in great danger."

Allowing Agent Drapper's summation to run its course, Agent Maddox looked over towards Agent Goldfield and said, "Call in back up and take this information he has on our guy and lets get all hands on deck." Then he added, "I'm making a call to Agent Forrester, Matt really needs to hear this." Before he made his call, he looked at both, Agents Smart and Drapper and extended his appreciative thanks, saying, "Thank you, gentlemen, for shining some light in this dark sewage tunnel we've been wading in for so long, good job, Team."

Chapter Forty - Eight

June 10, 2020 9:05am Wednesday
Spotsylvania, Virginia

Taking a day to collect his thoughts and figure out what his next move was, Detective McNealson decided to go to Detective Dabney's office again, to try and hash things out and make amends with him. Thinking back to how aggressive his conversation was and the look that was plastered upon Det. Dabney's face as he was leaving yesterday, only brought weariness and dread to McNealson over the last few hours, where he tried to formulate his next plan of action other than surrendering himself to prosecution, and possibly the loss of his whole career and closest friend.

After deciding to use the morning as productively as possible, he decided to reconnoiter the area around his home and work place, to see if, in fact the FEDs were still snooping around in his bushes, laying wait upon his arrival. But it wasn't until he cruised past his street that he saw, not only were they stationed in front of his home on the opposite side of the street, but they were actually posted at both ends of the street, just in case he got a wild hair up his ass and thought it wise to cruise on through the neighborhood, like some unsuspecting citizen, trying to go undetected. It was the most obvious set up, being that most of the cars on his street stayed parked in their garages or driveways, and there weren't many black FED issued SUVs with matching Federal tags as his neighbors, and they were never parked curbside in front of their homes, because he knew both home owners at the ends of each of the streets personally.

Pondering his next move, he thought it best to go around to the back of the house and climb the fence of the house whose backyard fence was adjacent to his own. But when he was signaling to turn down that street, he took notice that there was another unit, sitting across the street from that house watching the four homes directly in their view. The situation looked highly organized and was minimizing any potential advantage to advance upon his home, either by car or foot, nor to even exit the area without raising attention to himself, being that his neighborhood was a quiet and quaintly respectable community. He was very aware that they'd been put on notice about his little indiscretion with the law and how he's so nervy and unrelenting when it comes to standing up for what he believed in. After processing his thoughts and weighing out the pros and cons, he finally made the assessment that he should've picked his battles more wisely on this one and instead of provoking a wasp nest full of Federal bees into a frenzy, he should've left well enough alone, and passed on the information he had compiled on the inmates to the proper authorities who actually had jurisdiction over the case.

It wasn't until 20/20 hindsight came into focus that brought about this commonsense revelation which made him see that he was going gung-ho for a case that became personal for him and never really had ties or significance to him other than the FEDs being brought in and snatching a high profile murder case from under his feet. But also, it wasn't until he had talked to Agent Smart, back some weeks ago on the phone as he sat in his office, that things took a turn for the worse. He wasn't taking the verbal reprimand lightly the chin, nor was he turning the other cheek once the conversation was finished, because it was a known fact, that Detective Vince McNealson had serious issues with authority, maintaining law and order and following the protocols of departmental policies and procedures, when it came to chain of command. If Detective McNealson was the lead investigator of a case, all the defense lawyer had to do was, follow the trail of evidence that was collected, by asking the courts for a motion of discovery, then comb through that evidence and how it was handled through procedure and proper protocols and 9 times out of 10, the case didn't have a leg to stand on, because McNealson never adhered to proper departmental chain of custody evidence procedures.

It never failed being unveiled in the process of court proceedings. Most cases always got thrown out by the judge for violations of due process, failure to Mirandize a suspect before interrogating him and the mishandling of collected evidence, or the prosecutors would just throw in the towel and the court would dismiss the case due to the absentminded negligence of Detective McNealson, who would ruin a wet dream without even having to try. It was just a known fact, that to prosecute a case that was investigated by Det. McNealson and his partner, Matt York, they first had to reinvestigate and pick through their collected evidence like rubble, to locate plausible, usable untainted evidence before the process of going to trial. The best thing that Det. McNealson was known for, was his ability to pry a confession out of a rat, spring a leak out of an informant's faucet, and break in a case when he starts poking holes in statements and applying interrogation pressures, like the detectives on the television series "First 48", where the detectives use tactics and tricks of deceit to get a suspect to let their guard down and accept the conjured lies that the detectives are selling them as God's honest truth. They would divulge the truth and reveal their role in the incident. The detectives would say they would put in a good word with the prosecutors office, as long as they agree to give full details of their involvement and expose all of the other willful participants involved. Thus, making a deal with the devil, and sealing their fate in a penitentiary for the possible discovery of them ratting on someone in their case. That reputation as a rat, will follow them for the rest of their life. Once a rat, always a rat, it only takes one time telling to become a snitch, and once that label is placed upon someone in the penitentiary, they are ostracized. They become the new prey, where the words "hard time" takes on a whole new meaning. Most rats are either beaten up on a regular basis by other convicts for ratting, or robbed of all of their possessions, even raped or stabbed to death in worse case scenarios, depending on the status of the person they snitched on. In the end, about 99% of the snitches get discovered and exposed, ending up on a permanent protective custody status, where most are protected from the convicts, where they are treated even worse by the correctional officers that are hired to protect them and keep them safe, which is safe to say it doesn't pay to talk to the police and confess to a crime.

After traveling around the town of Fredericksburg for a couple of hours and mentally jogging through the many different scenarios in his head, Detective McNealson looked at his watch and decided it was early enough, but had to give Detective Dabney a fair amount of time to make it into the office to begin his daily job as a Detective for Spotsylvania Police Department Arson Division. Making a quick call to check to see if his calculations are correct, he made the call to Det. Dabney's office. The secretary answered the call asking, "How can I direct your call?"

When McNealson asked if Det. Dabney was in, the secretary said in a lively chipper voice, "why...yes, he is, but he's in a conference right now, can I redirect your call or take a message and he may return your call at his earliest convenience?" McNealson somberly said, "No, thank you, I'll just call back later," and hung up without hearing her reply or giving any formal parting farewells.

Once he ended the phone call, he knew that Det. Dabney was indeed in the office, so he chose to drive there to speak with him again and smooth things over a tad. He would try to regain his trust and utilize his connections to his benefit, or just have an ally in his corner who can become his eyes and ears at a distance. Smiling to himself, he realized he was really being a snake in the grass, but he had his reasons, and although they may not be reasonable or governed under the laws of the good conduct and justice for all, he truly believed as an officer of the law, that some people in the world didn't deserve rights and protections by the constitutional guarantees of justice. He felt that if you chose the opposite side of the law or fence to stand on, you lose your rights and condemn yourself to a miscarriage of justice under the thin veil that a choice to do right or the choice to do wrong, is a personal choice and there shouldn't be any flexibility in the law. Stand on one side, you are treated fairly, stand on the other, you are treated as an outlaw, because you are standing on the outskirts of the law, living your life outside the boundaries of lawfulness and clearly living in the land of lawlessness. This is the logic that McNealson adhered to, but he wasn't applying this same logic to himself as he's now running from the law, instead of turning himself in and facing the inevitable indictment that's gonna eventually not only send him to prison, but also ruin his career as a detective in law enforcement.

When pulling into the parking lot of the Spotsylvania Police Department, he sat momentarily to gather his wits about him so he can put on one 'helluva charade' to convince Det. Dabney that, although things turned ugly yesterday, he meant no harm. He also wanted to ask for his friendship and forgiveness, explain that he's just been under pressure with this case, and how it's taking a turn for the worse as the same killer has gone from state to state, killing other decorated cops under some bizarre fascination, and a deep-rooted hatred for officers of the law.

As he pulled the door handle of his Yukon and climbed out of his truck, Det. McNealson began to meticulously check himself in the tint of the driver's side window, making sure he looked like a well composed man, who has all his marbles even though he didn't feel anywhere close to having himself fully on point and pulled together. "But looks can be deceiving," he said to himself under his breath, as he looked into the window and winked at his own reflection. Placing his shades on his face, he shook any unnoticed wrinkles from his fitted sports jacket and proceeded to bend the front end of his truck, heading down the middle of the parking lot with a smooth casual gait, like he had no care in the world.

Suddenly, two black Ford Excursions sped up to the curbside, at the front of the lobby and doors popped open, with several FBI agents leaping out of the trucks in unison, falling in a protective detail formation, when none other than, Detective Joseph Dabney, was being escorted out of the front lobby of the building, surrounded by half a dozen cops and flanked by four sharp shooters at vantage points, with AR- 15, fully automatic assault weapons, sweeping the area for any potential threat, holding their positions until Detective Dabney was safely stowed away into the lead vehicle, as two more vehicles came storming into the lot, taking lead and rear cover of the two SUVs. One of the FBI agents who was climbing into the rear driver's side seat, halted his movements and locked eyes with Detective McNealson.

McNealson slipped quickly from sight as he slid between two parked vehicles, one being a red Ford Bronco, which provided him enough cover and time to duck down and weasel his way back to his own truck without being seen or caught in a pickle. This was quickly becoming a quagmire that had severe consequences laying at the end of the crossroad.

With fear rising inside his chest and his heartbeat pounding in his ear drums, McNealson lowered himself into a crouch and slightly peeked through the rear window of a car, trying to get a spy on the probability of him being surrounded and detained, in the middle this parking lot. Finally, the trucks sped off, after what seemed like eternity.

Agent Miller spun around the rear end of the truck to open the rear driver side door and saw an individual who was definitely familiar to him, but the figure moved out of his line of sight. He wasn't sure if it was Detective McNealson, so he told the driver to hold fast, as he thought he had seen something. The trucks waited, but the figure never resurfaced for him to positively identify him as the man they were seeking to detain, the same man whom just so happened to be the guy who made viable threats against the man they were presently securing in a vehicle to place in a Federal WITSEC program, pending the outcome of a federal indictment and trial. Allowing a few moments to pass, Agent Miller waved off his suspicions that the man they were actually searching for, was indeed, hiding in the same exact parking lot at the exact same moment they were moving a potential witness for security measures. They were on a mission and time was of the essence, so Agent Miller gave the go ahead to move out, while he kept his eyes peeled, looking out of the window for any suspicious movements or activities.

If he had, in fact, been confident in his initial sighting of the surrounding area, he would've called an extraction team to remove the package, Det. Dabney, and they would've set up a bottle neck perimeter around the lot and put the four sharp shooters in all four corners of the parking lot. Nothing in the area would move in or out of that parking lot, and an immediate lockdown of the area would have commenced, and their tactical team would have combed through every car and isle of that parking lot. There would not have been any room for mistakes and it would have come down to two choices for McNealson: Surrender without incident, or be shot down, with chances of survival being slim to none. The choice would be his to make, and the repercussions of that choice were also his to live or die with.

As they sped out of the parking lot, Agent Miller kept a keen eye over the area he thought he had seen McNealson, but wasn't quite sure it was actually him. Not seeing anyone fitting the description of the person he saw, he smiled to himself, saying, "I know I saw you, and there's no one who's even remotely close to who I know I saw. You get a pass on this one, buddy, sliver away, you little snake in the grass, sliver away."

When the trucks were gone from sight, Detective McNealson stood up from behind the automobile he had hidden behind, using it as camouflage, then quickly climbed into the front seat of his truck, and heaved a sigh of relief, as he slouched down in the seat, still frightfully hiding himself even though the threat was no longer present. With panic beating like steel drums in his chest,

McNealson shakily pulled out a pack of Newports from out of his jacket pocket and lit one with shaking sweat-coated hands. He placed the trembling cigarette between his dry lips, he took a deep pull and blew out a streaming white cloud of smoke, as he remained slouched down in the front seat, cowering in fear. Now, he could truly digest and absorb the feeling of why felons run, and the fear that runs through them when doing so. But he had come too far to turn back now, the bed was made, and it was time to lay in it. This wasn't his only choice, but he was choosing to finish what he started.

Once he smoked the entire cigarette down to the filter, he stubbed it out in the ashtray and remained docked down for quite some time, allowing enough time to pass before he felt positive that the threat of possible apprehension was completely erased from probability. With this assurance instilled in his mind, the panic receded and calm exchanged places with the panic, causing him to sit up, place another cigarette between his lips to chain smoke another one.

Starting the truck, he looked around and checked all of his mirrors before pulling out of the parking space. Without any well thought out plan of action, McNealson was playing all of this by ear, but he was definitely on a mission to find Stranger and bring his reign of terror to an end, before his career and his freedom was brought to an end first. Once again, he was faced with two outcomes. Just like every option in life, all are faced with, there are always two ways around, if you are being openminded to seeing all of your options.

Chapter Forty - Nine

June 10, 2020 8:30am Wednesday

Colorado, Interstate 25

Cruising along the interstate at a steady pace with morning traffic, Stranger turned on the radio, tuning the stations, looking for the morning radio buzz to hear what was being said on the news about the latest chain of events, in hopes, to come across the feed concerning last night's masterfully executed slaying that took place in plain sight for the public's viewing pleasure.

Smiling to himself as he mentally recalls the idiopathic nature of how he brought terror and shock to the world's living rooms and addressed the nation with a forewarning that shouldn't be taken lightly, for his browbeating came with a threat of reckoning attached, which was displayed like a live cinematic, pulse racing thriller, in a real life dramatic flare of public exhibition.

Snapping out of his recollection, the newscaster began broadcasting, "...a chilling incident that has taken place in a crowded restaurant parking lot of a McDonalds in Dallas which ended in bloodshed, as the patrons inside stood hopelessly by watching the suspect mercilessly commit a disturbing act of savagery when he bulldozed his SUV into the front lobby of the restaurant, intentionally mowing down two officers in the onslaught."

When the reporter finished summarizing the details of the event, she played a recorded message that was spoken from

Stranger's own mouth, after he had shot several bullets into the already wounded officers, fatally killing both and announcing to the world in ominous bravado, that "if any more black youth are shot unjustly by any officer of the law, in any state across the nation, 'I will commence my relentless attacks against the law enforcement with assiduous efforts to snap and cripple the Injustice system's back bone.'

"When the scene was thoroughly investigated, it was determined that two other officers were found fatally shot in their cruiser in what authorities say was a planned attack, and that this individual has been committing premeditated strikes of unique proportions for several weeks now. There's been a manhunt under way for this individual or individuals involved, and the FBI are asking the public for any information leading to the arrest and conviction of anyone who may be in connection with these homicides to call..."

Turning the station to tune into another news broadcast, Stranger sat quietly, before Mike's voice bombed from the rear seat, vehemently saying, "What the fuck, Stranger! I know my ears are deceiving me, Slim! Did that bitch just play a recorded message of your voice, verbally threatening the government, and they have a video recording of you committing those murders on the phones of all those innocent bystanders? Tell me you didn't, Slim! Convince me that all that hoopla was just a bunch of jaw jacking nonsense, conjured up for the entertainment of the viewing public... mutha fucka, are you just some dumb, or plain ole' plumb dumb?"

Mike's remark sent fire through Stranger's veins, as he erupted in anger for being talked down upon by Mike, saying, "Who the fuck you think you talking to, Mike? Your bitch ass ain't did shit but sit in the fucking shadows and whisper sweet nothings in my ear that your sweet ass was too damn scared to carry out yourself, Nigga, you ever in your mutha fuckin' life call me dumb again, I'll break every bone in your mutha fuckin' body and toss your bitch ass on the side of the highway like road kill, mutha fucka! Dumb? Nigga, dumb...what's dumb is to keep killing and no one even knows what the fuck I'm killing cops for. There's a reason and a method behind this madness! And keepin' it a secret sounds like the dumbest shit I've ever heard-"

Returning with his own spiteful comments, Mike came shooting back, "Bitch, huh? Is that how you see me now, Slim? I've been your nigga since childhood, we go all the way back to the jungle gym and hot wheels, nigga. I've been there when no one else was there for you, or for me, all we had was each other. Nigga I took bullets for you! And died in the process! No, fuck that! I died twice, nigga, for YOU! And now, you callin' me a scared bitch? Nigga, you and six niggas that act and look just like you couldn't break a fingernail on me, without me first breaking my foot off in your ass! You got me fucked up and twisted with that punk ass white boy sitting up front with you."

John turns his head, looking over his left shoulder in Mike's direction, who sat in the rear driver's side seat and said, "Keep my name out your mouth, Mike! Make my name taste like shit on your tongue! I'm tired of you venting on me every time you get mad. Stranger's right, all you do is talk, criticize and throw your opinions around like soft ass Nerf Balls when everyone in this car knows you're the last person on the planet to bust a grape, your ass ain't gonna throw a Crayola Crayon in a pre-school riot, mutha fucka! Shit, at least Lisa's ass was bold enough to willingly go with Stranger on one of these cop murders, your ass keep sitting in the back seat, like 'Driving Miss Daisy' and calling shots like you have ice flowing through your veins, shit, Lisa's-"

"Shut up John!" Lisa screams from the rear seat. "I'm not in this macho dick swinging contest of whose nuts hang the lowest. So, leave me out of it!"

Going silent for a second, John couldn't leave well enough alone, when he charged back, saying, " I'll leave you alone when I damn well please, Big Bird! And-"

SMACK!

Lisa's arm came flying out of no where from the back seat, slapping join in his mouth as he was about to insult Lisa, for no reason other than it's something that he's always done since they've known each other. Lisa yells heatedly, "I told your ass to leave me out of this and you're gonna stop disrespecting me, you little punk ass bitch, now shut the fuck up! Or I'm gonna climb my fat ass over this seat and beat your pink ass blue-black. Now, test me, John, and see what happens next."

Not wanting to infuriate Lisa anymore, John cracks a joke and says, "Damn, Lisa, was that a slap or a love tap, because my dick just got hard, I'm just sayin'..."

SMACK! SMACK!

Lisa sent two blinding slaps into John's face again, leaving behind beet red handprints in their wake. Lisa said, " Say something else, John, say one more fucking thing to me..."

John relented and says, "Alright, alright, damn..." Then he turns to Stranger while holding the left side of his face and said, "Do you got a Snickers Bar, she get a little feisty when she's hungry!"

Stranger was in no mood for John's antics, but instead, continued to send glaring looks into the rearview mirror, directed at Mike, which only made Mike ask, "What the fuck you keep staring at me for, Mr. Prime Time, give 'em something to talk about super predator. I mean, the joke's gonna be on you, in the end, when the walls come crashing down on your smart ass head, Mr. Know-It-All!"

"Oh, yea?" Stranger shot back, adding, "So, what would Mike, the hidden magician have me do instead? Continue killing like I'm some serial killer without a cause who just went crazy out of the clear blue and keep everyone guessing as to what my motives are behind the killings, huh? Mike, this ain't some sick, demented killing spree you're puppet mastering me through, I don't have wires tied to my limbs, Slim, I think on my own accord, I just so happen to take your thoughts and opinions into consideration."

Mike explodes in a loud voice, "Consideration!! Did you ever consider the impact of those statements you made on camera and the consequences they would bring? No! You didn't! What you thought? If you make a public announcement, that the law enforcement would quietly put down their guns and refuse to shoot someone in the line of duty, all because you made the national declaration to cease all fire or else. Who the fuck do you think you are? You're a nobody, Stranger, you've always been a nobody and when all this is over and done with, nobody is gonna remember you, except all the crazies in the world who glamorize serial killers, keeping the legacy of their acts alive. You're not gonna do nothing but get us all caught up by giving them all the missing pieces to this puzzle, instead of laying the trail of breadcrumbs for them to follow in hopes of catching up. That's why I called you dumb. 'Cause it was a dumbass move you did back in Texas, and a costly one too. Mark my words, Slim, and I'd hate to see the final outcome of all of this because if they start connecting all of the missing variables..." Pausing, Mike then added, "I'm gonna say this last thing and leave it at that, have you ever heard of the old saying, 'if it ain't broke, don't fix it'? Ponder on that, Slim."

Listening to Mike's last comment, Stranger realized he may have pushed things too far by giving them a definitive description of himself, but also, he wanted all the cops to know it's a life for a life and these murders are for a cause. So, he remained silent and kept his comments to himself, allowing the mood to change in the truck's interior as they continue to head down the highway. Stranger concluded that it was probably best to lay low for a while and find a quiet reserved hide away until they could figure out how much the FEDs knew and how close they were to catching up with him in their investigation, but he definitely struck while the iron was hot, and if another black youth lost his life by a cop anywhere in the nation, he promised he would start taking lives of cops all over again. Point served, the ball is now in their court. All he was waiting to see was who was willing to test his gangsta, test these deadly shark infested waters and test the ultimatum he had given. That's the million dollar question, that had no answer. So, Stranger would wait until time provided that answer for him.

Chapter Fifty

June 10, 2020 2:42pm Wednesday

Dallas, Texas

Flying into Dallas International Airport, the FBI team, Spl. Agents Smart, Draper, Maddox, and Goldfield, were briskly combing through case files and photo surveillance that were captured at some of the murder scenes over the past few weeks. After having to bypass the Oklahoma City casualty, they decided that the latest serial killing which took place the night before, in the middle of a crowded restaurant and parking lot, in the downtown area of Dallas, Texas, was their best option to follow up with their ongoing investigation, being that the killer actually provided them with a positive identification, and an actual motive for this recent rash of bewildering behavior, that seemed to have been some demented parody, with extremely exaggerated effect that they weren't made privy to, until now. When the video streams came flooding into the FBI headquarters, lead investigator, Spl. Agent Matthew Forrester, assembled a team to take over the Oklahoma City murders, and finish up with the evidence collection, and clearing the scene in St. Louis. They were on the clock and time was ticking down fast, until the next murder case file was slammed down on top of the many that were already at a dead lock, due to lack of evidence. It seemed to them that their perpetrator was very keen and careful in how he maneuvered, leaving behind barely any trace evidence to be collected, the only thing that he'd left behind intentionally, was a mutilated corpse and another cop's badge and gun from the prior murder, he was intentionally helping the FBI link the murders in an on going series. Hence, the making of the case apart of an artfully masterminded murder spree that only became dreadfully vile and disturbingly tumultuous as each subsequent murder progressed. It wasn't until now that the FBI had some credible information to go off, and their little engine was starting to pick up steam.

Spl. Agent Forrester began to recap the investigation findings of all the alleged copycat killings, only to spare them most of the gory details of those cases. When all was said and done, out of 11 copycat killings which happened in 10 states, 5 of those murders remained unsolved, 3 suspects were captured without incident, and 3 were shot down when officers tried to apprehend the suspects. Shoot outs ensued, ending in two wounded officers and three dead suspects.

Spl. Agent Forrester began issuing orders to the team and told them that they needed to catch their suspect fast, because after the Director of the FBI heard the recorded threat that was brazenly given without fear of apprehension. The shit began rolling downhill from the higher ups, and they were applying the pressure of a vice grip to get this renegade who was obviously committing murderous treason against authorities, whose basic jobs were to uphold the law, by protecting and serving. They didn't want a bunch of 'we're on top of it' promises, they wanted results and they wanted them yesterday. This was the last directive that was given, which wasn't an order, it was a demand, with the insinuation that heads were gonna roll if they didn't get on the ball.

Ending the conference call with the four agents, Spl. Agent Smart sat back in the plush jet seats and started vigorously searching through the emails that he'd requested of their alleged suspect, Ben Strange. After 30 minutes of reviewing all their possible information compiled of their suspect, he began trying to separate the trash from the treasure and building an image of the man they were now after.

With his mugshot in hand, Spl. Agent Goldfield asked, "So, that's our guy, huh?" He nodded his head without commenting. She then asked, "So, what do you think is our best approach to capturing him? You think we should put out a nationwide BOLO on him and ask for the community's help to rally against him?"

Shaking his head, no, Smart slowly answered, not sure he was making the right decision but he was weighing his options, when he said, "No, I think less is best on this one. I think leaving him in the blind, and thinking he's still free to run a muck without fear of being caught because we don't know who he is, is the best plan of action. We got a suspect now and we've connected the dots to the point we know who he is, why he's doing what he's doing, but when he's gonna strike again, and where he's presently at, those are the missing key variables in this equation, now we need to find the last variable, with what we have, then close this case and put away the worst serial killer this nation has ever seen since Manson and the Boston Strangler." Just then, an email pinged onto his computer screen and it was from the US Marshal Agent Clayton Vandoren.

Upon opening the email, he read the caption heading and started reading the contents which were enclosed. Halfway through the first few paragraphs, Spl. Agent Smart blew out an annoyed breath from his mouth, as his face scrunched up in a perturbed manner, as if what he was reading was really causing him distressed irritation and was just moments away from losing himself with all of the madness that was surrounding this case. Finishing the contents within the email, Agent Smart hung his head low and desperately tried to regain a sense of himself and his composure.

Seeing that something was bothering his partner, Spl. Agent Drapper leaned over the isle and tapped Smart's arm, "What's up, partner? Talk to me."

Looking up and seeing all of the other agents staring at him in concern, Smart chose to send each of the agents the email contents, being that he didn't want to recite any of the information he just read, because he was still reeling from it himself, he felt it was best to let them process the information by themselves just as he was trying to do.

As all the agents stared intently at their laptop screens, Agent Smart just closed his eyes and allowed himself some time to clear his thoughts before they landed and they were handed a sack full of puzzle pieces and asked to put it together in a matter of minutes. Hearing the other agents express their disbelief with audible discord while emotions began rising and falling, Spl. Agent

Cynthia Goldfield slams her laptop shut and silently stowed away towards the restroom with her eyes brimming with noticeable tears, just as Agent Drapper sat transfixed, reading. He removed his glasses and wiped his forehead with a handkerchief as he contemplated the jarring news he'd just perused through, unable to wrap his mind around the extreme circumstances that were exposed in the email which actually contained documented proof that was detailed in Dr. Emily Poole's personal bedside diaries. The information was jaw-dropping and precisely detailed.

When Spl. Agent Drapper began to talk to Smart, Spl. Agent Maddox cut in, saying, "I want that penitentiary under a full federal investigation right now!" voicing his displeasure at what was revealed in those personal memoirs and the admission that something very terrible was taking place behind those walls and razor wires of USP Lee County Federal Penitentiary.

Clamoring for his phone, and pressing a speed dial button, Spl Agent Maddox angrily said, "Get me Spl. Agent Forrester on the line and conference call the Director of the FBI and Director of Internal Affairs immediately! It's imperative that these gentlemen get enlightened about this new information that could potentially cause an avalanche of problems if they don't control this growing situation that has gone unchecked for quite some time, seeing that the information we've received and accumulated is incriminating and valid." Listening to what the person on the other end had to say, he said, "Yes, send me the Zoom link and thank you for your help, Stephanie!"

Ending the call, Agent Maddox checked his Breitling 1884 timepiece and leaned back into his headrest, saying, "This case is a fucking nightmare, and from the look of things, its all stemming from some seriously fucked up correctional officers and a rogue narcotics detective, whatever the trigger was, it most surely has something to do with some shady people implicating real true blue officers of the law." But just before going silent, Maddox added, "When I'm done with this tangled mess of a yarn ball, there's gonna be a lot of correctional officers pending charges, sitting in the unemployment lines regretting the mistake of abusing inmates under their care and the administration staff is gonna feel the heat, like a firing squad has rendered a verdict of guilt, as a judgement for allowing all of those atrocities to take place under their watch, watch all of the finger-pointing and blame pushing that's about to happen now."

With noticeable signs of anger etched in the contours of his face, Agent Maddox went dead silent. With all the venting and disquietness being lashed out of Maddox's mouth, Agent Smart was reminded of the task he'd assigned to one of his subordinate agents, and made a call to him, to see if the Grand Jury has come back with an indictment to proceed with a federal case of conspiracy against Detective McNealson, who was still at large and his two partners in crime who are detained already.

He was told that Detective Dabney was quietly tucked away in the WITSEC protection program, he told the junior FBI agent, that he was forwarding an email to him that he needed to be typed and placed in the indictment case file of all three officers under federal investigation and he also asked the agent to send another agent down to WITSEC to get a deposition from Det. Dabney and have him sign a waiver of rights and his immunity status, were the last orders he assigned, before ending his call and acknowledging that Spl. Agent Goldfield was casually coming forth down the isle towards him. He took in all of her subtle beauty. She stopped short of his seat, stared into his eyes and asked, "What?" with a pinkish blush to her cheeks. "Stop staring at me like that, you look goofy as hell, not to mention, thirsty."

Sliding into the seat beside him, she looked out the side window of the jet and said, "So, what did I miss?"

Spl. Agent Smart smoothly replied, "A lot of nothing, but I want to apologize for uhh..."

"Don't apologize for that, I catch myself staring at you from time to time. It's the law of attraction. We can't help it!" Spl. Agent Goldfield said, only to finish her comment by adding, "Besides, when this case is over, you can stare at me all you want, over dinner, my choice, deal?"

Smiling broadly, "That sounds like a pleasant deal to me... let's shake on it," said Smart.

Turning to face him, Goldfield extended her hand for a firm handshake, but said "I can think of better ways to seal this deal, but we're professionals." She winked at him in a flirtatious manner, as they shook hands and leaned back in their seats, just as the stewardess chimed in on the loudspeaker and alerted the agents that they would be landing momentarily, to buckle their seatbelts and remain seated until they've landed. Closing his eyes, Spl. Agent Smart was mentally preparing himself for what lie ahead, but felt good at knowing that they had a suspect of interest and they weren't far off of his heels. One slight mistake and this guy will be cornered, with no other way out but two ways, surrender or shoot out, there was no other options available to him...and surrendering seemed highly unlikely.

Chapter Fifty - One

June 11, 2020 6:30am Thursday

Alexandria, Virginia Waterfront

Relying on some trusted allies and friends, Det. McNealson found himself sitting in a seedy motel on the outskirts of Washington, D.C., on the waterfront area in Alexandria, Virginia, holed up like a fugitive, McNealson began racing through his thoughts, as the television set broadcasting the morning news announced that, another deadly shooting had taken place in Dallas, Texas, at a crowded McDonalds establishment, when the newscaster, reported that the alleged serial murderer spoke out for the first time, and the Channel 5 News Team had first footage of the suspect for the audience to view, McNealson hurriedly moved to catch an up-close look at the footage.

Kneeling in front of the TV with a purposefully attentive look upon his face, he waited for the footage to be aired. Suddenly, the masked face of the suspect was menacingly glaring in the direction of the person who was recording the incident as he began speaking in a threatening tone, promising the law enforcement a dreaded return if, any more innocent lives were taken by negligence of the police force, nationwide. Looking at the carnage that surrounded Ben Strange, he saw that there were two officers whose bodies lay crumbled in a mangled and contorted mess, but it wasn't the scene that caught his attention most, it was the final words that were spoken that gave McNealson an indirect clue that he could catch up and actually find Stranger. If his intuition was leading him correctly, he figured that, since he thought he was Moses, speaking with burning bushes, there was only a few places that he was sure that Stranger would hole up at finding some solace from detection, being that he told the world that he was going into hiding, then, Moses needed a mountain. And the closest mountain range that was heading due west would've been in the Colorado area, if his gut was steering him in the right direction, he believed that Stranger would be in the area of the Colorado Rockies Mountain Range, which are located in the Rocky Mountain Nation Park Reservation.

Smiling to himself, Det. McNealson began packing the little belongings he had, preparing himself to chase the wind on the notion of a whim. He felt this was a credible lead, no matter how small and insignificant the lead may have seemed, he was willing to go tracking clear to the middle of the United States and go rock climbing if he had to, just to catch Stranger and bring him to justice, since everything he had ever worked for, was being put on the line. He wasn't much of a gambler, but he realized with everything that he had placed at stake on this case, he was definitely going all in and going for broke. But this was one mouse that won't get to play, while he is away, before all was said and done, he was going to leave the police force with his final case closed on the books.

Once he took his shower and collected his things, McNealson headed through the door of the motel and before slamming the old squeaky hinged door closed, he took one last look at himself in the filmy mirror that hung on the wall above the dresser and saw his tension worn face saying, "Gotta do what I gotta do, ain't no turning back now." He then slammed the old, paint chipped wooden door closed and placed his sunglasses on his face. Stepping off towards his rental car that was rented under an alias by one of his closest friends. He now felt like a real fugitive on the lam, as he calmly glanced around the perimeter of the parking lot, looking for anything that looked peculiar. When he saw there was no initial threat, Detective McNealson made a quick advance toward his rental car, a Ford Escape SUV, climbed in and pulled easily out of the motel parking lot, heading west down the 495 interstate, only to take the I-95 south exit, to keep a steady course, with Colorado as his intended destination.

Turning his car radio to the morning news WPGC 95.5, a radio station which served the Metropolitan area of Washington, D.C., Maryland, and Virginia. He lit a Newport, inhaled the smooth menthal nicotine, and listened to Huggy Bear label someone the "Bama of the Week," laughing at the theatrics, the comedy skits and crank calls as he drove, every so often changing the channel to locate a news channel that would keep him abreast of the goings on and the latest news on Stranger, if there just so happens to have been another senseless killing of a child, Stranger was sure to come out of hiding to repay the debt, life for a life, as he threatened the nation he would, and McNealson believed he was every bit as capable of following through on his threat, if he wasn't captured first, which was why he was chasing the wind once again in hopes of catching him.

With an open file folder sitting in the passenger seat, McNealson looked over and lifted a mugshot photo of Stranger, out of the file and studied the picture of the man that had changed his whole life in a matter of a few short weeks. Shaking his head, he mumbles to himself, "This ain't over yet, Stranger. I'm hot on your ass, boy!"

Chapter Fifty - Two

June 11, 2020 8:01am Thursday

Dallas, Texas

Deciding to start out their day in two separate areas of the investigation, Spl. Agent Maddox shows up in the lobby where all the agents were meeting over the morning continental breakfast. When Maddox began issuing out assignments and partnering off the group to investigate certain aspects of the crime scene, being that there was also a new turn of events that they were made privy to. Maddox briefed the team on a newly discovered murder that was somehow connected to the McDonalds homicides in downtown Dallas.

As he began revealing the little he knew about the murder, he felt it would be best if the team switched partners and worked the respective cases from a different angle, which was to say, departing from the norm and reinventing the wheel, by approaching things with fresh mindsets, working in tandem to secure a renewed vigor to their ongoing seemingly perplexing case.

Spl. Agent Maddox said, "Agent Drapper, you're with me, you're the new Watson to my Sherlock, while Alfred Hitchcock there gets to work the other end of this case with Angela Landsberry over there," pointing out both Agents, Smart and Goldfield with a smile on his face, telling them that they were going to cover the murder that took place at a used car lot where one of the salesmen were slayed and found locked in the trailer office after the place was robbed.

Upon hearing the vague details, Agent Smart said, "So, what does a salesman have to do with this case?"

Agent Maddox stopped before answering, "I don't know, I was hoping that the two of you could help fill that missing piece in for me. You two seem to vibe well together, so use that vibe to help solve this case. All we know is that the victim's name is Albert Hammond, and he was working alone at the car lot on June 9th, his body wasn't found until the next morning on June 10th, and the rest is in your hands."

Before turning to walk away, Agent Maddox looked at Agent Goldfield and warned, "Cynthia, use your eyes and your head on this one, stay openminded and tie up the loose strings, leave nothing to chance."

As he turned to walk away, Agent Smart joked in a cheerful manner, "What, Mark? I don't get no pep talk to keep me focused on the directive I've been tasked with? I feel like I'm being discriminated against, and there's some secret feminist shenanigans taking place, which I'd like-"

"Quit it, Brad," Spl. Agent Maddox quickly remarked, cutting the morning joshing to a holt, and with an obvious smirk plastered on his face he went on to reply, "Brad, you don't need no damn pep talk, cause you're good at what you do and have a very keen perception of things. But, since you don't want to feel left out, Brad, your mission is to solve this case, and keep it professional, keep your nose to the ground and your head out of the clouds." Jibing with a knowing smile, Spl. Agent Maddox turned to look at Agent Drapper and said, "Let's roll out, partner. We got a long day ahead of us." With no other words being exchanged between the two, the pair headed out the front lobby towards the waiting caravan of FBI vehicles.

Looking at one another fondly, with radiant smiles upon their faces, Spl. Agents Smart and Goldfield grabbed up their personal effects and he, with a gentleman's chivalry, said, "Ladies first, after you."

Playing along with the charade, Agent Goldfield obliged with a dramatic curtsey and fancily pranced away, taking lead towards the front door, then looking over her shoulder, she threw the comment in Smart's direction, "You know, Mark manipulated this little get together to bring us closer..."

This caused Smart to reply back with a smile on his face, "I'm glad he did," as he watchfully appraised her feminine physique and the sway of her hips as she walked, while following closely behind her, exiting out of the lobby doors.

Arriving at the car lot and interviewing an older gentleman named Adam Abrams, the car lot owner and longtime friend of the victim, Mr. Hammond, it was quickly revealed that Mr. Abrams, was the one who had first discovered the body of his childhood friend, and employee. But as the information came pouring out, it was unveiled that Mr. Hammond was actually a retired Dallas Police Officer that was once under investigation by Internal Affairs for the use of excessive force, and several complaints of intimidation and extortion. Mr. Hammond had chose to retire by submitting his papers and taking his three quarters pension, before the case findings were complete and revealed. It was Mr. Abrams, who in fact made this information known about Mr. Hammond's past indiscretions in the line of duty. The preliminary findings in the investigation was a sealed in a confidential case file and no charges were ever filed against the retired Mr. Hammond. But, it was a known fact that Hammond was on the force for nearly 25 years and throughout those years, Mr. Hammond had quite a reputation for taking law and order to a whole new level. He was known to confiscate drugs and money from suspected or known drug dealers around the Dallas-Fort Worth and Oak Cliff area. Mr. Abrams admitted that Mr. Hammond came clean to him about his improprieties at work when he gave himself over to God and was baptized to cleanse himself of his sins. When he became a faithful member of his friend's local Baptist church, same church that Mr. Abrams had been a member of since childhood. Mr. Abrams gave Mr. Hammond a job, working as a salesman at his car lot because he was a redeemed Christian. With this knowledge, Agent Goldfield asked, "So, what made you think that Hammond wouldn't backslide and go against the grain with you?"

Shrugging his shoulders, Mr. Abrams rendered the question unanswerable, but chose to say, "I can't say what another person will or will not do, all I can do is give them the benefit of the doubt, to at least, burn a bridge with me. That's what the Bible says: "Love thy neighbor," and that gave me the responsibility to be, "Thy brother's keeper." God forgives and sheds his grace and mercy upon us all, so why shouldn't I be as my father, and do as my Father commands?"

Standing there transfixed, listening with a renewed belief in people truly walking in the light of Faith, Love, and Hope, Agent Smart asked, "Was there anything other than what was stolen that you'd like to bring to our attention, or do you think Mr. Hammond knew his killer?"

Shaking his head 'no', Mr. Abrams said, "The surveillance video feed was removed from the premises, and there was a 911 call made to dispatch, but was quickly excused as a 'non-emergency' by a man that I don't believe was Albert."

"Why would you say that, Mr. Abrams?" asked Agent Smart.

"Well, for starters, when the first responding officers came, they asked if I touched anything, and I told them 'no', then they wanted the video feed and I explained that the safe was left opened and the video recording unit that was inside had been removed. After they checked the phone for the last number dialed, they stumbled upon 911 as the last number dialed at 5:24pm, when they asked the dispatch to pull up the call log, they had me listen to the voice of the caller, and upon initially hearing the caller make the call in which dispatch placed them on hold, it was Albert's voice, but when dispatch came back from a short time on hold, they asked what the emergency was, but the voice on the line wasn't that of Albert. I knew it the instant I heard him talk. But it was so eerie to hear the man talking with casual nonchalance, so it told me that

Albert had enough time to make the call, cause he didn't feel something was seriously wrong, and decided against retrieving the loaded firearm that was left in the safe, which is no longer there nor was it used in this crime or left behind at the scene."

Pausing him in his recapping of the prior conversation with Dallas Homicide Detectives, Spl. Agent Goldfield chimed in, asking, "So, that gun that was stolen, what kind of gun was it and was it registered to you or Hammond?"

"Oh, yea," stated Mr. Abrams, "It was registered to me, a Glock 17, a 9mm 17 round mag, fully loaded."

"Thank you Mr. Abrams," said Agent Goldfield, "And I'm sorry to sound like I'm badgering you, but you never quite explained how you thought that Mr. Hammond didn't know his killer..."

Taking a second to answer, Mr. Abrams replied, "I did say, it's a fact that, if Albert truly felt or knew something wasn't right with the person, he wouldn't have tried calling the police first, he would've gotten the gun from the safe for protection. But it was the fact of him not knowing his killer which caused him to speculate and call 911 under the suspicion to have a unit come by to check things out, if he needed back up to assist him. Had he known his killer personally, he would've bypassed making the call and just went for the gun if he felt fearful that something was truly amiss. But it later revealed that a patrol unit did come by the lot around 5:45pm and they reported that there was no one on the lot and the place was closed and locked and that the lights inside the trailer were cut off. So, they went on with their patrol, because dispatch hailed for them to assist in a disturbance at a McDonalds, where they were fatally shot and died at the scene."

Upon hearing this news, Agent Smart stepped away and made a call to Dallas Homicide Division, asking for Detective Melvin Carr. When Detective Carr picked up the call, and the preliminary introductions were out of the way, he told Agent Smart that he had just gotten off the phone with their forensics crime lab techs and it was brought to his attention that the gun that was used and left at the scene of Mr. Hammond belonged to an Oklahoma City police officer. His name was Officer Eugene Chase, whose police issued Sig Sauer p220 .45 handgun was used as the murder weapon, but it was also revealed to him that another homicide case took place not far from the used car lot where Mr. Hammond was found murdered, but there was an obvious connection to both crimes. "How so?" asked Spl. Agent Smart.

Detective Carr began to relay the details of the second murder of four police officers in a crowded McDonalds parking lot and lobby. He said "The evidence that the suspect left behind connected not only Mr. Hammond's murder, but there was a police officer's badge that was left behind at the scene that belonged to the same officer in Oklahoma City by the name Officer Eugene Chase, bagde #512. Two firearms, one, a Glock 17, registered to the used car lot owner, Mr. Adams, and a Glock 27 that was registered to a St. Louis, Missouri Police Officer named-"

"Vernon O'Connel!" blurted Agent Smart, causing the

detective to stutter and say, "-uhh, ye-yes! How did you know that?"

"Because we've been chasing this killer for weeks now and we've kept account of how many guns and badges he's left at the subsequent scenes and in Officer O'Connel's murder there were several items that were taken, including his police uniform, and two of his firearms, one being his personal weapon and the other being his police issued sidearm, which was located at an Oklahoma City Homicide. Now that we know that both of these Dallas homicides are connected, we can positively say they are a part of our serial murderer's crime spree, and if I recall correctly, after seeing the video footage that was taken by one of the McDonalds patrons, the suspect who maliciously gunned down those officers in the restaurant lobby, was wearing a police uniform. If I'm correct in my assessment of this case, I'm willing to bet that the uniform belonged to Officer Vernon O'Connel of St. Louis Police Department."

Acknowledging that Agent Smart was correct in his assessment, Detective Carr went on to say, "An SUV was taken from the car lot, along with temp tags and a dealer's tag. The SUV was a black 2019 luxury Lincoln Navigator with black rims and the dealer tag was..." Locating the information, Detective Carr said, "Oh, here it is, it's umm...26511DT."

After jotting down this information, Agent Smart hurriedly told Detective Carr that it was imperative that he got this information passed on to his supervisor and told him that he or someone from his main office in the MidWest Region, would be in touch with him to seize control of all of the evidence and case file notes to transfer chain of custody from state jurisdiction to Federal.

When Detective Carr agreed to gladly hand over the case, and rid his hands of such a high profile case, Agent Smart bid him goodbye. Ending the call, he returned to the side of Agent Goldfield, who was still in deep interrogation mode and quizzically hammering out questions to Mr. Adams, when Smart said, "Agent Goldfield, there's been another development in the case, we need to wrap this up, there's nothing more here for us to investigate. We need to catch up with Agent Maddox and Drapper! I'll tell you the details along the way. Let's head out..."

Chapter Fifty - Three

June 11, 2020 8:51am Thursday

Dallas, Texas

Meeting up with Dallas Homicide, Detective Ross Wiesman to confer over the findings in regards to the multiple homicides at the downtown Dallas McDonalds restaurant. Spl. Agent Maddox told Agent Drapper to look over the evidence file and try to gather a compressed view of their case, while looking for other egregious aspects that could further shed light onto this case besides what they already knew.

As the two agents sat down at the conference table, in Dallas Homicide headquarters in Downtown Dallas, Texas. With Detective Wiesman meticulously elucidated over the initial findings of when he first inspected the scene, they were trying to piece together and rationalize the tirade of a speech that was delivered to a worldwide audience VIA Facebook live and YouTube. They couldn't ponder the thought of someone being so pernicious and subtly intimidating, just standing over the bodies of newly mutilated corpses without fear or consideration for human life, or even respect for those who uphold the law.

Going on to explain that after he reviewed the footage of all four officers' body cams and the cruisers' dash cams, it became apparent to Det. Wiesman that the murders were a part of an elaborate scheme, to bait and trap the officers by how the 911 call was made to summon the units to respond. But it wasn't the first unit to arrive that was attacked first, it was the second responding unit that was Unleashed upon first. Due to McDonalds having a surveillance camera system covering the parking lot, it showed the truck pulling into the parking lot, the driver getting out and peering around, before sliding beneath the SUV he arrived in, moments before the patrol unit pulled into the parking lot and came to an abrupt stop, just short of parking in front of the SUV, which they found to have been stolen from a town called Florence, in Kentucky.

But it was the way the guy creepily rolled from beneath the stolen Grand Cherokee that told Weisman that he was waiting for the second unit to arrive before he came out of hiding, which the dash cam and the surveillance of the parking lot showed. He was deliberately moving at blinding speed, leaping flatfooted onto the hood of the arriving patrol unit, and crouching into a shooter's stance with two guns leveled upon each officer who sat in the front seat totally caught off guard and released an unyielding assault of fatal shots into the bodies of, Officers Marquis Lampson and Titus Hawke Jr., both 8 year veterans on the Dallas Police Force. Then it was how fast he jumped off of the hood and quickly climbed into the awaiting SUV, and then drove straight into both officers, Sandy Wood-Pratt and Jeremy Thompson as they were exiting the lobby doors of the McDonalds, only to be struck head on and smashed into by the SUV's front grill.

Detective Weisman went on to say , "It was hard to view the final moments of the footage that each officer's body cam had recorded," then he finished the details of the story with how the suspect, exited the restaurant and calmly climbed inside the first responding patrol unit and pulled away from the scene, where the patrol car was later found at the dead end of a street four blocks away.

Reaching inside the case file, Detective Weisman pulled out forensic analysis and ballistics reports and told Spl. Agent Maddox: "The guns of both, Officers Wood-Pratt and Thompson, were removed from the scene along with their shields, and there were two guns recovered at the scene. One being a Glock 17, which was registered to a used car lot dealer, named Adam Abrams, who claims his weapon was stolen just hours earlier when his employee was robbed and murdered, obviously by the same suspect. The other weapon recovered was a Glock 27, registered to a St. Louis Police Officer who was recently murdered in Missouri by the name of Officer Vernon O'Connel."

Upon hearing the facts and realizing that the two murders that his team were investigating were both part of the same spree of killings, Spl. Agent Maddox thanked Detective Weisman for his help and asked that all the case files and evidence collected at both scenes be secured and transferred into the custody of FBI Crime Lab techs. Detective Wiesman cooperated with the jurisdictional procedures and assisted by expeditiously transferring chain of custody of the evidence, as well as all the video feeds of dash cams, body cams, and video surveillance footage.

It wasn't until Drapper spoke up and said, "Hey, Mark! I think

I have a hunch and a fair estimate on where our suspect is headed to or may be holed up at, but I think I need some more intel."

"As in what?" asked Spl. Agent Maddox .

"Like what vehicle our suspect is driving now, since he wrecked the vehicle he stole from Kentucky. I doubt he wrecked it without a back up plan already thought out. This guy's clever, but technology is more clever and more advanced these days-"

Just then, a call came in to Spl. Agent Maddox's cell phone. Answering, he listened to the caller, and said, "Yea, Brad, we know, we just got the full low-down on what happened and how both crime scenes are connected. But your partner has a hunch about what kinda vehicle he's traveling in, Whoa! Say that again!" demanded Spl. Agent Maddox, as a smile of contentment broke out on his face. He hastily told Spl. Agent Smart, "I need you to go back to the car lot and get the VIN number and find out if it has a global positioning system that can be activated or OnStar automobile assistance that we can enable through the Lincoln's dealership, GPS or even the Alexa navigational system, to get a location on the vehicle, then we'll be a step ahead of this guy, and he won't know that we've got him in our sights.

When Spl. Agent Maddox finished with Smart, he told him that they were to return to the hotel to regroup and prepare to assemble a team to aid and assist in the capturing of their suspect, but not before relaying his appreciation, by saying, "Great work Spl. Agent Smart, and your partner here, Agent Drapper makes a perfect Dr. Watson. Thanks for being a part of this team, see ya back at the hotel."

Ending the call, Spl. Agent Maddox sat back in the conference chair and looked over to Agent Draper, where Drapper quizzically asked, "So, what do we do now, Sherlock?"

"I prefer to bag and tag this guy, but I'll settle for a nice little quick surrender and capture," said Agent Maddox.

Nodding his head, Agent Drapper said, "Me too, Mark, me too…"

Chapter Fifty - Four

June 11, 2020 11:20pm Thursday

Interstate 40, Entering the State of Arkansas

Driving along interstate 40, Detective McNealson stared intently out of the windshield as the midnight hour drew near. Lost in thought, his throwaway phone rang, and upon answering it, he realized the incoming number was blocked. He listened to the caller relay some informative intelligence from an inside source that he had happened to stumble upon when making some inquiries to find out if he could, in fact, track down some in-depth details into what the FEDs had compiled on their investigation. Listening to an ally who now fed him information on how they were now on Stranger's scent and heading towards the Colorado Rockies area. Detective McNealson smiled to himself, he had caught a whiff of his suspect's position just from watching a Facebook live video from one of the restaurant patrons who had filmed the whole incident on his iPhone. The caller relayed the message that Stranger was in a black Lincoln Navigator and was presently holed up in the Colorado Rockies National Park area. But the FEDs were approaching the area with caution, in a covert operation, to get the whole area surrounded with a bottleneck perimeter to corral Stranger into surrendering without incidence. Detective McNealson believed that this was an impossible agenda to wish for, especially with the amount of calamity that Stranger had unleashed on the Nation's Police Force.

It wasn't until, after driving for several miles that McNealson took notice that there was a vehicle that he'd seen previously who seemed to be in pursuit of him, trying to look inconspicuous, but it was the lack of traffic on the highway at that time of hour that brought it to his attention. So, he finished listening to the caller debrief him on Stranger's supposed location, while he kept an eye trained on the car that trailed behind him, thinking to himself that he needed to see if the car that followed him was an actual threat.

McNealson decided to make an evasive move from the far left lane, darting across the lanes towards the exit that was quickly approaching. When the car that followed didn't pursue, he sat in park at the top of the ramp. He shook his head, as obvious thoughts of paranoia began to take desperate effect upon his mental. He was beginning to believe the likelihood that him being followed was all a figment of his imagination, so he stopped at the Exxon gas station just off the exit.

He refueled and grabbed something to eat before he got back on the road. While he pumped the gas and his mind began to wonder, he stood transfixed in an empty gas station lot. When the click of the gas pump broke his reverie, he travelled back to consciousness, yawning from exhaustion, from hours of riding along interstates, routes and exchanges, he climbed back onto the car and started the engine. He lit a cigarette and put the car in gear, but was frozen when the truck that he thought was following him earlier, eased past his front windshield and continued on down the road. He watched them depart in the opposite direction.

Playing the game of cat and mouse, Detective McNealson decided to make a maneuver of hide and seek. Moving towards the rear of the Exxon, out of clear sight of the vehicle that seemed to be following him over the last few hours, he waited. After a few minutes had passed and the dark blue Chevy Avalanche with dark tinted windows cruised back towards the interstate, getting on the ramp and heading west along, Interstate 40.

It was then that Detective McNealson saw that there was no doubt about it, that he was being tailed. But now he would make a major adjustment to his travel plans. Quickly pulling up to the side of the Exxon, he jumped out of his vehicle and ran inside the gas station and grabbed a road atlas from a display, double checking to make sure that he had grabbed the right one. He paid and then quickly made a frantic exit from the gas station lot and found another secluded location to contemplate the atlas and secure another travel plan, one that didn't have a trailing truck involved.

Once he had his new travel plans highlighted, he drove in silence and kept his eyes peeled in two separate directions, one was on the windshield and the other was on the rearview, but he definitely was looking out for any danger that could potentially derail his plans of apprehending Stranger, and bringing his reign of terror to a permanent end, as well as bringing him to justice.

Chapter Fifty - Five

June 11, 2020 11:30pm Thursday

Interstate 40, Arkansas

"So, where did he go?" asked Mayhem.

"I don't know! Let me check the GPS locator you put on his car," replied Mannimal.

After uploading to the laptop and synchronizing the GPS indicator app, it showed that McNealson was on a different course than the one they were presently on. "Well, you want to change course and keep the tail?" asked Mayhem.

Brewing over the question, Mannimal replied, "Naw, we know where he's headed and our inside source gave us the details we need to catch up with Stranger and give him heads up that the FEDs are closing in on him. I'm just pissed that Stranger deviated from the plan and can't be alerted to what's coming his way. If he'd have kept the cellphone that Emily provided him with for communication, he would know that the FEDs are following the OnStar GPS of the Navigator he's driving! That fool ain't thinking with his head, he's simply running off of emotions. But let's get moving, cause by morning, they should have him in the noose and be ready to hang him for the world to see. Time's tickin' and Mayhem, we gotta get there before McNealson does."

Sitting in quiet thought, Mayhem asked, "Hey, Mannimal, so how did you get this inside source to collaborate and switch sides?"

Taking a second to answer as he sat staring out of the

windshield at the road ahead, eyes locked on the lone reflectors that trailed down the highway ahead of them, Mannimal cockily answered. "When you're in between a rock and a hard place, and your family's survival hangs in the balance of your cooperation, you tend to make the right decisions when something you love is on the line. The man I got to set all this up, and got McNealson to think that he's helping him catch Stranger, when he's really guiding him to his death? That man is the man that helped put me in Federal Prison and testified to help the government secure my guilty verdict. Now his wife and three children are sitting in a basement, buried alive in a box fit for four, and he's gonna do everything in his power to keep them alive."

"Damn, Slim, that's some strategic shit you pulled off," said Mayhem.

"Naw, I've been planning this for years now, what that man don't know is; I already recorded his wife and kids pleading for him to help them and cooperate with my demands. Their pre-recorded voices are the bargaining tool I'm using and I'm not setting them free. No matter what happens, they good as dead in my book. At least they'll all die together as one family, and yea, I'll tell him where to find the bodies of his dead wife and kids when all of this is over, and let him dredge over the consequences of his actions for getting entangled in my affairs," said Mannimal.

"So, how did you get at his family?" asks Mayhem.

"I had Dr. Poole look him up and get the information into his family's whereabouts and location a year ago. I just showed up and took the whole family hostage and drove them away in their family caravan. What he don't know is, they're in the basement of his own father's vacation home in Eastern Shore, Maryland, down by Solomon's Island. I swear, the internet is the best thing to acquire a lot of personal information on someone, especially a cop who likes taking vacation pictures and posting them on their Facebook accounts for the world to see," replied Mannimal, with a malicious smirk on his face, as he recounted how he effortlessly took a Federal Officer's family and stored them away in a shallow grave, still breathing and praying for their savior to come and save the day. But that day is not coming and their savior is gonna shed tears for 40 days and 40 nights on his failure to protect his own family.

Shaking his head, Mayhem just smiled and said, "You vicious, Slim,cold blooded vicious," as he continued down the midnight highway and the silence ensued between them. "So, what we gonna do when we get to Colorado with all them FEDs searching about?" asked Mayhem.

Replying casually, Mannimal says, "They one track-minded, they ain't looking for us, they looking for Stranger's ass! We're hiding in plain sight." With a hand gun sitting in his lap, Mannimal finally said, "This is gonna be like killing crabs in a bucket. They got their agenda, and we got ours."

Smiling broadly, Mayhem just nodded his head in agreement and allowed the silence to lay like a blanket over the moment. They pushed forward with the Chevy Avalanche on cruise control, maintaining the designated speed limit as they headed out of

Arkansas, and into Missouri. Mayhem mentally explored the possibilities that he was gonna bring the old Mayhem back and release all the pent up fury he's been constraining since the abuse he'd experienced in the Federal Penitentiary.

Mannimal loomed over a plan of attack that was sure to come. He sat in the mind frame that teetered on the cliff edge of extremist and revolutionary. He saw no degree of balance and was laying in a bed of euphoric overkill. It was an intensity that was being subdued by a choke chain of melancholy patience.

Contemplatively, Mayhem and Mannimal were pondering their own display of wrath and justice. But they needed to catch up with Stranger before his final judgement lay at the feet of men with smoking barrels. There is no time to waste, and death is around the corner...Someone's death, that is.

Chapter Fifty - Six

June 12, 2020 5:32am Friday

Denver, Colorado

Filing into a crowded conference room at Denver Colorado FBI regional field office, Senior Investigator Spl. Agent Matthew Forrester came barging into the room with an ominous scowl on his face, while flanked by two agents. Taking the podium, he placed two thick files upon the flat surface.

Looking over the room of intent faces, Spl. Agent Forrester began the meeting with preliminary findings, giving a detailed description of the suspect, only to have a projector display a mugshot of Ben Strange up on the projector screen, while reciting a long list of charges that Stranger had either been charged in, with no available disposition, or found guilty of. These cases ran back as far as his teenage years, where he spent sometime in Sheltonham Boys Village Reformatory School in Upper Marlboro, Maryland, as well as other Reform Schools and Youth Centers that house troubled youth.

The cases compiled were from petty larceny, to theft, to gun possession, to drug distribution. But it wasn't until they dug deeper into Stranger's history that they found that Stranger had multiple run ins with the Prince George's Police Department in Prince George County, Maryland, and a few mishaps involving police within the Metropolitan Police Department in D.C.

After hashing over the incident report history of Stranger's behavior in the Federal Penitentiary, it became clear that there was no history of violence that could attribute to the vile acts that he was suspected of doing. But, with actual documents in hand, which was the diary of the recently deceased psychology Doctor, at Lee County USP Federal Penitentiary in Jonesville, Virginia, where there was documented proof that Ben Strange was a serious threat that was not to be taken lightly. These diaries also detailed private accounts of elusively mischievous acts that had taken place under Dr. Poole's watchful eye. These fantasies weren't acted upon, but were more of psychological infatuations that were a type of emotional foreplay which the late Dr. Poole wrote vivid desires of having sexual interest with several of the inmates under her care at the Federal Facility. Two of which are at large and unaccounted for. One of them recently escaped the Federal Maximum Security facility with the aid of Dr. Poole, whose diary depicted her having a strong lustful connection, that were only acted out in fantasies, by Dr. Poole. "The diary is a disturbingly detailed memoire of seduction and allurement that went far beyond the realms of professional ethics," said Agent Forrester.

Summarizing the accounts into the investigation that led back to Lee County Penitentiary and involved a key aspect of who and what Ben Strange was known for, and what his mental state was that seemed not to have a definitive answer because Dr. Poole couldn't quite put a precise psychological evaluation on record for Mr. Strange. "Due in part, that Ben Strange supposedly had a concoction of many different personalities, emotional, cognitive, and mental disorders, that ranged from bipolar depression to dissociative identity disorder to shadows, to mania and psychosis. It's uncertain what we're dealing with when it comes to Ben Strange, but we are certain that he won't hesitate to kill, or be killed if he's cornered, with no other option or a way out," said Spl. Agent Forrester.

After he handed the room over for questions, many were asked in regards to what tactical advantages were being put into place and who the captains were. It was also asked, if there were any proof that Ben Strange was acting alone in this spree of murders, and whether or not there could be any accomplices.

The room sat heavily brooding over that aspect of unknown variables, when Spl. Agent Forrester answered by saying, "It isn't known as of right now if Mr. Strange is acting alone or has an accomplice. I mean, other than that of Dr. Poole and another deranged lunatic by the name of Dominic Mann, who was known by the name of Mannimal, and if you remember some 8 years back, Mannimal was a serial killer who enacted extreme acts besides the murders on his victims with no sign of remorse or of sympathy. He was one of the worst serial killers of this century, it was unknown until now that anyone other than the suspect acted out these murders, but it is not being ruled out, that an accomplice or accomplices are involved in this carnage of serial murders."

Once Spl. Agent Forester finished the recap and gave out orders and team assignments, Spl. Agent Smart, leaned back in his conference chair and stared longingly at the projected image of Ben

Strange on the screen, asking himself, how someone could be so vile and angry?

When out of the blue, the voice of Spl. Agent Goldfield, brought him back to reality, when she said, as if reading his mind, "Some people have it harder than others, and some lose themselves in all the madness of it all, then some are just plain ole sick and demented. I believe he's just playing payback to all the officers who were or are targeting him and people of his race and ethnicity. This didn't just happen overnight, and there were no signs pointing to him as an erratic serial killer since childhood. No, something serious had taken place and he was at his wits end."

Turning to look at Cynthia in her stunningly beautiful crystal blue eyes, allowing his eyes to roam over the dark brunette hair that seemed to give an allurement about her that was insatiable to him the longer he remained in her company. It wasn't until hearing her thoughts about their suspect, that a lot of what didn't make sense began to make sense. Spl. Agent Smart didn't just appreciate Goldfield for her beauty, he was more attracted to her mind and her personality which had an effect on him quite like none he'd ever experienced before.

Once he considered her reasoning as a possible fact, he let the mood ease up as he sat forward and said, "You may be right Cynthia, I never tried looking at it like that, but it don't give him the right to unleash this sort of terror."

Causing Agent Goldfield to say, "You're right, it doesn't, but there is a lot we don't know. But whatever triggered this onslaught remains a mystery to everyone, other than the man who is committing these murders. Our job is to catch him and put him away so he can't cause any more harm to unsuspecting innocent people, whether they are civilians or law enforcement."

Rising from his seat, Spl. Agent Smart looks deep into Spl. Agent Goldfield's eyes and says, "Well, let's catch this guy so we can plan our vacation and go on our honeymoon!"

Smiling, Agent Goldfield said, "Chivalry is dead, huh? When were you going to tell me that I was getting married to you? My, aren't we confident!"

"Yea, I'm an oracle, I can see the future, and hold up...Yep! Yep! There are also little ones running around with a cute little yellow lab in that picture frame, too," said Agent Smart.

Walking away from the conference table, Agent Smart looks back and notices that Agent Goldfield is still sitting with a smile plastered on her face. Breaking the daydream effect, Agent Smart said, "Shall we? Snap out of it, it's destiny..."

Turning to leave the room with a smile of contentment upon his face, Agent Smart believed that this was a smooth way to convey his feelings for Cynthia, and he saw just how much the effect had on her. She was gonna be his wife in a very short time to come. He'd finally met his match..

Chapter Fifty - Seven

June 12, 2020 6:20am Friday

Colorado Rockies Mountain Range

Strolling about a hiking trail on the mountainous range of the Colorado Rockies, Stranger and the others are taking in the beautiful sight, as the sun comes peeking above the horizon and the birds are singing about.

John says, "Hey, Moses, where the fuck are these burning bushes that we're supposed to be having deep contemplative conversations with?" This in turn, causes Mike to join in on the jest saying, "'Yea, Stranger, you got us up here in the high elevation of the Rockies and ain't no damn bushes burning or speaking. Shit, you told the world you would be talking with bushes and bringing forth a new prophesy or some shit, didn't you?"

Mike laughing at his little jab at Stranger, began to hoorah and grab at his stomach in total clowning effect to make Stranger mad. John chimed in with another foolish remark, saying, "See Stranger, come here, look at this." Stooping down to put his ear to a scraggly dried bush as if he was listening, John said, "Okay, I'll…okay...okay...okay...uhhh huh...yea, yea, yea, okay, repeat that...ok, I'll let him know..."

Standing up abruptly, John says, "Stranger, guess what? I just got this dried twig of a bush to relay a message to me, it told meee...to tell youuuu..." elongating the vowels to sound condescending, "that you're standing on the wrong mountain range and that you're not Moses, or a prophet, and you need to watch the company you keep because you hanging with a cow that's manipulating you, a retard who thinks he's smart, but in reality, he's really a moron who's gonna get you caught up with all his stupid psychological babble and don't be deceived by his looks, because he just looks smarter than he really is." As John takes a gander around at the bunch. He realizes that no one is laughing at his snide remark and jokingly says, "Come on now, you know that was funny! You're just mad cuz the joke's on you!" Laughing alone at his own jest, he walks to the edge of the mountain to look over while everyone stares at him in angry silence for how John always makes jokes at their expense.

Then Mike says, "You know what, John? I can push your white ass off this mountain top and won't no one care or feel indifferent for me doing so."

Lisa suddenly screamed at John in fury, yelling, "Fuck that shit! I told your ass about fuckin' with me!" Storming forward with her fist balled up in a tight clench, she began throwing punches at John's face, landing several on his chin and cheekbone, as John tried desperately to get away. He began backing up, towards the cliff edge inches away from falling before Mike swiftly intervened and grabbed both of Lisa's arms as she threw a slew of powerful punches, dazing John with her fierce blows until he stood befuddled and scared with his arms covering his face to keep from being assaulted any further by Lisa's continuous blows. Lisa screamed at him saying, "I told you mutha fucka! Stop fuckin' with me!" Steadily throwing her hay makers, landing more than she missed, "And you better quit callin' me a cow, you bitch made mutha fucka!"

After Mike separated Lisa from her barrage of furious punches, Mike turns around in a tight spin on his heels and lands a right hook, solid upon John's temple and cheekbone area, knocking him unconscious on his feet. John folded like a lawn chair, when his legs went spaghetti limp, causing him to crumble and buckle under his dead weight. Laying on the rock surface of the mountain trail, John was rendered comatose and left to lay motionless, as the others stood by and watched him sleep as silently as a newborn baby.

A few minutes passed before John stirred awake and stared up at the sun, and asked, "Did you just stand there and let your cow kick me into unconsciousness?"

Lisa lunged forward in a desperate attempt to unleash another fury of blows upon John, when Stranger said, "Y'all chill out, and John! Get your stupid ass off the ground before I let Lisa beat your ass again! She told you to stop disrespecting her. A hard head make a soft ass."

Leaning up on his elbows, John looks in Lisa's direction and says, "Lisa, I don't know if those punches jarred something inside me or not, but I think I'm in love, or maybe I'm still punch drunk and the effects haven't worn off yet. Either way, will you marry me?" saying these words like he was serious, he waited for her answer.

Lisa only stared at him with hatred in her eyes and said, "Fuck you! Yea, I'll marry your ass, and beat you senseless every single day of our miserable lives together!"

Which makes John reply, as he climbed to his feet, dusting himself off, "Good! That settles it! Me and you are married and Moses over there resided over our wedding." Looking in Stranger's direction, John adds, "If I can't beat her, I might as well join her. I need someone to protect me from the Hulk over there," pointing a stern finger over in Mike's direction, he then walked over to Lisa and stood in front of her and said, "I'm sorry my darling wife, I won't disrespect you any more, now let's go behind one of those burning bushes over there and consummate this marriage."

Not being able to stay mad at John's wild and crazy antics, Lisa turns to walk away, looks over her shoulder with a smile and says, "John, you make me sick," Then she turns to Stranger and said, "Come on Stranger, let's go talk, I need to ask you something..."

Standing, at a distance from the other, Lisa began her inquisition by staring deep into Stranger's eyes and saying, "My eyes aren't deceiving me, I see that you have some unsure concerns weighing heavy on your mind. But, so do I, Stranger." Looking harder with uncertainly in her callow face, the youthful friend comes out of hiding and Lisa says, "Since the beginning of all this, I went from state to state, listening to every thought you allow your mind to brood over, and yet, I said nothing, keeping a lot opinions to myself. But the point I'm trying to make is: Why? Why all this,

Stranger? I mean I understand that it seems like our race is under siege and we're dying by our own protectors at an alarming rate these days, and hardly any are being penalized or held accountable. They are justifying their actions with excuses, reasons like our past criminal records that have nothing to do with the present, and I see how the police are stereotyping us and giving us astronomical numbers of time to do in the penitentiaries for nonviolent crimes-"

"No! You don't understand, Lisa " yelled Stranger, cutting her words short, "They ain't just being biased, they think all blacks are bad! They think everyone had a fruitful glorious life without crack fiends for parents, or a system who ships children around like cattle. They want us dependent on the system and to remain poverty stricken, excepting every pitiful handout and stimulus they give with a laundry list of do's and don'ts attached, and the police are the worst criminals of all criminals. They'll break the law just to uphold the law, where they deem facts as their own agenda. There's no clear line of right and wrong. If a black drives around drunk and kills someone in a car accident, thats a manslaughter. It will carry the maximum sentence, whereas a white man gets probation, and he's back drinking and driving by the end of the week at a Country Jamboree with all his down home buddies. A black man can't possess a gun to protect himself, though."

"Yeah, he can, Stranger," screamed Lisa, "he just needs a license to carry it, that's all, get a license..."

"For what, Lisa? To have one, and get shot down for being black with a gun, if you're pulled over on a stop and frisk," said

Stranger, arguing back with another sharp point of view of his own. "They don't ask anymore. They're killing us at traffic stops! Running up in innocent people's houses with the wrong address, and shooting people. Planting evidences, abusing the arrested people in their care, assaulting us and no one's paying for all those murders! *No one!*"

Stranger argues, venting his anger and showing signs of breaking under the heated change of views, while his lips and jaw shook with a tick, as the tension showed visibly on his face. "Lisa, you don't have no idea what it's like being in my shoes or every black man in America, who's under the gun and could fall at the drop of a hat all because some cop thinks he's cleaning up the community by falsifying evidence and violating our civil rights and due process rights, and even coercing the witnesses to testify in cases with false testimonies. Lisa, they do this everyday in every state across America, and no one cares! The courts turn a blind eye, Congress keeps passing laws with countless gateways for them and hurdles for us to surmount, but they leave the trap doors for the government to wiggle themselves out of situations where they violated our constitutional rights. Just look at the 'Qualified Immunity', they can't even get into trouble for killing us! Why is it that a man can have a gun case and the gun wasn't even used in a crime, or a crime of violence, but he gets 15 years to life for that gun? More time than people who commit manslaughter, murder or child molestation! Or rape!" yelled Stranger, as he turns his back to Lisa and looks over the mountain scene.

Lisa stands there at a loss for words before finally answering, "I understand your anger and confusion of how the law is applied to our race, but is this the best way to go about it? Making all cops pay for a few cops-"

"A few! The fuck you mean, 'a few' Lisa? On average, there's 8 out of 10 cops who are racially profiling us, and a lot of those cops are our own kind, going along with their counterparts because they don't wanna look like they're against the Police Force. It's all a farce, Lisa! This all new age slavery and the Klan don't wear hoods no more. They're in Congress, they wear suits and robes and uniforms! Their badges are their shields to uphold and break the law as they see fit. I told you before, that Justice isn't blind, that bitch sees 'Just Us' just fine! It's a new world order with a race depleting point of attack: When we push, they push back, then we take a stand, they take a stand on our backs and bring our communities to weakened knees, they are tearing black families apart, and taking our communities and turning them into prominent white dwellings. Kicking out our families, its gentrification with no remorse. And we as a people aren't even considered men, because the constitution once considered us as three-fifths of a man! It's written in the constitution of the United States of America as so. So, if we aren't considered full men, then what are we? Animals? Beasts of the wild, with no religion and no flag, just creatures in their eyes and we are being treated worse than animals, killed in the streets by the ones who are supposed to protect us."

"Hey, Stranger, come look at this. Hurry up, Slim, come

look!" said Mike from a distance, as he and John stood at the mountain's ledge, looking down along the mountain side.

Approaching the mountain's edge, Stranger looked over and saw a lot of movement around the Lincoln Navigator and said, "Man I know that ain't cops, is it?" Urging Mike to reply.

"If it ain't, it sure looks like it, and it seems there's another car down there that they are-Oh shit! Look! The car took off with the cops on foot, chasing him! Damn, Slim!" Mike says excitedly, as he watches the car peel off and break away from the cops who surrounded him on foot.

"It looks like there's about 20 of them cops down there chasing that car!"

"Naw, Slim, they aren't there for him, they there for us, look at how they were positioned, they were everywhere, surrounding our truck, look...look at where they're all coming from, like they were hiding or something," said Stranger.

This caused Lisa to tearfully ask, "What now, Stranger?"

"Yea, Moses, what we gonna do now?" asked John, with a hint of sarcasm in his question.

With no answer to give them, Stranger turned and walked away but replied by saying, "Let's go! I'll figure it out in a minute. First off, we need to leave this area, we may have to do it on foot for now, but need to move! Now!"

Storming away, he hot-footed along the mountain trail with the others in pursuit. Stranger knew things were coming to a head, and he needed to think fast and come up with a plan before their feet touched flat ground...

Chapter Fifty - Eight

July 12, 2020 7:00am Friday

Colorado Rockies National Park

Driving to the Colorado Rockies National Park, Detective McNealson talks to Agent Albert Finely as he guides him to the location of Stranger's stolen Lincoln Navigator.

Frantically, Agent Finley says, "It shows it's a half of a mile due west of your present position." Searching with his eyes and looking for the vehicle's description, McNealson turns down a road that was heavily surrounded with foliage cover and trees that aligned the area like a wall of dense forest.

When he came upon an area that enclosed a parking lot, where campers and RVs sat arranged in rows, he continued on the path he was driving, when finally Agent Finley spoke softly into the phone, saying, "Here! The truck is right there, within a few yards of your position, I'm hanging up now-" Click!

The phone line goes dead. The cellphone hums a lost signal. McNealson tossed the cellphone into the passenger seat atop the field file that he'd looked over a hundred times since this little scavenger hunt began, back in Alexandria, Virginia.

Perusing the area, his eyes fell upon the parked Lincoln Navigator with huge black rims and thin rubber band like tires. He knew he had found the truck, so he quickly parked his Ford Escape and climbed out with his glasses shading his eyes from the bright morning sunlight.

Approaching the SUV from the rear driver's side like he was an occupant of the RV that was parked to the SUV's left, he got within close proximity of the truck. He took a quick glance into the SUV's dark tinted windows and saw no one inside the truck. Reholstering his weapon, he decided to take a look around the area and see if he could spot anyone that fit the description of the mugshot face he'd had in his file of Stranger, or even come close in resemblance. Looking about, the feeling of unease came upon him, and knowing how to follow his intuition, he knew something was unsettling. He was certain, when across the parking lot there sat several vehicles that didn't quite fit with the vacation setting of automobiles that would come to a National Park.

It wasn't until a door opened up one of the dark colored Crown Vics that drew his attention, as he made a hasty retreat back to his SUV in a desperate attempt to flee from what was an apparent sting to apprehend Stranger. When the agents began to descend upon him, McNealson responsively moved towards his SUV, jumped in the driver's seat and started the truck. He quickly looked for an exit strategy because the surrounding agents began to encircle the truck as he crouched low in the seat, in fear of being fired on, as 15 or more agents in suits and tactical gear had him penned. But it was the incoming influx of camper and vacationers that drew their attention away from him long enough for McNealson to slam the Ford Escape into gear, and ram his foot down on the gas petal, panicking in an effort to abscond the threat of being arrested by the agents.

One of the agents whom he had seen back in Spotsylvania, Virginia, when Detective Dabney was being taken into protective custody, came beating the butt of his firearm on the passenger window, chasing along side the truck as he was kicking up dust and gravel from the rocky ground that made up the parking lot.

Finally, in a brazen attempt to keep from being shot, McNealson drove the passenger side of the SUV in close proximity of the other parked recreational vehicles that were aligned in rows along the edge of the parking area. The agent saw that he was about to be crushed and pinned between the escaping truck and a parked camper, so he quickly ended his pursuit and hunched down in a shooter stance to try and take out the rear tires of McNealson's SUV. Just then, a child came running into view, chasing a ball into the parking lot, which caused all the agents to hold fire as the child's parents came running to retrieve their son from the ensuing chaos that the child was unaware was taking place at the moment.

With that little break in time, McNealson sped away and bent the corner of the parking area at breakneck speed, trying to get away from the force of agents that actually had him in a tight grip. He made it out by the grace of God, and he continued to tear away down the road to flee the area, but slowed once he saw that there was no hot pursuit of cars on his tail.

The team captain screamed into the earpieces of the surrounding agents. "Retreat! Retreat! That is NOT the prime target! I repeat! That is not the prime target, get back in position now! The target is still at large."

Slamming the walkie talkie down in angry frustration, Spl. Agent Maddox yelled, "Find out who broke cover and chased that truck, find out now! I want his ass on a platter, I didn't give an order to break out of surveillance! So, what the fuck did this person think he was doing?"

Listening into his ear mic, Agent Drapper said, "They're saying the guy in the Ford Escape was Detective McNealson, the man that's been indicted on federal charges concerning this case. They were trying to detain him."

Yelling at the top of his lungs, Spl. Agent Maddox said, "Fuck him! Fuck him! Fuck him! He's not the primary objective right now, I could give two fucks about Detective McNealson, he's been a pain in our ass since the beginning of all of this! Now look, I bet my pension that we just blew our only chance at catching this sick mutherfucker! All for what? A fucking renegade homicide detective who is about to go to federal prison? Fuck! Fuck! Fuck!" Spl. Agent Maddox vented angrily, beating his fist on the steering wheel. "Now I have to tell Matt Forrester that we blew this assignment, and we may have given this Ben Strange guy a fuckin' way out! We fuckin' had him! All we had to do was hold our position, now look! Look at all this fuckin' chaos, look at all the civilians just staring at us like we're sitting ducks. That Stranger guy ain't coming back to this truck now, he'd be a damn fool if he did, and we can all agree he ain't a fool."

Throwing his sunglasses on the dashboard, Spl. Agent Maddox lowered his head to the steering wheel and said, "Send all units back into position, and tell whoever broke protocol to write up a report and get ready for an ass chewing, because one is definitely coming, not only for him but for my ass as well."

A voice came on the mic, "It was me, sir. Special Agent Miller, I saw Detective McNealson and I just reacted. I'm sorry, sir. I'm on the report now..."

Chapter Fifty - Nine

July 12, 2020 8:00am Friday

Colorado Rockies National Park

Climbing out of the thickets, Stranger, Lisa, Mike, and John all moved about the area, trying to find a way out of the National Park without drawing any unwanted attention to themselves, when they happened to come across what looked like a small cottage from the rear.

John said, "Hey Stranger, that looks like a ranger station, how about we stop and ask for directions-"

"Hell Nawl, Slim!" said Mike, interrupting. "We better try getting away in the woods before approaching that station."

Then Lisa said, "It looks like there's no one there, we should follow Mike's suggestion."

Closing in on the ranger station at the rear window, Stranger ignored what the others were saying and quietly peeked in the window with a stealthy approach. After a few seconds, Stranger said to the others, "Wait here, I'll be back." Then he rounded the side of the wooden cottage.

Pulling a hunting knife from his belt lining, Stranger stuck the knife in his hoodie pouch and entered the front door. Sitting in a chair with hiking boots casually up on the desktop, a ranger leans back and says in a solemn tone, "I'm Ranger Greenway, how may I help you, sir?"

Taking a few moments to scan the open room, Stranger said,

"I would like to get directions to find my way back to the campsite area." Huffing his irritated breath at being brought out of his relaxed slumber, the ranger sat up and slammed his boots down on the floor. Heaving himself out of the chair, he walked towards the National Park grounds map that was displayed on the far left side of the room. Lumbering towards the map, the ranger said, "We are here," pointing to the red X that was marked.

Before he could say anything further, Stranger said, "Thank you, Ranger Greenway, and plunged the tip of the serrated blade of the hunting knife into his ear, twisting the handle, causing a crunching, squishy sound to echo in the hollow room. Ranger Greenway collapsed in a fallen heap into the floor. Stranger viciously yanked his knife out and stood over him. Tilting his head back to look in his dead ranger eyes, he said, "You know I hate cops, but I really hate Park police even more, we have bitches like you running around D.C. like you some real tough guys!" Then to add insult to injury, Stranger slammed the knife down hard into the gaping mouth of Ranger Greenway until the blade broke through the skin at the back of his neck and lodged into the wooden floor.

Taking a look around, Stranger saw that there was a browning 10mm handgun on his hip and removed it from the holster. He decided to make this kill a part of his long endless spree, when he rips the silver ranger badge from his uniform and laid the badges and guns of both officers from the Dallas Police Department on his chest, those being Officer Sandy Wood-Pratt, badge #2821 and Jeremy J Thompson, badge #5993.

Noticing a set of keys on the key chain, Stranger roughly tore the keys from the belt loop and headed towards the front door. Taking another look around, he turned the sign that hung on the door to 'closed' and quietly shut and locked the door, heading over to a beige Ford F150 extended cab. Stranger whistled and the others came into view from behind the rear of the the building, quickly moving towards the truck to climb in.

Speeding away, but not erratic enough to draw any unwanted attention, Stranger and the others left the park in search of another hideaway to wait until nightfall, John said, "Lets see what's on the radio."

Stranger turned the station to find a special newscast of another deadly shooting of a 22 year old unarmed man and his 21 year old girlfriend in the New York City area, which caused Stranger to look into the rear view mirror at Mike's face and say, "You know what this means, right?"

Nodding his head slowly, Mike said, "Round two of our killing spree is about to start. You warned them, Slim. You gave them a warning and they didn't take heed. Now we make em pay, and make em pay in a major way..."

Hearing Mike's words ringing in his ears, Stranger remained calm and quiet, as he navigated his way out of the Colorado Rockies National Park, thinking to himself, 'Wait until nightfall, I'm going to unleash on these bitches, they saw terror before, but this is gonna be the icing on the cake... the total age of both of those young people that they just killed in New York, I'm accumulating that many bodies, that's 43 bodies-in 24 hours. That's gonna make headlines for sure... ' Changing the station to music, Stranger looks into the rearview mirror, as Lisa sat with tears streaming down her face, looking sadly into his eyes.

Chapter Sixty

July 12, 2020 8:35pm Friday
Downtown Denver, Colorado

After hearing the news of what took place that morning out at the national park, with the spoiled operation and the surprising revelation that Det. McNealson was actually on the scene, it had thrown Agent Smart for a loop. He would have never guessed that Det. McNealson would have shown up all the way in Colorado, although he has seen his fair share of mind boggling things in his lifetime. But it wasn't until Spl. Agent Goldfield who sat along side him, voiced her opinion by saying, "You know Brad, I've been thinking, how would Detective McNealson know exactly where that truck was located? I mean how did he find that truck? I think there's someone involved in this case that's helping him out. He's evading capture, yea, that's one. But to show up out here in Colorado, at the same precise time that our team is sitting on our suspect? The same suspect that he's been infatuated with, trying to capture? It seems-I mean, he's not hiding from us, he's chasing this Stranger guy! Thinking if he catches this guy before us, he's gonna kill him."

Looking over from the driver's seat, Spl. Agent Smart said, "If he does that, he'll be doing us all a solid, in the name of Justice. But hey if we catch him first, then that will be fine with me too. Either way about it, the man's gonna go to death row and get the lethal injection. We got something for a serial cop killer that will make him wish he'd lived a normal blue collar life."

As they stopped at a red light, a truck pulled up beside them, beating their system and checking Spl. Agent Goldfield out. As she took a gander at the occupant's direction, she rolled her eyes and sucked her teeth at how men were always catcalling and carrying on like she was a dizzy, dumb broad who was loose in the britches and an easy lay.

When Spl. Agent Goldfield said, "Brad, I'm thirsty, can you pull up at that store over there?" pointing to a convenience store to the opposite side of the street.

But Spl. Agent Smart said, "You sure you don't want something to eat? We can stop for a quick bite to eat…"

Hesitating a little bit, Cynthia said, "No, I'm good, we got to get a line on this guy, he's somewhere around here, we got the state troopers on high alert for the stolen Ford F150, damn, can you believe that guy actually killed a park ranger while only less than a few hundred yards from a Federal Apprehension Task Force in the area? He's really bold, I tell you."

"Naw, he ain't bold, he's scared, he knew he was in a pinch and if he'd come out of that mountain or woods or wherever he was hiding, he was as good as got, so he's running on adrenaline, if you ask me," says Smart.

Pulling into the convenience store and parking in front of the store, Spl. Agent Smart looked over at Cynthia and said, "You look tired, I'll run in and get what you need."

Pausing to think, she said, "Get me a Red Bull and some

Skittles, please. I need some sugar and energy." Smiling mischievously she added, "If you want, you may want to grab some, ummm...Trojans..."

Surprised at her comment, Spl. Agent Smart asked, "What? You serious?"

"You did make me your wife, didn't you?" she replied, smiling sleepily. "Plus, I need to get laid, I ain't had no good-good in a long, long...long time," she added, exaggerating the 'Long' in her statement as if it's been a very long period of time since she had been romantically involved.

Smart leaped out of the car and headed into the store, as Spl. Agent Goldfield leaned her head onto the soft headrest and closed her eyes, thinking about how her life was turning out for the best.

Suddenly, the door is opened and she is yanked halfway out of the seat while the seatbelt is still holding her in the seat. She is trying to fight the man off of her as she reaches for her gun, but was stopped when the sharp blade of a knife was jammed under her chin.

As she gurgled on her own blood and stared into her killer's eyes, she realized that she was looking into the most beautiful golden hazel eyes of a cold blooded killer. He then unbuckled her seatbelt and pulled her out of the car, with the door slamming shut, once she laid flat on the pavement of the parking lot. With a powerful thrust of a sawing action, her head was decapitated from her shoulders and tossed to the side by a handful of her beautiful blonde hair.

As Spl. Agent Smart came out of the store and climbed in the front driver's seat, he realized that Spl. Agent Goldfield had gotten out of the car, although he hadn't seen her enter the establishment.

He waited for her to come out of the store and it wasn't until he just so happened to look over at the passenger side and saw that her firearm was on the floorboard, that he realized something was very wrong. When the truck beside them began to back out of the space, a woman getting out of the car parked one spot over, started yelling and screamed, pointing to the ground.

When Spl. Agent Smart jumped out of the car and ran around the other side of it, his stomach dropped and he fell to his knees in a weakened emotional despair as he gathered the beheaded body of Agent Cynthia Goldfield in his shaky arms and the tears came flooding over the brims of his eyes.

With fear racking his body, he looked around desperately to seek help. He looked up and locked eyes with the worse sight he had ever imagined he would see. Pulling away was a dark blue Chevy Avalanche, with the passenger window lowered. Mannimal smirked a devious smile and dropped the blood-smeared knife on the pavement as the truck pulled away with a screech of its tires. Those golden eyes of satan, tore a hole in Smart's heart, as he kneeled frozen in fear, staring at the killer of his future wife drive away, while he couldn't pull himself to let her dead body go long enough to pull his weapon and unleash every bullet he had in his firearm into that truck and its occupants.

Mannimal's face was a scary sight to see behind a locked door, but to experience it in real life, in society, after he'd just lost the love his life, was something else entirely. He was never gonna get this out of his head, as he looked over and saw that Cynthia Goldfield's head lay decapitated and strewn about on the ground, he was truly heartbroken and shattered like a delicate China dish.

Unable to speak or utter a word of help, Spl. Agent Smart kneeled in a puddle of blood, holding Spl. Agent Goldfield's body to his, pleading for her to forgive him for not protecting her. Begging for her forgiveness for not returning the favor and pulling his firearm, gunning down Mannimal and whoever was driving that Avalanche.

A few minutes later, he called backup and waited in tears, wondering how he was going to explain this.

Chapter Sixty - One

July 12, 2020 8:45pm Friday

Downtown Denver, Colorado

The streets of Denver were clustered with cars, as paramedics and police cars drove at high speeds towards an apparent emergency. When Detective McNealson came to a halt at a stop light, he looked down the street towards all of the commotion in a convenience store parking lot, and saw there was a scene with yellow tape barricading the area off from the onlookers. Though unable to see what was actually taking place, he knew from experience that the scene was a homicide, so he rubbernecked to catch a glimpse. It wasn't until he got close enough to see what was happening that he saw a crowd of FBI jackets grouped tightly together with sorrowful despondent looks upon their faces. He proceeded past the scene, continuing with his slow observation of the surrounding area, trying to keep his attention on the road as well, being that he was on the radar. When the cellphone rang, he answered and listened to Spl. Agent Finley tell him of the new twist that had just taken place.

Upon hearing the news that an agent had been savagely slain in a convenience store parking lot by the escapee, Dominic Mannimal Mann, and that there was an APB out for the Chevy Avalanche, McNealson was flabbergasted that the serial murderer was supposedly still in the downtown area of Denver on top of all of that. But it wasn't until Agent Finley said that the suspect he was after had stolen a Park Ranger's Ford F150 that gave him a clue of what to look for. But he was also informed that the Denver Police Department was involved with the apprehension team for not only Stranger, but for Mannimal and himself as well. After giving McNealson all the information and reminding him to be careful of what was coming his way if he was spotted by law enforcement, well wishes were spoken, and the phone line went dead. McNealson placed the phone in the cup holder and signaled right to get off the main avenue, to try to get some clarity of the situation by coming up with another strategy, because driving around the highly patrolled area wasn't a smart move on his part. After parking on the next street, Detective McNealson sat in the front seat of the rented Ford Escape, pondering his next move, as he lit a Newport and inhaled a long pull of smoke. He sat contemplating how he was in a real bad fix and searching for Stranger was like seeking a needle in a haystack.

It was right then that his eyes caught a glimpse of someone very familiar, that could actually fit Stranger's description, but it was the beige Ford F150 with a Park Rangers decal on the back of the cab's window that gave Det. McNealson the notion that it could be Stranger who had just passed by him on the street.

In urgent despair, McNealson started his SUV and jumped into traffic, making U-turn in the middle of the street as cars honked horns for his blatant disrespect for the traffic laws. It wasn't until he had completed his turn that Mannimal and Mayhem caught sight of the vehicle that was recklessly making a U-turn in the middle of a heavily congested street, brazenly breaking traffic laws.

Mannimal said, "Slim, I know my eyes aren't deceiving me, I think that's the detective we've been following." He pulled out the GPS locator on his laptop and said, "Well, lo and behold, look what we have here, if it isn't Detective McNealson," staring at a highlight green dot that was just ten yards in front of their location. "Follow that bitch, he's on something, Slim!" Mannimal heatedly said.

Reaching into the backpack that sat on the floor board, Mannimal pulled out a chrome Smith & Wesson .45, cocked and chambered a round into the head, then sat back tightly in the front seat with his eyes peeled on the blue Ford Escape. When they maneuvered onto the main avenue, Mannimal maintained visual contact and told Mayhem, "Get closer to that SUV," but when the light changed to red, stopping traffic to a dead halt, they noticed Detective McNealson jump out of his vehicle. Slowly and stealthily, he began moving down the crowded lane street approaching a beige pick up from the rear. When Mannimal saw this taking place, he and Mayhem quickly reacted, leaping out of their vehicle leaving the doors wide open as they ascended upon the action sneakily, while occupants sat in their cars awaiting the light to change.

Hands engaging the Glock 19 from its holster, McNealson peered hard through the drivers side mirror to make sure he was approaching the right person, as Stranger sat with a stoic look on his face, staring directly ahead, with his lips moving, talking to someone, as if carrying on a real conversation with someone in the truck with him.

Once Detective McNealson passed the tail end of the pick up truck, he crouched down and tightly slid alongside of the truck bed, raising his gun eye level in case Stranger detected his movement. Keeping a close eye on the mirror, McNealson was a couple of feet from the drivers side door, slowly moving, trying not to draw any attention. When Stranger looked left, he didn't immediately take notice to McNealson's presence until the passenger in the car next to him sat with a fearful look on her face as her eyes sat staring backward and were bulging out of their sockets.

It was too late, as Detective McNealson grabbed a hold of the door handle, popping the front driver's side door. He raised his service weapon eye level at Stranger.

Peering deeply into those cold black eyes, McNealson said, "Now! Get your dreadlock ass out of that front seat and do it real slow, I'm a hair trigger away from blowing your demented head off your shoulders, Mr. Ben Strange, Move! Now! Or I'll-"

"You ain't doin' shit, bitch!" yelled a voice behind him, cutting his words short mid-sentence.

Spinning around, he was eye to eye with two individuals who both stood with guns raised on him at close range. Hesitant to what was about to happen, Detective McNealson slowly raised his weapon above his head in surrender and said, "Come on, Mannimal, this ain't gonna end well."

"Naw, it ain't Detective, not for you, that is certain," said Mannimal.

"Fuck all this talk!" said Mayhem, and pulled his trigger,

sending a hot slug into the face of McNealson just as Stranger cautiously climbed out of the pick-up truck, and leveled the barrel of Park Ranger Adam Greenway's Browning 10mm, to the back of McNealson's head, and discharged two slugs simultaneously, as Mannimal began pulling his trigger, riddling the body of Detective McNealson with a mess of bullets that were meant to send him to the upper room.

Once Detective McNealson's body hit the ground in a pathetic slump, Mayhem, Mannimal and Stranger looked at one another for a second and smiled. Hearing the sirens of police cars nearby, Mannimal said, "Nice the to see you, Slim, but now's not the time for a reunion. Get ghost, Slim! We'll rendezvous in a more secluded area, head south, I'll follow."

Mayhem was already heading back to the Chevy Avalanche, yelling for Mannimal to 'come on.'

Mannimal winked his golden eyes at Stranger and said, "I told you I had your back, Slim." Turning quickly on his heels, Mannimal ran back to the SUV. To make a clean getaway, they smashed into the car behind them, allowing them to make room for the Avalanche to maneuver out and into traffic.

But a concerned citizen used his car to block Stranger's truck from pulling away when the car in front of him backed the tail end of their car into the front grille of Stranger's F150, penning him in and making it impossible to maneuver out of the spot.

Stranger climbed back into the driver's seat. He tried desperately to slam the truck in reverse and make room, when he saw Mannimal's Avalanche come speeding down the crowded side walk, mowing down anyone who stood in their way.

He knew Mannimal and Mayhem were in the clear. Now he needed to get out of the pinch he was in...

Chapter Sixty - Two

July 12, 2020 9:15pm Friday

Downtown Denver, Colorado

The light brings Stranger to a stand still, listening to the music play and keeping a keen eye on the traffic in front of him, John says, "You know what we should do now that those cops killed another young black couple?"

Not answering John's question, Stranger just grips the steering wheel, and waited to catch another cop off guard. Looking sternly around, he notices through the driver side window that a white lady had a look in her face of sudden shock and fear. Following the path of her eyes, Stranger turned his head, seeing that there was an unknown face staring at him, pulling on the door handle as the interior light popped on, alerting him that a door was ajar. But the handgun was pointed directly his at face, and staring down the barrel, Stranger saw things were at a deadly crossroad now.

Hearing the words of Lisa sing in his ear, when she said, "Oh my God, Stranger! No! That man is gonna shoot!"

Then Mike said in a casual and fearless tone, "Go out with a bang, Slim, it's now or never."

While John sat motionless, scared shitless to the point in which he was lip-locked speechless.

Lisa added, "No! Stranger! Stay in the truck, ram the back of that car in front of us and get us out of here, now! I said NO, Stranger!"

Being that Stranger was climbing out of the truck's front seat with a fearless look in his eyes. The cop demanded Stranger by his government name, to get out of the truck, and to do it slowly, screaming at him in an authoritative voice, "Now! Move!"

In doing so, Stranger caught the eyes of someone he'd known as family, and those golden eyes that spoke of death and determination, when the voice came as clear as melody. Stranger heard the words, "You ain't gonna do shit!"

The man spun around, caught off guard, when he was staring at two good friends of Stranger's, who both had the drop on him. The man raised his weapon in surrender, which was of no help to him when Mayhem pulled his trigger, just as Stranger climbed out of the truck and lifted his Browning 10mm, sending two blasts to the back of the man's head before the cop began to crumble to the ground. Stranger's fiendish partner, Mannimal, began unloading a bombardment of hollow tips into the chest and stomach of the man before him.

When the man hit the surface of the pavement, Mannimal and Mayhem stood there looking into Stranger's eyes, then smiled a maniacal grin. The sirens came whooping towards them, Stranger heard Mannimal's voice say, "Nice to see you, Slim, but now's not the time for a reunion, get ghost, Slim, we'll rendezvous at a secluded area, just head south, and I'll follow you!"

He threw the command at him as he retreated backwards and sprinted back to a blue Avalanche. Mayhem hit the gas and slammed the cars in front of him and behind him to maneuver out of the closed in spot they were currently trapped in. It was the wink that Mannimal gave him that told Stranger he had his back before he had turned to sprint away.

Just as Stranger climbed in his F150, the car in front of him reversed and slammed its rear end into the truck's front grille, trying to restrain Stranger from maneuvering, out of the traffic jam. But Stranger reversed the F150 and slammed hard footed on the gas petal, peeling tires and crushing his rear end into the car behind him as a speeding truck came jetting by, driven by Mayhem, mowing down pedestrians in his path. Stranger saw them leap hard off the sidewalk bending the corner heading south, evading the force of cops who were now coming to a screeching halt at the intersection, blocking any way of escape.

Looking into the side and rear view mirrors, Stranger saw a catastrophic situation surrounding him as cops and Federal agents fell in and were approaching him on all sides.

Lisa, John and Mike sat in awe as they saw the predicament they were all in, the time had come and this was the beginning of the end.

Lisa argued that they should just give up and surrender, where Mike yelled, "Ain't no fucking surrendering, Slim, get out and fight your last fight, hold court in the streets, gangsta! Fuck that!"

John became just plain ole John, when he said, "Stranger, let me get one of them cigarettes, seems like now is the time to pick up a new habit."

Taking one out the pack and lighting the end, Stranger tossed the pack at John and said, "John, shut the fuck up."

As he took a few deep hits and expelled the smoke through his nose, Stranger decided his plan of action and said, "Everybody out! We ride together, we die together," making John rethink the remark and reply. "Hey, hey, hey, Stranger, nobody ever said anything about dying alongside your crazy ass." The look that Stranger gave John was enough for John to retract his statement, when he said, "Alright, alright, let's face the music cowboy, it's showdown at high noon. But I wish the Moses in your ass could part the red seas now and get our ass out of this mess."

The door popped open and Stranger climbed out, and proceeded to the intersection, with his Browning 10mm firmly in his grip. Standing in the middle of the intersection, he turned to look around as he saw a multitude of officers and agents staring down on him behind sighted firearms. Still smoking his cigarette, which now dangled from his lips, Stranger peered around and said, "All this for me! Looks like a welcome home party!"

With Lisa, Mike and John, standing beside him in a semi-circle, he said, "Seems like you're not too happy when the rabbit's got the gun! No matter what, I took out as many of you bitches as I could, and if I wasn't surrounded by you now, I'd take out even more of you. But I got some last words to say!"

"Fuck your last words Ben Strange, my name's Agent Smart and you're under ar-"

Lifting his gun, Stranger got off two shots in the agent's direction before a battalion of bullets came hailing down upon him, ripping him to shreds from all directions.

When the smoke cleared, Lisa, Mike and John stood over Stranger's dead body and said their final goodbyes, Lisa said, "I love you, Stranger, but now it's time to go."

Mike said, "It's been real, soldier. I'll never have another friend like you."

Which left John with the final remark, when John stood over Stranger's body, shed a tear drop, and said, "Well, Slim, life's a bitch and then we die."

Then he turned and walked away singing the Reaper's lullaby as he went for the last time. The cops surrounded Stranger's sprawled out body and John sang, as he, Lisa, and Mike faded away into thin air for the last act, as if, they never existed at all.

Time is frozen, casket closing, the flesh is empty, the soul is set free, no longer are you breathing, death has chose a season, for you to go to sleep, eternally in peace, eternally in peace, Stranger's only real friends disappeared, along with the life and times of Ben "Stranger" Strange.

§§§§

It was Mannimal who stood amongst the commotion of the crowd, blending with his hoodie hood lowered over his head. He was watching the whole scene and saw that Special Agent Smart's gun was the first bullet that hit Stranger. He would make him pay dearly for that mistake.

Turning away, he got lost in the crowd of onlookers with

Mayhem following closely behind. Both, with their fingers on their triggers, just in case someone wanted to play the hero...

But today wouldn't be the day to play hero, not with Mannimal, Unleashed again .....

To Be Continued...

STAY TUNED

If you loved Stranger's adventure with making those responsible, pay for the lives that they have taken without just cause...

Check out Sincere Echoes' next installment

Unleashed Again: Mannimal's Retaliation
(City Under Siege)

Coming this summer 2024... From Free Taboo Publishing, LLC www.freetaboopublishing.com

Also available on Amazon.

About the Author

Sincere Echoes, is a native of Washington DC. He's a member of a youth organization called: Freeminds book club and workshop, where he's debuted many of his literary works through the genre of poetry in several outlets publishings, literary magazines and books, designed to uplift and rebuild the youth on a level of positivity and structure.

Sincere Echoes is married and a father of 3, who is purpose-driven, with a talent for writing that's been laying dormant for decades, whereas, his talents for poetry hasn't gone unnoticed or unrecognized by the many who has encountered his work throughout the years..

Now the caged has awakened and unchained his first literary novel, of many to come; Unleashed, A Stranger root of wrath part 1.

www.ingramcontent.com/pod-product-compliance
Lightning Source LLC
Chambersburg PA
CBHW050914030726
47503CB00007BB/2296